THE
WISHING
PEARL

✦ A DIAMOND ESTATES NOVEL ✦

NICOLE O'DELL

BARBOUR
PUBLISHING

Published by Barbour Publishing, Inc., P.O. Box 719, Uhrichsville, Ohio 44683, www.barbourbooks.com

Our mission is to publish and distribute inspirational products offering exceptional value and biblical encouragement to the masses.

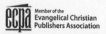
Member of the
Evangelical Christian
Publishers Association

Printed in the United States of America.

Dedicated to Frank and Pam Smith,
my Ben and Alicia Bradley.
Frank, you were larger than life when I first arrived
at Teen Challenge more than twenty years ago,
and you still are a truly powerful force in my life.
Pam, your nurturing soul was a joy to me then,
and it still is today as you model what it means
to be a godly wife, mother, daughter, and friend.
You two are a special gift from God,
and I'm so grateful, decades later, that we've
walked this life together. I love you both.

Acknowledgments

My first words of thanks go to my Savior, Jesus Christ. Not only did He rescue me from my own poor choices, but He gave me the privilege to share His truth through my passion for writing. I feel so fulfilled by what He's allowed me to do, and I am humbled that He would choose me. . .but so grateful that He did.

Next, I owe so much to my hubby, Wil, who has so selflessly given of his time and some of his own ambitions to allow me the freedom to live as a full-time writer in a house with six children. What a rare man I've married. I love you, Wil.

And those six kids of mine: Erik, Natalie, Emily, Logan, Megan, and Ryleigh. I pray the words I write will touch your life in some way, for among all the youth of this world, you are my first calling, and I love you so very much. Thank you for being who you are, and for loving me for who I am.

Grandma Party—with a name like that, need I say more? You're such a bright spot in my life, and your unfailing support and encouragement of me are so appreciated. You are the best mom and most awesome Grandma Party in the world! I love you.

I owe a debt of gratitude to my wonderful agent and friend, Chip MacGregor. Chip, you've taught me a lot this year, and I don't just mean about publishing. Your humility, kindness, and humor have spurred me on whenever I got discouraged. I can't thank you enough for believing in me when your broca and I joined forces to make you take me on as a client and then for continuing to suffer my incessant e-mails. Bless you.

And Valerie Comer. What's there to say? Not only have you taught me more than I ever knew I needed to know, but you've held my hand over every single word on every single page that

I've written. Often more than once. I hope my readers realize that this book wouldn't be what it is without your fine-tooth comb. Thank you for your commitment and, most of all, your friendship.

My writer-sister-friends. Jenny B. Jones, Cara Putman, Kim Cash Tate, Cindy Thomson, Marybeth Whalen, and Kit Wilkinson. God knew I needed you guys. I'll never stop thanking Him for uniting us as a tiny little family in the world of books. Your prayers over my writing, my family, and my walk mean so much to me, and I'm honored to be able to pray for you and share this journey with you, too.

To my CYAW critique partners who had a part in this book: Ann Miller, Lynn Rush, and Diana Sharples. Thank you for dropping everything to take a look when I needed you. Your input meant so much to me, and I'm forever grateful.

Friends at Barbour Publishing. Not a day goes by that I don't thank God for your constant support of my work. You have believed in me since day one—still shaking my head in wonderment at that—and you continue to call me one of your own. Thank you for working tirelessly to see the shelves filled with more books for young adults.

Cynthia Gramm. . .my heart friend. Thank you for the years of prayers and prodding. You're the best sista friend a girl could have. I love you. Don't forget to save a seat on the sea of glass if you get there before me. If it's me who arrives first, you know I'll be waiting.

Chapter 1

Even the happiest of songs could sound mournful on the oboe if played just right. Olivia Mansfield pulled the instrument from between her lips and traced her fingers along the silver tracks and keys that reminded her of the braces she wore on her teeth last year. The oboe understood her. It sang her somber song. Melancholy and forlorn, her band director once called it. Perfect words to describe its cry *and* Olivia.

Buzz. Olivia jumped as the intercom in her bedroom suite intruded.

"Are you almost done with that incessant noise?" barked a crackling voice.

Five more minutes had been the plan—but not anymore. She hurried to the wall and jabbed the TALK button. "I'll be at least another half hour, *Chuck*." Charles hated when Olivia called him that, almost as much as he hated the sound of the oboe. Which wasn't nearly as much as he hated her.

"Well, hurry up."

The speaker clicked and fell silent.

Olivia tipped the bell of her instrument in the direction of the door and blew a long, angry note, loud enough to make her stepfather's acne-scarred skin crawl just like he made hers every time he came near. She *could* wait and practice later when he wasn't home, but why should she? Only two more years of high school band and then, hopefully, a prestigious music school somewhere very far away. Making that dream come true required practice—lots of it. It wasn't her fault Charles couldn't tolerate the sound.

The door to her room flew open. Mom rapped her knuckles on the frame then bustled in looking perfect as usual in her designer clothes and impeccable makeup. Her big brown eyes surveyed the room.

"Hi, Mom. Thanks for knocking." Olivia gave her a raised eyebrow then continued her song. If her room were smaller, it might be considered a pigsty. Luckily, the enormity swallowed the mess, making it look only mildly untidy. Hopefully Mom wouldn't complain too much about all the dirty designer clothes littering the walnut floors.

"Sorry. I'm just in a hurry." Mom rushed over to the king-sized four-poster bed and yanked the silk duvet cover up over the rumpled sheets. "I wish you'd take better care of this beautiful room, Liv. Charles has been more than generous to pay for all of this and everything else you'd have only dreamed of having—like this Egyptian cotton."

Yeah, Charles had bought Olivia all that stuff, but only so he'd look good to everyone else—certainly not to make *her* happy. "I never asked him for any of this." Olivia swiveled in the desk chair she'd pulled to the center of the room and gestured at her expansive quarters. The sitting area looked like a high-tech home theater pictured in a magazine, and the marble and granite bathroom would have satisfied a queen. The jetted tub *was* nice, but Olivia would never admit that to Charles. "Besides, I'm going to get in the bed in a couple of hours anyway, so why bother?"

Mom's spiked heels clicked as she strode across the room, swept up a pile of dirty clothes into her arms, then dumped them down the laundry chute near Olivia's bathroom door. "You know,

Norma can't wash the laundry if you don't drop it down."

Whatever. Norma could come up here and get it if she wanted it—she sure got paid enough. Time to change the subject. "Where are you going anyway?"

"Don't you remember?" Mom turned to the mirror while she spoke and tucked a nonexistent errant hair back into her long dark waves.

When would she cut her hair into a more age-appropriate style—at least shoulder length? "Don't tell me this is your shopping weekend in Chicago."

"Yep. Tonight's a fancy downtown dinner with the girls and a night at the Ritz. Saturday is for shopping on Mag Mile and dinner again. Then we'll work off the calories with a lakefront bike ride on Sunday."

Two nights? Home alone with Chuck? "Will Jake be here?"

"Probably for some of the weekend. But he's definitely going to want to get out and have fun with his friends—he's only got three weeks left before he leaves for college. Try not to get in his way too much."

"That's my job. Stay out of everyone's way." Why should this weekend be any different? Olivia slumped in her chair.

Mom stacked some books that had slipped to the floor from Olivia's built-in bookcase. "Just try a little harder to be nice to Charles. He's never been anything but wonderful to you."

Gag. "No, Mom. Daddy was wonderful. Chuck. . .exists." Olivia threaded her fingers through the layers of her silky black hair to find the purple streak she'd added a few days ago. She twisted it around her fingers and put the ends in her mouth.

"Quit that. Do you know how many germs are in your hair?" Mom swiped the clump of hair from between Olivia's lips. "Now give me a hug. I'll be home in a couple of days. Just try to be pleasant. Okay?" She pulled Olivia back to arm's length and smiled as she slid her hand down the back of Olivia's head. "I'll buy you something special—purple to match that streak of rebellion in that gorgeous hair of yours."

Great. A present. Mom's answer for everything—she sure hadn't acted like that when Daddy was alive, and she wouldn't have even if she'd had the money. Olivia mumbled her thanks as Mom hurried from the room, high heels clacking on the wood.

Olivia rushed to lock the door, her plan the same as every other day: stay out of everyone's way. Nothing new. Probably shouldn't have started the weekend off with the oboe serenade though—much better not to draw attention to herself. But it was too late to worry about that. Her eyes drilled holes in the intercom. A shame she couldn't see through it into the rest of the house. Go down and make peace, or stay hidden as long as possible? It would help if she knew whether he was already drinking.

She gazed around her room. The huge LCD television with its projection system along one wall of the sitting area. The dorm-sized refrigerator stocked with soda and snacks hidden in the alcove beside the bookcase. The swimming pool of a bathtub. Yeah, she'd just stay up here. It's not like she'd be suffering some great hardship—as long as *he* left her alone.

Olivia's stomach fluttered at a knock at the door. *Not him. Not already.* "Who is it?"

"It's me. Open up, Liv."

Phew. Just Jake. Olivia flipped the lock and threw the door open to find her lanky brother filling the doorway.

Jake held up a plate with two slices of thick Chicago-style pepperoni pizza. "Brought you some dinner."

Olivia smiled as his garbled speech brought to mind the hours upon hours she let him hold fingers to her lips or place his hand over the muscles in her neck as he tried to learn to speak even though he couldn't hear.

"You mean there's actually some left after you plowed through it?" Olivia faced him so he could read her lips. She raked her fingers over her open palm in the sign for *plow* as she accepted the dish.

"I have no idea what you're talking about." Jake folded his arms across his chest. "Besides, I ordered two larges." He winked one of those brown eyes all the girls seemed to love. "Gotta gain more weight before basketball season." He rubbed his flat stomach and puffed out his cheeks.

"Right. You'll never be fat." Fun problem—to have to *gain* weight. Olivia motioned for Jake to step all the way in then secured the door again before taking her dinner to the overstuffed sofa in her sitting area. She pulled her legs up and nestled into the corner with her plate resting on her knees.

Jake tipped his head toward the locked door. "You hiding out from King Charles?"

"How'd you guess?" Olivia took a big bite. "Mmm. This is so good." Sauce dripped onto her chin. She caught it with the back of her hand then licked it off.

"Gross." Jake shook his head, black curls bouncing. "Well, I'm going out with some of the guys from the team in a little while. Stay in your room, okay?" His gaze darted around the room. "Need anything before I go?"

"Need anything?" Olivia stared at the fringe on the edge of the East Indian area rug. "Yeah. I need you to take me with you." She touched her clenched fists together then pointed at Jake.

"You'll be okay if you stay out of sight." Jake put his hand on the door. "It'll be fine." He ducked his head under the frame on his way out, glancing over his shoulder with a nod and a wink.

That's what you think. Olivia locked the door behind Jake. If only he didn't have to leave. Tonight or ever.

Alone. Again. Olivia thought she heard the ticking of her digital clock. Great. Now she was going crazy imagining things. No way could she sit in that room alone with a thundering sense of doom all night. But who could she call? *Jordyn!* She'd never been inside the mansion, but she'd told Olivia to text her anytime. Sliding her sleek new cell phone open to expose the keyboard, Olivia tapped out a plea. CAN U COME OVER? Charles would leave her alone if someone else was with her. Olivia stared at her phone, willing the text message notification to chime a reply.

In less than sixty seconds, the phone vibrated and beeped the text tune. SURE. 4 A LITTLE WHILE. IN TROUBLE—HAVE TO BE HOME BY 10.

Jordyn in trouble? *Impossible.* Olivia chuckled. Well, ten o'clock was better than nothing. Maybe he'd be passed out by then anyway. . .or just getting started. She shuddered. GR8. C U SOON. HURRY.

Olivia knelt on her bed and parted the gauzy curtains at the window overlooking the four-car garage. Soon the farthest door lifted, and Jake's black sports car roared to life. Another present from *Chuck.* At least her brother wasn't completely fooled by him like Mom seemed to be. Olivia watched Jake back out of the driveway and squeal his tires as he sped away. She fell back on her bed and crossed her arms over her eyes.

What would she do when he left for college? Who would look out for her then? He'd hardly ever be back, with school during the week and basketball games on the weekends. Not to mention the parties. Besides, if she were him, Olivia would never come back.

Funny, even though Jake was two years older and twice as big as his little sister, Olivia had felt protective of him through the years. Helping him learn to talk. Learning sign language herself so she could help him communicate when people didn't understand his muted, halting speech. Shielding him from teasing kids. Now Jake was the strong one—popular and athletic, good-looking—plus he'd learned to read lips and speak very well. He'd be fine at college. Jake didn't need her anymore, but what would she do without him?

Right on time, fifteen minutes after the text message, Olivia's door shook with a knock. She threw it open, reached one arm out, and pulled Jordyn in. One quick glance up and down the hallway assured Olivia that Charles was nowhere to be seen. She shut the door and locked it as fast as she could.

"How'd you get in the gate?"

"Your brother passed me on his way out, and he let me through. He said you were the only one home—"

Hmm. Guess Charles went out. That could be good or bad. Only time would tell.

"—and to just let myself in." Jordyn's blue eyes grew misty. "He's so hot." She fanned herself with the blunt end of her blond braid and swooned as her backpack slipped off her shoulder and landed with a heavy thud on the floor.

Olivia pretended to gag. "Eww. He's my brother."

"I'm just glad he's not *my* brother if you know what I mean." Jordyn wiggled her eyebrows.

"Oh man. Cut that out. You're giving me the heebie-jeebies."

"Hey, can you teach me sign language? Maybe I'll ask him out." A dozen bangle bracelets slid to the crook of Jordyn's elbow as she held up a hand. "What's the sign for *date*?"

Olivia brushed Jordyn's arm down and giggled. "I don't think so. My brother's *way* too good for you." At least Jordyn passed the deaf test. Olivia could never be friends with someone who acted uncomfortable or nervous around Jake. Many so-called friends had fallen by the wayside when it became clear they barely tolerated Jake.

Olivia grinned. "So what do you want to do?"

"Ooh!" Jordyn squealed and flopped onto her stomach across the bed. "I brought treats." She reached down and hefted her backpack up to the bed beside her then pulled out a six-pack of beer, dangling it from the plastic ring hooked on two fingers. "Let's party."

Oh no! Olivia stared at the beer. She'd never really drank alcohol before. Did she want this to be her first time? Was she ready to take that step? Charles would literally kill her if he caught her drinking. Plus the last thing she needed tonight was to be buzzed while alone in the house with *Chuck*, especially since she had no idea what it felt like to drink or how alcohol would affect her. But wouldn't Jordyn laugh at her for being a beer virgin? Maybe Olivia could just sip it, and Jordyn would never have to know it was her first time.

Olivia searched the room—and her brain—for ways to stall. "Where did you get that?" She tried not to look nervous.

"From my dad's stash. He won't miss it. He never does."

"You mean you've done this before?" Kids at school talked about drinking all the time, but Olivia hadn't had much opportunity to witness it, let alone try it.

Jordyn squinted. "What do you mean? Of course I've done it before. You mean you *haven't*?"

"Oh sure. . .um. . .just not a whole six-pack, and I've never taken it from here. You know. . .just at parties and stuff."

"Well, there *are* two of us. You're going to have to share, silly." Jordyn plucked a can from the plastic ring and held it out to Olivia.

She peeked at the clock on her bedside table. Seven o'clock. They still had three hours before Jordyn had to be home. One beer wouldn't hurt, would it? And it should be worn off by then anyway.

"I think I'll just have one tonight though." Hopefully Jordyn didn't see Olivia's hand shake as she reached out for the beer.

"Great. More for me." Jordyn pried open her tab with her fingernail, and a big flake of her neon green nail polish chipped off and fluttered to the floor. She hoisted her can in the air and tipped it toward Olivia before guzzling at least a third of it. Wiping the foam off her mouth, she let out a belch. "The fizz always does that to me on the first drink." She giggled.

"Classy." Olivia shook her head and popped the top of her own can. She took a discreet sniff. Lots of people seemed to like beer, so maybe she would, too. Olivia took a hesitant sip. It tasted quite different than the sweet champagne she'd had at weddings. Foamy, fizzy, and bitter. The way *Chuck* put it away, she figured it would taste a lot better than it did. But maybe it would grow on her.

Olivia couldn't pry her eyes off the sight of tiny Jordyn, with her blond hair in schoolgirl braids below her ears, chugging the last of the beer from her first can. She looked like a little girl playing dress-up in her mommy's clothes.

Bringing the can to her lips, Olivia took another bubbly sip. It wasn't horrible—maybe slightly better than the first drink— but it still wouldn't top her list of favorites with Diet Dr Pepper and cream soda. What she wouldn't give for a big frosted mug of those two mixed together over a bunch of crushed ice. So far the beer thing didn't seem that exciting, let alone tasty.

Jordyn pulled another can from the plastic ring and started right in on it. Within an hour she had three empty cans scattered around her. She rolled from her perch on the bed and stumbled toward the bathroom. "I'll be right back, after I. . .well, you know." She slurred her words then laughed like it was the funniest thing she'd ever heard.

Olivia smiled and shook her head. Why did alcohol make smart people so stupid? On the other hand, she hadn't thought of Charles or his whereabouts in a long time. Maybe she'd discovered the key to coping in her family—get drunk and stay that way to escape from reality. One beer sure wouldn't cut it though. She took a sip of her beer. *Ick.* It just didn't taste good. No matter how many times she tried it, she just couldn't get enough down her throat to make a dent in her fears.

By nine forty-five, all the beer had disappeared, leaving only crushed cans as evidence. How was Jordyn planning to get home in time for her curfew? Surely she didn't plan to drive after drinking five beers. Besides, Charles was probably home by now. How would they get her out of the house without running into him?

"Well, it's time for me to go." Jordyn stood up and swayed before she found her balance. She reached in her pocket and pulled out a set of car keys. *"Vroom, vroom."* She made a steering motion.

"You can't drive like this." Olivia reached for Jordyn's keys. "No way."

Jordyn jerked the set of keys away and dangled them overhead and out of reach. "Don't be so bossy, Livly. Get it? Like lovely, but Livly. Get it?"

Oh no. Jordyn was in bad shape. She could hurt herself or someone else or get in really big trouble. Or all of the above. The way she saw it, Olivia had three choices. She could try to get permission from Charles to take Jordyn home. But then he'd want to know why Jordyn couldn't drive herself home. That wouldn't work. Second choice: sneak Charles's keys and do it anyway. Yeah, that would work if she had a death wish. Plus he'd probably search her room while she was gone.

That reminded her—hide the empty cans before Charles came up for a visit. Olivia scooped up the three cans on the floor and two from the rumpled comforter. Where was the sixth one? She searched under the bed and behind the television.

Jordyn giggled and slinked a hand into her jacket. She pulled out a half-full beer and lifted it into the air. "I was saving a roadie." Raising it a couple of inches higher, she chimed, "Cheers," then polished it off and crushed the can. Without another word, she dropped it into Olivia's garbage, turned on her heels, and made her way in a sort of zigzag pattern across Olivia's room toward the door.

Third option. "If you won't stay, let me at least call you a taxi." There had to be numbers in the phone book for that, right?

"Yeah, and I'm supposed to explain that to my parents how?" Jordyn waved her hand. "Stop being such a baby. I'll be fine." She peered into the mirror and straightened one of her cockeyed braids. "I do this all the time. Everyone does. Besides, this is nothing, really."

Olivia felt for the cell phone in her pocket. Maybe she should call Jordyn's parents. Jordyn would probably hate Olivia for it, but at least she'd be safe. But then everyone would know Olivia had turned in her new best friend. No one would want to hang out with her, and she'd be alone again. She'd never made friends very easily. How smart would it be to betray the one good friend she'd found? But what kind of friend would let Jordyn drive drunk? Even if she made it home and nothing happened tonight, what about next time? Olivia would have to talk to her about this. She couldn't just sit back and let it continue.

"Bye!" Jordyn sailed through the door, her braids whipping behind her.

Frozen in place, Olivia let her go.

Chapter 2

"Hey! Open this door. I will *not* have locked doors in my house!"

Olivia bolted up from her sound sleep, pulled the covers to her chin—not that they could protect her. . . . Nothing could. She peeked at the clock. One in the morning. "I'm sleeping. Can we talk tomorrow?" Olivia tried to keep her voice from trembling. *Please go away. Please go away.* Would Charles break the door down again?

"You will open up right now, young lady." Charles stopped rattling the knob after he bellowed his demand, obviously expecting her to obey. And judging by the slur in his words and past experience, Olivia figured she'd better. Like her entire body, her feet felt numb under the covers. How would she force them to walk to the door? She searched her suite for one last chance at help. Anything.

All the way on the other side of the room, her cell phone lay on the desk where she'd plugged it in to charge before she climbed into bed. Could she get to it and call Jake before opening the door? Probably, but—she shuddered at a recent memory—if she made Charles wait, he'd bust in and everything would be much worse for her. What about dialing 911? What would she say to them if she called? That her stepfather wanted her bedroom door unlocked? The police wouldn't care about that. Charles hadn't laid a finger on her yet, at least not tonight.

Jake would care, but he wouldn't be able to get home in time, and what could he do anyway? What could anyone do?

"I'm waiting and I am *not* happy." Charles spoke with a measured, even tone. He had no intention of going away.

Olivia stretched a shaky foot toward the floor and slid from her bed. Goose bumps layered upon goose bumps covered her from head to toe. Why hadn't she worn something more modest to bed? She tugged at her teeny shorts and stretched the bottom hem of the tank top that barely reached her waist. A mammoth sweat suit would have been way better. Where had she put that thick robe she'd gotten from Grandma last Christmas? Still in the box buried under a pile of shoes on the floor of her cavernous closet, most likely—which was all the way in the bathroom. She'd never make it there and find it in time.

"Charles, it's just—I'm tired." *Please go away. Please.*

"I don't care if you're tired or not. I'm your father. You'll do what I tell you to do."

My father? Olivia clenched her fists and bit down on her tongue, drawing on every ounce of her self-control to not correct Charles's last statement. He didn't even deserve to say her beloved daddy's name, let alone pretend to fill his shoes.

"If I have to break through this door, you'll be very sorry. But don't think I won't do it." Charles rapped on the door in a sinister rhythm. *Tap. Tap. Tap. Tap.*

She'd lost. Or had she given up? Arguing would only make matters worse and wouldn't change his mind anyway. So what was the point? Olivia sent her mind and heart fluttering out the window to a far-off land while her body crept to the door. She slowly unlocked the fate she'd been living for years.

৯

"Mom, we need to talk." Olivia strode into the kitchen as her mom snatched her bag from the dark granite slab.

With a set of car keys in her hand, Mom sighed and looked beyond Olivia toward her escape, the garage. "Can't it wait? I have a spa appointment."

No. Not this time. Olivia stepped between her mom and the door, blocking the way out. "It's really important. I've been trying to talk to you all week since you got back from Chicago."

Mom swung her keys in front of Olivia's face like a pendulum. "I'm already running late, and they make you pay for the appointment even if you don't show up." She took another step forward and waited for Olivia to get out of her way. When Olivia didn't move, Mom pointed the remote start toward the garage and pressed the button. Her Mercedes roared to life. "I know! Why don't you come with me? You can get a pedicure, too. We'll talk there. You can tell me all about the boys you like and the new styles that are coming out."

Boys she liked? Styles? Could the woman be any more clueless? "This is serious. It's not pedicure talk." *Choose me, Mom.*

"Oh, Liv, anything goes during a pedi." She cupped her hand around her mouth and dropped her voice to a whisper. "Those people don't speak very good English anyway."

"Whatever." The conversation sure hadn't unfolded the way Olivia had hoped it would, but she might as well go along for the ride. Maybe they could talk on the way. She picked up her purse and followed the trail of her mom's perfume out to the luxurious car. "When are you going to hire a chauffeur?" Olivia turned her head away and rolled her eyes as she climbed into the front seat.

"Um. I've considered it, but that might be a little extrava– Hold on. Did I hear sarcasm in your voice?" Mom tapped her perfect fingernails on the steering wheel.

Clueless.

"So, Mom." Olivia tried to get back on the subject as she

fastened her seat belt. "We really need to talk."

"So you mentioned." Mom checked the rearview mirror and backed the car onto the driveway. "I hope this isn't about Charles. One of these days you're going to wake up and regret how you've treated him."

"You have *got* to be kidding me." Olivia's eyes welled up. Why wouldn't Mom see the truth about Charles? Why wouldn't she ever take Olivia's side?

Mom's lower lip puckered sympathetically. "You missing your dad, sweetie?" She rubbed Olivia's thigh.

"Would you listen to me?" Olivia blinked back the tears. "This has nothing to do with Dad." Except for the fact that Daddy never would have let anything bad happen to his little angel. "This is really hard to say. Charles. . .he. . .he scares me." *He hurts me.*

Mom clucked her tongue and nodded. "I know. He told me you two had a disagreement and he forced you to open your door. Liv, you know he doesn't like locked doors. Thinks they're unsafe."

A disagreement? That was what he called it? "No. That's not at all how it happened." Olivia took a ragged breath to calm her racing heart. *Just say it.* "He shook my door and pounded on it in the middle of the night. He rushed in on me when I opened it and then twisted the door handle until the lock broke so I can never lock it again. Then he pulled the chain lock right off the wall. I cowered in a corner while he stood over me and yelled at me—stuff I don't want to repeat." Olivia held up her hand to ward off any comments while she gathered her thoughts. "And Mom, I–I'm afraid he's going to do something bad to me someday. He says things to me, and it's scary when he looks at me. It creeps me out." If Mom only knew that the *someday* of Olivia's fears had already come—long ago—and many times.

But Mom wouldn't even face the *possibility* of the truth. What would she do if she knew the reality?

Mom whipped around and stared at Olivia before shaking her head and returning her gaze to the road. Her knuckles turned white from her grip on the steering wheel. "If you're saying what I think you are, you should be ashamed of yourself. Charles has done nothing but make your life wonderful. And you've been ungrateful every step of the way."

Unbelievable. She still had no intention of defending her daughter against her husband? Olivia shrank back into the leather upholstery. That was exactly why she could never tell her the whole truth. Mom would never believe her, and the whole thing would get back to Charles as though *she* had done something wrong. And then. . .well. . .he'd kill her.

What would it take to just disappear? Permanently.

"Now, I'm not going to tell him you said these things. But you need to get a grip on yourself. This has gone too far, and I don't want to hear another word of this nonsense." Mom shook her head and picked up her cell phone. She pressed a speed-dial button and waited. "Yes, this is Mrs. Virginia Whitford. I have an appointment for a pedicure in a few minutes. I am suddenly in desperate need of a massage, too. Is it possible to squeeze me in?" She paused. "Great. Also, my daughter, Olivia Mansfield, would like a pedicure. Sure, I'll hold."

Mom needed a massage? *Right.* Olivia was quite sure their talk had been very rough on her. How had her mother allowed herself to become this creature? When she and Dad were married, they had no money, but they were so in love. Olivia remembered the view from the backseat of their minivan where she and Jake would watch Dad play with Mom's hair. Jake would roll his eyes at Olivia and make gagging motions at the lovey-dovey stuff. Olivia always laughed at his silliness, but deep down she loved that they were so affectionate. It meant security.

Mom and Dad held hands, giggled at private jokes, and whispered about exotic vacations they hoped to take one day. Their actual family vacations usually involved checking into a Holiday Inn, traipsing through caves, swimming in the hotel pool, and maybe visiting an amusement park now and then. But they were happy. All four of them—at least they were until she was seven.

Quite different from the vacation her *new* family took last summer. A week in the south of France. It had sounded wonderful during the planning stages—but Charles spent the whole time on his computer when he wasn't barking orders and complaints at everyone in sight. Mom took up permanent residence in the spa, and Jake chased bikinis. *Fun stuff.* If Daddy had been there, he'd have explored with Olivia, and they'd have sat on the beach making up stories about the rich ladies in the funny hats. Come to think of it, Mom would have been right there with them. What had happened to her?

"Fantastic. We'll be there in a few minutes." Dropping the phone into her cavernous designer bag, Mom turned to Olivia. "Now, let's put all of this behind us and have a girls' day. We'll get pretty and then go to lunch after the spa. You can even pick the place." She reached her hand over to lift Olivia's chin and gazed into her eyes. "Everything's going to be just fine. I'm really glad we had this talk."

Yeah right. *Just fine* was a dream that went up in smoke the day Daddy died.

⑤

Olivia rushed into her room, shut the door behind her, and then slumped against it to catch her breath from the long bike ride. She pulled the Home Depot bag from its hiding spot under her sweater, then tucked it under her pillow to deal with later—once she could sneak some tools to her room. Hopefully Google knew how to install a chain lock. Not that a new lock on her door could help her now. Much too little and far too late. Charles had made it clear that he could make her do anything he wanted her to do. Open her door. Listen to his berating shouts. Accept his apology. . .and his touches. *Sick.* Still, a new lock offered some measure of security, which was much better than doing nothing, and she had run out of fresh ideas.

There was always the option of going to the police. But no, Olivia had gone over that scenario a thousand times in her mind. The first thing they'd do is contact her mom. She'd seen how effective talking to Mom proved to be. Mom would be furious that Olivia had aired her lies to Charles's adoring public. She'd convince the police that nothing was wrong and say Olivia was just a spoiled little liar. Charles would find out once and for all that he could get away with anything—not even the police would do anything about it.

On her way to her desk to fire up her newest electronic keep-quiet bribe, she slipped the leather belt from the loops of her jeans. *Oops.* Olivia grabbed the waistband of her jeans as it slipped a few inches down her hips. Had they stretched out? She passed her full-length mirror and stopped short as she saw her reflection. Who stared back at her? From the way her favorite jeans draped across her hip bones, Olivia had lost at least ten pounds in the past few weeks since Mom's weekend away. After a year of unsuccessful dieting, how had she not noticed this sudden success? When had she stopped caring? Go figure—a lost appetite equaled weight loss—who knew? If she lost more, she'd just disappear completely. She could hope.

Olivia leaned closer to the mirror to look at her face. Her skin had a porcelain-doll effect after using the two-hundred-dollar set of new makeup Mom bought her on their girls' day

at the spa a couple of weeks ago. Her deep brown eyes, huge
as always, seemed different. Older. Likely the dark circles had
something to do with that. She ran her tongue over her teeth.
The braces had wiggled them into perfect position, and the
Zoom! whitening treatments made them dazzle. The purple
streak and chunky layers added a bit of edginess to her sleek
black hair. She looked nice—even she had to admit it. Was she
pretty?

Too pretty, maybe?

Maybe *Chuck* would leave her alone if she didn't look
good. But Olivia doubted it. He just wanted to prove he was in
charge. Nothing she did would change that.

"You're on your own," she whispered to her reflection. With
Jake leaving and Mom oblivious, Olivia only had herself to
depend on. Being a good little daddy's girl hadn't gotten her
anywhere. And Daddy was gone now anyway. Not much in life
really mattered anymore.

Maybe it was time to just have fun. Why not? Might as well
live a little. Maybe she could find that numbness she'd tasted
the other night with Jordyn. *Yep. I'll stay numb by getting a little
crazy—live life like an out-of-body experience.* Then maybe things
wouldn't hurt so much.

That decision made, it was time to stir up some excitement.
Olivia rushed to her desk and powered up her customized
metallic purple laptop. The instant-message screen popped up
just as her cell phone buzzed with a new text. The messages
were identical—from Jordyn. Busy l8r? We're cookin up a
party.

Perfect. Olivia slid her phone open and punched out a reply.
Works 4 me! Where? When? Ask and you will receive, right? A
party was just what she needed.

The phone chimed in a matter of seconds. Brett's house.

OUT BACK. ALL NIGHT.

SOUNDS GR8. C U THERE.

A quick look out the window revealed two open garage doors—Mom's Mercedes sat in one side and the other stood empty. Charles hadn't arrived home from the office yet.

Like a bird facing the blue sky beyond an open window, Olivia skipped every other step on her way down the marble staircase. "Mom?" She poked her head into the study. Not there. Olivia flitted through the dining room and the family room—empty. Finally, she heard the clanging of pots in the kitchen.

"Hey, Mom." Olivia waited at the arched entrance.

Mom held a recipe card between her teeth as she measured out a teaspoon of vanilla. "Mm-hmm?"

"Can I borrow the car tonight? I want to spend the night at Jordyn's." A little white lie wouldn't kill anyone.

Mom's eyes lit up. "Sure, sweetie. That sounds like fun."

That was almost too easy. Mom actually seemed relieved. And no lectures about how newly licensed drivers shouldn't have other riders in the car? No seat belt instruction? Nothing? How weird.

"I'm going out tonight, too." Mom gestured toward her baking project. "Girls' night at Mary's, and I'm in charge of dessert. I'll take Charles's BMW so you can drive my car."

"Cool." Olivia turned at the doorway. "You know, Mom, you could always get me my own car. Then you wouldn't have to share."

Mom grabbed an apple from the bowl of fruit on the counter and pretended to throw it at Olivia. "Very funny. You know how I feel about that. You need at least a year of driving experience before you get your own."

Blah. Blah. Blah. "Well, it was worth a try anyway."

Olivia rummaged through the junk drawer when Mom turned toward the oven. There. A hammer should do the job. Olivia slid the tool up her sleeve, then took the stairs two at a time on the way back to her room to install the new lock. With any luck she'd be gone long before *Chuck* got home. With a little more luck, she wouldn't be back that night at all. But if she had to come home, at least she'd be able to lock her door.

Chapter 3

Olivia stepped through the wrought-iron gate into Brett's backyard, a private beach on the north shore of Chicago's Lake Michigan. The stars glimmered in the water just beyond the roaring bonfire. Students she knew from school and some much older teens she'd never seen before milled around the yard, the moon lighting their way. Olivia grinned. She'd had enough of being the good girl all the time—what did she have to show for it anyway? It was far past time to let loose and find out what life was all about.

"Livly!" Barefooted Jordyn came running toward her wearing a frayed denim miniskirt, a sheer tank top, and sunglasses. She grabbed Olivia's hand and danced in a circle.

"You're crazy! And you've got to be freezing." Olivia shook her head and rubbed her arms against the chill in the autumn air. "Can you even see with those dark glasses on?"

"Who needs to see? I let my heart lead me." Still gripping Olivia's hand, Jordyn looked her up and down. "You look hot tonight. You're going to have to let me borrow that top sometime. I love off-the-shoulder shirts."

"I wasn't sure I should wear it." Olivia adjusted the single strap and pulled down the fitted waistline of the stretchy purple top.

"Are you kidding? It's perfect, and those jeans are to die for." Jordyn twirled one more time and pulled Olivia toward the party. "Come on. There's some people I want you to meet."

She lowered her sunglasses and peered over them, wiggling her eyebrows. "College boys." She let go of Olivia's hand, flipped her ponytail over her shoulder, and set off toward the bonfire.

"Are Brett's parents home?" Olivia searched the yard for signs of an adult.

Jordyn lowered her glasses again.

If she couldn't see, why didn't she take them off?

"You can't be serious. Did you see that huge keg over there?" Jordyn pointed to a silver barrel on the patio. "No way there are adults of any kind at home. Speaking of the keg. . ." She grabbed Olivia's hand and dragged her toward the patio. "We need beverages."

"Um. I don't know. I'm not big on. . ." But why not? Her new outlook on life dictated that fun was the only thing that mattered now, right? No holding back.

Jordyn pumped the keg handle and held a red plastic cup under the spout, letting it fill with a frothy golden brew. She thrust it into Olivia's hand and raised her own cup. "Cheers!"

Olivia leaned her face forward and raised the cup to sniff it. The sprinkles of popping fizz tickled her nose. "Cheers." She forced herself to drink several long gulps. It didn't taste as bad as she remembered from the other night. Still not exactly *good*, but definitely not *bad*.

"Okay then." Jordyn beamed. "Let's top off our drinks and go find those college boys I told you about." She pumped the handle one more time and filled their cups.

Olivia held her arm out to let the foam flow over her fingers and into the grass. When it settled, she took a big drink and plodded after Jordyn across the rocky yard. The heels of Olivia's boots stumbled on the rocks every few steps, but that was nothing compared to how Jordyn's bare feet must have felt. Yet she plowed on.

Halfway to the roaring fire, which blazed at least four feet high in a sandy area near the lake, Jordyn turned around with a cigarette dangling from her lips. "Got a light?"

"No. I didn't know you smoked." What else didn't she know about Jordyn—and about life?

"Oh yeah. On and off since I turned thirteen. Everyone does."

Another moment of truth. No holding back. "Can I bum one off you?" Olivia's voice squeaked like a little mouse.

"Sure!" She tapped one out of the pack and handed it to Olivia.

She hoped Jordyn wouldn't notice her hand shake as she took it.

"Let me find a light. I'll be right back." Jordyn ran off, leaving Olivia alone on the grass with a half-empty beer, staring at an unlit cigarette.

If only *Chuck* could see her now.

Jordyn jogged back to her with a packet of matches.

Olivia studied Jordyn's moves as she struck the match, held it to the cigarette between her lips, and sucked in until it caught. She inhaled deeply and closed her eyes for a moment before exhaling a powdery white plume.

Olivia's turn. Fumbling to light the match without dropping the cigarette, Olivia had to try three times before it sparked and a flame appeared.

"I hate using matches." Jordyn looked at her fingertips. "I've burned my fingers so many times. I usually make sure I have a lighter. I even know one girl who lit an acrylic nail on fire. It looked so funny all twisted and melted."

Olivia smirked in pretend agreement and lifted her hand to her mouth with the cigarette poised between her first two fingers like she'd watched Jordyn do. Inserting it between her lips, Olivia pulled in thick, smoky air as the tip glowed red in the flame. She tried not to let any of it into her lungs, but the taste alone made her sputter and gag. Choking back the coughs, she gave it another try, this time inhaling a little bit of the smoke. The nicotine burned her lungs—Olivia imagined them turning black like in the videos at school—but she held it in anyway.

"I guess it went down the wrong way at first."

Jordyn nodded. "Sure. Happens to me all the time, especially when it's been awhile."

After a few more drags, Olivia felt like an old pro. It tasted gross—exactly like an ashtray smelled—and why did it make her head feel thick and woozy? Didn't matter, looking cool was totally worth it. If she chugged her beer after each drag, it chased the smoke taste from her mouth and helped control the coughing.

Olivia drained her drink. With half a cigarette remaining, she nudged Jordyn and tipped her cup over. "I'm going to go get a refill." She nodded her head toward the keg, feeling happy for the first time in weeks. Months. Years. In fact, she couldn't remember why she hadn't been happy all along.

Jordyn held up her empty cup. "I'll join you. But we're coming right back to this spot. I've got my eye on a real hottie."

"Oh, I'm sure you do." Olivia giggled and spun around toward the house, running smack into a brick wall. She stumbled forward and dropped her cup in the grass as an arm reached out to keep her from falling. She squinted her eyes against the darkness, expecting to see the familiar face of a student from school. It definitely was a familiar face.

Jake.

"Oh, sorry. Here, let me help you." Jake stumbled through his words as he felt for her cup in the grass while maintaining his grip on a can of Coke.

Didn't he know it was her? Olivia glanced to her right and her left. Maybe she could get away without him looking at her. What if she just started running into the dark? Could she make it to the tree line before he recognized her?

Handing her the empty cup, Jake leaned in toward her face. His eyes grew wide at first, and then they sparked with anger. "Liv?" He turned her toward the light and looked into her eyes. "What are you doing here? Are you drinking?" He tipped his cupped hand up to his mouth.

Oh man. Jake would be so mad. Should she lie? No point, really. She held an empty cup of beer in one hand, and a lit cigarette dangled from the other. There'd be no convincing him that she was innocent. She opened and closed her mouth as if to speak, but no words came.

He pressed two fingers hard to his lips. "You're smoking, too?" Jake's eyes grew wide, and he yanked her away from the group. He pulled the cigarette from between her fingers, threw it onto the grass, and ground it to bits.

"So what? I'm sixteen. You don't have to worry about me." She turned away after she finished signing.

Jake pulled her chin back around until she faced him and shook his head. "No way. That's not how this is going to go. You're coming home with me right now." He signed so fast he gave up trying to speak the words. He only did that when he was really mad. "I'm not leaving for college with this to worry about. Mom's going to have to deal with it."

"What?" Olivia spoke through a clenched jaw. "You'd better not tell Mom. How could you do that to me?" So much for Jake being on her side.

"You did this to yourself, Liv." Jake's face softened. "I love you." He crossed his forearms and pressed his fists to his chest.

"I don't want to see you go down this path—no good can come of it. Come on, let's go. Is Mom's car here?" His eyes roved up and down the rows of parked cars.

Olivia nodded and stared at the ground. Where was Jordyn? She could talk their way out of this.

"We'll take hers home, and I'll come back for mine tomorrow." He squeezed her elbow and steered her toward the street.

Olivia pulled against his grip on her arm and finally jerked free. She tugged on his wrist and stepped in front of him, forcing him to look at her face. "Jake. You can't tell Mom. She'll tell Charles, and then who knows what will happen?" She lifted her hands in despair.

"Mom has to know, Liv. Maybe she won't tell Charles. But that'll have to be her decision."

Oh, she'd tell him. No question about it. And he would use it against her—any excuse to punish her was enough for Charles.

"I'm concerned about you." He waved two fingers from each hand in circles in front of his face. *Worried.* Jake helped her into the car. "I can't leave for school if I'm worried about what you're doing to yourself."

"What *I'm* doing?" Olivia sighed in disgust. He'd never get it.

"What does that mean? What are you getting at?" Jake shook his head when she remained silent. "I wasn't the one drinking and smoking tonight."

"That's not what I meant." Olivia turned her head away as she mumbled.

"I don't know what you're talking about. Maybe Mom can get to the bottom of this."

Olivia snorted. *Only if she doesn't have a massage appointment.*

The ride home passed too quickly. They sat at the base of the long driveway while Jake punched in the security code for the gate. Olivia had one more chance to change his mind before it was all over. She touched his arm to make him turn and look at her. "Jake. Please. Don't tell Mom." She fought against the tears burning in her eyes. "Mom *will* tell Charles." She rubbed her flat palm on her heart. "Please."

Jake gripped the steering wheel. "Liv, I love you. I wouldn't do anything to harm you on purpose. I'm doing what I think is the best thing."

Olivia leaned her head back against the seat and squeezed her eyes shut. "You don't understand. It's. . .it's different for you." One lone tear leaked out of her right eye. She wiped it away before Jake could see it. Maybe she should just tell him everything. Surely he'd keep her secret then. Olivia opened her mouth to speak. . .then closed it. She just couldn't do it.

"It's for your own good." Jake pulled up to the garage and waited for it to open.

My own good? Like Jake had any idea what she needed. This sure wasn't it. Olivia got out of the car, went into the house through the front door, and stormed up to her room. She slipped the chain into the lock and pulled the chair in front of the door, wedging it under the handle—something she wished she'd done last time. Perhaps that would keep Charles out. No, nothing could.

Wonder what Mom and Jake are saying. Didn't really matter. If they were going to have a conversation about Olivia, they were going to have to do it without her.

But wait. If she didn't face Mom now, it might come up sometime when Charles was around. It might be better to talk to Mom while he was out of the house—especially with Jake there as a buffer. Plus there was still the chance Jake decided not to fill Mom in on *all* of the details of the evening, and there was only one way to find out.

Olivia popped a piece of gum into her mouth to mask the smell of smoke and beer, sprayed herself with just a touch of body mist—too much would be a dead giveaway—and crept down the stairs, avoiding the squeaky parts. She approached the arched entryway to the kitchen and peeked around the corner.

Mom stood at her usual spot behind the island with her forearms resting on the granite slab. Jake towered just across from Mom with his back toward Olivia.

"Olivia's smart. She'll be okay. She's just testing the waters a little bit." Jake shrugged. "We all do it." Jake wasn't signing, which meant he'd calmed down enough to concentrate on speaking his words clearly. Just the way Olivia had taught him.

Mom shook her head. "Yes, but there's more to it with Liv. She's never gotten over losing your dad." She spoke carefully and deliberately, allowing Jake to read her lips. "And she hates Charles so much for trying to take his place." She lifted her head and closed her eyes. "I'm just not sure she's not going to take it too far." She signed *too far*.

Wait. She thinks Charles trying to take Daddy's place is the problem? And what did she fear Olivia would take too far?

"Have you considered getting her counseling?"

"I mentioned it about a year ago, but Charles had a fit." Mom shook her head. "He hated the idea and forbade me to pursue it." She smacked her pointer finger against her open palm.

I'll bet he did. No way he'd let someone go digging around in Olivia's head, unearthing dirty memories and dark secrets, revealing him as a monster. She'd heard enough. Olivia pulled her shirt down to cover her belly, squared her shoulders, and breezed into the kitchen like nothing was amiss. "What's up?"

she signed to Jake and then went right to the fridge and grabbed a Coke. "I'm thirsty." She drew a line down her throat with her pointer finger.

Mom sighed and rubbed her temples—not too hard though. Of course she wouldn't want to bring back the wrinkles she'd recently had removed. "Care to tell me what happened tonight?"

"Oh, the party?" Olivia gave a sheepish grin as she signed her words toward Jake. "I just did something stupid. It's no big deal. It was my first time—you could even ask Jordyn. I probably looked like a complete dummy. She could have taught me a thing or two."

"Oh?" Mom raised an eyebrow. "So maybe you're spending too much time with Jordyn, then?"

Oops. Backtrack. "No. No. It's not her fault. I know I'm responsible for my own choices. I made a mistake. It won't happen again."

"Okay. I'm counting on that." Mom smiled and took a sip from Olivia's can.

Phew. That wasn't so bad. Would Mom really let it go that easily? Olivia took a long drink and waited for more.

"So I was thinking." Mom's eyes shifted from Olivia to Jake. "How about we go to church on Sunday?"

Olivia sputtered and almost spit out her Coke. "Church?" *Where'd that come from?*

"I ran into Jodie Swinley at the mall today. She said that she and Pastor Tom were doing great, and the church has grown a lot since we were there a few years ago."

"I don't know, Mom." Jake shook his head. "What's the point? I'm going to be leaving in a few days. I plan to find a church when I get to Michigan."

"Yeah, I'm with Jake." Olivia grimaced. "I don't think it's

a great idea." Church was the last place she wanted to go. And what if Charles went with them and she was forced to act like they were a happy family? *Eww.* "Who wants to get up that early anyway?"

"Well, it was only a thought." Mom pulled them both into a hug. "I just want you guys to stay on the right path. Maybe church would help. Promise me you'll think about it."

Jake nodded; then his eyes darted to Olivia. "On second thought, maybe we *should* go. Not like it would kill us."

"I promise I'll think about it." *Sorry, not happening.*

※

"I'm packed up and ready to go." Jake stood in Olivia's doorway with a backpack slung over his shoulder. He looked so tall and grown-up standing there—like a man.

"You're headed out, huh?" Olivia tried to sound lighthearted, even though her heart was breaking.

"Yeah, Coach wants us there for a meeting today, so I have to leave now." His eyes traveled to the floor. "I'm going to miss you, Liv."

Olivia nodded but couldn't look at him for fear of crying again. What would she do without him? How could he leave her? Didn't he know how scary every day of her life was? Then again, how could he know if she didn't tell him?

Jake loved her. Olivia had no doubt about that. Maybe she should tell him. *Right now.* Before he left and it was too late. No way he'd leave if he knew the truth about Charles and what had been going on the past few years.

She lifted her face and turned to her brother with every intention of blurting out the horrible truth. But there he stood, looking every bit like a panting golden retriever in his Michigan sweatshirt with a basketball tucked under his lanky arm. He couldn't wait to get to school and play college ball. He was so excited, and he deserved it. She couldn't selfishly ruin it for him, no matter what it meant for her. Olivia loved her brother more than life itself. He needed this, and her pride for him was far stronger than her fear for herself.

"Play for me?" Jake gestured to the oboe near the music stand in the center of the room and made the sign for *song*.

Olivia laughed. "I've never understood why you like to watch me play. You can't even hear the music." She went to the chair and sat down on the edge, her back straight and her oboe poised.

Jake shook his head. "No. But I can feel it." He had tried to explain many times how he felt the strains of the melody floating through the air and rising up from the floorboards. "Mostly, though, it's the look you get on your face that speaks to me. It's when you're the happiest, and that's the sight I want to take with me."

Olivia placed the reed between her lips and closed her eyes as she began to play the piece she'd been working on: "Adagio for Oboe Concerto in D Minor." She swayed lightly to the swells of the song—felt every note in her soul. As the last melodic breath faded away, she opened her eyes.

Jake was gone.

Chapter 4

Only hundred-dollar bills? There had to be a dozen in Mom's wallet. Would she notice if one disappeared? Olivia thumbed through the cash, hoping to find a twenty. Her gaze darted toward the bathroom door. Once that shower stopped, her decision time would be over. Mom had given Olivia her fifty-dollar weekly allowance earlier that day, but it needed to cover lunch at school plus extras for the whole week. Jordyn said a case of beer cost close to twenty dollars. Her friends would probably want a couple of those.

Mom would never miss a mere hundred bucks. If she did, she'd just assume she'd spent it somewhere and forgotten about it. She could drop that much over lunch and not even blink an eye.

Olivia shifted from one foot to the other. Her friends waited in the driveway, and Olivia really wanted to be gone before Mom got out of the shower and before *Chuck* got home. The thought of seeing Charles made her shudder—plus he'd probably embarrass her in front of her friends by saying something stupid or acting really nice to them.

Just do it!

Olivia plucked a bill from her mom's wallet and shoved the money into the front pocket of her jeans. *Snap.* Wallet closed, she put it back in Mom's bag, tightened the turquoise leather drawstring, and draped the strap across the purse exactly like it had been before she opened it. Hurrying from the room, she let the door softly close behind her and waited until it clicked before she finally gasped for air. Amateur! Hardened criminals didn't forget to breathe.

Oh boy. She'd just stolen money from her own mother. She'd really crossed a line this time. What if she got caught? Not like it mattered. Mom couldn't really do anything to her. Could she? Visions of her laptop, her car privileges, and her recent freedom all flashed before Olivia's eyes. Okay, so Mom *could* do something. But Olivia wouldn't get caught—she'd make sure of it.

The rush of running water turned to a trickle then slowed to drips. Time to get out of here.

Olivia hurried down the stairs, an overnight bag hanging from her shoulder. She'd be sleeping at Jordyn's again. Or so she'd told Mom. If it turned out to be anything like the last party a few weeks ago, there'd be no sleeping. And at least with Jake away at college, there'd be no chance of an unpleasant encounter, like when he caught her drinking at that very first kegger.

Olivia stepped onto the front porch and grinned at her friends as she pulled the towering front door closed behind her. She could already hear the bass thundering from the cloth-top Jeep. Jordyn, in the driver's seat, danced and bobbed her head to the beat. Tara's red hair fanned out across the backseat next to Bailey's shiny black hair. Who was that scrunched next to Bailey?

Olivia settled into the passenger seat and turned around. "Hi, I'm Olivia."

"Hey. I'm Emma, Bailey's sister."

"She's in college, and she has a fake ID." Jordyn grinned and slipped the car in reverse just as Charles pulled around the curve and started toward the house.

"Hurry. Go. Go. Go." Olivia turned and put her hand on the seat behind her, pretending to talk to the girls so Charles wouldn't expect her to wave. "What's he doing?"

"He never even glanced at us." Jordyn sounded confused. "What's your problem?"

Olivia waited until they rounded the curve that took them out of sight of the house. *Phew.* "No problem. At least not now." She unrolled her window a little and let the fresh air flow across her face.

"Um"—Emma turned backward in her seat and peered out the back window—"I just have to say, your dad is gorgeous."

Olivia shuddered. "He's my stepdad, and he's disgusting."

"I don't know, Liv. He really is cute." Bailey winked. "That spiky brown hair. Those dark eyes and huge muscles."

Gross. Were they serious? "Trust me. You want to stay as far away from him as you can." Olivia looked each girl in the eye. "Promise me?"

"Okay. Okay." Bailey laughed. "Someone's sensitive about her stepdaddy."

Tara grinned. "He's not my type anyway."

"Yeah, me neither." Jordyn flipped down the visor and checked her teeth in the mirror.

Olivia couldn't help but notice that Emma eyed her a little longer than the rest. Did she suspect? Surely not. But it would be a good time to change the subject. "Can we take the top off the Jeep?"

"Yeah." Emma leaned forward between the front seats. "It is kind of stuffy back here. My little sister's big rear end is taking up so much room."

"Ha. Nice try! You couldn't fit into my jeans if your life depended on it." Bailey crossed her arms in mock protest.

"Settle down, you two. Don't make me come back there." Jordyn peered into the rearview mirror. "We could take the top off, but October nights get really cold and it's hard to put back on in the dark. I'll just kick on the AC a little bit."

"Yeah," Tara piped up. "Can you see us five, totally buzzed, trying to get this top on at two in the morning?"

"Speaking of buzzed"—Jordyn peeked at Olivia—"we're good for an ID." She gestured her thumb at Emma. "But we're counting on you for the funds. How did that go?"

"Well. . ." Olivia plastered on a sad face and reached into her pocket. "I could only get this." She pulled out one crumpled bill and smoothed it on her leg before waving it in the air with a grin.

"A hundred bucks?" Bailey bounced on her seat.

"That will buy some great stuff. How much of it can we use?" Emma fished out a cigarette and tipped the pack toward Olivia.

"As much as you want. Use it up. Let's have fun." Might as well go all the way. If she got caught, Olivia wouldn't be in any less trouble if they spent only half of it. She took a cigarette from Emma's pack and pressed in the car lighter.

"Yeah, don't forget we're buying for Aaron and Brett, too." Jordyn turned into the parking lot of Discount Liquors. The Jeep bounced as she ran one tire over the curb before pulling into a spot. Olivia scooted out and flipped the seat forward and held it while Emma unfolded her long legs from the backseat.

"You'd think you guys would show a little more respect to the one with the ID and let me sit in front." Emma climbed over Bailey's legs and wedged herself between the front seat and the door.

"Well, it's my car. I have to drive." Jordyn put up her hands.

Olivia waved the money. "And I have the cash."

"Point taken." Emma snatched it from Olivia and straightened her clothes then set off toward the store.

"Don't forget smokes!" Jordyn shouted.

"I hope they don't give her any trouble." Olivia shielded her eyes from the setting sun and watched Emma enter the store.

"She'll be fine. Emma totally looks older than nineteen. Plus her ID is perfect." Jordyn got back in her seat and took out a nail file.

Olivia nipped at a hangnail and tapped her feet on the floor mat. She turned down the radio—then Jordyn turned it up. The wait dragged on forever. "It's been like fifteen minutes, you guys. Should we go in there?" Olivia didn't understand how they could be so calm. She expected a police car to careen into the lot with lights blazing and sirens blaring any minute.

"No way! Are you nuts? They'll definitely question her if we're hanging around." Bailey shook her head. "Besides, she's never had any trouble before."

"Here she comes." Tara pointed at the front of the store, where Emma pushed a full shopping cart through the automatic doors.

"Phew. I was getting worried." Olivia pretended to wipe sweat from above her eyebrow.

Jordyn chuckled. "You need to lighten up, girlie."

The four girls scampered from the car. Jordyn yanked open the back hatch while they waited for Emma to navigate the heavy basket up the sloped parking lot.

With the shopping cart pressed against the Jeep's bumper, they loaded the car. The four cases of beer barely fit in the tiny space behind the backseat. "We'll never drink all of this." Olivia shook her head at their stash. They'd bought way too much alcohol. What if someone got sick—or worse—like in those videos they showed at school?

Olivia bit her lower lip. What if she did something stupid? Maybe she should just back out now—before she did something she'd regret. . .before it was too late.

"Sure we will, or we'll share. Best way to get reinvited to a party is to show up with extra booze." Emma tossed a pack of cigarettes to each girl.

Olivia stared at the little box in her hand. It seemed much more serious to have her own pack rather than to bum a single cig off a friend now and then. Having her own sort of meant she'd crossed a line and become a real smoker. Did she want to be one? Money wasn't really her concern. She got a nice allowance, and there seemed to be an endless supply of money in Mom's purse—Olivia simply needed to help herself when her allowance ran out. Was it the health aspect? No. She didn't care about that—having fun was all that mattered. Did she find smoking fun? Not exactly. It tasted gross and smelled horrible. So why did she do it? Olivia tapped the cigarette on the dashboard then raised it to her lips along with the lighter. She flicked the flame to life and drew a smoky breath into her lungs.

Because it felt good—that's why. It felt good to go against the stream, do bad things—at least these days it did. Plus it calmed her down and gave her confidence. She felt cool with a cigarette in one hand and a beer in the other. Leaning her head back on the seat, she let the wind from the half-open window blow onto her face and whip her hair around in swirls. She blew the smoke out into the wind and watched it disappear, wishing she could follow.

⑤

The security monitor beeped as it came out of hibernation mode, signaling a car had approached the front gate. Mom and Charles were gone for the day, so Olivia would have to get it. She groaned and leaned out from her bed to peek at the tiny display on her nightstand. She couldn't quite make out the driver, so she squinted harder at the screen. She grabbed her head, hoping to quell the throbbing as the nausea rose in her stomach—a clear reminder of the party the night before.

Jodie Swinley? No mistaking her long brown 1980s permed hair with the poodle pouf on top. What was her former pastor's wife doing here? Olivia hadn't spoken to Jodie since the last time she attended youth group around Christmas three years ago. Mom said she'd run into her a week or so ago but hadn't said anything about her coming by.

Ugh. Perfect timing. Olivia pulled her pillow over her head. She could just ignore the beep.

But Jodie pressed the buzzer again. Then again. It appeared she wasn't planning to go away.

Olivia groaned as she leaned from her bed to press the button to open the gate. She only had a minute or two while Jodie waited for the iron doors to creak open so she could squeeze her car through and then make the drive up the long, winding driveway.

What could Olivia do to make herself presentable in a couple of minutes? She slid from her bed and hurried to the bathroom. While she brushed her teeth, she ran a comb through her messy and most likely smoky hair. She fumbled in the medicine cabinet for aspirin, which she popped into her mouth and guzzled down with a full glass of water. Her skin looked ghostly, but that couldn't be helped. She'd run out of time. A quick spritz of lavender body spray, and then Olivia slunk down the stairs just in time to hear Jodie's knock.

"Hi, Olivia." She reached out and pulled Olivia into a tight embrace.

Did Jodie actually stiffen at the sight and smell of her, or was that only Olivia's imagination? "Hey, Jodie." Olivia hugged her back, hoping it was still okay to call her Jodie. "I haven't seen you in, like, forever. What brings you by Chez Whitford?" She stifled a yawn, which only made her head throb harder. *Come on, aspirin; do your trick.*

"Oh, I saw your mom out shopping the other day, and then we spoke on the phone yesterday. Didn't she tell you? I thought I'd come by to visit with you for a little bit." She raised her eyebrows. "Judging by the eye roll, it looks like things might not be going so well?"

Olivia stepped back to let her into the foyer. "Mom told you stuff about me, huh?" Her voice echoed across the marble floors and up the spiral staircase to the three-story ceiling.

"She's a little concerned about you." Jodie followed Olivia into the den and perched on the edge of a sofa.

"Trust me. She's not worried about *me*." Olivia whipped her head side to side. Her brain felt like it bounced inside her skull like a pinball. She fought the urge to rub her temples. "Mom just doesn't know how to keep me from messing up her perfect world."

"Olivia. Alcohol? Cigarettes? Lying? Come on. Of course your mother's worried about you." Jodie's heavily made-up eyes darkened as she looked Olivia over from head to toe.

"If she's so concerned, why hasn't she talked to me about any of it herself?" When Jake told her about that party, she just blew it off. Never brought it up again. "This is the first I've heard about this."

Jodie raised her shoulders. "I don't know, hon."

"She can't be bothered to deal with me herself, apparently. Instead, she called for reinforcements so she can dump it on you." But at least Mom hadn't told Charles. Though that could change at any moment.

Jodie's eyes narrowed. "What's going on with you? This isn't the Olivia I once knew."

"It's been awhile since you've been around. How do you know this isn't the real me?" Her eyes burned with that telltale sting. *Don't cry. Don't cry.* "What does it matter anyway?"

"Oh, hon. It does matter. You're so important to a lot of people. And the reason I know this isn't the real you is that God doesn't break His promises." Jodie squeezed her eyes shut, her lips moving.

Olivia rolled her eyes. "Prayer isn't going to help things, Jodie. Sure won't bring my dad back. He prayed to God with his very last breath—I heard him. Look what it got him. Prayer isn't going to wake my mom up. And it sure won't get rid of *Chuck*." Olivia walked to the window, her back to Jodie. "So, if you don't mind, I'll just keep doing what comes naturally. Then we'll all get to see who the real me is."

The floor creaked when Jodie stood and stepped behind Olivia. She put her hands on Olivia's upper arms, making her flinch. "I think you're hurting. I think you want someone to fight for you. Will you let me in? Let me be your friend?"

I've got friends—ones who understand me. Olivia sighed. "You and Pastor Tom are still my friends. But there's nothing you can do. I'll be all right. It's really not as bad as Mom made it out to be, I'm sure. Just normal teenage stuff—you know, everyone experiments with that stuff. No big deal." Olivia shrugged. "But I've got homework to do and a band concert tonight." *And a nap to take.* She stepped toward the door.

"Hang on. I'll leave you to your homework in just a second." Jodie reached into her bag and pulled out a glossy pamphlet. "Would you do me a favor and take a quick look at this?" She handed it to Olivia.

"Diamond Estates? What's that?" The front-page picture of an old stone building nestled in the mountains was kind of cool—might be a haunted house. Olivia turned the booklet over in her hands to read the back. "Colorado? It says they help troubled girls." *Ah, so that's it.* She held Jodie's gaze with fire in her eyes. "You're trying to say *I* need to go to a place like this?"

"I'm only making sure you know your options. That you do have choices." Jodie held her hands up, palms out. "No need to get riled up. It's just that sometimes it's good to completely remove yourself from your current situation in order to make a fresh start."

"Fresh start? My whole life has been one fresh start after another." Olivia shook her head and strode to the front door. "I'm certainly not going to go looking for another one anytime soon." She flipped the page over and looked at the front again. "Besides, Charles would never agree to pay for something like this." He'd be paranoid that they'd uncover his deep, dark secrets. She tried to give Jodie back the brochure.

"Well, just hang on to it—you never know. It's a good place—totally subsidized by donations from people and churches all over the country. Charles wouldn't have to pay a dime unless he wanted to contribute." Jodie stepped onto the porch. "I'll be praying for you, hon."

"Don't get me wrong. I appreciate your concern, and I know you mean well. But this sort of thing isn't for me."

"Okay. Call me if you need me. Anytime." Jodie squinted from the sun. She opened her mouth like she had more to say, but turned and went to her car without another word.

Olivia closed the front door and glanced at the pamphlet she clutched in her hand. Shaking her head, she crumpled it and dropped it into the trash can on the way to her room. Yeah right. Like she'd go to Diamond Estates. She hadn't done anything to deserve kiddie jail.

It would take an act of God to get me to that place.

Chapter 5

Her symphonic band concert in an hour, Olivia tore through her jam-packed closet for something to wear. She thought back to how desperate she'd been to try out for the elite band. Then to make it—what an honor that had been. Now she didn't even want to go to the first concert of the year. She wondered what would happen if she skipped it to hang out with her friends instead. She'd get kicked out most likely, and that wouldn't take her very far in her dream of music school scholarships and orchestras. But did she even care about those things anymore?

A one-hundred-dollar bill, fresh from Mom's purse, burned a hole in the pocket of her jeans. That along with her fifty-dollar allowance were the makings of a pretty great party, plus a week of smokes for her *and* her friends.

No. She had an oboe solo. They'd kill her if she didn't show up. At least the concert started at six, so there'd be plenty of time for partying afterward. *Okay, concentrate. Black skirt or a black dress?* She moved to the deep recesses of her closet and flipped out the arm that held a cascade of her fanciest dresses. Dark fabric swished at the back of the row. Olivia reached for it around the pink chiffon and yellow silk, hoping to discover some classy couture number she'd forgotten about. When she pulled the shiny black dress out, realization slammed into her stomach like a wrecking ball.

Her unsuspecting hands sizzled with shock as she held her funeral dress from nine years ago. Daddy's funeral. How had she forgotten that she'd hung it back there on the rack as a memento?

Olivia slumped down on the floor of her closet and clutched the fabric to her chest as memories of the day she'd worn that dress assailed her.

The tops of her new patent-leather Mary Janes were already scratched from crawling around on the maroon carpet with her cousin Patrick. She swung her legs and counted the scuff marks as she sat in the velvet chair and waited for the people who just kept coming and coming. They all wanted to hug her. Some of them smelled good, like soap, so she didn't mind too much. But some of them smelled really bad—like food or bad breath. Why didn't they stay home to take a shower and leave her alone with her daddy?

The day before, when they thought Olivia slept curled up on the couch between them, Auntie Sylvie told Mommy she should let Olivia go play at a friend's house, that she was too young to be at the funeral. But Olivia wanted to be there because Mommy said she wouldn't see Daddy again. Did she mean ever? No. Daddy would never leave her forever. She was his angel.

Finally, the music started playing, and Mommy clutched Olivia's hand and helped her walk past all the people to sit in the front row. It felt strange all the way up in front by the pastor. Mommy and Daddy usually liked to sit in the middle so they could hold hands without the pastor seeing them. Well, they didn't exactly say that was why, but they sure did hold hands a lot.

Daddy's box came rolling down the aisle. Jake helped the big men push it. He looked like a grown-up man in his suit. Wait. The lid was closed. Where was Daddy? "Mommy, when do we get to see Daddy in the box again?"

She shook her head, her face white like a ghost. "Livvie, it's done. The men shut it."

"But I didn't get to say good-bye to him." Olivia felt hot tears coursing down her cheeks. "I want my daddy," she whispered.

Mommy shook her head and scrunched her eyes shut.

Olivia's heart pounded, and she jumped to her feet. She slipped from her mother's grip and dove for the floor in front of the casket, shredding her tights and her knees. She pounded her hands into the carpet, kicked her feet, and screamed, "I want my daddy!"

Exhaling, Olivia tried to shake the details from her mind and wiped at streams of tears with the skirt of the tiny black dress she clutched. She rubbed her knuckles and cringed at the memory of how she had beat them to a pulp on that ragged carpet.

The wails! Oh, the sound of the women wailing—Olivia had never forgotten it. When she had nightmares of hell, those were the sounds she heard. Mom later explained that they just couldn't take the sight of the little girl agonizing for her daddy. The grief was too much for many of them to bear, and they had to leave. Too much for Mom, too—she disappeared, never even tried to comfort Olivia as she crouched on the floor in desperation.

Enough. Olivia stood to her feet, grabbed a black pencil skirt and a ruffled blouse. She hurriedly pulled on tights and donned her Manolo pumps. She looked in the mirror. Should she hide the purple streak to make Mom happy? Olivia twisted it under a dark layer and secured it with a clip then stared at her reflection. Definitely a pretty hairdo—conservative—but it just didn't look like her. She whipped the clip from her hair and ran a brush through it.

That was more like it. Mom would have to deal with it.

೫

Olivia took her coveted first-chair position next to two other oboists in the symphonic band made up mostly of students a year ahead of her. On this special night, the band would be featuring an original arrangement taken from the musical score of *Phantom of the Opera*.

Even though she'd never seen the live play, the music had haunted her as she practiced. It affected her deep down, unlike anything she'd ever played on her oboe. Olivia had been awarded the solo from her favorite piece in the score. Mom was there to watch—not Charles though. When he'd heard she had the solo, he ranted that it wasn't even in the play. He even accused her of making it up. Olivia's teacher explained that he was right, her solo wasn't actually in the play, but it was in a scene in the movie version. Happy with the compromise, Olivia figured she and Charles were both right—called it a draw. Charles hadn't liked that very much. Big surprise.

The lights dimmed, and a hush fell over the audience as the conductor raised his arms. The musicians came to attention like soldiers on a battlefield and poised their instruments, ready to play.

BAM!

The show started with a thundering note and a cymbal crash. Olivia lost herself in the swells and strains of the beautiful music. All of her doubts and fears melted away as she coaxed perfection from her instrument. Song after song, she remained in complete control while she played—in fact, it was the only time in life that she felt truly in control.

Her turn. A real solo in front of an audience. Olivia's hands trembled as she readied them over the delicate instrument, waiting for her cue. And. . .there. She played her own heartbeat. Olivia let her pain, her joy, her sorrow, and her laughter flow from her soul through her fingertips. She'd never felt more vibrant as the music of her heart filled that auditorium, alone.

What was it that made her feel so alive as she played at that moment, more alive than any other moment?

Then it hit her. She felt heard.

⟡

"A hundred and fifty bucks sure doesn't buy what it used to," Olivia joked as she helped her friends load the carton of cigarettes and four cases of beer into the back of Jordyn's Jeep.

Emma laughed as she tucked her ID back into her wallet. "I'm pretty sure this will get us through the night."

"I might have a little surprise for us, too." Tara grinned and patted the purse slung across her chest.

"What is it?" Bailey yanked at the strap.

Tara held tight and clamped it down with her elbow. "You're just going to have to wait until you finish your third beer." Her eyes twinkled.

"Why third?" Bailey chuckled. "You're such a weirdo."

"Where are we going anyway?" Olivia watched out the side window and then swiveled to look out the back.

"You'll see." Jordyn winked.

"All right, I need to get out of these clothes. Let me know if someone's coming." Olivia reached under her skirt and rolled her tights down from the waistband then pulled them off each foot. "Hah. Here, watch this." She hung them out the window and let the empty legs flap in the wind.

"You're going to lose—" Jordyn gasped as the tights slipped from Olivia's grip and got swallowed into the night.

Olivia laughed. "Whatever." She pulled her skirt off and lifted her hips off the seat to slip on her jeans. There. The hard part was over—now for the top. She unbuttoned her blouse and got her hoodie ready to pull on. *Just do it. One. Two. Three.* She slid her arms out of her blouse and sat in her bra as she fumbled with the sweatshirt.

HONK!

A semitruck barreled by blaring his horn and blinking his brights.

"Great. Now I'm flashing the whole world." Olivia squirmed into her shirt and zipped it. Why hadn't she worn a cami under her shirt?

"Well, at least you look good while doing it. And. . .here we are." Jordyn turned into an upscale community and punched a code into a little box, kind of like the one in front of Charles's house. A mechanical arm lifted to let them enter. "This is where my dad lives. He has an old storage unit on his property that he let me turn into a hangout a year ago. He'll never know we're out there."

"Wait a second." Emma chuckled. "You're telling me we're going to your childhood hideout? Do you have a stash of forbidden makeup and a No Boys Allowed sign on the door?" She laughed and gave Bailey a high five. "Is there a club initiation?"

"Very funny. You won't be teasing me when you see it." Jordyn pulled forward and then reversed the Jeep into a parking space near the community clubhouse. "Dad's property is that way." She pointed across a dark ravine. "We'll go through those bushes on the other side and be right by the. . .place."

Tara snickered. "You were going to say clubhouse."

Bailey covered her mouth, but the giggles still escaped.

"Yeah, right." Jordyn rolled her eyes. "Now, you guys are going to have to be really quiet until we get in there. Dad doesn't know we're here."

"What would happen if he found out?" Olivia imagined an angry man bursting in on them. She'd had enough of that to last a lifetime.

Jordyn heaved a case from the trunk and handed it to

Emma before taking one herself. "He'd want to hang out with us, and then he'd drink all of our beer."

Olivia grabbed a case and followed Jordyn and the others into the trees. "You mean he lets you drink? That's awesome."

"Sure. After the divorce, he decided he wanted to be the cool parent, so basically anything goes. Most of the time it's great. Now, shh." Jordyn lifted a finger to her lips as they passed through a backyard.

They cut across several yards and arrived at a shed. Jordyn dug under the floor mat, pulled out a key, and unlocked the door. "Don't turn on any lights until I make sure the blackout shades are pulled. He could see this place from his kitchen window if he happened to look out."

They stepped inside and waited.

Bang!

"Ouch!"

"You okay?"

"What's going on, you guys?" Was someone else inside? Olivia turned toward the door, ready to bolt.

Something rustled and a switch flipped, drenching the room with light. Brightly colored overstuffed furniture sat around a wide-screen plasma TV. A refrigerator stood in one corner and a microwave in the other. A dinette sat in the center of the kitchenette on top of plank wood flooring. Cool clubhouse.

Jordyn hunched over, rubbing her shin. "Banged it on the coffee table. Man, that hurts so bad, I'm afraid to look." She pulled up the leg of her jeans.

"It's skinned, but I'm pretty sure you're going to make it." Olivia rolled her eyes at Bailey.

"This is an awesome place." Emma peeked in the fridge.

Jordyn turned on the stereo and tossed everyone a beer. "Toast?" Jordyn popped open her can and raised it in the air.

"To a great year of partying and lots of hundred-dollar nights!"

They touched their cans together and guzzled a big drink.

Emma lit up a cigarette. "How come you never told us about this place before?"

"I don't know. I didn't want to bring anyone here to hang out with my dad—it's embarrassing—and it never occurred to me to sneak in here. But, hey, what's the worst that could happen? We'd just have to share our beer with him."

"Well, that's fine. We have plenty. But we aren't sharing this." Tara reached into her purse and pulled out a white napkin that she laid down on the coffee table.

Everyone drew close and peered over her shoulder as she unfolded her little package to reveal several thin, nubby cigarettes with pinched ends.

"Is that what I think it is?" Olivia's heart raced. Marijuana. Weren't they taking things a bit too far? "I don't think I'm up for that." Didn't they know how much trouble they could get into? Could she be in trouble for even being in the house with it?

Emma brushed her off. "Come on, don't be a baby. You're doing it."

"Let's smoke it now in case your dad finds us later and we can't." Tara put it to her lips and flicked the cigarette lighter.

Olivia stared openmouthed. She stood in a room with someone smoking pot. How could that be? It came about so easily. First beer, then cigarettes, now pot. This couldn't be happening.

She looked at each of the girls. Who were these people— these girls she called her friends? She didn't even know them— or, better yet, they didn't know her. Or maybe they did. Maybe this was how it started for everyone, and they knew Olivia would be ready.

A smoky sweet smell filled the room as the first nubby stick made its way around the circle. It would be passed to Olivia. Do it, or don't do it? A defining moment. She had one foot in the party scene, and one foot back home with Daddy—except Daddy wasn't there. So what was her decision going to be?

She might as well take a chance. Who knew when there'd be another opportunity? And if she didn't like it, she'd just not do it again. No need to make it such a big deal, right? She was a smart girl—everyone said so—so she'd know when she'd had enough. As the little rolled cigarette passed in front of her face, Olivia watched her hand rise to accept it. A foreign object—like it was someone else's hand pinching the marijuana between her fingers. Olivia lifted it to her lips and sucked in the heady air. She held it for several moments—until she just had to breathe—like she'd seen the other girls do.

The pot went around the circle a few more times until only a few nubs lay in the green metal ashtray. Olivia couldn't tell if the haze filling the room had come from the smoke or if it was because of her own dizziness. She held her hand up in front of her face and giggled at her wiggling fingers. What was so funny? Olivia had no idea. *Life* was funny.

The other girls joined in, cracking up at nothing until tears ran down their cheeks.

Tara took several deep breaths and held her stomach. "Why are we laughing?"

"I don't know," the other three girls replied in unison, which sent them into another fit.

"I'm going to the bathroom. Nobody leave, okay?" Bailey slurred her words.

"Where would we go?" Olivia giggled.

"I dunno. I'm just saying." Bailey turned toward the bathroom. "Hey!" She pointed her finger and flung a wobbly arm at Jordyn. "Do you have any mac 'n' cheese?"

"Oh, I love macaroni and cheese." Tara let out a belch, which started her on another round of laughter.

"Oh yeah! That sounds so good." Jordyn stumbled to the kitchenette and flung open all the cabinet doors. "Found some." She held up two boxes of spiral Kraft and opened the refrigerator door.

Emma located a pot under the stove and filled it with water.

Jordyn stood in front of the open fridge for a full minute. "What am I looking for?"

"Milk and butter for mac 'n' cheese?" Emma asked.

"Oh, right." Jordyn bit her lip. "I have yogurt." She moved a few things around and pulled out a jar of powdered coffee creamer. "I know. We'll mix this with water to make milk and use yogurt instead of butter."

Olivia finished her beer and rose to help, holding on to the countertop as she made her way. "That'll probably be even better than the regular way. Maybe we can patent that recipe and get independently wealthy."

"Here, put some of this in there, too." Bailey handed Jordyn a jar of bacon bits.

"Ooh! Perfect." Emma pinched a few bacon bits and placed them on her tongue.

Thirty minutes later, after a big bowl of bacon-macaroni-yogurt-and-cheese and a couple of more beers, Olivia held her stomach and moaned. "I don't feel so good."

"Now that you mention it, I'm not feeling too hot either." Bailey zigzagged in the general direction of the bathroom.

Olivia sank to the floor and crawled to the sofa. She climbed onto the cushions and dropped her head on a velvet throw pillow. "I'm just gonna lay here for a little bit. Save me some more of the good stuff."

Chapter 6

Hot coffee breath tickled her cheek, but it hurt to even think about opening her eyes. She threw an arm over her head and moaned. So bright. Whoever was there didn't seem to be planning to move anytime soon. If those girls were about to do something to her with cold water, she'd have to kill them.

Okay. Open your eyes. You can do it. Olivia pried one eye open and found a man staring at her, just inches from her face.

No!

Oh wait, it wasn't Charles. Then who? Olivia let her eyes rove a little farther down the man's face. *Uh-oh.*

"Nice of you to join the living, missy." The policeman shook his head.

Olivia searched for the girls and evidence of their party.

Oh boy. Busted—big-time. Jordyn, Emma, and Bailey sat at the dinette with all their contraband piled in front of them. Tara was nowhere to be seen. Lucky girl—she must have left before the cops arrived. Olivia furrowed her eyebrows at Jordyn, who had her head on her arms.

A thirtysomething man with a Santa Claus beer belly, wearing pajamas, nodded toward Jordyn. "No, Officer. I didn't know they were here. But, like I said, she's my daughter. If I'd known she and her friends were the ones hanging out in here, I wouldn't have called the police." He glared at Jordyn and shook his head. "I'm sorry for the trouble."

Jordyn peered up at her dad with puppy eyes. "I'm really sorry, Dad."

"Well, problem is we're here now." The officer leaned his mouth toward the radio on his shoulder and pressed the button. "We've got underage drinking. The use of a fake ID—she's only nineteen, but that's still an adult supplying minors with alcohol. Plus possession and the use of a controlled substance." He lifted the ashtray and shifted it, exposing all three of the butts. He held it up to his buddy. "They smoked at least three. No wonder this one crashed out on the sofa." He gestured to Olivia.

Oh no. Olivia didn't feel so great. Her stomach roiled at the sight and smell of the ashes, and her head felt like it might split in two. She swallowed a few times as her mouth started to water. "I. . .I. . .have to. . ." Olivia covered her mouth as her stomach heaved. She knocked over a chair in her rush to get to the bathroom, where she vomited into the toilet. She feared she'd never be able to breathe again as the spasms rocked her body.

Her stomach empty, Olivia wiped her mouth with a wad of toilet paper and splashed cold water on her face. She stared into the mirror. What would happen now? What had she done? Would she go to jail? Had they called home already? Mom would be so disappointed. Charles would probably kill her. There was one sure way to find out for sure what was going on, but she didn't want to go back out there. Ever.

"Miss?" A light knock sounded at the door. "You've had plenty of time. Come on out."

Olivia creaked open the door and stepped across the swaying floor back into the kitchen. The cabin stood completely empty except for the police officer who had called her out from the bathroom. His name tag read OFFICER MARK STAPLETON. "Where are my friends?"

"They're in the squads. We're ready to take you home now."

He held the door open and helped steady her by the elbow as she wobbled onto the gravel path.

Olivia hung her head and followed him through the backyard and around the house to the waiting police car with its lights flashing. She slid into the backseat beside Bailey. "Where is everyone else?" Olivia whispered as the police officer stood outside the car speaking into his radio.

"Tara took off around the back when the cops pulled up. They're leaving Jordyn here with her dad. Emma got arrested and hauled off to jail." Bailey's voice caught, and her chin quivered.

"What?" Olivia's stomach sank. "Why her and not us?"

Bailey rubbed her forehead. "Come on, Olivia. She's nineteen, used a fake ID, bought liquor for minors, and smoked pot. What do you think?" She shook her head. "Look, I don't want to talk right now, okay?"

Olivia slid down in the seat and turned away from the window, hoping no one she knew would see her. The ride took forever, and yet no time at all. She felt every bump as she fought back waves of nausea and scrunched her eyes against a glaring headache. Oh, what she would give to have the chance to do this night over again.

They approached Bailey's house first. Her dad stood on the porch with his arms crossed on his chest. The cops must have called him already. Did that mean Mom and Charles had received a call, too? Olivia's stomach convulsed. She swallowed and lifted her face to gulp fresh air as the door opened for Bailey to step out of the cruiser.

Olivia watched Bailey shuffle up the sidewalk with her hands in her pockets and her head hung low. It reminded Olivia of the look on a prisoner's face when he walked from his death-row cell to his final destination. Would Bailey even get a last meal? She couldn't watch any longer and slid even farther down in her seat, avoiding the scene on the porch.

After a few minutes, the policeman returned to the car and pulled out of the driveway without a word to Olivia. He turned in the direction of her house.

My turn.

❧

"If no one answers the door, I'll have to bring you with me to the police station." Officer Stapleton rang the doorbell again. He turned his mouth toward the radio on his shoulder and pressed the button.

Olivia shook her head in horror. "But. . .but I have the security code. I can just let myself in the house." Maybe Mom and Charles wouldn't have to know after all.

"I have to turn you over to your parents. I can't just drop you here and leave." He pressed the buzzer one more time. "Looks like you'll have to come with me." He stepped off the porch and motioned for Olivia to follow as he spoke into his radio.

Oh no. Please! At that moment headlights shone on them like the spotlights that illuminated Olivia at the concert just hours before. If only she still sat in her seat with her oboe in hand, then none of this would be real. Olivia wanted to look away as the sleek BMW pulled up beside the squad car with its flashing police lights. She didn't want to witness the expression on her mom's face as she put the pieces together or the anger that would surely darken Charles's face. But, like watching a train wreck, no matter how hard she tried, she couldn't tear her eyes from the scene.

Peering out the car window, Mom's eyes roved up and down the length of Olivia's body, checking for injury, no doubt. She glanced at the closed garage doors.

Don't worry, Mom, your precious car is safe and sound.

She turned back to Olivia, her face a picture of defeat.

Or was that fear?

Charles's red pockmarked face looked subhuman in his rage. Of course, he instantly assumed she'd done something wrong. In this case, he happened to be right. He was about to have the perfect opportunity to play self-righteous, indignant father. Or whatever role he chose.

They climbed from the car. Mom hesitantly approached the officer, still gripping the carryout container holding the remains of her dinner.

Standing with his feet apart and his hands on his hips, Charles thundered, "I demand to know what is going on here!"

Officer Stapleton's head jerked back in surprise at the outburst. He glared at Charles. "Sir, you need to calm down."

Charles glared back at the police officer and pointed one white-knuckled bony finger at his face. "I want some answers. Now."

I'm going to throw up. Olivia's hands grew clammy, and her stomach burned and gurgled. Feeling woozy, she dropped down to the porch step so she wouldn't vomit all over the policeman's feet.

With the back of her hand pressed against Olivia's forehead, Mom sat beside her on the porch. "Was there an accident? Are you hurt?"

"What are you thinking sitting down like that?" Charles stormed across the driveway to tower over Olivia. "Show some respect and stand up. What have you done?" Without waiting for a reply, he turned to the officer again. "I demand some answers. And Ginny—get away from that little twit until we get them." He glared up at the dark sky, shaking his head in disgust. "Is she hurt, you ask. Stupid woman. She's obviously drunk."

Stepping between Charles and Olivia, Officer Stapleton put his hand on his belt near the Taser. "Sir, you're going to need to calm down immediately, or we'll have to move this discussion to the station."

Charles closed his mouth and folded his arms across his chest, his eyes piercing the night with hate.

Officer Stapleton nodded at Mom. "I'm sure she doesn't feel well, ma'am. She's had a lot to drink and some marijuana."

Mom gasped and covered her mouth. "Is that true?" She lifted Olivia's chin and peered into her eyes. "What is going on with you? How could you do that?"

"I don't know." Olivia put her head in her hands.

"You don't know?" Charles sputtered through clenched teeth as his face morphed into mottled blotches of red and white. His eyebrows rose to a peak in the middle like little horns.

Olivia watched his ears turn beet red and expected smoke to billow from them at any moment. His hands clenched and unclenched several times, like he wanted to strangle something. . .her.

"I'm through with you." Charles looked from Olivia to the cop and back to Olivia with complete disgust before storming into the house. The door slammed violently, and the house seemed to shudder in fear.

Olivia's eyes pled with the police officer. *Take me with you.* She faced a rough night if she stayed in that house. As long as Mom stuck around, she might be okay. But once Mom went to bed. . .being arrested would be a much better option.

"Ma'am, is everything going to be all right here?" He peered closer at Mom's face. His eyes widened. "Don't I know you from somewhere. . .um"—he checked his papers—"Mrs. Whitford?"

Her hand still covering her mouth, Mom nodded. "You're Mark Stapleton. We used to go to church together when I was still married to Olivia's dad—before the accident."

"Oh wow. You're Ginny Mansfield." The officer grinned. "I haven't seen you in ages. How are y–" His face darkened. "Oh, I'm sorry. I was surprised to see you and forgot what was happening here for a moment. How unprofessional." He stuck his hand in his pocket and extended a business card to Olivia and one to her mom. "Please call me if you run into any trouble or need anything—either of you. My direct line is on there."

Mom took the card and stared at it blankly, her eyes dull and chalky. It didn't look like things were computing for her. She opened her mouth and closed it several times. No words came.

Officer Stapleton sighed. "You know"—he reached into the car and pulled out a pamphlet from under the visor—"I don't normally do this, but in this case, I just can't help myself. I hope it's okay." Officer Stapleton handed the glossy brochure to Mom.

"Diamond Estates?" Mom turned the paper over and studied the back.

How could that be? The old stone castle pictured on the front proved it was the exact same brochure Jodie had given Olivia earlier that day. Coincidence was one thing, but this seemed like some sort of cosmic conspiracy against her.

"It's a place where troubled girls can get real help in all areas of their lives—physical, mental, and spiritual. The director, Ben Bradley, and his wife, Alicia, are doing some amazing work there—even their son, Justin, pitches in. I've been out there to help twice. Building projects. . .stuff like that. Wonderful thing they've got going on."

"But. . .we don't need. . . Olivia's not troubled." Mom shook her head, her eyes confused.

He put his hand on his radio. "I'm not going to say any more. I could get into trouble for even bringing it up to you while I'm on the job. Just take a look at it. You know your situation far better than I do." He gave one swift nod and got into his cruiser. The flashing lights stopped as the window rolled down. "You call me anytime, okay?"

Olivia nodded but refused to look at her mom.

He gave a soft smile, the corners of his eyes crinkling with kindness, then drove away with a wave.

When the rumble of his motor and the beam from his headlights faded into nonexistence, Olivia stood trembling. Exposed. "Mom?"

Mom's head snapped back, and her eyes popped wide open. She shot a look up to Olivia's bedroom window, her face dark with fear. "Olivia. I don't want to talk about any of this right now. You need to go into the house. Go to your room and lock the door—stay out of sight for the rest of the night."

"But. . ." What was going on? Mom actually seemed scared. Had Charles hurt her, too? Could it be that she knew the truth? If so. . .how could. . . ? No. Surely Mom would have done something to put an end to it if she'd known.

"Just do as I say. Right now." Mom pulled her gaze from the upstairs window and jerked her head toward the house. "Go."

Olivia scurried past her, through the front door, and up the stairs as though an unseen ghost was gaining on her. She could feel its evil presence all around her but had no idea where it hovered. She propelled her body toward her room with the force it would require to speed through quicksand and finally reached her doorway.

She panted as she looked both ways down the hallway. Seeing no one, Olivia stepped inside her room and slipped the chain into the lock. Safe. Olivia slumped back against the door and gushed a big sigh of relief.

A sinister taunt came from the direction of her bed.

"Running from someone?"

Chapter 7

Dread fell like a cloak over Olivia's body. Like a robot, she inched herself around until she faced the right side of her room.

There he sat, on the edge of her bed, with a lecherous grin on his face. His legs were crossed, and his hands were clasped around his knees. He'd seem relaxed to a stranger, but Olivia saw the white-knuckled grip Charles had on his leg and the twitch that pulled at his right eye and the corner of his mouth.

Olivia reached behind her head and released the chain lock. Not that Mom would come—she never had before.

"What do you think I'm going to do, beat you, girl? You think you're worth my effort?" He snorted and pulled a half-empty bottle of amber liquid from behind his back. He lifted it to his lips and took several long gulps.

A beating would be a welcome reprieve from his usual repertoire. It didn't matter. Whatever he did to her, Olivia was done cowering in a corner. She'd stand up to him for once.

Charles drained his bottle and threw it at the wall, where it shattered, raining millions of glass tears onto Olivia's floor. He swiped his forearm across his upper lip and shook his head. "No. I don't care anymore. I've given you everything I could think of. Everything your money-hungry mama could think to demand, that is. But I'll never live up to the saintly image of your dearly departed *father*."

You've got that right, you psycho creep.

"So I'll tell you what. I'm going to leave you alone. In two years, you'll never have to see me again. Who knows, maybe sooner if I shake my leg until your mom falls off. Which might be much sooner rather than later, since I saw her flirting with that pig outside." He stumbled toward her and jabbed a crooked finger in her face. "Just stay out of my sight. I don't want to hear a peep out of you or that ridiculous oboe ever again." Charles teetered out of the room and down the hallway like a pinball bouncing off the walls.

Hmm. Did he mean it? Would he really leave her alone? Doubtful. It would probably be like every other time he made some kind of promise so she'd lower her guard; then he'd strike. He probably only left her alone tonight because he worried Mom might come looking for him. When Olivia had been younger, things with Charles had been much worse for her because she was a scared little girl and he knew it—and loved it. Now, at least he had to stop and wonder what he could get away with. Maybe he figured he'd used up his luck.

Olivia snatched her purse from where she'd dropped it on the floor and pawed through it like a desperate junkie. Maybe a smoke would settle her nerves, or at least her stomach. She crept to the bathroom, avoiding the creaky spots on the wood floor, and sank onto the edge of her bathtub. Her trembling hands fumbled to pull a cigarette from the pack and strike the match. She brought them toward her lips, the flame flickering as an extension of her jitters. How had she come to this? Olivia opened the window a crack and blew the smoke out, hoping no one would smell it.

Now what? Hide out forever? Run away? Turn into the perfect good girl? Olivia took a long drag. Why did none of those seem appealing, let alone like real possibilities? She slid into the empty bathtub and rested her head on the inflatable bath pillow. Maybe she could live right here, in the bathroom.

After Olivia had started on her second cigarette, a soft knock sounded at the door. She jumped.

"Olivia?" Mom's voice sounded normal—sunny even.

"I'm. . .uh"—Olivia looked down at her fully clothed body—"taking a bath."

"Okay. When you're done, buzz me. I want to chat with you."

Chat? A police escort home only warranted a little *chat*? Olivia shook her head. Not that she wanted to be in trouble exactly. Well then, what did she want? Normalcy. Security. Love. Apparently too much to ask for around here.

Olivia took her time getting into heavy flannel pajamas, sprayed her room with deodorizer in case the smoke smell lingered, then buzzed her mom. "Where are you?"

"Oh, don't worry, dear. I'll come to you."

Dear?

Olivia climbed into bed to wait and pulled the covers up to her chin. The effects of the alcohol and pot had finally worn off, and she just wanted some blessed sleep. It was three o'clock in the morning, after all. Maybe if Olivia were out of it before Mom got there, she'd leave quietly without trying to have her little talk. *Ha.* Not likely.

Mom opened the door and crossed the room to Olivia's bedside.

Thanks for knocking.

"Mind if I sit down?"

"No. Go ahead." Olivia shifted over a little bit while Mom made herself comfortable amid the mounds of down pillows, wincing as she leaned back against the headboard.

Olivia sighed. "Let's have it."

"Have what?" Mom pulled her eyebrows together in

confusion. "Oh, you mean you think I'm going to yell at you?" She waved a bruised hand. "Liv, I'm past that. You're sixteen, and you need to make your own choices. I want us to be friends. Friends don't yell."

What? Friends. Where had that come from? No! Olivia wanted a mom, not a friend. "What do you mean?" And where'd she those big bruises on her arm?

"I mean that I want us to enjoy each other, go places together, and confide in each other. That can't happen if I'm being a grouch all the time." Mom's eyes widened with hope. "Maybe if we're best buds, you won't feel the need to hang out with those other *friends* of yours. They're nothing but trouble, you know."

Best buds? "I guess." Probably best to say whatever it took to get Mom to leave. It was the only way Olivia would get to sleep. She was already losing the struggle to keep her heavy eyelids from closing.

"Besides"—Mom fingered the fringe on a throw pillow— "I. . .I need you." Her chin quivered for a fraction of a second before she put the mask back on. "I'm going to go now. You sleep." Mom kissed her on the forehead. "Oh, wait. Friends wouldn't do that, would they?"

Olivia murmured something unintelligible.

"Sweet dreams." Mom's singsong voice trailed off as she left the room.

Finally alone, Olivia tried to let her body relax. Would she be able to sleep, or would she lie there staring at the ceiling for hours wondering if Charles would show up? Her eyes fluttered. She could barely keep them open. Then the relief came.

"The answer to my dreams. . ." Daddy sang Olivia's special song while he rocked her in their favorite nighttime spot next to her big-girl bed. He snugged the quilt around her shoulders and squeezed. "I love

you, my sweet angel." Daddy pressed his lips on the nape of Olivia's
warm neck.

At four years old, even she knew she had grown too big to be
rocked to sleep, but she just couldn't get into bed without hearing
her song. And her neck would tingle all night without Daddy's
special kiss.

"Now, come on, you little staller, it's sleepy time." Daddy patted
her on the bottom as she scampered off his lap and hopped into bed.
He pulled the covers up to her chin and pressed them tight all the
way around her body.

"You forgot down by my toes, Daddy." Olivia nestled into the
covers while he snuggled the blankets tighter around her feet. "I
miss Mommy while she's working at the hospital. But it's nice to
have our special time together, isn't it?"

"It sure is, Livvie Love." Daddy grinned and tucked the covers
around her one more time. "Now, Olivia, I'm going to kiss you good
night one more time. I'll be in the family room and then in my bed.
Remember our deal? I know you're safe, so I'm not coming back
if you call out—you need to obey Daddy and go to sleep without
yelling for me."

"Okay. I love you, Daddy."

"I love you, too, angel." Daddy kissed her forehead. "Sleep
tight." He left the door cracked open when he stepped into the
hallway.

Olivia watched the light flicker from the television down the
hall. Would Daddy come if she screamed? He said he wouldn't. But
just maybe. . .

"Daddy?"

What if she yelled two times? He said he wanted to teach her to
fall asleep on her own—that she was a big girl. But Olivia didn't
want to be a big girl. She wanted her daddy.

"Daddy!"

"Daddy!"

Maybe louder would help. "Daddy!"

Olivia bolted upright, scared of the sound of her own scream. She felt her cheeks, knowing they'd be damp. That dream always made her cry. She tipped her head toward the door and waited for footsteps that never came. Apparently no one had heard her cry out.

Or no one cared.

✴

"Livvie? Rise and shine!"

Olivia pried open one eye to a throbbing headache and sunshine streaming in through her already-opened window shades. She propped up on one elbow. Did she hear running water?

Mom popped out from behind Olivia's closet door. "How about these jeans with this cute top? It's purple to match your hair."

Olivia waited for the standard sarcastic comment about her streak. Nothing. Not even a roll of the eyes.

"What's going on? What are you picking out clothes for?"

"We're going shopping to celebrate our new friendship." Mom grinned and clipped toward the bathroom in her high heels. Hadn't the woman ever heard of bedroom slippers?

"The water's perfect. Come on and shower up so we can hit the stores."

Those poor stores. Olivia swung her legs over. No point arguing with Mom when she had her mind set on something, especially when it involved shopping. Might as well go along with it. Besides, new clothes never hurt anyone. She shuffled to the bathroom and stepped into the double shower as big as some bathrooms she'd been in. Maybe the water would wash away her headache. She adjusted the spray nozzle to pulsate and let the hot water beat at the back of her neck until steam filled the room.

"Where are we shopping?" Olivia called from the shower, positive her mom was still puttering around her room.

"We're going into Chicago. Shopping for the good stuff on Mag Mile." Mom's voice escalated in excitement as she listed off the top designers they'd descend upon this afternoon.

Didn't she know no one actually called it *Mag Mile* except tourists and television reporters? Olivia finished her shower and toweled off. Completely ignoring the outfit her mom had hung on the dressing bar in her closet, Olivia riffled through her racks of clothes to pick out something her mother would hate. . .*best buds* or not.

Frayed denim miniskirt, black tights, thigh-high boots— Mom might not like the outfit, but she'd never complain about Chanel boots—and a tight black shirt, which she pulled down to expose her shoulders and the straps of her purple cami. *Perfect.*

Olivia blow-dried her hair and even added some touch-up color to her purple streak with the mascara-type wand the hairdresser had given her. Extra-heavy dark eyeliner and sparkly eye shadow. A dozen narrow silver bracelets tinkling on each forearm. Three pairs of earrings and a cuff around the top of her ear. Ready. Oops. She almost forgot. After a minute of rummaging through her jewelry drawers, Olivia found it. A fake lip ring.

Olivia walked into the bedroom as Mom finished organizing the bookcase. She turned around and managed to not even blink an eye at Olivia's appearance.

"Great! You're ready." Mom smiled as she inspected Olivia's outfit. "You look cool."

Olivia pasted on a grin, trying to hide her disgust. Daddy

never would have let her out of the house like that, but her new BFF thought she looked *cool*? Whatever. Wonder what Mom would think if Olivia lit up a cigarette. She'd have to try that later.

🌀

Arms laden with packages, Olivia struggled up the stairs to her room. She might be the only teenager ever brought home by a cop and then rewarded for it with an extravagant shopping trip the very next day. About to drop it all, she set everything down in the hallway outside her room so she could open the door. She barely touched it, yet it swung wide open. *Huh?*

Olivia crept into her room, leaving the packages where they sat. She didn't sense anyone in the room, but Charles could be hiding anywhere. What was he up to? Olivia glanced back toward the hallway, and something caught her eye. Her lock dangled from the chain with splinters of wooden door still attached. Her eyes moved to the door handle. The brand-new knob dangled from its hole on both the inside and outside of the door. Useless. *Someone* had twisted it until it broke—just like the last one he'd destroyed.

That's it!

Olivia stormed down the stairs into the kitchen, where Mom stood opening Chinese take-out containers. Charles sat in the breakfast nook, waiting to be served, no doubt, with a full glass of wine in front of him. Olivia searched the countertops and saw an open bottle on the service bar still three-fourths full. So he hadn't had much to drink yet. Perfect timing.

She took a deep breath and stared her mom down, ignoring Charles. "We have to talk. Now."

Mom opened her mouth and shot a look toward Charles, who sat back watching the scene unfold with a smug look on his face. He'd gotten to Olivia, and from the looks of things, he knew it. . .and enjoyed it.

Olivia held up a hand. "No, Mom. Don't brush me off this time. I'm serious. If you don't want to talk, don't. But I'm not leaving until I'm heard." Even saying that much felt good to Olivia. But where to start? "First of all. . .he"—Olivia tipped her head back toward where Charles sat behind her—"ripped the locks off my door. Where does he get off doing something like that again?" She didn't look back to see Charles's reaction.

Mom shot a panicked look at Charles and went to stand right in front of him, forcing Olivia to look in his direction like she always did. Always trying to force peace between them.

Mom shook her head. "No, Olivia, don't overreact. He told me about this. He doesn't want you to lock your doors. What with the cigarettes, the pot, the alcohol, and the cops. He only wants to monitor what's going on a little better."

Charles sneered and winked at Olivia from behind Mom's back. So much for leaving her alone—Olivia had known that wouldn't last.

"Mom!" Olivia pointed at him. "He's taunting me, and he even winked at me."

By the time Mom whipped her head around to look at him, Charles was the perfect picture of a thoughtful and concerned parent.

"He's not taunting you, Livvie. He's understandably upset with all that's happened."

"Okay. Well, then why did he have to rip the locks off the wall and destroy my door?"

"Honestly, Liv, it's not your door." Mom would defend him until her dying day, apparently. Which just might happen.

"Fine. But there's more." Olivia looked at the floor, wishing it would swallow her whole. "This is hard to say." She lifted her eyes to her mom's. Just beyond Mom's body, the camera of Olivia's brain zeroed in, and Charles's face came into sharp focus.

His face held no rage. No hate. No lust. His face promised pure threat. He wasn't *trying* to scare her with the dark glint in his eyes and the firm set to his jaw. It was simply fact. Then he mouthed three words. Words she knew she'd never forget. Words that chilled her to the bone. *I. Dare. You.*

In the next instant, Charles's face turned kind and loving as he reached forward for his wife's hand. He tugged on it until she stepped backward. He pulled her to his lap. "What is it, Olivia?" His voice sounded concerned.

Olivia gave up. She might as well not even fight him anymore. There was no point. *He wins.* Mom would never let Olivia get the truth out, and even if she did, she wouldn't believe her. Charles promised new levels of revenge if she spilled the truth. There was nothing she could do. Nothing. Charles had won yet again.

Time to backpedal. "Look, it's just. . .I don't think it's right for a teenage girl not to have a lock on her door. What would it take to get it back?"

Charles helped Mom stand up then stood and walked to Olivia. He took her hands.

Olivia cringed at his clammy touch.

Clueless Mom smiled at her loving family.

"Liv, if I've made my point well enough, I'll fix the lock. Not the chain lock, only the doorknob. It's not safe to chain yourself into a room."

"You know, that's true, babe." Mom nodded at Charles and then turned to Olivia. "I've heard stories about people being trapped in a fire because of those chains on doors."

Oh yeah? Like when, Mom? What stories? Didn't really matter anyway. It wouldn't have kept him out if he'd wanted in. "Okay.

When will you fix it?"

"Is tomorrow soon enough?" The edge had returned to his voice, daring her to push him.

"Sure. Thank you." Olivia turned away and shuffled up the stairs. What had she done to deserve this? She'd been a good girl—until lately. But she'd never hurt anyone. She had prayed as a little girl. Daddy prayed. Even Mom prayed. But their prayers never got answered. On second thought, they did get answered every single time. They got answered by God thumbing His nose at them and piling on more and more tragedy. They got answered with a resounding *NO*.

Why did she even have to be alive?

Chapter 8

The inside of her head clamored like an orchestra during warm-up while Olivia plodded through the hall on her way to first period. Lost in thought, she felt hands clamp over her eyes. "Hey!" Olivia grabbed at some fingers and spun around. Phew. Just Jordyn.

"What's got you so distracted? I called your name a bunch of times." Jordyn furrowed her eyebrows.

"Oh, nothing. Just didn't hear you."

"Well, come with me. I've got a surprise." Jordyn pulled Olivia's sleeve and guided her to the back restroom in the old junior-high wing—the only bathroom in the school without stalls. As soon as the door closed behind them, Jordyn locked it. "Look what I've got." She reached in the front pocket of her jeans and pulled out a little plastic baggie holding four joints. "These ought to get us through the day, wouldn't you say?"

Olivia gasped. "We can't do that here! Are you crazy?" She fumbled for the door.

Jordyn pried Olivia's fingers from the door handle. "I do it all the time. No one ever comes back here, and the smoke detectors are disabled. Can't you smell it in here? Everyone does it—well, everyone who's anyone. It's been going on for years."

"Are you sure?" Olivia shook her head. "I don't want to get in trouble with the police again or get a suspension or something." Who cared about Mom and Charles? "Look at what happened to Emma."

"Trust me." Jordyn put her hand in the bag just as a light knock sounded on the door.

Olivia let out a yelp. "See?" she hissed.

"It's only Bailey. Let her in."

Olivia unlocked the door and opened it a crack, blocking with her foot so it wouldn't open too far.

Bailey pushed on it until she could squeeze her body through the opening. "Sheesh. What's the problem?"

"Oh, she's chicken." Jordyn nodded at Olivia. "Something tells me she'll be just fine in a minute though." She giggled and handed a smoldering joint to Olivia.

"Where's Tara?" Olivia took a drag and passed it to Bailey.

Bailey rolled her eyes at Jordyn. "Ever since the thing with the cops, she thinks she's too good to hang out with us. That we're a bad influence on her."

Jordyn nodded. "I guess her mom smelled pot on her and took her to talk to a pastor. He supposedly talked some sense in her, so now she's steering clear of us bad influences for a while. She'll get over it."

"Fine with me." Bailey shrugged. "Less we have to share."

"Now, *that's* a great point." After a few long drags, Olivia felt no fear—of anything. That was how she needed to feel at home. Maybe high was the best way to float through her day. And why not? There was no real reason she couldn't smoke some pot on her own—why wait for Bailey or Jordyn to provide it for her? "Hey, where can I get more of this myself if I want to?"

Bailey winked at Jordyn and laughed. "We thought you'd never ask. Welcome to the jungle."

ॐ

"So I heard you were looking for me." A hand snaked around Olivia's head to press on the locker beside hers.

She jumped at the raspy male voice in her ear and dropped the stack of books she'd pulled from her locker. She whirled around to find a complete stranger behind her. A creepy one with a metal ring through his lip and black greasy hair tucked behind his ears. "Who are you?"

"I'm Emma's boyfriend, Seth. I used to go here." His stringy black hair fell over his eye as he cast a shady glance down the hallway. "We probably don't want to talk about making a transaction right here, do we?"

"What kind of *transaction*? What are you talking about?" Maybe he had the wrong person.

"I was told you want some of what only I can provide." He lowered his voice and nodded, imploring her with his eyes to catch on.

"Oh!" Olivia put her books back and slammed her locker door. She had no intention of cracking a single one of those boring tomes, so why lug them home?

Seth followed as she made her way out to the parking lot.

"I have a hundred bucks on me. What will that buy?"

"Shh. Are you insane?" he hissed. "Lower your voice. People aren't that crazy about a drug deal going down on school property, you know." Seth glanced in every direction.

Drug deal? That sounded so criminal. But that *was* what she was doing, wasn't it?

"A hundred bucks will set you up for a good while. And when you need me again, you won't have any trouble finding me." Seth reached for her book bag and let something slide out of his sleeve into the bag.

Olivia dug into the pocket of her jeans, pulled out a crumpled bill, and handed it to him in plain sight.

Seth chuckled and shook his head. "Girl, you need to get a little sneakier before we meet again." He pocketed the money and lumbered off across the school yard like something out of a movie.

🌀

Standing on her front porch, Olivia lifted a tired hand to wave good-bye to Jordyn and twisted her watch to the front of her wrist. Ten o'clock on Saturday morning. Mom would most likely be out shopping. What about Charles? Olivia rummaged in her bag but couldn't find a garage door opener to see if his car sat inside.

No matter what, she couldn't let him see her—bloodshot eyes, ragged clothes, alcohol on her breath, an aura of cigarette smoke. If he saw her. . .she didn't even want to think about what would happen. But if Olivia could get to the shower before anyone spotted her, she'd be fine. No other choice—she'd have to make a dash for it and hope for the best.

Olivia punched in the security code to unlock the front door and stepped into the house. The massive wooden door swung to a close. She grabbed it and eased it into position so it wouldn't slam. The click of the doorknob seemed to reverberate throughout the house, along with Olivia's heartbeat. She froze and listened for a moment. Silence.

Starting toward the stairs, her footsteps echoed in the foyer. No other sounds at all. Perfect! The house even felt empty. Tiptoeing past the family room, she thought she must've gotten lucky. Mom and Chuck almost never went upstairs—they used the intercom to beckon her when they wanted her—so once she made it to her room, she'd be home free.

Then it happened. With one foot on the bottom step, she heard the sound she'd been dreading. Her mom's voice called from the kitchen, "Liv, is that you?"

Oh no. Sound normal. "It's me. I'll be right down. Have to go to the bathroom. . .bad!" What was Mom doing home on a

Saturday morning? Why wasn't she out shopping?

"No need to go upstairs to find a bathroom, silly. There are three on this floor alone. Then come in here. I've got something I want to talk to you about."

Oh great. "O–okay. I'll be right there." Olivia hurried into the powder room in the hallway and splashed water on her face. She dropped her knees to the floor and rummaged in the cabinet under the sink for some kind of perfume or body spritz. Lysol? It would have to do. Holding the can at arm's length, Olivia misted her body with the aerosol spray. She gagged on the institutional smell, but she had no choice. Once the cloud settled, she squared her shoulders, smoothed the wrinkles in the clothes she'd had on since the day before, and tested her breath in her cupped hand. Gum! Olivia dug in her bag for a piece and popped it into her mouth. Enough stalling.

Mom wrinkled her nose when Olivia entered the kitchen. "What is that smell?"

"Oh, I just used some Lysol to. . .um. . .freshen up the bathroom." Olivia tottered as she climbed atop a stool at the massive island. She steadied herself by gripping the granite as she selected a banana from the fruit bowl. As she peeled it, she tried not to look at her mom.

After an eternal pause, Mom cleared her throat. "Olivia, I had wanted to talk to you about going somewhere, just the two of us today—" Her voice sounded stern.

Her hands frozen on the half-peeled banana, Olivia tried to smile. "That s–sounds nice." She still didn't look at Mom.

"—but I can clearly see that last night was a repeat of a few weeks ago. In fact, you're still drunk, aren't you? You're slurring and stumbling. You reek to high heaven of who knows what." Mom cleared her throat. "You leave me with no choice."

Olivia put down the fruit. That didn't sound good.

"We're going to check out that place Officer Stapleton recommended, Diamond Estates."

The words fell like bombs exploding in Olivia's pounding head.

"I'm really worried about you." Mom rubbed her newly wrinkle-free forehead with her manicured fingers. "I tried being your friend, but that didn't work. And I have neither the time nor the energy to deal with you. It's beyond my capabilities."

Mom didn't have the time to deal with her? What else did she have to do with the hours in her day? She didn't work. She didn't volunteer. She didn't go to the gym. The problem was simple: she just didn't want Olivia to get in the way of her *me* time, as she called it. *Traitor.*

"Since your dad died, it's seems like we've lost our way." Mom looked up at the ceiling.

Olivia stared at the floor. *We've* lost the way? Last Olivia checked, she was the kid in the relationship. Wasn't it the parent's job to *lead* the way?

"We don't go to church. We never talk."

Whose fault was that? Olivia had sure tried—at least early on. Though she had a lot to say, her face remained stone cold.

"And you're slipping out of control." Mom took a deep breath. "You took money from my purse, didn't you?"

How did she know about that, and why hadn't she brought it up before? "No! How could you accuse me of that?" Should have known. Mom was clueless about everything, but she would surely notice *money.*

"Olivia, I'm not stupid." Mom sighed. "Did you honestly think I wouldn't realize a hundred-dollar bill had disappeared— more than once?"

Uh-oh. "I'm sorry."

"You stole money from my purse. You lied to me about

where you were going to be. You drank alcohol—a lot, from the looks of things—and we both know this isn't nearly the first time." She gestured to Olivia's face. "You smoked, too, I'm guessing. In fact, let me have your purse."

Olivia clutched her bag to her chest. "Mom! This is my private property. How dare you?"

"You're a minor, and you're living in my house—nothing is private property."

"This isn't *your* house! It's *Chuck's* house. Nothing here is yours." Olivia had never screamed at her mom like this. "You want it? Here!" She took her pack of cigarettes out of her bag right in plain view. Maybe if she fessed up to the cigarettes, Mom would think they were the only problem and not go digging around for more. Olivia thrust her bag at her mom and planted her fists on her hips.

"I really hate doing this." Mom peered into the bag and shook it a few times to move the contents around. "Is there anything I should know about in this purse? You can spare us both the humiliation by just telling me now."

"I'm not embarrassed at all. Have at it." She leaned back against the counter and waited. As long as she didn't look in the zipper pocket on the front of the purse.

"Olivia, I don't want to have to search your things. How about you just come clean with me. What's in here?"

"There's nothing in there that would matter to you." Beer tabs, cigarettes, matches. . .the marijuana. But so what? There wasn't a thing Mom could do to her that would matter—if she even cared.

Mom sighed and pawed around in the bag for a minute, then zipped open the pocket on the front. She looked inside and gasped as she pulled out the baggie. She pinched it between two fingers and dangled it inches from Olivia's face.

Mom's dark circles looked magnified through the plastic.

"So it's come to this, Liv?" She dumped it into the garbage disposal—bag and all. "We're going to Colorado whether you want to or not. It's only a visit—a tour of Diamond Estates." She spoke matter-of-factly, leaving no room for debate. "Charles already knows I've been thinking about it. We're leaving on Monday. It won't be bad—maybe we'll have a ski day or find a spa somewhere, but we're going."

Olivia stormed from the kitchen, a mallet shattering her heart with each stomp up the stairs. Slamming her bedroom door behind her, she flopped on her bed. No tears—experience had proven there was no point. No prayers—no one listened to them anyway. No dreams—they all turned to nightmares in the end. She'd bet anything Mom planned to buy Olivia a one-way ticket and not bring her home. After she booked a spa day for herself, of course.

Abandoned. . .first by God and now by Mom? Didn't see that one coming.

Chapter 9

The airplane slipped beneath the fluffy clouds like a scalding fire poker through a marshmallow. What had been a sunny afternoon blanketed in white fluff turned into an angry day canopied with sinister storms. How could the clouds look so perfect and happy on one side but vengeful and dangerous on the other?

Olivia white-knuckled her armrests as the plane bounced up and down and listed from side to side as it made its descent. As they neared the ground, she held her breath. There seemed no possible way the unsteady plane could make safe contact with the earth at such a speed.

Mom let out a tiny snore and shifted in her seat. How could she sleep through all the chaos while Olivia's life flashed before her eyes?

The moments before The Accident flooded Olivia's memories. She squeezed her eyes shut against the vision of her daddy hitting the roof of the car. Why hadn't he fastened his seat belt after he secured Olivia in hers? Oh, how life would have been different if only he'd done that one thing. That one decision, or lack thereof, ruined everyone's life—forever.

The plane broke out of the turbulent air as it flew low and parallel to the ground while making its final reach to touch the earth. The wheels made contact with the asphalt, and the plane bumped along topsy-turvy until it skidded to a stop. A collective sigh of relief was heard and felt throughout the plane.

"Oh, did we land?" Mom yawned and stretched her arms above her head.

Olivia exhaled and unpeeled her cramped fingers from their grip on the armrests.

The intercom beeped. "This is your captain speaking. I'm glad to be on the ground. How about you?"

Cheers erupted throughout the cabin.

"Well, be assured, it wasn't nearly as bad as it probably felt—you were safe the entire time. On behalf of myself and the rest of the flight crew, I thank you for your patience with the turbulence. If you have a connecting flight, you'll be met at the gate with your flight information. Please be aware that some flight times have been adjusted due to the weather. And if this is home for you, welcome to Denver."

Olivia snorted. *Home? Never.*

"Come on, Liv. Let's get out of here." Mom picked up her carry-on, and Olivia grabbed hers from the overhead compartment. They wedged into the narrow aisle, waiting for the dad in front of them to gather a stroller, car seat, and four carry-ons while the mom wrestled a cranky toddler. The dad glared at a teenage boy who stood behind them, lost in whatever blared through his iPod.

Olivia wondered if he really had music on, or if he was just pretending so he could avoid his family. Olivia chuckled. *I feel your pain, kid.*

Finally off the plane, they took a series of escalators, glided on two moving walkways, and navigated several long corridors before they found the exit to the carpool lanes. "This is what I love about not checking bags—no waiting." Mom smiled as they bustled past the passengers waiting at the baggage carousel and stepped outside.

"Uh-huh." Olivia stared at the ground.

"Okay. That's it." Mom pulled Olivia over to the side, away from the waiting cars. "Listen to me, Liv. We aren't here as a punishment. We're only here to see if maybe these people could be of some help to you. Believe me, it's not what I want. But you've slipped away from me these past couple of years, and I want my daughter back."

Then be my mom. Simple as that.

"I know you think I've changed. I know you think I don't know a thing about real life anymore. But I hope you realize, losing your dad was hard on me, too. I still miss him every single day. This hasn't been as easy on me as you seem to think."

Olivia nodded, counting the tiles around her feet.

"Would you give it a chance. . .please? Worst thing, we hate Diamond Estates but get in a day of skiing and go home. How bad could that be?" The lilt of hope filled her voice.

"Promise you're not planning to leave me here against my will?" Olivia tried to sound defiant but suspected that it came out more like the plaintive mew of a kitten.

"Oh, Liv. You can't possibly think I would do that." Mom pulled Olivia into a tight embrace. "I would never leave you here like that. I promise."

"Okay, then I'll try to relax." She offered a hesitant smile. "Are we really going to get to ski?"

"Most like– Oh, here's our ride." Mom pointed to a white van with a magnetic logo on the side that read DIAMOND ESTATES, WHERE THE FINEST GEMS ARE PULLED FROM THE DEEPEST ROUGH.

The driver pulled the van over to the curb a few yards beyond where they stood.

Mom handed Olivia a bag. "Here we go."

Olivia followed a few steps behind, through the exhaust

fumes, as her mom pulled open the door and spoke to the driver.

A boy about her age, probably a year older, with piercing blue eyes, stepped from the van. He nodded at Olivia, and a lock of his shoulder-length wavy brown hair fell in front of his face. "I'm Justin. I'll be giving you a ride up the mountain and then taking you on a tour of the grounds until my dad gets back from the hospital."

"I'm Olivia." She climbed into the van and shut the door without another word. What must Justin think of her? Obviously she was a *problem child* or she wouldn't be there. How embarrassing! But whatever he thought probably came pretty close to the truth.

"He's cute, but he needs a haircut," Mom hissed at Olivia before Justin made it back around to the driver's seat after loading their bags.

"Shh, Mom." Olivia rested her elbow on the armrest and laid her forehead in her hand. Mom could be so embarrassing. *But cute? Try again, Mom. How about gorgeous? Like he should be in a magazine.*

Justin climbed in and pulled away from the curb.

"So, you said your dad is in the hospital? Is he okay?" Mom touched Justin's forearm.

"Oh no. It's not him who's sick. He's picking up one of the residents who's been in the hospital for a couple of days and is ready to come home." Justin peeked at the mirror. "She's been sick, but she's fine now."

"So, if I remember correctly, your dad is the director of the program?"

Nothing like giving the kid the third degree, Mom.

"Yes, ma'am. Dad is Ben Bradley, the director, and my mom, Alicia, helps out when she can. She also works as an emergency-room nurse at the hospital where Dad is now."

"Oh. Interesting. I'm a nurse, too. Well, I was until. . . Well, I'm not working outside the home right now."

Hah. Ask her how much she works inside *the home.* Not that he would care. Olivia closed her mind to the chatter and gazed out the window at the flat interstate terrain. After about forty minutes, they began their climb into the higher elevation. The windshield wipers did their best to bat away the falling snow as the van wound its way up the mountain road.

Justin didn't seem the least bit concerned about the travel conditions.

After about twenty minutes of climbing, the van made a sudden sharp turn toward the tree line. Olivia squealed and clutched the door handle, her eyes scrunched tight against the coming crash. At the last second, just before they would wreck, she peeked with one eye and spotted the narrow driveway carved between the clusters of tall spruce.

Justin slipped the vehicle between the trees and parked in a small clearing. He turned off the ignition. "Here we are."

Mom fanned herself with her leather gloves. "Phew. Thought we'd had it there for a minute."

"Sorry." Justin's neck reddened. "I forget how that turn can seem the first time. I should have taken it slower."

Heart still beating wildly, Olivia stepped out of the van onto a blanket of fresh snow that crunched beneath her boots. Snow didn't do that very often in Illinois—it usually slopped like slush and threw dirty globs onto the back of a person's leg with each step. She breathed the fresh mountain air deeply into her hungry lungs. Would the mountain itself gasp in horror if she lit up a cigarette out here? She gazed up the mountain into the dense, snowcapped forest, then turned in the other direction to look behind her.

There it stood. Just beyond the clearing towered the amazing stone structure pictured on the cover of the brochure Jodie and Officer Stapleton had given her. "What is that building?" Its character was undeniable.

"It's an old monastery—you know, where monks lived in seclusion and served God by letting go of all worldly goods."

Sounds like fun. "It's really old."

"It was built in the 1800s, and Mom and Dad converted it for use as the main quarters of Diamond Estates." Justin stepped closer and gazed lovingly at its stone arches. "Isn't she beautiful?"

Olivia wasn't sure *beautiful* described it best. "It's pretty amazing, that's for sure. Those stained-glass windows are incredible. I've never seen anything like them."

Mom stepped closer. "That one depicts the Garden of Eden, and that one over there with the rainbow, that's Noah and the Ark."

"My favorite is the nativity window, but you have to go around back to see it from the outside." Justin grinned, the corners of his eyes crinkling. He gestured toward the long porch that led to the front doors. "Shall we go inside?"

"Does it even have heat?" Olivia stepped onto the porch and shivered at the thought of the cold, damp building.

Justin's laugh echoed through the mountains. "Yeah. You're going to be surprised when you get inside. Everyone always is." He gestured to the ornate entrance with its carved wooden doors that arched at the top. "After you." He pulled open a front door even taller and more massive than *Chuck's*.

They stepped into a foyer that dwarfed the one at home. Olivia hadn't thought that possible anywhere. She gazed up at the high ceilings and intricate carvings. Large lighting fixtures hung low enough to cast eerie shadows to the ceiling, and actual candles flickered in wall sconces. If they were trying to creep her out, they were doing a great job of it.

"Are there candles burning every day?" That seemed like a lot of work, not to mention a fire hazard. Probably expensive, too.

"Oh no. My dad likes to do it for effect when someone's coming for a tour." Justin smiled and shook his head. "Kinda silly, I think. But whatever. Just do as I'm told." He opened another big wooden door with the same rounded top as the front doors and stood back to let them pass. "This is the library."

They stepped over the threshold into a different world. Windows lined the far wall, floor to very high ceiling. They overlooked beautiful craggy mountain terrain. Along the other three walls were books. Many thousands of volumes. Each of the walls of shelves had a tall, narrow ladder that slid on rails so a reader could access anything, no matter how high. In the center of the room were two rows of three long wooden tables with six chairs each.

Olivia walked to the far wall and ran her hand along the book spines.

"That's where the schooling takes place." Justin pointed at the tables. "Five days a week, five hours of instruction with an hour for lunch in the middle."

"Do you come here for school, too? I'm just curious—not trying to be nosy." Mom took a step toward him.

Nosy? You, Mom? Never.

"No. I go to an outside school. A school for the performing arts—actually, we passed it on the way from the airport. Mom and Dad think it's best that I not be the only guy in a room full of teenage girls all day long." Justin chuckled. "They're probably right."

Mom nodded. "I bet you'd be the subject of all kinds of catfights if you were around here every day."

Olivia didn't even flinch as she continued to feign disinterest, pretending to read book titles.

"It's hard because, for the girls, this is their life for a year or more—it's huge for them. They're alone and scared—all looking for something to cling to." Justin shrugged. "For me, it's just more of the same. Girls come and go, and no matter how close I might become with someone, when they leave, they really leave. I almost never hear back from any of them. Plus I've learned that, for them, being interested in a boy can only get in the way of what they're here to do."

"You're a very wise young man, Justin. I did wonder if the girls are allowed to date while they're here."

Olivia stopped on *A Tale of Two Cities* and listened, but didn't turn around.

"No. There's no actual dating of any kind. In fact, no male/female alone time at all. Every once in a while someone will kind of match up with a boy at church or something. Those sorts of crushes or mini relationships aren't really encouraged, but they're part of life, I guess—it happens. Personally, I don't see the point. Every girl here knows it's only temporary. Dating like that makes no sense to me."

"Well. Maybe you can talk some of that sense into my Olivia."

"What?" Olivia shouted and whirled around from the book wall. What was Mom talking about? Olivia had never had a boyfriend. Never even been on a date.

"Oh, I'm only kidding around. Relax."

Great. Now Justin would have the wrong idea about her. But why did Olivia even care?

Mom walked to the window and looked out over the slope to a valley. "Wow, Liv. You can see the tops of trees down below. Truly spectacular."

Olivia made no move to look outside. "Mm-hmm. Spectacular." She refused to get sucked into the scenery. If she showed any interest, Mom would start unpacking her bags.

"Speaking of the girls, how many live here at one time?" Mom tilted her head toward the tables.

"Anywhere from twenty to thirty. If I'm not mistaken, there are twenty-three here right now." Justin pointed to an office. "There are also three live-in staff counselors—Donna, Patty, and Tammy. You might have a chance to meet them later. Just so you know, Tammy's deaf. But she can read lips so well you'd almost never know."

"I know sign language," Olivia mumbled. "My brother's deaf."

"Really? That's cool. I've always wanted to learn how to do it." Justin strode to the door. "If you'll follow me, I'll show you the dining area and kitchen."

Cool? Well, at least Justin passed the deaf test. She'd expected him to offer condolences for Jake's condition like most people did when they first learned of it. Nice surprise.

"I'm just wondering, Justin, are three staff counselors enough to handle thirty girls?"

Right, Mom. Like you really care. As long as you *don't have to handle them it doesn't matter. And don't you mean thirty* troubled *girls?*

"It seems to work, Mrs. Whitford. Things are pretty structured around here. Dad, with Mom's help as much as possible, has things running like clockwork."

They walked down a long hallway lined with windows and turned a corner at two metal swinging doors with portholes— the kind of doors Olivia would expect to see at a restaurant. Justin pushed on one of the doors and held it open.

It felt like stepping through a time capsule and jumping

far into the future. No hints of an old monastery remained in the industrial kitchen. Aluminum, chrome, and steel covered everything from top to bottom, and two double ovens spanned the far wall. Rows of metal workstations gleamed down the center of the long room. Four deep sinks, two enormous dishwashers, a stove with eight burners, and a real restaurant-style griddle formed the back wall.

Olivia whistled. "Boy, they mean business in here, don't they?"

"Who does the cooking?" Mom peeked around a corner.

"There's a full-time cook on staff. Marilyn oversees the meal planning and prep, and she orders the food every other day to assure the produce is fresh and the refrigerator is stocked." Justin walked across the room toward two gleaming steel doors and pulled down the handle to open the massive one on the left. "This side is the freezer, and next to it is the fridge. When I was little, the girls used to trick me to go in there and then they'd hold the door closed so I couldn't get out." He shivered. "I'm still terrified."

Mom laughed and stepped inside.

Olivia followed but tried not to look impressed at the shelves of fresh produce and frozen meats. "What if a girl doesn't like whatever's on the menu for a particular meal?"

"That happens. We ask the girls to try everything, but there's always a little table with stuff to make a sandwich of some kind. That's the only option other than the prepared meal." Justin beckoned them to follow. "This way, ladies."

Olivia walked behind Mom around the corner and found a row of six microwaves and dozens of cabinets with locks on them. "Why are these locked?"

"The residents are allowed to buy their own snacks or special items like soda. Each girl has a cupboard with a lock where she can keep her own things."

"Is there a lot of theft going on that makes it necessary to lock things up?" Mom's eyebrows knitted together.

Justin chuckled. "Oh no. Much less than at your high school, I'd assume." He nodded at Olivia. "But anything we can do to prevent temptation, accusations, or confusion is good."

Mom held up a finger. "Now, you mentioned that the chef oversees the meal planning and preparation. That must mean she has help with the cooking. Who does that?"

"Everyone does." Justin seemed to be selecting his words carefully. "My parents believe in raising up self-sufficient people. Anything the girls can help with, they do. Cooking. Grounds keeping. Shopping. Laundry. Cleaning. The jobs rotate every week."

"That sounds fair." Mom nodded.

Easy for her to say. The term slave labor *comes to mind.*

"One other question. You keep saying 'we.' What exactly is your role here?"

Good question. Olivia's ears perked up.

"I'm basically the groundskeeper. I organize the outdoor chores and some mountain activities. I make sure that anything that needs to be taken care of outside gets handled."

Olivia walked to another set of swinging doors and peered into the dining room. At least ten round tables sat around a humongous stone fireplace with glass on all sides. It reminded her of something right out of a ski lodge. One gigantic picture window stood in place of a wall along the back of the dining room. Its view took in the same mountainous valley as the windows in the library did. Even Olivia had to admit it was truly spectacular. Not that she had any intention of letting them know she thought that. She spun her back toward the window. "What kind of fun happens around here?"

Justin chuckled. "I'll leave some of that to my dad to describe for you. Just understand that the primary goal here is to do hard work."

Olivia lifted her eyebrows and snapped her gum toward her mom. *See. They turn bad girls into slaves here.*

"Oh, I don't mean work like chores. Of course, there *is* some of that." Justin leaned back on the counter. "But I'm talking about the work that needs to be done on the inside. That's often much, much harder."

That was difficult to believe. Visions of scrubbing floors on her hands and knees, washing towels on a washboard, and being up to her elbows cleaning toilets assaulted her mind. Nothing could be worse than that.

"Oh look." Justin nodded toward the door. "Here comes my dad."

Olivia turned in the direction Justin indicated, and her jaw dropped.

Chapter 10

A man looking like he'd jumped right off the set of a wilderness movie burst into the room in designer jeans and Western boots. His emerald-green flannel shirt showed off his rugged mountain tan and gleaming white teeth.

Olivia gasped as he rushed toward them with his arm outstretched.

"I'm Ben Bradley. It's so good to meet you." He pumped Olivia's hand then turned to Mom. "Mrs. Whitford, a pleasure." He shook Mom's hand. "I trust you've been given the grand tour of our humble estate?" He gave a movie-star grin and smoothed his salt-and-pepper waves.

What was the deal with this guy? Olivia had expected a stodgy old man who shuffled up and down the hallways in bedroom slippers carrying a big ring of keys, not a book-cover-worthy lumberjack.

"We haven't gone upstairs yet, but they've pretty much seen everything down here, Dad." Justin smiled and backed away with a tiny bow. "Ladies, I haven't been home since early this morning, and I have chores and homework to finish. You're in good hands now. So, if you don't mind, I'll see you at dinner."

Dinner? Oh great. It would be hours before they'd get away from here. Maybe that was when Mom planned to sneak away and leave her behind. She'd promised she wouldn't, but Olivia refused to let her guard down. Did Justin know something she didn't? Olivia had tried to read his eyes, but, except for the twinkle, they were blank.

She'd kill for a cigarette. "Um, Mr. Bradley?"

He shook his head. "No, no. Please call me Ben."

"Okay. Ben? Is there a place I can go have a smoke?"

Mom gasped. "Olivia!" Her cheeks reddened, and she turned to Ben. "I don't know what's gotten into her."

Book-cover Ben smiled. "Sorry. No smoking on the grounds." He glanced at his watch. "Okay, it's four fifteen. We'll finish up the tour and then have dinner when the girls get back."

"Where are they now?" Off to work the mines for the day? Olivia pictured the seven dwarfs coming home with pickaxes over their shoulders. *Heigh-ho, heigh-ho! It's home from work I go.*

"They're horseback riding. They enjoy long rides on the mountain several times a week. There are stables and ten horses on the grounds—twelve if you count the two new foals born this past spring." Ben steered her into the dining room. "Here. I'll show you. Look right over there, through those trees. See that clearing? That building houses the stables, and just beyond that is a pasture."

Olivia gazed out on yet another picturesque scene. Several inches of powder blanketed the ground, and bales of hay had already been put out for when the horses returned hungry from their ride.

Mom squealed. "You love horses, Olivia!"

"Um, thanks for the reminder." Olivia turned away from the window—they might mistake her attention for interest. Which it most certainly was *not*.

"What's that building beyond the horse pasture?" Mom reached an arm past Olivia's face to point to a smaller stone structure of similar architecture as the main house. Almost like those replica playhouses that sat in people's backyards.

"That was an infirmary—a mini hospital actually. We aren't using it for anything right now, but we have lots of potential ministry ideas for the future—all in God's timing though."

"You could use it as the dungeon." *Oops. Probably shouldn't have said that.*

Ben turned away, ignoring Olivia's comment.

Mom glared at Olivia as soon as his back was turned. "What are some of your ideas?" She spoke in a sickeningly sweet voice.

Ben gazed out the window. "I'd love to see it as a place for girls to start out their time with us. A place for deeper treatment—more individualized—until they're ready for the less intense environment here at the main house. It would be better equipped to deal with depression, suicidal tendencies, things like that. Or, alternatively, it could become a home for unwed teen mothers. It's up to God though."

"You have wonderful ideas, Ben." Mom turned away from the window. "Not to change the subject, but I was wondering: how do mealtimes actually work?"

"Take dinner, for example. The girls are required to be here at five thirty sharp to eat. If they're on kitchen duty, it's four thirty. We pray over our food, and then they go through the line." He gestured at a cafeteria setup. "The meal is healthy and well balanced, including a dessert."

Oh boy. That sounded simply delightful. Gag. Olivia rolled her eyes.

"What if the girls get hungry before bed? Speaking of bed, what time is lights-out?" Mom stepped in front of Olivia and shot her another dirty look.

Ben gestured for them to follow him back into the hallway as he spoke. "There's a snack time every night at seven thirty.

The girls can choose to have whatever we provide that day, like popcorn, ice cream, or cookies and milk. Or they can have something out of their own cabinet." Ben laughed. "We have one Ding Dong addict right now—she can't go to sleep without one." He winked. "During the week, lights-out is at nine o'clock. Weekends at ten thirty."

"Seriously?" Olivia hadn't gone to bed at nine o'clock since fourth grade. And did he say cookies and milk? He had to be joking.

"Have you seen the game room?" Ben gestured for them to follow. His long strides were difficult to match, but they scurried along after him, two to every one of his.

At the end of the long hallway stood a plain, narrow door. Ben inserted a key and pushed it open and then stood aside to let them enter first.

Olivia walked into yet another world—this one a teenager's heaven. The room, complete with skylights and bright fluorescent lighting, held more than a dozen beanbag chairs, some stereo equipment, two exercise bikes, three treadmills, a video game system, and a Ping-Pong table. In one corner she noticed a bookcase full of board games next to a card table. The best part lined the opposite end of the room. A screen hung on one wall with theater seating in front of it, and a projector was positioned directly overhead. Nearby stood an old-fashioned popcorn maker. Okay, so more went on than just work here. But still.

Ben followed her gaze. "It's pretty neat, huh?"

"To say the least." Olivia nodded. "Although my private bedroom has most of this stuff."

Mom ground her heel into the top of Olivia's foot and glared at her while stepping closer to Ben.

"Ow, Mom." Olivia shook her foot. "That hurt."

"A donation from one church funded this whole room. They saw a need and met it—in a big way." He ran his hands along the back of one of the leather chairs. "In fact, several members came out here to do all the work. True servants, let me tell you."

"I believe I may have met one of those folks." Mom brightened. "Mark Stapleton, an old friend of mine, told me about this place and that he'd done work here. Do you know him?"

"Do I know him? Mark Stapleton has been a huge blessing to us. He covers us in prayer and offers consistent financial support as well as physical help whenever he can. He had a big part in the construction of this room."

Mom smiled. "That's wonderful." She turned in a full circle, taking it all in. "How often do the girls use it?"

"They're in here some of each day, depending on what's going on. We monitor their time on electronics like video games, but we allow plenty of time for everything in moderation."

"How do you control things like that?" Olivia crossed her arms and raised an eyebrow at Ben.

"It's not as bad as it sounds. We just limit the number of hours this room is open. Everyone gets to choose what they want to do while they're in here." Ben smiled. "Oh, I almost forgot to mention. Once a month there's a free day where the girls can do whatever they want to for twenty-four hours. No bedtime, no food restrictions, no game-room limits. It's all up for grabs. Everyone has a blast on free day."

Once a month? Hah! That was how Olivia lived her life every single day. "Interesting."

"We want to teach the girls about balance. There's a time for everything—including recreation."

"That makes perfect sense, Ben." Mom gazed into his eyes.

Was she actually flirting with him? *Gross.*

Ben flipped off the lights and pulled the door closed then tested the lock.

"But why is it kept locked?" *Like Fort Knox around here.*

"Well, Olivia, we try to keep things pretty scheduled. We believe that the best way to keep teens out of trouble is to keep them busy." He nodded at Mom and then turned back to Olivia. "If we left that door open all the time, girls would spend hours and hours a day in there. But that kind of activity is done only after it's earned—schoolwork, chores, fresh air. . .that all comes first."

"That's how it should be, Ben." Mom sighed. "I wish I'd instilled priorities like that back when I had the chance. Instead, I made Olivia's private bedroom very much like that game room back there."

"Yeah, that's a mistake many parents make. But it's never too late to set things right."

Mom didn't look convinced. "Not sure I have the energy to do that unless something else changes first." She jerked her thumb at Olivia.

"Sometimes those types of adjustments need to happen simultaneously. One of the aspects of Diamond Estates that we haven't talked about yet is that we require a counseling connection with the family." Ben turned the corner down another long hallway.

"A counseling connection?"

"Yes, Mrs. Whitford." Ben turned back to Mom. "That helps us assure that the girls don't just come here and exist separately from their families. We require a joint counseling session by conference call once a week and a private call with either parent at least once a week. We feel that it's necessary to prepare the home environment to be ready to accept a changed girl and to support those changes so they last."

Mom grinned. "That sounds like a wonderful thing, and it makes perfect sense."

"Yeah. Before we started this aspect of the program, girls just returned home and often went right back to their old lifestyles because no one was prepared."

Or, better idea, Olivia could run away with Jordyn and never look back. They could move into the city and get an apartment or something. Could she convince Jordyn to go with her?

They followed Ben past the public bathroom.

"I'm going to take a detour in here, if that's okay." Olivia tipped her head toward the door.

"Sure. You can meet us in my office when you're finished. Just follow this hallway and take the second door on the right."

Olivia pushed through the swinging door and hurried into a stall then quickly shut and locked the door. She lowered the lid and sat down on the toilet. A moment alone. Finally. She dropped her head into her hands and fought back tears. What was she doing here? How had her life become such a mess? No doubt Mom and Ben were talking about her right now. How troubled and hopeless she was.

Oh, Daddy. Why? Why did you leave me?

Where were her smokes? She fumbled in the pockets of her hoodie and pulled out the little box. She put one to her lips and lit it like a starving person at her first meal in a week. She inhaled the heady smoke and held it in her lungs.

The bathroom door squeaked and banged into the wall as someone flung it open.

Olivia gasped but didn't let any smoke escape. She lifted her feet and wrapped her arms around her knees so they wouldn't slip down again and sat perfectly still. Hopefully no one would find her hiding out in a stall like a scared little girl. Smoking.

Feet slapped on the tile in angry stomps across the room. The intruder flipped the faucet on full blast and let the water stream into the sink.

Masked by the noise of the water, Olivia slowly let the smoke stream from her body. Hopefully the air fresheners would mask the smell and the person would leave quickly. She flicked the cigarette into the toilet just as the water turned off.

Ssssp. The cigarette fizzled out as it sank.

Peeking through a slit, Olivia saw a blond ponytail bobbing as a narrow set of shoulders shook with unmistakable sobs. Oh no. Should Olivia go to the girl? She didn't know her, and whatever her problem was, it was none of Olivia's business, but how much worse would it be if she got caught hiding—

Whoosh!

The sensor triggered the autoflush when she shifted positions. Oh no! She lowered her feet. Maybe the crying girl would think Olivia was just using the restroom and not realize she'd been hiding in there. *Just act natural.* Olivia clicked the latch and let the door swing open.

No such luck.

A set of icy blue eyes glared at her. The tears were gone, but the redness gave away her pain. "Who are you, and why were you hiding? And what's that smell?"

"I wasn't hiding."

"Yes, you were. I checked for feet." She turned back to the sink. "But whatever."

"Is everything okay?" Olivia took a step toward the tiny powerhouse. Maybe someone had hurt her. Could it be Ben?

"Look. You'd be real smart to mind your own business. . .whoever you are. And if I were you, I'd go back to where you came from before you get caught smoking in here."

She flung her ponytail over her shoulder and stormed out of the bathroom.

Olivia took a deep breath and waited a moment before leaving the restroom in case the girl was out there. Peering down the hallway, confident she was alone, Olivia hurried to Ben's office and slid into the seat beside her mom in front of a large desk and several mismatched bookcases.

Controlling her breathing so they wouldn't ask questions, Olivia shielded her eyes from the bright sun coming through the window.

Ben adjusted the window blinds to avert the bright afternoon sun. "Is that better?"

"Oh, it's just fine. Thank you." Mom blushed. "No need to worry about us."

Ugh. Quit gushing, Mom.

Ben pulled a folder from the file cabinet behind him. He swiveled and placed his forearms on his desk in one swift motion.

Olivia snapped her gum and crossed her arms, waiting for Mom to drop the bomb that she had no intention of bringing Olivia home with her.

"Well, you've had the grand tour. You'll meet some of the girls and staff in a few minutes. You basically know what we're about here at Diamond Estates. But I want to share something with you—something that might surprise you both." Ben pursed his lips and rocked back in his chair. After a moment he looked in Olivia's eyes with a solemn expression. "If this weren't just a visit—if you had come here planning to stay with us—I'm sorry to say, I'd have to send you back home with your mom."

Mom gasped.

Olivia's eyes widened. *Hah!* Maybe there was a God after all.

And maybe He *did* answer prayers. She had to bite her bottom lip to keep from laughing out loud.

"Why is that, Ben?" Mom's attempt at an even tone sounded strained.

Don't be too disappointed, Mom. Guess you're stuck with me. Olivia smirked and raised an eyebrow. *I'm not even good enough for this place.*

"Well, Mrs. Whitford, I hope you can understand." Ben pulled on his square chin, accentuating the deep cleft. "We're here to find the diamonds in the rough. We work hard to uncover God's finest jewels by chiseling at the layers of pain, sin, fear, and whatever else is piled on top of the beauty. We are completely ineffective at that work when the pearl wants to stay in its oyster, so to speak."

"But—"

Ben cut Mom off and turned to Olivia. "Basically, dear, you have to want to be here. You have to want Jesus to get ahold of your life. *You* have to want to change."

Mom closed her mouth.

"There are girls all over the country who come here because they are desperate to let go of their messed-up lives and give God complete control." Ben tipped back in his chair with his hands clasped behind his head. "Not only will we not fill one of their spots in the program with a girl who doesn't want it, but we also can't let a bad attitude permeate the house and negatively affect the girls who have come to do the hard work and surrender themselves fully. Sometimes negativity sneaks in the back door when we're unaware. But we can't just stand back and welcome it into our midst."

Olivia parted two of the vertical blinds with her fingers and peered out at the bright, snowy mountain-scape while he spoke. Did she want to change her life? What about God? Maybe it was time to let Him back in. Parts of her heart felt hollow and longed for those long-ago Sunday school days when she'd memorized Bible verses and sang silly songs about floods and armies that somehow made her feel close to Jesus. But He didn't answer her prayers then—when she needed Him most. And her prayers in years since had continuously been ignored. Why bother turning to Him now?

"Can you understand that, Olivia?" Ben spoke in a near whisper.

The metal strips fell back against the window. Olivia looked from her mom to Ben and shrugged. "I guess."

Ben frowned and held her gaze for a few moments. He blinked first. "Mrs. Whitford, you should pray—pray for Olivia, her decisions, her faith. The staff and I here at Diamond Estates, we'll pray, too. I sense in my heart that there's something truly special about your daughter. That the Lord is calling out to her. Unfortunately, this program requires dedication, and it isn't effective when girls come kicking and screaming."

Mom's brimming eyes begged Olivia. "I'm so fearful for your future—for what you're going to do next. Don't you have *any*thing to say?"

What could she tell them? Did Mom expect her to beg? That wasn't happening. The conversation needed to end. Now.

"When's dinner?" Olivia's aloof response probably came off as very rude, but the conversation had grown too heavy and she felt like a kitten cornered by rabid dogs. Was she expected to make this easy for them? After all, she hadn't asked for the visit, and she certainly didn't want to stay. This wasn't her idea, and it wasn't her job to make *them* feel at ease.

Mom turned to Ben, her shoulders slumped, and lifted both hands as if to say, *I give up.*

With a nod and a resigned sigh, he checked his watch. "Dinner is now. Shall we?" He stood and waited for them to rise then led them from the room. An awkward silence reverberated through the hallway on the walk to the dining room until Ben cleared his throat. "Mrs. Whitford, please don't worry too much. Everything takes time—at least the things worth waiting for. Sadly, girls often have to hit rock bottom before they're ready to reach up a hand for help. We'll pray for some kind of intervention—a miracle—before it comes to that."

Olivia raised her eyebrows. *Hello? I'm still here.* She resisted the urge to wave her hands in front of their faces. Instead, she listened to the *click-clack* of boots on the stone floor—hers and Ben's. The *tip-tap* of Mom's stilettos sounded silly in the enormity of the old building.

Ben stepped in front of them to allow a pack of three girls, led by the blond from the bathroom, to pass in the other direction.

Mom tugged at Olivia's hand. "You're being so rude." She spoke through clenched teeth.

"Mom, shh." Olivia peeked back at the girls. The two followers were giggling—at her, most likely. How embarrassing. Then her eyes locked with the leader of the pack. Her ponytail had swung around and hung down her front like Lady Godiva. But it was those brown eyes that caught Olivia's attention. They were full of anger. For what? Olivia hadn't done anything to her except try to help. It wasn't Olivia's fault that she'd been crying. From the way it looked in the bathroom, someone had hurt her pretty badly. And it sure wasn't Olivia.

Just as quickly as the hate flashed in her eyes, it disappeared. She flipped her hair back over her shoulder and pranced away, the other two close at her heels.

"Here we are." Ben opened the door and ushered them into

the noisy room. He waved at the dozens of girls who shouted a cheery greeting to him. At least he seemed well liked—unless something in the water made them act like zombies.

Ben steered them to the cafeteria line where he handed them each a plate. Mom went right for the salad bar. Olivia hung back and surveyed the room. Clusters of four to six teenage girls of every size, shape, and ethnicity shared the tables. Some eyed her suspiciously, some just looked on in interest, some completely ignored her. Those were the ones who made her nervous.

Ben helped her select some food and then walked her to a table of three of the most blatant ignorers who hadn't even glanced at her yet. He set down her tray in front of an empty seat and slid the chair back for her to sit down.

Great. Could he make this any more awkward?

"Just enjoy yourself here with the girls, Olivia. Your mom and I are going to talk privately over dinner." Ben smiled at each girl. "Introduce yourselves and make our guest feel welcome, okay?"

Were grown-ups always so clueless?

"So. Whatchu in for?" A tiny girl with a thick Spanish accent chewed on a toothpick and narrowed her eyes to suspicious slits.

Was she serious? "Excuse me? I'm not *in* for anything."

"Ju-Ju. Come on. Give her a break." A beautiful girl—like an African princess—turned to Olivia. "I'm Tricia. What's your name?" Rather than reaching out for a handshake, she took a bite of her lasagna.

"I'm Olivia. It's nice to meet you, Tricia." With the emphasis on *Tricia*. She turned to Ju-Ju and smirked. "I'm not *in* for anything. In fact, I'm going home tomorrow."

"You'll be back." A pretty girl with long shiny brown hair

and sparkly blue eyes spoke with confidence. "I'm Skye." She reached out her hand.

Olivia accepted the handshake. "No, I'm quite sure I won't be back." What did Skye know anyway? Olivia blew on her french onion soup.

Tricia, Skye, and Ju-Ju looked from one to the other like they shared a secret. "It's too late. You've fallen under *the spell*." Skye wiggled her fingers like a magician as she spoke.

"The spell?" The place got creepier every minute.

"God's will is like a spell. You're on the path, and He ain't about to let you go now. You might as well not fight it." Skye chuckled. "Unfortunately for the three of us. . .we had to learn the hard way."

"Got that right." Tricia's eyes clouded over as she looked out the window. "If only I'd known then what I know—"

Ju-Ju snorted. "Oh, get real. Like either of you would have done a single thing differently. You"—she pointed at Tricia—"wanted the boys' attention a little too much, and you'd have done anything to get it. And you"—Ju-Ju jerked her thumb at Skye—"hated your preacher papa too much and would do anything to get back at him. You were both going down no matter what." She shrugged. "So what? You're here now, and she's going home. But she'll be back soon." She gestured toward Olivia. "After *Diablo* does a little more work on her."

Tricia shuddered. "You say that so coldly. . .so matter-of-factly. Like it's not important."

"It doesn't really matter though, does it?" Ju-Ju shrugged again. "*La chica* could change her mind, beg to stay. . .but she won't. Which is fine. It's her journey. But mark my words"—Ju-Ju pointed at Olivia—"you'll be back."

Over my dead body.

Chapter 11

"This party's a bust. We're out of here." Jordyn's blood-red eyes shot daggers toward her boyfriend who stood across the room, flirting with another girl. She jerked Olivia away from a pot-smoking cluster where she'd just taken a huge hit. "Brett's being such a jerk. I'm totally through with him, and I want to leave right now." Jordyn stormed toward the front door.

Olivia nodded and followed, holding in her breath for as long as she could. When she ran out of oxygen, she blew the smoke from her lungs and gasped for fresh air. "Hold it a sec. Where's Bailey?" Olivia searched the faces in the dark room, hoping Bailey might be in better condition to drive than Jordyn seemed. Olivia obviously had no business getting behind the wheel either.

"She's not coming. She said she's staying over with Aaron." Jordyn scowled. "Right there's another couple who should break up. Like Aaron isn't cheating on her. *Please.* I'm through with men—I guess Bailey'll have to find out the hard way that they aren't worth her time." Jordan tripped over the threshold of the front door and stumbled out onto the porch. The heel of her right shoe snapped off and flew into the bushes. She clutched the railing until she steadied herself.

"Are you sure you're okay to drive?" Olivia watched Jordyn's unsteady swagger down the driveway. Not good. "We could always call a cab."

"No. There's no way I'm leaving my car here overnight. That would mean I'd have to deal with Brett tomorrow when I came to pick it up. No thank you." Jordyn waved a hand back and forth. "Besides, what would we tell our parents if we got dropped off in a taxi?" She shook her arms and jumped up and down a few times. "I'll just suck it up. It'll be fine. Not like it's the first time I've driven after a few drinks." She almost toppled over as she climbed into the driver's seat and pressed a button, trying to unlock the door for Olivia, but the window buzzed down instead. And then back up. It took her three tries to find the right one to pop the lock.

A *few* drinks? Olivia shivered outside the car with her hand on the door handle. Should she refuse to get in? Pretend she felt sick? Maybe she should call Jordyn's dad to come get them. He seemed pretty cool about stuff. He could pick them up and let them crash in the shed. But Olivia didn't have his number, and she doubted Jordyn would give it to her. It seemed like Jordyn drank and then drove every single week—maybe she was used to it and *would* be fine. But when would her luck run out?

The window lowered an inch. "You coming or what?"

"I'm coming." She slid into her seat and pulled the belt tight around her as she hooked the latch into place. Everything would be okay—or it wouldn't. Didn't really matter either way.

Feeling queasy from the mixture of pot and alcohol, Olivia put her head back against the seat and closed her eyes while Jordyn peeled out of the driveway. *No, no. Don't sleep.* Olivia lifted her head with a wobbly neck. She should talk to Jordyn, keep her awake. But Olivia's eyes felt like they had anchors on them, weighing them down. It was so hard to stay awake. She had to try. Maybe she'd rest her eyes for just a moment and then sit up and help Jordyn stay awake for the rest of the drive.

Everything went black.

✺

"Start an IV. We'll sedate her while we repair. . ." The unfamiliar voices went in and out of clarity.

Where am I? Olivia tried to open her eyes, but the lids seemed to be superglued shut. People talked around her—she felt the tingle of their touch sometimes—on her arm, her foot, her shoulder. Her head buzzed and her ears rang—but nothing hurt. Where was she? She pulled strength from her deepest recesses and tried to fight against the urge to drift off again.

"Two more stitches should. . ."

Stitches? Wake up. Wake up. Her eyes still refused to open. What did she remember last? Out with Jordyn and Bailey. The party. Jordyn said Brett had been acting like a jerk—not like that was news. They broke up, and Jordyn wanted to leave. Olivia couldn't recall anything after that—she found it difficult to think with the constant ringing in her ears. Beeping. . . Where had the beeping come from? Wait! Olivia remembered getting in the car with Jordyn, but then nothing. Had they been in an accident?

"Doctor?" A woman's kind voice hovered in a whisper near Olivia's ear. "Her pulse has increased a bit, and her eyelids are moving. She may be waking up." It must be a nurse's light touches that Olivia felt flutter on her body from time to time. Was Mom in the room somewhere?

"Okay." The same man who talked about stitches answered. A doctor? "Give her ten more milligrams. Let's not have her awaken while we're sewing up her face."

My face? Olivia wanted nothing more than to touch her cheeks. Was she hurt badly? How many stitches? What else was injured? But she felt no pain. . . . How could that be? How about Jordyn?

The buzzing in her head grew louder and her thinking hazier. The darkness fought a valiant battle against consciousness. It won.

ॐ

"Livvie? Are you coming to? It's Mommy here with you."

Mommy? Since when did she refer to herself as that? *Things must be bad.* Olivia felt the light brush of a kiss on her forehead. Memories of being a little girl in her parents' bed watching Saturday morning cartoons comforted her. Somehow she knew the beeping she heard was not from the television. What was going on? It took all her might to force one eye open. She steeled herself against the bright light and opened the other eye. "What happened?"

"Shh. Don't talk. Just rest. There will be plenty of time for talk later." Mom sniffled. "We almost lost you, Livvie Love." She blew her nose in a shriveled tissue.

Olivia warmed at the familiar sound of a nickname she hadn't heard for almost a decade—except for in her dreams. She tried to lift her head, but it felt like a bowling ball. Her eyes closed, and her mind blanked as she gave in to sleep again.

When she woke, hours or maybe only minutes later, Mom stood right beside her bed, looking calmer than she had before. Did that mean Olivia's prognosis had improved? "Mom." It took all of Olivia's energy to speak in a whisper. "I need to know. What happened?" She blinked her eyes and turned toward the empty bed across the room. "Where's Jordyn?" Why wasn't she Olivia's roommate?

Mom shook her head.

"Tell me." Olivia had only moments before she'd drift off again—she felt the weight pressing on her eyelids. She had to know. . .now.

After a deep, ragged breath, Mom took Olivia's hand—the

one without the IV—in both of hers and rubbed the top of it with her thumb. "You and Jordyn were in a car accident. Jordyn ran the car into a tree going eighty-five miles an hour."

Olivia gasped and tears stung her eyes. "How is she?" *How am I?*

"Jordyn didn't have her seat belt on." Mom choked on a sob and squeezed Olivia's hand. "She didn't make it."

The acid bubbled up from Olivia's stomach. She whipped her head to the side and fumbled in her dizziness for the basin the nurse had laid on her pillow.

Mom held back her daughter's hair while she vomited, her own tears dropping onto the back of Olivia's head and running down her neck.

Olivia fell back against the bed and frantically searched the space within reach. She wanted to throw something—smash it against the floor. But she couldn't protest—what was the point? Couldn't punch the wall. Couldn't move. She could cry, but what good were tears? She'd sure cried her share over the years, but they'd never brought her daddy back. They never changed a thing. Useless like her prayers. "I wish it had been me instead, like it should have been. . .the first time." God must want to punish her. If He even existed. Olivia sure had her doubts about that.

"Don't say that." Mom put her hand on the top of Olivia's hand and squeezed. "Please don't say that. I don't know what I'd do if something happened to you."

The dam broke, and the flood of tears poured forth from Olivia's eyes.

The door opened, and a nurse poked her head in. "Everything okay?" She bustled to the bedside with a syringe and injected something into an IV port.

Mom rubbed Olivia's hand, the room silent except for the

beeping. Would the monitor stop making noise if her heart broke in half? Apparently not.

Tears continued to stream from Olivia's closed eyes down her cheeks, soaking the bandage that ran beside her ear, from her chin to her forehead. Her eyelids fluttered, and no matter how hard she tried to fight it, she started to drift off.

Probably thinking Olivia was already asleep, the nurse whispered, "She took it pretty hard, huh?"

"Yeah. She was in the car when her dad died many years ago—when she was seven. He hadn't had his seat belt on either—like her friend Jordyn. Poor Olivia." Mom sniffled. "This brought back some horrible memories for her, I'm sure."

❧

Wriggling her head, Olivia freed her long braid from beneath the trap of the seat belt across her chest. Why weren't they home yet? The drive from Daddy's work took forever tonight. Olivia poked her thumbs in her ears, wiggled four fingers, and stuck out her tongue at the reflection she saw in the rearview mirror. She leaned the side of her head against the cold window on her left then had an idea. She huffed on the widow, expelling steamy breath to frost the glass. She dragged her pointer finger up and down, erasing the fog, leaving her most important message behind: I Luv Daddy!

Olivia nodded in satisfaction and grinned. Her eyes caught her face in the mirror again. She giggled at the cavern where her two front teeth used to be and pressed her tongue in the hole. She'd wanted to lose those teeth since she was six, but it took them a whole year to fall out! It felt gooey and weird—kind of like Jell-O Jigglers. Mmm. Maybe Mommy made some today. Maybe even red ones shaped like hearts or green ones like Christmas trees. Green ones were her favorite.

Flip. Flap. Olivia flicked the zipper on her coat with her mittened hand. Her fingers were getting sticky with sweat.

"Jingle bells, jingle bells. . ." Daddy sang along with the song on the radio. He loved Christmas music. He loved all music, but Christmas was his favorite. Especially on a night like this—snow falling around them. . .perfect snow for building a snowman. Maybe they could do that after dinner.

"Jingle all the way." Olivia joined in. "Oh, what fun. . ."

Daddy gasped.

Olivia froze in horror—something seemed very wrong, but she didn't know what it meant.

Headlights beamed through the front window, coming right for them. Daddy would get them out of the way in time, right? Olivia wanted to look at him, but she couldn't tear her eyes off the beacons that grew bigger and bigger with each passing moment.

"Stop him, Daddy!" Olivia clenched her fists and scrunched her eyes closed.

Tires squealed. The impact jarred her entire body. Would the seat belt snap? The sound of crunching metal and breaking glass seemed unending. Screams filled the car. Hers or Daddy's? Sounded like both.

It didn't hurt—like an amusement park ride. But when would the tumbling stop?

"Oh God, save my angel!" Daddy cried out into the night as Olivia watched his back hit the roof of the car. A final roll, then the world went black.

The turn signal click-clicked, click-clicked. No other

sound could be heard.

"Daddy?" Olivia whispered into the darkness. She felt funny. Almost like she hung from the sky. She tested her seat belt—it felt tight across her chest and belly. Her legs dangled. Why couldn't she see? Where was Daddy? Her heart pounded and her body trembled. "Daddy? Where are you?"

Silence.

"Daddy? I'm scared." Olivia scrunched her eyes shut, this time to pray. Jesus, make it all go away. . .please. *She slowly opened one eye then the other. "Daddy!"*

What should she do? It was getting cold in the car, and the snow blew in through the broken windows. Maybe Daddy needed help. Olivia reached down by her right hip, felt among the folds of her puffy winter coat, and released the belt. She dropped with a thud to a flat surface, but her arm got twisted and stuck in the seat belt above her. She crouched on what must have been the ceiling to free her arm. How weird that the ceiling was under her feet.

Olivia reached over and tried to open the door, but it was upside down and stuck in the snowbank. The other side! She crawled across the ceiling and fumbled for the door handle. Stuck. She could feel her heart beating in her chest. What if no one found them?

"Daddy?" She tried again. Her tiny plea was answered by nothing but the whir of the wind.

In the pitch black of the snow-covered car, Olivia pulled off her gloves and patted the area around her. "Daddy, why aren't you saying anything? Where are you?"

The car seemed kind of tilted. Like it rested on a hill or a slope of some kind. Olivia had to hold on to the seat to crawl toward the front of the car, where she groped for contact. Finally, she felt her dad's nylon ski jacket in front of her.

Scurrying under the seats so she could be near him, Olivia smelled the comforting scent of his familiar cologne. She reached out a cold hand and touched his face. Warm wetness. She pulled back her hands and pressed her fingers together. Sticky. What was that? It felt like glue—only warmer.

"Over here," a man's voice called from right outside the car.

"I see it." The second person sounded farther away.

Olivia sighed in relief as she saw lights flicker through the snowfall. "Daddy, they found us. It's going to be okay. You can wake up now." Silence.

"Hey! How many people are in there? Are you okay?" The first man yelled through the window with a gravelly voice. He sounded pretty old. Like thirty.

"Me and Daddy are here. Daddy's taking a nap." Olivia's teeth chattered, so she cuddled her shivering body as close to her father as she could.

"Hey, Mike, bring the shovel. I think we need to hurry. You call 911?"

"Yep—as soon as I saw the accident. They're on their way."

A siren wailed in the distance. The shovel was put to work. As the snow cleared from the windows, light from the rescuers' flashlights began to seep into the car. Olivia felt Daddy's cheek again. Even more glue. Where was it coming from?

Finally, they cleared the area by Daddy's door and managed to pry it open just in time for Olivia to see the ambulance pull alongside their overturned vehicle. The lights made pretty red swirls on the mounds of snow.

"Hi, sweetie. What's your name, and how old are you?"

The ambulance man crouched down by the door, letting the flashlight shine on his face.

"I'm Olivia, and I just turned seven."

"You've been very brave, Olivia. Are you hurt anywhere?" He pointed the light on her body.

"No, but my daddy has glue all over him."

"Glue?" The nice man squeezed through the door and shined the powerful light onto Daddy's face. He gasped.

Blood covered Daddy's head and soaked his coat. A shiny red puddle spread from beneath his back.

Olivia's jaw fell, and her stomach retched. She looked from her daddy's head to her blood-covered hand and screamed.

And screamed.

Olivia opened her eyes, expecting her hands to be covered with Daddy's blood. Instead, she found herself in a sterile hospital room, hooked up to beeping and whirring machines. She clenched the damp sheets to her chest. A droplet of sweat trickled from her forehead into her right ear. Her heart raced beneath her fists as her ragged breath fought to gain control.

As the horse hooves thundering in her chest calmed, her mind caught up and Olivia remembered why she lay there in a hospital bed. Her hands flew to her face. The bandages still covered her left cheek and ear. Wonder what lay beneath those bandages. Did she even want to know? Why did she have to wake up at all? Blessed eternal sleep would have been so much easier than this new reality.

Two accidents, neither one a dream. When would the nightmare end?

Chapter 12

"Knock, knock. You up for a visitor?" Jodie poked her head into the room.

Olivia winced when she tried to nod. She touched her bandages and wondered how bad she looked. Mom said her face was swollen and bruised, but no one would let Olivia see a mirror. "Head hurts so bad." The throbbing felt like a drumbeat.

"I know, sweetie." Jodie stepped over to the bed. "I brought you some flowers." She held up a vase of cheery daisies.

Olivia nodded and gestured to the window ledge. "Thanks."

Jodie set them down and spread the flowers in the sunlight. "I heard what happened last night." She covered Olivia's hand. "I'm really sorry about your friend."

Olivia blinked. "Everyone dies." Her breathy voice was a barely audible whisper.

"What'd you say, sweetie?" Jodie leaned closer.

"Nothing." Best not to repeat it, or they'd put her in the psych ward. Then again, that might be the best place for her.

"Where's your mom?" Jodie looked around the room even though Mom obviously wasn't there.

"Shopping." Olivia swallowed, finding it difficult to talk. "She was here earlier. Decided a concussion and twenty-two stitches deserved new pajamas." She lifted the cup of water from her bedside tray and sucked on the straw, letting the water touch her cracked lips. "Might go home tomorrow."

"I heard." Jodie sighed. "Any news about when the visitation will be?"

"Tues. . .day." Olivia's voice choked on a sob. She closed her eyes to the horror of the reality she faced in the coming week, and forever.

"I'm not going to stay long. You need your rest." Jodie squeezed her hand. "Can I pray with you before I go?"

Olivia blinked. "Please."

"Our precious Lord Jesus. . ."

At the mention of His name, Olivia broke down. Hours, months, years of grief poured out from her body in buckets of tears that washed over the bandages on her face, soaking through them and stinging the rips in her flesh. Her shoulders shook; her hands trembled. She felt Jodie's arms encircle her and pull her close, but Olivia didn't hear another word Jodie said. Finally, when she'd cried her last tear, Olivia opened her eyes.

Jodie desperately prayed, pleading with God over Olivia. Her lips moved, and her hands were white as they clasped a well-worn Bible. "Olivia. I feel an urgency. I feel like God is asking me to talk to you about this right now while He's got ahold of your heart. Get out of this, Liv. Go to Diamond Estates. Find healing. Find peace. Find Jesus." Jodie scrunched her eyes and squeezed Olivia's hand. "Please."

Olivia blinked twice.

༄

Dressed for the visitation, Olivia sat on her bed. How could she put one foot in front of the other and walk out of the house to go to something like this? What would it be like? Jordyn had been so young, so beautiful. Her parents must be beyond devastated. Surely they blamed Olivia for not doing something—anything to stop Jordyn from getting behind the wheel that night. What should she say to them? What *could* she say? It probably didn't matter. They wouldn't speak to her anyway.

Olivia put her fingers on her temples and tried to smooth away the tension and the questions plaguing her. Why hadn't Olivia insisted they call a cab? She could have taken the keys from Jordyn, called home for a ride, or even staged a simple protest by not getting into the car. Was she just as guilty as Jordyn because she went along with it? Maybe even worse because she knew better. Why hadn't she told Jordyn to put on her seat belt? And why had Olivia allowed herself to fall asleep? If she had just stayed awake, maybe she could have kept Jordyn alert. Why hadn't she just said no in the first place? The endless questions would never have answers.

Her fingers traveled down her face and traced the length of the three-inch wound running down the side of her cheek, in front of her ear. She walked back to the bathroom to cover it with a patch of surgical gauze. The doctor had she didn't need to bandage it, but it looked so red, so angry—gross with all those stitches.

People keep saying it could have been a lot worse. *Duh. Just ask Jordyn.* But, even so, it would be a permanent reminder that nothing ever went right for Olivia.

And nothing lasted forever. . .except for scars.

Time to go. One last deep breath, and Olivia pulled herself away from the mirror and reached in her closet for her black jacket to go over her charcoal sheath dress. She needed to find Mom and hurry her up.

"Livvie?"

Startled at the sound of a man's voice in her bedroom, she hurried from her closet, half expecting it to be Charles. But thankfully he'd ignored her since the accident. Olivia peeked into her room then squealed and jumped when she saw who stood there beaming at her. She immediately winced as her sore body reminded her it still wasn't quite ready for excitement. "Jake! What are you doing here?"

Her big brother pulled her into a tender hug.

She let her head drop onto his comforting chest and soaked in the security only he offered. Olivia held on as though she clung to a life preserver in the middle of a vicious ocean.

"I came as soon as I could get away. I needed to see you—to make sure you're okay." He pulled back and looked in her eyes. "You *are* okay, aren't you?"

Olivia nodded. "Nothing that won't heal. Well, except for this." She pointed to her wound.

"Oh, that's nothing. What a wimpy scar." Jake tried to make light of it with his words, but his eyes were sad.

"Yeah right." Olivia smiled for the first time in days. "You coming to the funeral home with us?" *Please.*

Jake nodded. "If it's okay with you."

"Thanks." She tapped her fingers on her chin in the sign for *thank you* and breathed a deep sigh of relief. Jake would get her through the visitation and the funeral that afternoon. He'd be her rock.

"I brought you something. I want you to have it—at least for a while." Jake dug in the front pocket of his jeans and pulled out a gold ring.

Olivia gasped and reached out a finger to touch it then shrank back like she'd been bitten. "You can't give Dad's wedding ring to me."

"We're calling it a loan. I think you need it more than I do right now."

She nodded as she accepted her father's wedding ring and slipped it onto the chain she wore around her neck, letting it drop under her dress. Placing her hand on her chest, covering the dangling ring, Olivia closed her eyes and drew strength from her father's eternal promise.

"Ready?"

Olivia exhaled a shaky breath and nodded. As ready as she'd ever be. It was time to go.

After a short drive, the trio walked through the front doors of the funeral home and up to the registry book where Mom signed them in and included their address.

Olivia shifted nervously and glanced both ways down a stately hallway. Ghostlike forms milled in and out of doorways. Some nodded at each other as they passed, but no one spoke. Where had they put Jordyn? Would the casket be open? How would she look in death?

Mom gestured at a sign directing them to the room on the right.

Entering the visitation felt like getting in line for a beating. The collective pain of the grieving crowd was like a dark storm cloud overtaking the room. Not a dry eye among the mourners. Did everyone know who she was? Did they blame her for the accident? If they did, they were probably right.

Dozens of people stood queued for their opportunity to approach the open casket. She recognized some teachers and students from school. Bailey and Emma stood huddled in line with their parents. Olivia turned to Jake in a panic and clutched his hand. "Do I have to go up there?"

Jake offered a gentle smile. "You only do what you feel comfortable doing. Maybe it'll get easier in a little while." He scanned the room. "Which ones are her parents?"

Olivia located Jordyn's mom lying on a sofa. "She's over there on the couch. Is she asleep?" Olivia squinted and peered closer.

A plump gray-haired woman with a tissue tucked into the

neckline of her black dress leaned in with a whisper. "Penny was having a horrible time of it, and they had to give her something to take the edge off. Jordyn was her only child, you know. She's sleeping off the effects of the medication." The woman shook her head and dabbed her bloodshot eyes. "Unthinkable what she must be going through."

"Thanks," Olivia mumbled as Mom steered them to three seats in the middle of the room. Mom had told her people didn't always wear black to funerals anymore, but it seemed like everyone had to this one. Olivia watched as person after person approached the casket and leaned over to say a prayer, touch Jordyn's hand, or, in some cases, kiss her cheek.

What would it have looked like if it had been Olivia in that casket? Whose faces would have peered down at her? Mom. Jake. Jodie and Pastor Tom. Jordyn. Kids from school. Some teachers. Charles? Maybe, but he hadn't come to the hospital— not that she'd wanted him to—but who knew if he'd even bother coming to her funeral?

Daddy. She'd always known he'd never be at her graduation or her wedding—but it never dawned on her that he wouldn't be at her funeral either. If she'd died instead of Jordyn, she'd be *with* Daddy already. Would he be sad to see her, knowing it meant she was dead? She sure didn't want to go be with him under circumstances like these had been. She wanted to make him proud, live a long life, give him grandbabies to love from heaven.

Was Daddy disappointed with her choices and the way her life was going? He had to be—that is, if God let him see the bad stuff. That's *if* there was even a God. Did Olivia even deserve to go to heaven? Would God let her in? She shuddered at the chilling thought that she might not make it—if there even *was* a heaven. But there had to be, because if there wasn't, that meant Daddy was gone forever. Jordyn, too. Impossible.

Maybe the time *had* come. . . . Time to make some changes.

She'd already pretty much told Jodie she'd go to Diamond Estates. Even though Olivia's reply had been weak blinks from a hospital bed, Jodie seemed to have gotten the message. Maybe that place *could* help her get it together and find some answers to the questions she'd been asking for so long. Maybe it *was* the right thing to do. In Jordyn's honor. In Daddy's honor.

How would she tell Mom? Not like Mom would fight it or anything—she'd probably help her pack. What if Charles said no? He might not want to let her out of his sight. Well, if he said no, she'd just run away to Diamond Estates anyway—if they'd have her. If they wouldn't, she'd just have to disappear. Her life depended on it. . .in more ways than one.

Toward the end of the visitation, when the line died down, Olivia gathered her nerve. She stood up, smoothed her dress, and sucked in a rattly breath.

Jake slipped his hand into hers and shifted in his seat as if he planned to rise and accompany her to view Jordyn's body.

Olivia pressed his hand and shook her head. "I need to do this alone," she signed.

He nodded and rested back in his chair.

New Louboutin pumps slipping on the carpet, Olivia made her way to the front. Up close, the figure in the casket resembled Jordyn, only. . .not. Like one of those cheesy wax-figure renditions they made of celebrities. A caricature only reminiscent of the beauty she had once been.

It occurred to Olivia that she'd never seen Jordyn with her blond hair loose and flowy like that. It was always braided or tied back in a ponytail. Olivia reached out to touch her friend's hand then reeled back as the feel of Jordyn's icy skin shocked her. There was no life there. It wasn't gross or weird. It just wasn't anything.

Olivia remembered seeing her daddy lie like that. Then

Mom had taken her out while they closed the casket. Over the years, she'd been so resentful toward her mother for that choice. Still hated her for it. Olivia's breath caught as she realized her mom had been right to do it. To have a memory of her daddy like the sight she saw before her was bad enough. But to see the casket close on him—Olivia shuddered. Letting a seven-year-old see such a thing would have been cruel. Wow. Mom had been right.

Olivia felt movement near her arm. She turned her sore neck just enough to see Jordyn's mom out of the corner of her eye. Olivia took a single step toward the haggard woman and became enveloped in a hug. "I'm so sorry." Olivia sobbed on the shoulder of a woman she'd met only one other time. A shattered woman who faced the unimaginable task of burying her teenage daughter that very day.

"Jordyn thought you were very special, Olivia." Penny didn't look her in the eye. "She wanted to be just like you."

"*She* wanted to be like *me*?" Jordyn was the cool one. She had it all together.

Penny nodded. "She saw something in you. Please promise me you'll honor her memory by doing something great with your life. Something greater than *this*." She gestured to her lifeless daughter. Penny's knees began to buckle, and she reached out for support. Her ex-husband stepped in and offered his arm.

He turned to Olivia. "I guess I thought you girls were smarter than this."

Olivia nodded and gulped back her sobs.

The funeral director asked everyone to leave the room so the family could have a few moments alone with Jordyn before the service started.

Olivia, Mom, and Jake left the room as the director pulled the door shut.

"This is when they close the casket, isn't it?" Olivia whispered.

Mom nodded, her lip quivering.

At that exact moment, Jordyn's parents were behind the closed doors looking at their daughter for the last time ever on earth. Parents didn't lay their children in the ground—it was meant to be the other way around. It seemed so unnatural and wrong. Final. It wasn't supposed to be like that. Weren't teenagers invincible?

A few minutes passed before the doors swung open again. The guests were directed back to the seats in the center of the room, in front of the eternally closed coffin.

Penny's head rested on her ex-husband's chest. The trembling of her shoulders was visible from even five rows back where Olivia looked on.

The minister droned. His words blended into one long buzz in Olivia's ears. She just couldn't get past the reality that Jordyn wouldn't get a do-over. A stupid decision. One drunken car ride cost her the rest of her life.

The permanence of it resonated in Olivia's soul. She could have been the one in that casket.

Next time, she probably would be.

Chapter 13

On the way home from the funeral, Olivia broke the silence with her news. "Mom. I've made a decision." She took a deep breath and then let the words tumble out in one long blurb. "IwanttogotoDiamondEstates."

Mom's gaze darted to the rearview mirror and fixed on Olivia. Understanding flickered in her eyes as the words sank in.

Jake's eyebrows furrowed, and he turned to look at Olivia in the backseat, his eyes full of questions.

"When did you decide this?" Mom's knuckles were white on the steering wheel.

"Pretty much in the hospital. Jodie and I talked about it, but I had to think things through before I made up my mind." Olivia straightened her back and nodded. "Now I'm sure it's the right thing. It's what I want to do."

"I think it might be the best move, too. I mean, I'll hate to see you leave—especially now. But the alternative we saw today doesn't appeal very much either." Mom's shoulders dropped a couple of inches as she exhaled. "I'll be honest; I'm relieved."

Easier than Olivia had expected it to be, but what would Charles say? "Mom, if it's okay, I'd like for us to make all of the arrangements before we tell Charles about any of this."

Mom pursed her lips and shook her head. "I don't like that at all. It's really not fair to him to decide something so important without involving him."

Not fair to him? What about fair to me? Deep breath. "I'm positive that if we phrase it to Charles like it's an option, like he has a say in the decision, he *will* say no."

"Hmm." Mom drummed her fingernails on the steering wheel and chewed her lip. At least she seemed to be listening for once.

Jake watched the volley of conversation without jumping in.

"But if we stand up to him and tell him how it's going to be, at least I have a chance." Olivia waited for an answer. Her whole future depended on this.

Jake cleared his throat. "I have to agree with Liv on this one, Mom. I'm not exactly sure what he'll say, but I do know Charles—he won't make this easy."

"Okay." Mom didn't sound convinced. "He's not going to like it one bit. But we'll try it your way."

🌀

"Diamond Estates, this is Ben Bradley. Can I help you?"

He answered his own phone? "Mr. Bradley? Ben? This is Olivia Mansfield. I visited about a month ago. I'm not sure if you remem–"

"Olivia! How wonderful to hear from you. Of course I remember you." Ben's voice sounded warm and welcoming. Good sign. "In fact, we just prayed for you in our staff prayer time this morning."

"Thank you." *I think.*

"What can I do for you?"

"Well, if it's still possible. . .I mean, if there's still room. . ." The words stuck like a lump in her throat. At the last minute, she'd gotten nervous and wanted Mom to make the phone call for her, but Mom thought it would mean more coming directly from Olivia—proof that it was what she wanted. But how could she come right out and say it?

"Yes, Olivia?" Ben obviously had no intention of making it easy for her.

Olivia drew a shaky breath. "I'm ready."

"That's all I needed to hear. How soon can you get here?" Ben's tone grew more serious as he got down to business.

"Is Monday okay?" That would give her five days to pack and say good-bye to her friends.

"It's *okay*, if it's the soonest you can arrange. But these next few days before you arrive are going to be tougher on you than you realize. You should get here as soon as possible—I'd think Friday would be doable."

"I could probably arrange that. I'm not going to be sad about leaving or anything though—if that's what you're worried about." Scared, maybe, but not sad. "It's not like I'm going to change my mind."

"Let's shoot for Friday—you can call me later today when you've made the arrangements. I'd also like to speak with you tomorrow. Be aware, there are evil forces at work that want you to fail. You've declared you're seeking change, but you aren't equipped yet with the tools to stand up in the face of temptation and peer pressure. This is a very vulnerable time."

"There won't be any peer pressure—my best friend is dead."

🌀

How do I pack up my whole life when it all belongs to someone else? Olivia stowed many of her favorite things—jeans, casual tops, yoga pants, and running shoes—in two large Louis Vuitton suitcases. One matching hanging bag held some dressier items that Mom made her pack. No way she'd need them in a house full of teenage girls, but there was no convincing her mother. She'd use her backpack as a carry-on, but she'd wait until the next day to fill it with books, snacks, her laptop, and her iPod, since her flight wasn't until noon.

Olivia stuffed three extra-large trash bags with the rest of her designer wardrobe, which she stacked in the corner of her closet and marked for charity. She hoped Norma would find them and take care of the donation before Charles noticed them. He refused to give his things to people who, as he said, couldn't bother getting a job. But Olivia had no use for them anymore. She had no intention of returning to Charles's house. Ever. No matter what. In fact, if she could manage it, she'd leave the next day without even saying good-bye to him.

Did he even know she was leaving yet? Mom had said she would tell him last night, but Olivia hadn't heard any screaming or crashing of lamps against the wall. She'd probably chickened out—which might be for the best since Mom had plans to be out for a few hours tonight. Charles wasn't home either—Olivia hoped that didn't change before Mom got home. She only had to get through one more night, and she'd be free of *Chuck* forever. Except in her memories.

With nothing left to pack, Olivia decided to treat it like Christmas Eve—go to bed to hurry morning's arrival. Plus the sooner she slept, the less time she'd have to worry about things she couldn't change, like where Charles was and when he'd be home.

As she nuzzled her face deep into her fluffy pillow, it occurred to her that she had no one left to say good-bye to. Jordyn was gone. Bailey and Tara hadn't spoken to her since before the funeral. Her childhood friends had long since been abandoned when she chose her all-new lifestyle and new friends. Jodie had already come by earlier that day—at least someone cared.

What was she doing? Was she really packing up and moving out the very next morning? Olivia squirmed in her bed, the sheets tangled around her feet. Maybe she should rethink things. This was such a severe reaction to some normal life events, natural consequences, and experimental teen choices. She wasn't bad enough to need a treatment facility—a group home.

Wait! Those thoughts were exactly what Ben warned her to watch for. Olivia remembered his exact words during their most recent phone call that morning: *"Thoughts and doubts will assail your mind, trying to convince you that you're right and everyone else is wrong. They'll tell you that you don't need a place like this. Just remember what to watch out for, and be intentional about shutting those voices down before they wreak havoc on your resolve."*

Olivia flopped over onto her back and covered her face with a pillow. It didn't stop the doubts thundering in her ears, but it made her feel stronger and safer from them while she drifted off to sleep.

CRASH!

Olivia's eyes flew open, and she scurried off her bed toward the window. The sheet was twisted around one foot, and she fell flat to the floor. She shook her leg and pulled at the sheet until her foot came free then scrambled to the window to see what the noise had been.

Grabbing the windowsill, she peered out to the driveway below.

Charles! He'd crashed the car into the garage—he seemed to have been aiming for his side of the garage and missed by just a few feet. His Beemer was folded like an accordion, sticking halfway out onto the driveway amid a pile of bricks. He pitched and teetered across the pavement. Dust swirled in clouds around him as he made his way to the front porch, fumbling with his keys and a bottle of almost-gone amber liquid. He glanced up at her window and locked eyes with Olivia before entering the house.

Oh no! She frantically searched every corner of her room. Where could she hide?

Okay, Olivia. . .think!

He would come up the front stairs, and judging by his stagger, it would take a bit longer than usual for him to get to her. Would a locked door keep him out? No way. She'd been trying that defense for years. Could she hide? She could try, but she had no guarantee he wouldn't find her, especially since she knew he had seen her in there. And if he did find her, it would be so much worse.

Her only hope was to climb out the window. If she timed it just right, he'd be stumbling up the stairs while she was scaling the side of the house. But where would she go once she got to the ground? Then again, did it even matter? She could just start running. He'd never catch her—not in the condition he was in, and his car certainly wasn't drivable.

Olivia pressed her ear against her bedroom door and heard nothing. Charles hadn't made it to the stairs yet. She ran back to the window, threw it open, and leaned her head out just in time to see him step into the house and slam the front door. Not a moment to lose.

She couldn't jump; it was way too far. *The ladder!* A long time ago, Mom had stored an emergency one in the bench of Olivia's window seat in case of fire. Olivia threw the cushions to the floor and dug in the chest like a dog searching for a bone at the beach. Sheets, pillows, and blankets flew over her head as she cast them out of her way until she finally found the rope ladder at the bottom, still wrapped in its original packaging. *Ugh.* Why hadn't they taken it out of the plastic wrapper yet? Good thing there wasn't really a fire! Then again, that might be preferable to the monster trudging up the stairs looking for her.

The ladder finally ready, she hooked it to the windowsill

and watched it unfurl as it dropped down to barely skim the ground. Olivia slipped her arms into a hoodie and stashed her cigarettes and cell phone in the pocket.

Deep breath.

She flung her legs out the window and dangled near the knotted rungs until she could steady herself enough to grab on. She shimmied down, hand under hand, letting her legs hang free. It would have taken too much time to actually climb down. *Cool.* She was stronger than she thought.

When she had just a few feet left, she dropped to the ground and glanced up at her window. What about the ladder? She tried flinging it to unhook it from the house, but that didn't work. But so what? Let him find it. He'd be mad, but she'd be gone. Safe for the night on the run, and then, after tomorrow, safely tucked away for a while on a snowy mountainside in Colorado.

Olivia ran down the long driveway toward the street. She needed to get past the gate before he found her, or she'd have to run into the woods lining the property and try to climb the fence without being spotted. She could probably outrun him—especially when he was drunk—but she wouldn't test her luck.

Yes! Charles had left the gate open after he'd driven through. He hardly ever did that. Score one for luck. Olivia scurried through the gate and then darted into the trees for cover, hoping the rest of the night would go as smoothly. *Just make it to morning.*

Breath in white smoke clouds around her face, Olivia maintained her speed on the uneven ground. When she stumbled, she reached out to steady herself with a tree branch or rock. After ten minutes, she slowed to a jog then a walk. There was no way Charles could find her in his present state. Besides, he wasn't the type to search too hard. He liked to lie in wait for his prey, like a spider watching its carefully spun web.

Olivia dug her cigarettes out of her pocket and lit one with shaky hands. She sucked in deeply, letting the warm smoke fill her lungs and calm her nerves. She glanced at the pack she gripped with white knuckles—what would likely be her last pack of cigarettes. She turned the box sideways and peered inside. She counted six remaining. That would get her through until her flight. Then what? How hard would it be to quit now that she had been smoking almost a pack a day for a few months? Oh well, nothing she could do to change it now. . .and at least she had them to get her through that night. *Just make it to morning.*

She ducked under the mechanical arms at the entrance to the semi-secure community where Jordyn's dad lived. She'd hide out in the little cabin behind his house if the key was still hidden where Jordyn had shown her. If not, she'd sit behind a bush and shiver all night—better than whatever Charles had in mind. Ducking into the shadows as a car approached, Olivia sighed with relief when it turned into a driveway before it reached her.

What was happening at home? Olivia shuddered as she imagined Charles ransacking her room, enraged at being outsmarted. Did Mom know yet? Maybe Olivia should call her. *No, phones work both ways.* If Mom was worried, she'd call. Olivia tapped her screen to bring it to life, making sure the battery was charged. Full bars. No recent calls. Maybe Mom hadn't discovered Olivia was gone yet.

The little cabin, secluded on three sides by trees, beckoned to her from across the backyard. Her heart sank as she remembered the night they teased Jordyn about having a hideout—until they saw how cool it was. That night was rough—drugs, cops, trouble. If only they'd learned from those mistakes. *Oh, Jordyn. . .*

Olivia shook away the memories and hurried to the entrance, eager to get inside, and dug in the rocks until she found the key. Using her cell phone for light, she checked the place out before stepping all the way in. Satisfied she was alone, Olivia stepped over the threshold and glanced back one last time to make sure she wasn't followed. Making sure she locked the door securely behind her, she collapsed on the couch.

§

Was that a phone ringing? Olivia winced as her neck muscles knotted and pinched when she tried to sit up. Where was she? Bright light shone through the horizontal slits in the window blinds across the room. As she squinted at the unfamiliar surroundings, memories of the night before slowly flooded in.

Olivia scrambled for her phone. It must have slipped from her hand to the floor when she'd fallen asleep. She pressed the CALL button seconds before the last ring sent Mom to voice mail. "Hello?" Olivia braced herself for yelling.

"Hey, Liv." Mom sounded as cheery as ever. "Where are you? Go for a walk to say good-bye to the neighborhood?"

Olivia shook her head. Mom. . .clueless again. No surprise there. Best to keep Mom in the dark for now and just get out of town in one piece. So did that mean Charles pulled in the rope ladder and left everything alone? He must have, or Mom would have sounded worried. Hadn't she seen the garage and the car though?

"Liv? You there?"

"Yep. Sorry. I got distracted by something." *Act natural.* "I'm heading back home now for a shower."

"Okay. Well, you'd better hurry. We need to leave in about an hour."

"I'm on my way." Olivia stood and stretched her back.

"Sounds good. Oh wait! Did you have a chance to say good-bye to Charles, or do we need to stop by his office on the way to O'Hare?"

Olivia's stomach retched at the thought of standing in the same room as *Chuck* ever again. "No need. We've said our good-byes."

"Great. I'll see you soon, then."

Olivia slipped her phone into her pocket and sighed. Mom could try to sound a *little* sad instead of like she was leaving for a trip to a beach resort. Maybe the thought of having Olivia out of the house *did* feel like a vacation to her. Well, she'd be getting her wish in a few short hours, and then she could have *Chuck* all to herself.

Forever.

Chapter 14

Could God find Denver, Colorado? Was He there already? Did He know Olivia was coming, that she was looking for Him? Would she even know it if she happened to encounter Him somewhere? Why didn't she sense Him yet at all? He was going to have to meet her halfway if He wanted to be found. Olivia would never manage it on her own. She glanced at her mom in the aisle seat beside her. Mom was certainly no help.

God, if You're real enough for me to feel Your presence, I'll believe. If she knew His presence was real, even for just an instant, Olivia would give her life to Him and follow Him. But if He stayed absent, if the prayers remained unanswered—unacknowledged—then she'd just have to move on. To what, she had no idea. To something. Or maybe nothing.

Would lightning shoot out like a claw from those clouds in the distance and strike her for giving God an ultimatum? Olivia leaned her head back on the airplane seat. She pondered her past and how it might blend with her future as the plane cut through the storm clouds. The sky appeared so different than it had the last time she'd flown to Denver just a couple of weeks ago—like a different place completely. That time, the flight had been bright and clear until the descent. Then the plane pitched and dropped from the turbulence until she'd felt sick. This time, the sky above the clouds roiled violently. She could barely see out her window as they flew right through the storm for most of the flight.

"Eww. Liv, put this under your head. Do you know how many people have leaned back on that same chair?" Mom brushed off the seat back and spread out a towel for Olivia.

"These seats are leather. They're not like the cloth seats in coach." Olivia smoothed the scratchy towel as best she could and put her head back against the seat so she could resume her cloud watching.

Mr. Ben had told her she'd probably be at Diamond Estates anywhere from nine to eighteen months depending on how she responded to the program. Maybe she should drag it out to eighteen months on purpose since she didn't want to return home. She'd be just shy of eighteen if she made it last that long. On the other hand, what if she hated it there? What would she do for more than a year? She had nowhere else to go if things didn't work out. She gazed through the tiny airplane window over miles of stormy clouds—so high above the earth with no home in any direction.

Finally, they broke through the darkness and found promise beneath the clouds. The sun shone a beacon upon the craggy mountain peaks covered with sparkling snow. Patches of still-grassy foothills beckoned from below. Her last visit had been so stormy that she never got a good glimpse of the Rockies in the distance. Now she gazed on mountains as far as her eyes could see. What a glorious sight. Surely they weren't an accident, right? Something or Someone had a hand in creating something so amazing. If God were anywhere, it would be in Colorado. Had to be.

"Are you getting nervous?" Mom's eyebrows furrowed together.

Olivia shook her head. "A few days ago I was, but not anymore. I mean, sure, I have questions, and the unknown is kind of scary. But. . ."

"I know what you mean." Mom nodded. "I can't wait to find out more about what you'll be doing specifically. It will ease my mind some, I'm sure."

"It is what it is, Mom." Olivia stared, unblinking. "Seriously, I'm staying. No matter what." What choice did she have?

"I know that's your plan. . . ." Mom bit her bottom lip, smearing lipstick on her teeth.

What wasn't she saying? "But what?"

"Well, I don't want you to get mad and think I'm interfering, and I sure don't want you to give up too easily, but I decided to stay in Denver for three days. I want to be nearby in case you change your mind."

That was just the sort of thing Mr. Ben had warned her about. Well-intentioned sabotage. "I wish you'd just support what I need to do, Mom. But whatever. You do what you have to do." It didn't really matter though. By dinnertime, those huge front doors of Diamond Estates would close behind Mom as she said good-bye. Olivia wondered when she'd see her again. Weeks? Months? What about the upcoming holidays? How would that work out? The sacrifice might turn out to be a bigger one than she'd anticipated. Hopefully it would be worth it.

"This is the pilot speaking." The intercom buzzed with light static. "We're about to begin our descent into sunshiny Denver, Colorado. I'm told the slopes are prime for you early season skiers and the lower elevations are enjoying a beautiful fall day. Couldn't ask for more out of the exquisite Rocky Mountains. If you're continuing on from here, a flight attendant will help you locate your connecting flight. If this is home for you, welcome."

Olivia's mind jumped back to the last time she'd heard those words. She'd been adamant that she'd never call this place home, but somehow, home it had become. For better or worse.

❧

"Welcome back to Denver." Justin's black knit shirt stretched at the shoulder seams as he heaved their bags into the trunk space of the van.

Had he been that muscular the last time they'd been here?

Mom shielded her eyes from the sun as she gazed at the landscape around her. "It's great to see you again, Justin. Wow. It's so much prettier here than I remember."

"Well, the last time you came we were in the middle of an early fall storm. If I remember correctly, visibility was low due to rain down here and snow up higher." Justin gestured at the mountains. "What do you think now?"

"Actually, I'm a little surprised they're so far away. In the plane it seemed like we'd be right up on them."

"Yes, ma'am. The low areas are about half an hour away— which is right where we're headed—then another half hour to get home." Justin held open the van doors. "Ready?" He secured the side door for Olivia while Mom settled into the front passenger seat.

Mom nudged her while Justin walked around the van to the driver's side. "What a nice boy," she whispered.

"Shh. You're embarrassing me, Mom." Nice boy or not, he'd never be interested in a Diamond troublemaker. Justin saw dozens of bad girls come through the program every year. He probably had some good stories to tell. Besides, dating would surely be off-limits for her. This wasn't going to be the time or place for her first real boyfriend. Even so, Olivia turned her head slightly to make sure her scar wasn't visible to Justin if he turned around to look out the back window while he drove.

"I know we talked about dating in general last time, but I was wondering if you had a girlfriend outside of Diamond

Estates." Mom pounced on him the instant he pulled the vehicle from the curb.

Olivia wanted to sink through the seat, out the back of the car, and onto the mountain road they traveled on. She couldn't remember her mother being so out of touch when she was younger. But now that she'd mentioned it, *did* he have one?

Justin coughed. Choked was more like it. "No, Mrs. Whitford. I don't have a girlfriend right now." His neck reddened, and he turned down the heat.

"Can I ask why?"

No, Mom, you can't! How rude. Olivia leaned forward an inch and craned her neck toward Justin.

"Not enough time or money." Justin whistled. "Girls are expensive."

"That's very true." Mom giggled.

Ha. If Justin only knew he was talking to the most expensive one ever.

"Plus things never seem to go quite my way in that department." His mouth smiled, but pained eyes were reflected in the mirror.

"Oh, I'm really sorry to hear that." Mom patted him on the shoulder. "Time heals all wounds."

Olivia touched her scar and shook her head. *That remains to be seen.*

⑤

Waiting for Ben in the same chair she'd used the last time she'd been in his office, Olivia fidgeted with the strap of her backpack while Mom picked at invisible lint on her wool slacks. What if Ben sent Olivia home like he'd said he would have last time? She'd never go back to *Chuck's* house. She'd just have to run away. Girls younger than Olivia had done it and survived. She wouldn't be the first and probably not the last teenage runaway.

But what reason would Ben have to refuse her entry to the program? Her attitude had completely changed. And they'd spoken several times during the past few days. He wouldn't have her come all the way out there only to make her turn right around and go home. Would he? As long as she acted respectfully and—

The office door flew open and banged on the wall behind it.

Olivia's heart leapfrogged over her stomach. She dropped her backpack and gasped in shock at the explosive intrusion.

Ben burst into the room in pressed khakis and a royal blue button-down shirt, the exact color of the brightest glints in his eyes, with a slender gray pinstripe to match the silver in his hair. The sleeves were rolled up just enough to expose the sinewy muscles in his forearms. Like father, like son. Olivia shook her head. She had to stop examining Ben like that no matter how good he looked—it was creepy.

Ben flashed a warm grin as he sank into his chair. "Ladies, I'm very pleased to see you both. This is a direct answer to the prayers of a lot of people." He rocked back in his seat and clasped his hands behind his head. "I'm sure you have tons of questions, but first, let me go over some preliminaries that might address some of the things you need to know. I'll describe the daily schedule. Then we'll talk about the rules and how to earn privileges." He raised his eyebrows and waited.

"Sounds good to me," Mom answered, returning his smile.

Get on with it already.

Ben pulled a little booklet the size of a checkbook from his desk and handed it to Olivia. "This is the schedule. You'll notice each day is broken down into hours. Preprinted in the calendar is what you'll be doing at that time. Beside each event is space where you can write notes to yourself. For example"— he reached over the desk and flipped the book open to that day's page—"next to the space for school time right here, you can list what you actually need to do that particular day—assignments, supplies you need, whatever. We print a new one of these every other month."

Olivia thumbed through the pages while he talked. "Uh, hold on a sec. According to this schedule, it looks like we have to get up at six every single day? I never get up that early. Ever." What would they do to her if she overslept?

"That's right. Everyone gets up early to start the day off with the sunrise. Except for Saturdays when you can sleep until eight o'clock."

Ooh! How generous. "Why so early though? Don't teenagers need extra sleep?" Olivia fought to keep down the sarcasm in her voice.

"Most teens sleep so late in the morning because they're up too late at night. We make sure that doesn't happen here at Diamond Estates. It all works out."

Olivia slumped back in her chair. This was not going to be easy.

"Also about mornings, you'll notice you're allotted thirty minutes to shower and dress for the day. If you need more than that—many girls seem to—"

You think?

"—then you'll need to rise earlier or find a way to shorten your morning routine." Ben riffled through his own copy of the schedule. "At six thirty, you're to be in the prayer commons. We have an hour of scripture reading and prayer every single day. That's the one thing that never, ever changes."

Olivia nodded slowly. What had she gotten herself into? Mom had offered to take Olivia back home if she had second thoughts and wanted to leave. Home meant no curfew, no chores, no alarm clock on the weekends—no *prayer* time encroaching on her sleep. But home also meant Charles. *No thanks.* Plus there were other reasons she'd come to Diamond Estates. Olivia had to keep reminding herself of those things so she wouldn't lose sight of the goal. Change. Faith. Hope. Important goals, right? Only time would tell if they were worth it.

"When prayer time's over, you go to breakfast. At eight thirty, after the meal and the cleanup, school starts. On Saturdays it would be ten thirty by then and you'd leave for an activity of some kind. Horseback riding, skiing, shopping—whatever the staff has planned. I think tomorrow is snowshoeing."

Oh joy. Tromping through snow with webbed feet and a bunch of people she didn't know sounded like *great* fun.

"Sundays after breakfast, we head down the mountain to church."

Olivia's jaw dropped. "You mean we'll go to a real church?"

"Sure. Why is that such a surprise?"

"I just assumed we would stay here most of the time. Like, you would do church here." Olivia shuddered at the thought of the whole group filing into a public church. People would know they came from Diamond Estates. They'd be like those prison cleanup crews in orange jumpsuits on the roadside. How embarrassing.

"Nope. We join the real world for church." Ben winked. "You'll love it."

The hint of laughter that always laced his words made things seem less intense, but Olivia had no plans to let her guard down. This place was hard-core whether Ben would admit it or not.

He put his calendar on the desk. "This might seem very rigid. I don't want you to worry though. We do like a lot of structure around here, but we also love to throw in some changes now and then just to keep things lively."

Mom sat up straighter. "Okay, so that's the schedule. What about the rules?"

Ben swiveled his chair and slid it across the plastic mat. He reached into his file cabinet and pulled out a few sheets of paper. "This is the part everyone hates, but it's necessary."

It couldn't possibly be worse than the schedule.

"Here's a copy of the rules." Eyes sparkling, Ben handed one to each of them and then sat back with his hands behind his head again.

He didn't have to enjoy this so much, did he?

Olivia scanned the list of ten items. *Oh boy, this ought to be good.* Moving her eyes back to the top, she read each word carefully.

1. No smoking, alcohol, or drug use of any kind.

Duh. We covered the smoking issue last time. But don't they even let people smoke in prison?

2. No lying, cheating, stealing, or fighting.

What's left?

3. Absolutely no leaving the premises without permission and an escort.

Heaven forbid.

4. No dating or fraternizing with boys at church or other activities.

That settles the question about Justin's availability.

5. Strict adherence to wardrobe guidelines is required at all times. See attached dress code.

Can't wait to see that.

6. You will be on time to all scheduled activities.

If the stars line up just right and I don't have to share a bathroom with anyone, maybe.

7. You will exercise adequate hygiene procedures—hand washing, regular showers, laundering your clothes, etc.

Gross! The fact that it has to be a rule must mean some girls don't do those things.

8. You will always speak respectfully to staff members and kindly to residents.

Or. . . ?

9. You will act appropriately and politely at all times, on and off the estate grounds.

Blah. Blah. Blah.

10. You will put forth your best effort in all things: schoolwork, spiritual growth (prayer, Bible study, etc.), chores, recreation.

So in other words, my life is over?

Olivia put the paper down on her lap and lifted her eyes, trying not to let the dismay show on her face, but not sure she succeeded. As long as she didn't cry. Anything but that.

"I think you've seen that the rules aren't anything unexpected." Ben smiled, his eyes dancing. "Do you have any questions?"

"They mentioned a dress code?" Olivia's stomach churned. She couldn't believe she'd asked for this life. How would a dress code and a ridiculous schedule help her find God?

Ben handed her another sheet of paper. "Again, nothing unexpected, I'm sure." He ticked items off on his fingers. "If you hang your arms down to your sides, the hems of your shorts and skirts can't be higher than your fingertips. You're allowed to wear one set of earrings—no other body piercings. Makeup can't be extreme, gothic, or gaudy."

Who decides what's gaudy?

"Spaghetti straps or strapless tops aren't allowed, and the straps of undergarments must always be covered. And no bare midriffs whatsoever."

"What about her hair?" Mom gestured to the purple streak.

"Are you going to make her get rid of that?"

Olivia froze, her eyes still on the paper. Now, *that* could be a deal breaker.

Ben shook his head. "No, probably not. We allow some forms of personal style as long as it's tasteful." He turned to Olivia and looked her in the eyes. "We're not trying to fit you into a mold. We just want to help you become a healthy expression of who God made you to be."

Olivia forced herself to look into Ben's eyes. What would he say when he found out what Olivia already knew? God didn't care about her.

Ben stood up. "Shall I show you to your room?"

Chapter 15

Weren't you supposed to walk *down* to a dungeon? Eerie sconces flickered dancing shadows onto the stone walls of the stairway leading up to the bedroom quarters. Ben went first, carrying Olivia's largest suitcase. Mom followed, and Olivia trailed behind, half expecting to hear the sounds of moaning or clinking chains.

Ben broke the awkward silence with his booming voice. "Typically, this staircase is off-limits to visitors and even to me for the most part. I rarely have a need to approach the girls' rooms and find it's much better if I don't. I only come up here if I'm giving a tour or signing in a new resident, and only then if the girls are cleared out."

Good. No midnight visitors.

He opened the door at the top, letting bright natural light bathe the dark stairway. "These doors aren't locked until every girl is out for the day, and then they're unlocked when it's okay for them to be up here."

Olivia nodded and stepped through the door he held open, following Mom into a gleaming hallway. The skylights overhead let in the sunlight beaming on the white walls. Not a single stone anywhere. No candles either. Finally, some sense of modern. Three white doors lined each side of the hallway with a seventh door at the end. Olivia ran her hand along the smooth wall as they walked toward the first door.

Ben passed it and opened the second one then stepped back for them to look inside. "Each room is exactly the same. There are two sets of bunk beds. The two dressers and desks are shared by the same two girls who share the bed. The closet is divided into four parts. Each room has a bathroom with a double sink and a shower."

No jetted tub? Two of these rooms shared by four girls would fit into her private bedroom in Charles's house—with some room left over, probably. Could have been worse though. Olivia had expected a dormitory-style area with rows of metal cots like in war movies. At least she'd only have to battle three others for bathroom space—better than twenty or more.

Ben motioned for them to step into the room. "This one has an opening. I think you already met your roommates, as a matter of fact."

Olivia heaved her backpack up to one shoulder and stepped inside. The remains of someone's flowery perfume lingered. Better that than the smell of sweat socks or someone in need of rule number seven. On the right side of the room, one bed had a floral comforter with little hearts on vertical vines and a fuzzy pink heart pillow. Olivia couldn't help but roll her eyes at the wall space around that top bunk, which had been hosed with pictures of puppies, dolphins, and ocean scenery. The girlie girl who slept there must have long hair because every imaginable color of claw hair clips gripped the length of the white bedrail.

The lower bunk had an orange blanket with purple and brown throw pillows. Pictures covered the wall inside the bunk area. Olivia peered a bit closer at the group photo of what appeared to be a large family of mostly African Americans. They looked like nice and happy people—smiling like someone had just told a joke. Olivia realized for the first time that she'd never really known a black person before—there weren't many at her school.

Right in the center of about eight kids of all different ages sat Tricia, the gorgeous girl she'd met the last time she'd been there. Tricia flashed pearly white teeth, showing off supermodel good looks. What could she have done to have landed herself at Diamond Estates? With such a big, happy—seemingly loving—family, what did she have to worry about? Ju-Ju had said that Tricia liked boys too much. How much too much?

So if the bottom bunk belonged to Tricia, the cutesy stuff above must be Skye's. Which meant. . .*Oh no.* Olivia pivoted in slow motion toward the other side of the room, afraid to look at the bed. The top bunk sat untouched. Her eyes roved to the bottom, and dread sank like an anchor in her stomach.

"You can just set your things down here." Ben pointed to the space in front of the bed. "Your bunk mate, Julia—Ju-Ju—can show you what to do with it later."

Olivia's mouth hung open as she stared at Ben. Surely he was joking. He couldn't possibly mean that of every possible roommate in the whole place, Olivia had to share a bunk bed with a girl who already hated her. What had begun to look like a bleak existence of rules and dress codes was rapidly graduating to impossible. Were things going to work out after all? Could she live under those conditions?

Yes. She could. No matter what Ju-Ju or any of the other girls threw at her, she could handle it. After all, she'd endured living with Charles for years.

"You're awfully quiet, Olivia." Ben leaned back against the wall. "Tell me what you're thinking."

"I'd like to know, too." Mom stared at Olivia's face.

Feeling her eyes stinging and her chin about to quiver—quiver? She wasn't four years old. Olivia tried to keep her composure. It wouldn't help at all if Mom saw her cry. And what if the girls came up here? No tears. "I. . .I just don't know.

It's so different than what I'm used to." Olivia bit her lip. "There are so many rules and so many girls. What if they all hate me?" *One already does.*

Ben nodded. "Some might."

Mom gasped and stared at Ben with her mouth hanging open.

"Listen. This is the real world. When you put twenty to thirty girls under one roof, there are going to be personality clashes. That's just the way it is. We'll help you cope with those things."

This is insane.

"However, you'll forge some friendships here, maybe even some unlikely ones, that will stick with you for the rest of your life." Ben paced the room. "Time and time again I get letters and calls from girls who share with me that in some ways their time here was the hardest time of their lives."

Oh? How comforting. Olivia rubbed at a snag in the berber carpet with the toe of her shoe.

"But they also say it was the absolute best time of their lives in the most important ways." Ben placed his hands on her shoulders and stared into her face. "You see, it's the contrast of God's hand reaching out to you and finding you against the backdrop of life's pain and struggles that makes the experience so rich. Since you and the other girls are being honed in similar fashion, you come out of the refinement process united in a special way."

He dropped his hands and shrugged. "The choice is yours. You might as well give it a chance. What have you got to lose?"

He's right. The alternative held no greater promise. If she left Diamond Estates before at least giving it a try, her life would be in shambles. At least here she had some hope. Olivia nodded. "I'll stay." *For now anyway.*

"Okay. This is it, then. Time to say good-bye to Mom." Ben gave a brisk nod. "It's best to make a clean break—like pulling off a Band-Aid—rather than a long, drawn-out farewell."

Mom paled, and her eyes filled with tears.

Ben strode to the door. "I'll step outside for a moment, and then I'll walk you out, Mrs. Whitford." He pulled the door almost closed behind him.

"Are you sure, Livvie?" Mom grasped Olivia's hands and searched deep into her eyes. "This is what you want?"

Not what she *wanted*, but what she needed. "I'll be okay." Hopefully Olivia sounded more confident than she felt.

"All right. I'll be in Denver for three days—my flight is on Monday morning. If you need me, you call me and I'll come get you."

Olivia nodded and held her gaze. *What else, Mom? Tell me you're sorry. Tell me you'll fix it all and make life right for us. Please.*

Gulping back a sob, Mom rushed through the doorway without looking back.

Olivia stood in the center of her new room and waited for tears, but none came. The time for crying had passed. It was time to square her shoulders and face the unknown like a big girl. Should she unpack? But that would mean looking for empty drawers, and the last thing she wanted was for someone to come in and think she was snooping around in her things. She could at least make up her bed.

Thankful Mom had insisted she pack her favorite blankets and pillows, Olivia opened the duffel bag that held the vacuum-sealed packages. She unzipped the one that held the squished comforter. It let out a big *swoosh* as it took in air and puffed up to full size while she tried to tuck her luxury king-sized sheets around her twin-sized mattress. The extra material bunched in clumps under the mattress and made it too lumpy, so she pulled the sheet off and folded it in half. That was better. Sheet in place, Olivia flapped her comforter in the air and watched it sail into place over the bed.

The door opened and Ju-Ju stepped inside with her arms folded across her chest. "Well, well. Looky here." She snapped her gum.

Skye followed her inside. "We told ya you'd be back ree-ul soon."

Why hadn't Olivia noticed Skye's Southern drawl before? Must have been too nervous. So she'd be living with a Southern belle, a beauty queen, and a bulldog? Fun times.

"Hi, Skye. Hi, Tricia." Olivia nodded at the shy but beautiful black girl hiding behind Skye.

"What? No hello to me? I'm the welcome wagon." Ju-Ju popped her gum again.

"I wouldn't say hi to you either, if I were her. You're not being friendly at all." Skye put her arm around Olivia's shoulders. "Don't mind Ju-Ju. She acts tough, but she's really an old softy once you get to know her."

Ju-Ju snorted. "You'd be hard as nails, too, if you'd raised yourself living on the streets of New York. Kinda hafta be."

Tricia narrowed her eyes behind the longest eyelashes Olivia had ever seen. "These aren't the streets though. You can cut the act and get real for once."

"Anyway. . ." Skye glared at them. "We have a new roommate, and Ben asked us to show her the ropes. So let's quit the bickering." She surveyed Olivia's stuff.

"These are yours." Tricia pulled open the top three drawers of the dresser and then shot Ju-Ju a look. "If *someone* would get her junk out of them."

"They weren't being used. So what?" Ju-Ju scooped up some

paperback books, a few framed photographs, a pair of fingerless leather gloves, and some other items Olivia didn't recognize and shoved them under her bed, then turned and pointed her finger in Olivia's face. "Listen. You need to get one thing straight." The tiny little spitfire put her hands on her hips and bobbed her dark curls from side to side as she talked. "Don't you even think about touching my stuff. Got it?"

Or what? "Yeah. I get it. I'm not going to touch your stuff or anyone else's. But not because *you* said so." Olivia pointed her finger at Ju-Ju. "Now *you* get one thing straight. Don't ever point that finger at me again. I'll treat you with respect if you do the same. Simple as that."

"So it *is* true—you got that nasty scar in a knife brawl like the other girls said." Ju-Ju closed her mouth, spun around, and huffed out of the room. No one said anything until the sound of her stomps had faded into the distance.

Olivia exhaled. *That went well.* "What's her problem?"

"Oh, go easy on Ju-Ju. She's really had it rough." Skye's smile wavered at the corners.

Tricia nodded and sat on her bed. "Yep. She might be tough to get along with at first, but once you break through, she's the most loyal friend you could want."

"Why should I go easy on her? She's plain rude. That thing about the knife brawl. . .uncalled for." Olivia shook her head. "How old is she anyway?" Olivia dropped to her knees beside her suitcase and began to unzip it.

Skye bent to help Olivia get the bag open. "She's about to turn sixteen, but she's been on her own since she was twelve. Her mom and brother got killed in a drive-by shooting by a rival Mexican gang." Skye's eyes teared up. "She'll tell you stories about how she survived the past three and a half years. You'll understand more about her then."

"Well, I don't see her opening up to me about her deep, dark secrets anytime soon. But I'll give her a chance. I just hope she lightens up—soon."

"What's in this little case?" Skye held up the black plastic box and turned it over in her hands.

"Oh, that's my oboe." Olivia wondered if she'd ever get to practice. Ju-Ju would probably hate the sound as much as Charles did. Good-bye scholarship if that turned out to be the case.

"Oboe? Cool!" Tricia pulled out a longer black instrument case from under her bed. "I play the flute. Hey, maybe we can practice together sometime."

Had there ever been an oboe-flute duo before? Was the world ready for something like that? Was Olivia?

✨

"New girl. What's your name?" A large aproned woman in a white chef's hat held a bag of potatoes in her chapped hands.

"I'm Olivia." She stepped forward hesitantly into the sea of teenage sous-chefs, most of whom she hadn't even met yet.

"Okay, Olivia. I'm Marilyn, the cook. You'll be on potatoes tonight." She set the bag down next to three others just like it. "They need to be washed well. Poke a few holes in them with this." She held up a meat fork. "Then place them on the rack in the oven. Turn them after twenty minutes. Can you handle that?" She winked—the first sign of personality from her ruddy face.

"Sounds easy enough." Olivia shrugged and pulled a potato from the bag. At least she didn't have to peel them.

"So, my girls are on cooking detail tonight?" A thin woman in an amethyst velour warm-up suit walked into the kitchen signing her words as she spoke. She approached Olivia with her hand outstretched. "I'm Tammy." She shook Olivia's hand then laid one hand flat and brushed the other one across the top of it. Then she put two fingers upright and parallel to each other. "It's nice to meet you."

Olivia had turned to put some potatoes in the oven but set them down instead and adjusted her stance to make sure Tammy could see her lips. "Nice to meet you, too." She spoke clearly and enunciated every word while she brushed the palms of her hands together and pointed at Tammy.

Tammy's eyes opened wide. She probably wasn't used to people, especially teenage girls, using sign language when they met her. "I'm your counselor. I take care of the girls in your room and the room right across the hall from you. You and I will get together once a week for a counseling session, and I'm here if you have any problems or concerns anytime at all. I'm really glad you're here, Olivia." She touched Olivia's hand and smiled then took a cart loaded with dishes and pushed it out to the dining room, where another group of girls bustled around setting up for dinner.

"Tammy's awesome. You'll love her," Skye whispered as she stepped behind Olivia at the worktable.

Tricia nodded. "She's my favorite of all the counselors."

"Where are the other two?"

"Patty's out in the dining room." She steered Olivia to the little porthole window on the swinging door. "She's the supershort one with the curly red hair. Her group is on setup and teardown this week. Donna's girls have laundry duty." Tricia grimaced.

"What? You don't like Donna or laundry?"

"Both, I guess. Donna is stunning—like *America's Next Top Model* gorgeous—so people think she's going to be cool. But she's so moody."

"Yep. I used to be in Donna's group when I first got here."

Skye nodded. "She can be tough to read. Sometimes she's great, but you never know when she's going to get crabby. But she has a good heart deep down. You just have to work hard to see it."

Tricia lifted a giant colander of green beans into the sink to be rinsed. "She's a perfect example of how beauty can be more of a curse than a blessing. Sometimes it's better to be unattractive than to be beautiful and have to fight hard to stay that way."

Olivia chuckled. "Well, if anyone would know about that, it would be you. But I wouldn't mind the chance to find out for myself."

"You say that. But you have no idea. . ." Tricia shook her head. "Besides, you *are* beautiful."

"Not like you."

"Trust me. It's caused me more problems than anything in my life. Still does to this day. Gaining weight like I have recently is the kiss of death for someone like me. I mean, everything good about myself is wrapped up in how I look. . .and now. . ." Her eyes welled up with tears.

"Oh, for Pete's sake. Tricia, get a grip. You've gained what? Five pounds?" Ju-Ju looked her up and down.

"Eight!"

"I love ya, but you're just fishing for compliments now. Talk it out with Tammy, and let's pick a different subject. One not quite so pink and girlie."

Tricia's eyes clouded over just before the smile lit up her face. She gave a swift nod. "You're right."

Notes to self: no girl talk with Ju-Ju, and steer clear of Donna.

Chapter 16

The girls filed out into the hallway and blended in with the other semi-sleepwalkers coming out of their rooms. They shuffled silently to the prayer commons. Olivia fought the urge to ask how many of them were happy about this little facet of their morning routine.

Should be interesting. The prayer commons was the one room she hadn't seen on the tour. They walked all the way past the dining hall, through the foyer, and toward a huge arched doorway beside the front door.

Olivia's jaw dropped as she stepped into the majestic prayer room. The stained-glass windows visible from the front yard lined the cathedral-type space. There, on the far side, was the nativity scene window Justin said he liked best. She gazed up to the carved ceilings that were pitched like those of an old church. A small stage with the pipes of a huge organ lining the wall behind it faced the back of the room. What could that be for?

The cobblestone floors felt bumpy and uneven under her feet. Olivia imagined a dozen monks on their knees, laying those stones in vowed silence. Area rugs had been scattered around the room to create clustered groupings with chairs, couches, love seats, and oversized beanbags in odd formations.

Olivia hung back as girls repositioned their seats in groups or found a private place to sit by themselves, presumably to pray. But Olivia bet sleep reigned at the top of their agenda, far higher than prayer. At least it did hers. She followed her roommates' lead and dragged a beanbag chair to the corner by the window depicting Jesus praying in a garden. Olivia scrunched down into her chair and waited. Did they pray out loud? She had no intention of doing that—ever.

Ben stepped to the center of the room and cleared his throat. He lifted his hands, raised his face to the early morning sunshine streaming through the dewy window portraying Christ's resurrection. And he began to pray. "Father, I thank You for another beautiful day. I open our quiet time with a simple request that You meet us here."

Oh? Maybe Olivia would feel God's presence right here in the chapel.

Ben finished praying and then released them to their own private time with God—whatever that meant.

Olivia closed her eyes and then peeked around the room through tiny slits at the other girls. One or two actually did seem to be sleeping, but some of the others, like Tricia and Ju-Ju, had their eyes closed as they moved their lips. Skye and a few other girls were writing in journals. Several read their Bibles, and a couple of clusters seemed to actually be praying together. Were they kidding her with this stuff? There was no way she could make it through this every single day and not embarrass herself by snoring. She'd have to find out if there was some stiff penalty for sleeping during prayer time.

Okay. Focus. At least she could try it out and see what the fuss was all about.

What did she feel? Nothing, really. If she closed her eyes, she didn't even sense the presence of the other girls, let alone some unseen and likely unreal deity who hadn't ever been there for her before. What did she expect? Lightning bolts to course through her body? An earthquake? It would take something big like that to make religion real to her.

🌀

"What's the point of snowshoeing, anyway?" Olivia smoothed the lumps and tugged the blanket to cover the corner of the sheet that hung down the side of the bed. *Good enough.* She straightened her pillows to help cover the mess. Where was Norma when she needed her?

Breakfast sat like a lump in her stomach. She wasn't used to eating rich food this early, especially not french toast and sausage. At home, the most she ever ate in the mornings was a granola bar and a can of Diet Pepsi.

Skye flipped her legs forward and vaulted off the covers she had just smoothed. "Oh, it's great. You'll love it."

"Yeah. I'm usually not one for outdoor activity"—Tricia smoothed her hair—"and even I don't have a problem with snowshoeing. I wouldn't go as far as to say I love it. But I don't mind it."

"I think I'd rather sit by the fire in the library and read a book." Any chance of that happening?

"Tsk-tsk." Ju-Ju shook her head. "All I ever hear out of you are complaints. Sounds like you just want to buck the system. You're not going to get very far in this place like that, girlie."

Tricia groaned. "Ju-Ju, would you just lay off of her? You hate being out in the snow, too."

"Whatever." Ju-Ju rolled her eyes. "At least I know when to keep my mouth shut and go with the flow. Unlike our little princess here who thinks the world revolves around her." The bathroom door slammed as she went inside.

"Look, I know you guys like her, but I'm really having trouble finding her appeal. And it's just getting worse between us. What can I do to fix things with her?"

Skye looked at Tricia, and they both shrugged. "Oh, just

give it time." Tricia waved her hand in a brush-off.

"Now, don't you worry your purty little head about it at all. It'll be just fine."

Hard not to smile at Skye's sweet Southern drawl. A sharp rap on the door made Olivia jump.

Skye rushed to the door and pulled it open. "Mornin', Tammy."

Tammy grinned and stepped into the room wearing a bubblegum-pink snowsuit and a headband to pull down over her ears. "Morning! You girls about ready for a beautiful day on the mountain?"

Olivia groaned. "Hiking through the snow really isn't my thing, but I guess I'm along for the ride whether I like it or not."

Tammy nodded and turned to Olivia. "I know this is all new to you, but we're about wholeness healing here at Diamond Estates. Your mind, body, and heart are all connected. Recreation takes care of the body part. School is for the mind, and church, prayer, and other spiritual things are for the heart."

"I get that recreation is important, but is there any reason we can't choose our own form of recreation?" Olivia made a mental list of the many things she'd prefer to be doing on this cold, snowy Saturday. Reading. Practicing her oboe. Sleeping. Coloring her hair. Painting her nails. Snowshoeing ranked at or very near the bottom—only higher than napping on a bed of nails. On second thought, at least that involved a nap.

Tammy looked into her eyes. "Let me ask you something. Are you used to getting your own way? Have you had to share much in your life?"

Not much more than beer money. "I pretty much always get my way." Something niggled at Olivia, telling her that was all about to change.

"Well, one of the things you'll learn while you're here at

Diamond is that life doesn't always work like that. We have varied activities so everyone gets to do what she enjoys. But we all participate together as a family. Might as well get used to the idea." Tammy turned and fixed Olivia's bed-making attempt.

Uh-oh. Olivia took Tammy's subtle hint that halfhearted efforts weren't going to fly.

"Ready to go?" Tammy smiled.

Skye, Tricia, and Ju-Ju, dressed for the cold weather, held their gloves and goggles. Olivia scrambled to catch up—thankful Mom had made her pack winter gear. She'd better start acting more agreeable—no reason to get off on the wrong foot with everyone. They probably already thought she was a spoiled brat. She was stuck there, for better or worse, and complaints were only going to cause her more trouble.

They tromped outside to meet up with the other twenty girls and two counselors by the shed, where they'd fit themselves for snowshoes. She'd get to meet the infamous Donna, who hadn't come to dinner the night before because of a headache. She seemed to have recovered just fine though. Her beautiful blond waves peeked out from the purple hat atop her head. Olivia could see her sea-green eyes from several yards away. Donna probably wasn't tall enough to be a supermodel, but she sure had the body and exquisite looks for it. What would someone who looked like *that* have to be moody about? Tricia had said it wasn't always easy to be beautiful—that was hard to believe.

"You must be Olivia." Donna grabbed her hand and pumped it twice. "I'm Donna. It's really great to meet you."

"It's nice to meet you, t–" Olivia spoke to Donna's back as the counselor strode away. *Okaaay.*

"C'mere, Liv." Skye beckoned from the end of a bench. "Pick from this here pile." She gestured to a pile of woven snowshoes with leather straps. "These are the best ones."

They all looked exactly the same to Olivia, so she grabbed a pair and carried them outside, away from everyone. She gazed up the mountain into the stillness of the wild. Rustling in those trees could be bears, deer, antelope, wild boar—okay, maybe not wild boar, but how should she know? She wondered what it would be like to face a bear. Mom once said that elderly Indians, when they knew their life was coming to an end, would tie themselves to a tree to let the bears eat them rather than become a burden to their families and suffer through a painful death or debilitating illness. How much of a burden was Olivia?

"Olivia!"

"Ah!" She squealed as a male voice boomed her name from the trees behind her. She put her hand on her thumping heart and patted her chest. "You scared me!"

Justin laughed. "I'm sorry. I wasn't trying to sneak up on you. It never occurred to me you might not have heard me coming down the path."

"It's okay." Olivia smiled and fanned herself. "I'll live. I think." She peered down the snow-covered gravel driveway. "Where did you come from? I don't see a car."

"Oh, we live just over there." Justin pointed beyond the stables at a white two-story farmhouse—the type postcards always depict with smoke rising from the chimney and an apple pie steaming on the windowsill.

"That's nice you live so close. Makes things easier, I'll bet."

"Some things, yes; some things, not so much. But it all works out in the end." Justin smiled and leaned on a tree, his chestnut waves skimming his shoulders.

"Justin, come on over." Ben waved from the doorway to the shed, looking like something out of a Winter Olympics ad from 1985 in a royal blue belted one-piece snowsuit that had obviously been quite pricey in its day.

"Oops. Didn't see Dad arrive. Gotta go." He jogged over to his dad and nodded along while Ben seemed to be instructing him.

Justin grinned and waved at Olivia as he ran back into the trees.

"Girls! We ready?" Ben surveyed his array of snow bunnies. He slipped his hands into his waterproof gloves—the male version of her own—and nodded toward the woods. "We'd better get started. Alicia's doing all sorts of cooking for when we get back—she has a special afternoon planned." Ben pulled on his gloves and began the trudge up the hill into the forest.

"Tammy?" Olivia turned to her right and tried to smile so she wouldn't be blamed for complaining. "How far do you think we'll go?" She signed some of her words but also let Tammy read her lips.

"I'm not sure on the mileage—that would depend on the route he takes." Tammy signed as she spoke. "We'll be out here for at least three hours." With her right thumb and first two fingers, she made three circles around the face of her raised left hand representing a clock.

Three hours? She hadn't spent that much time doing any kind of physical exertion outdoors since she was a little girl on a bicycle. Maybe not even then. Olivia knew she had two choices. She could hate every minute of it or try to enjoy herself. Nothing would change the fact that she was stuck out there for the day, so she might as well try to get something out of it. But what?

"Do you hear what I hear?" Tammy pointed to her ear as she spoke in the same kind of halting, rounded words Jake used. He had trouble with his *r*'s, too.

Olivia tried to listen but shook her head. "All I hear are pine needles crunching and people breathing hard." What could a deaf person possibly hear that Olivia couldn't?

Tammy smiled. "Listen." She cupped her right hand around her ear.

Olivia continued her clomp up the trail, grabbing on to tree limbs for support. She tried to concentrate on whatever Tammy thought she heard, but the squeak of the snowshoes pressing into the snow was the only sound that filled Olivia's ears. "Nothing." She shook her head.

"He calls out to me when I'm in His house." Tammy stopped climbing. She lifted her face, closed her eyes, and breathed deeply.

No one told me she was a nutso. "Whose house? Who calls out to you?"

Tammy gestured at the forest all around her. "This is all God's house. Isn't it perfect? He made it just for you to enjoy with Him."

Aha. It was God talk. But if Tammy felt Him here, why didn't Olivia sense Him at all? Was Tammy crazy to say she felt God, or did God simply not care about Olivia? In her reality, those were the only two options. He wasn't there at all, or He just wasn't there for Olivia. Simple. Time was running out on her ultimatum with God. Olivia needed to know what to believe, but He didn't seem to be planning to answer her prayer anytime soon, if at all.

That was enough. Olivia needed to get away from Tammy and the God talk, so she reached for a branch and prepared to take a fork in the trail and climb on her own for a few minutes. She stepped up on a ledge and pulled on the branch closest to her face.

WHAM!

The lights went out as what felt like a dump truck full of snow piled on her head and slid down her face into her parka and beneath her shirt. Olivia sputtered and shook as she tried to free herself from the snow attack. "Who. . . ? What happened? How. . . ?" The ice-cold snow burned the warm skin inside her jacket. She frantically dug beneath her shirt, pulling out melting clumps of snow and shaking them off her freezing hand onto the ground, spraying anyone who stood near. She gave up after a minute and looked up. Twenty-three girls, three counselors, one director, and one very guilty-looking son of a director stared at her, openmouthed.

"Are you okay, Liv?" Skye lifted her sunglasses.

Ju-Ju raised her eyebrows and smirked.

Tricia dug in her backpack and pulled out a sweatshirt, which she handed to Olivia. "This is probably too big for you, but you can use this to dry off or put it on. We can shield you while you change."

"Too big? More likely it's way too small. But thanks." Olivia dried her stinging cheeks with the sleeve.

Justin stepped forward. "I'm really sorry. I don't know what to say."

"Why would you be sorry?" Olivia dried her chest and neck with the other sleeve of Tricia's sweatshirt. No way was she going to change shirts out there in the great outdoors. . .oh right, God's house.

"Um. It wasn't technically an accident." His neck and the tips of his ears turned red. They seemed to do that a lot.

"Justin? What are you saying?" Ben's voice grew stern.

Justin mouthed *I'm sorry* to Olivia before stomping over to his dad, hurrying as fast as his snowshoes would allow. "I was only having some fun. I thought it would land on you, Dad. I didn't realize it was so much snow. It was a stupid prank. I'm sorry."

"Oh, son. I'm not mad. I always love a good practical joke. You just need to be careful." Ben gestured toward Olivia. "There's always the potential of an unintended victim. Come on over here with me while the girls help Olivia get straightened up." He put his arm around Justin and led him to a clearing where, judging by Justin's face, Ben started right in with a lecture.

A long, slender hand with delicate fingers waved in front of her face. "Earth to Olivia." Tricia brushed off Olivia's concern with a wave of her hand. "Don't mind Justin. I doubt he'll be in any trouble. It's just that he's not really allowed to make friends with us. He's supposed to stay all business."

"Oh? I wonder why." Olivia knitted her brows as she watched Justin lope off in the other direction.

"Well, you really can't blame his parents. There are lots of girls coming in and out of here every year—messed-up girls at that. It would be easy for him to get off track if his parents weren't careful."

"He kind of insinuated that he recently had to get over a rough situation with a girl." Olivia shielded her eyes from the sun and watched him disappear in the trees. "What's the deal with that?"

Tricia jerked her head back and squinted. "He told you? Hmm. I'm surprised he mentioned it."

"Why?" Olivia stepped closer to Tricia. She *had* to know.

"He's usually more private than that, and I'm sure his dad hoped the story would fade away."

"What story? And where did he meet her?" Surely Tricia would know that much. Olivia figured she had to be from Justin's school based on what he'd said earlier.

"Oh, she was a Diamond girl." Tricia chuckled. "You can imagine how upset his dad was when he found out. Actually, I was surprised Ben let it continue at all. Then it ended badly, and now we're not allowed to have boyfriends at all."

"Is it someone who's still here?" Couldn't be. Olivia surely would have heard about it by now.

"I'm not saying anything else." Tricia shook her head. "I don't know many of the *intimate* details, and honestly, you'd be better off leaving that alone."

Leaving what alone? The story or the boy?

Too late for both.

Chapter 17

Olivia slumped down in her seat as the two-van caravan pulled into the church parking lot. If she slunk all the way to the floor and hid under the seats, maybe no one would notice and she could wait out the service in the van. Thankfully, they weren't forced to wear orange jumpsuits, but the dress was bad enough. Who wore dresses to church at her age?

She peeked out the window, careful not to raise her head high enough for anyone to see her. The place was the size of a mall. *Oh wait.* The sign boasted a bookstore and a coffee shop inside the building. It *was* a mall. Cars filed in through four entrances, and people streamed from their vehicles.

Some suited men, standing tall and proud, escorted ladies in full Sunday dress—gloves, hats, high heels—with Bibles hanging from their wrists in handmade quilted covers. Young children were dressed in adorable outfits—cute, although too matchy-matchy for Olivia's taste. Rebellious teens hung back, the agony in their eyes revealing they'd rather be anywhere else. Olivia saw one girl hitch up her skirt a fraction of an inch. Her mom saw it, too, and yanked it back down.

Olivia gave a mental high five to a long-haired dude who had the nerve to wear a T-shirt with a beer advertisement on it. Judging by the grins, handshakes, and slaps on his back, he seemed well liked by everyone. Didn't they see his shirt? Were they going to let him into the church in that?

Ah, there they were, the happy families. Moms and dads held hands or swung toddlers between them. They were the types of families that would stop for lunch on the way home from church, change into play clothes the minute they got home, and then spend the afternoon doing yard work together. It wasn't that she begrudged them their happiness. It was just. . .well, why couldn't she have had a family like one of those? She almost did. . . .

Were people watching as the Diamond Estates vans pulled into the spaces in the back? She didn't want to make eye contact with anyone to see for herself. The thought of the disapproval that would surely fill their gaze didn't appeal to her one bit.

The girls poured from the vans and headed across the parking lot toward the church in a double-file line. Dread filled the pit of her stomach as Olivia walked beside Ju-Ju and in front of Skye. Tricia trailed right behind. The two rows offered Olivia another reminder of criminals. She imagined them like a prison gang in an old movie, shuffling along, dragging the chains that bound them to each other at the ankles.

"I've been working on a chain gang. . ." Olivia sang a few bars of an old spiritual before she could help herself.

Ju-Ju choked.

Skye giggled and covered her mouth.

Several other girls glared back at them, their eyes shifting from one to the other—probably trying to figure out who sang the words.

Tammy pretended not to hear her. Oh—she probably *hadn't* heard her.

The Diamond girls entered the auditorium. Many of them waved and greeted people as they made their way down the aisle. Some even stopped for a quick hug along the way. The people seemed nice enough—but there was no way everyone

THE WISHING PEARL

would be like these first few she'd seen. Clearly the gossipers and finger pointers just hadn't arrived yet. They'd show up soon—they always did.

Ben walked swiftly as he led them to the right and up toward the front. He held his head high. Why wasn't he embarrassed by his ragamuffin brood of troublemakers?

Four rows of chairs stood empty with RESERVED signs on the sides. *Ha.* They made the Diamond girls sit up close—probably thought they'd get more out of the service that way. Plus people could keep a better eye on them. So much for sitting in back, hidden from prying eyes.

The girls settled into seats. Olivia sat between Tricia and Skye. Ju-Ju took the end seat and crossed her ankles in the aisle, her body pivoted away from the girls. Olivia cast her gaze down at the floor. Disapproval would be bad enough, but what if she saw pity in people's eyes—or worse, fear? What if they clutched their purses or held their child's hand a little tighter in case she were a knife-wielding thug? She'd die of embarrassment. Olivia had never been the object of a stranger's scorn before—that she knew of—and she didn't like how it felt one bit.

What might they think brought her to Diamond Estates? Probably assumed it was drugs or something worse.

A life-controlling problem. Ben had explained that girls who came to Diamond Estates didn't have to be addicts or criminals. They simply had to have a life-controlling problem that, according to Ben, in Olivia's case, meant she didn't have Jesus. Her own selfish desires, he said, were directing her life. She needed to surrender that control to *the Lord*.

The Lord. It sounded strange. Like an otherworldly paranormal being. At least Jesus sounded more relatable—more real. But surrender to Jesus? She had no idea what that even meant. And how could she surrender to someone she couldn't even find? Maybe He was right there in that two-story church auditorium with its basketball nets anchored to the ceiling. Did the bright, shiny tape on the padded floor outlining the boundaries of a court have anything to do with Jesus? How about the stage with the glass-enclosed drum set? Would that be what helped her find God? Why did it seem so impossible for her when everyone else seemed to understand Him and make Him a real part of their lives so easily?

Olivia stared at the pocket on the seat back of the maroon chair in front of her. Visitor cards. She fought the urge to laugh. They probably didn't want to know who she was. Just a Diamond girl—a temporary seat warmer who would disappear once she'd done her time. Maybe that did make her a visitor. After all, she sure wouldn't be there forever.

She pulled out a card and read the information it asked for. Name. Address. Family members. Phone number. And then there were several boxes to check about how long she'd known God. No box said *Complete stranger*. Funny, the only question she knew the answer to was her name. She put the card back in the slot and glanced to her right before she could help herself.

Someone leaning against the back wall looked familiar. Olivia squinted.

Mom?

What was she doing here? Olivia stared in horror as her mother, fully dressed in head-to-toe couture, tried to go unnoticed. Her flashy clothes sure weren't acting as camouflage. Wasn't it poor form to mix designers? Mom never cared. The more glitz and glamour she could pour onto her body, the better—in *her* opinion. But why was she there? Olivia could get in trouble for the contact. She wasn't supposed to see any family again until she moved to the next level of the program. Leave it to Mom to think the rules had nothing to do with her. Didn't she care about how her actions affected Olivia? At least she didn't seem to be trying to get to her. Yet.

The stage came to life as the musicians took their places and the vocalists stepped up to the microphones. Olivia whipped her head around at the sound of an electric guitar. *In church?* Without prompting, the people stood and clapped to the beat. Tricia joined right in and seemed to be enjoying herself, even swaying to the music. A peek to the left revealed a slightly more reserved, but participating, Skye. Beyond Skye stood Ju-Ju, grinning and clapping offbeat, but she sure didn't seem to care. It was the most life Olivia had seen in Ju-Ju yet.

But what about Mom? Olivia tried to find her out of the corner of her eye and almost didn't see her slip into a back seat. Thankfully, Ben hadn't seen her yet. Olivia had no idea what to do. She peeked at the people in the seats around her. Could she sneak out of her row, go up the side aisle, and hide in a bathroom? Maybe Mom would be gone before she came out. But the people around her were engrossed in the music. Many closed their eyes as they sang and clapped. Some had a hand raised and others had both in the air, waving. Others stood stoically, mouthing the words but clearly not in their comfort zone—much like Olivia. She'd never be able to sneak past them all without causing a big ruckus.

Maybe if she told Tammy she was sick, they'd just take her home and she could avoid Mom completely. But Tammy stood four rows in front of her, in the midst of a group of people Olivia had never seen before. They appeared to all be hearing impaired because an elegantly dressed gray-haired woman stood on the edge of the stage right in front of the group and signed for them. Olivia would cause a big scene just trying to get a message to her.

After four or five songs—Olivia lost count—several prayers,

and the passing of the offering plate, the preacher invited them to sit for the sermon. Sinking into her seat, she at least felt safe from her mom's prying eyes for the moment. Olivia pressed her toe against the bottom edge of the hardcover Bible in the seat back in front of her. She pushed it up an inch with her black leather boot and then let if fall back down with a *thud*.

Her boot had gotten scuffed somehow. *Hmm. Wonder if Mom will keep the Chanel thigh-highs or give them away.* Not like Mom could get them over her own thighs. Olivia slid a little lower in her seat and squeezed her eyes shut.

"Livvie, sit still," Mom hissed through her teeth as the preacher finished his prayer.

Daddy pulled her onto his lap and scooted closer to Mom. "Now, if you don't settle down, Livvie Love, you'll have to go to your kindergarten class."

"Okay, Daddy. I'll be good." Olivia felt her curls bounce against her cheeks when she nodded her head. It tickled, so she did it again. Mommy always made her sleep in curlers on Saturday night so her hair would look pretty for church. "I don't want to go to that class. Those kids are dumb." Daddy squeezed her arm and pulled her back against his chest as the elderly couple behind them stifled a giggle.

The people in front of them had funny hair. Olivia just wanted to play with the man's ponytail. Maybe she could ride him like a horsey. The lady had short spiked hair, like a porcupine. Weird animal people.

". . .nearing the close of my sermon. I once heard that a sermon should have a good beginning and a good ending. In the best sermons, they're as close together as possible." The preacher laughed along with the congregation at his joke.

"Daddy, that wasn't funny at all." Olivia sent the elderly couple behind her into another fit of giggles, and the man with the

ponytail turned around to wink at her. Olivia gasped when she saw that his black-and-gray beard was as long and scraggly as his hair.

The preacher stopped laughing, and the smile left his face as he cleared his throat. "In all seriousness, folks, this is it. This is what it all comes back to. Where are you with Jesus? Do you know Him as your personal Savior? I'm not going to preach another sermon, so I'm just going to ask you. Do you want to know Jesus? If you want a personal relationship with Him, raise your hand." He looked across the congregation and nodded as several people put up their hands.

Olivia slipped her tiny hand into the air and smiled at the preacher. "It's okay, Daddy, right? I can know Jesus if I want to, can't I?"

"Yes, Livvie Love, you can know Jesus. In fact, I'm sure He's smiling at you right now because He wants to know you, too."

So what happened? If He'd been smiling at her *that* day, if He'd met her as she made her way to the front of the church and stood beside the preacher to ask Jesus into her heart, where had He gone? Olivia strained to hear the bars of the old Sunday school songs.

"Jesus loves me, this I know. . ."

She dug in her memory to find some hidden snippets of Bible verses she'd memorized.

"For God so loved the world. . ."

What happened? If—and that was a big *if*—she knew Him *then*, why didn't she know Him *now*?

He took Daddy.

There it was. Fact. Unemotional reality. There was no denying the truth she'd found in her soul. She blamed God. In a way, the realization freed her. On the other hand, even if Olivia reached out to God now—or soon—maybe He'd be so mad at her that He wouldn't respond to her plea. Surely it wasn't okay to blame God for things, right? Didn't people get in big trouble for that in the Bible?

". . .stand and join me in a closing prayer." The preacher lifted his hands as he prayed.

Oops. Olivia had missed the whole sermon. She hoped there wouldn't be a quiz on the ride back to the center. She stood to her feet and peeked at the people around her. Everyone's eyes were closed. Tricia moved her lips in prayer. Skye had a serene and peaceful look on her face. Ju-Ju turned and met Olivia's gaze for a moment. She gave one nod. That was all it took. It was a nod of assurance and understanding—acceptance.

Olivia blinked and let the corners of her mouth curl up just a fraction. Enough to take Ju-Ju's move a half step further. Ju-Ju didn't respond to the mini smile. Not that Olivia had expected her to—she'd stepped outside of her comfort zone enough for one day. Olivia would take what she could get. At least there was hope.

". . . Amen."

The worship team launched a final song as people began to collect their belongings.

Mom! Olivia had almost forgotten that when she turned to leave with the group, she'd be confronted with the one person she didn't need to see—wasn't allowed to see, actually. Should she go tell Ben and let him deal with it? At least then he'd know she had nothing to do with her Mom being here. They couldn't blame her for something someone else did. If she didn't tell him right away, Ben might think she and Mom had set it up ahead of time. That was all she needed. So hard to know what to do.

Olivia turned and climbed over Tricia's feet and squeezed out into the aisle against the flow of traffic. She tapped Tammy on the shoulder.

Tammy spun around. "Olivia. How did you like the service? Wasn't it wonderful? I want you to meet Ben's wife, Alicia."

As much as she wanted to dive right into her problem, Olivia shook Alicia's warm hand. "It's nice to meet you."

Alicia grinned and exposed two of the deepest dimples Olivia had ever seen, then pulled her in for a warm hug. "It's great to meet you, too, honey. I hear you play a mean oboe. Can't wait to hear it."

"Thanks." As difficult as it was to pull away, Olivia unfolded her comforted body from Alicia's motherly arms and cast a glance toward the back of the church. "Listen. I don't mean to be rude. But I have a little problem. My mom's here."

Alicia looked around the emptying sanctuary.

Tammy stood up on her tiptoes, shaking her head. "I don't see her anywhere, hon."

Olivia searched the room. Rows and rows of empty seats, a few clusters of chitchatters and people praying, and someone wrapping up cords on the stage. Mom was gone. "Where could she be?"

"Maybe she just wanted to see you, and then she left." Alicia put an arm around Olivia's shoulders and steered her toward the door. "Let's join the others and try to put it behind us for now."

Could it be as simple as that? Had Mom come all the way there simply to make sure her daughter was okay, and then left without causing a scene?

They headed through the lobby and toward the back door. Olivia glanced in every direction, expecting her mom to pop out from behind a door or a pillar and yell, *Surprise!* But they made it all the way to the exit and still no Mom. Maybe she *had* left. She knew it was against the rules for Olivia to have outside contact at this early stage in the Diamond Estates program. Maybe she was following the rules after all. Possible, but not likely.

Olivia, Alicia, and Tammy entered the parking lot, and

Olivia immediately noticed a crowd of people in the center of the parking lot. She bobbed her head to each side, trying to see through the crowd to find out what the attraction was.

Then she heard it. The whiny shriek her mother used when she wasn't getting her way.

Then she saw it. *Oh no.* Olivia wished the ground would open up and swallow her whole.

Chapter 18

"I demand access to my daughter, Olivia Mansfield, this instant." Mom had her freshly done nails on her Donna Karan hips as she tapped her Louboutin stiletto on the pavement. They'd better watch out. Those things were a deadly weapon—she could poke someone's eye out with those spikes if she wanted to. Like a ninja.

"Mrs. Whitford, please calm down. You're causing a scene. Let's talk over here." Ben put his hand on her arm and tried to steer her to the van and away from the cars queued to leave the parking lot.

Mom shook off his hand, planted her feet, and pointed her finger at Ben.

Olivia groaned and turned to Tammy and Alicia. "What do I do? I didn't ask her to do this. Am I going to be in trouble? Will I get sent home?" *Because I'm not going.*

Alicia pulled Olivia into a tight embrace. "Don't worry, honey. You're not in trouble. This isn't your fault at all. But now we have to deal with it. We have two options for how to handle this. One, you get into my car that's parked over there." She pointed to a sedan near the side entrance. "We'll leave and let Ben handle this and get the girls back to the center. Or, two, you go deal with your mom and try to defuse this situation once and for all. Your call."

Olivia wanted nothing more than to climb into the back

of Alicia's car, duck down out of view, and return to Diamond Estates without having a big public confrontation with her mom. She could let Ben handle Mom—he dealt with difficult people all the time. But that wasn't fair to everyone else. Plus all the girls would get to witness even more of her mom's temper tantrum when she realized that Olivia had left. *Ugh!* "I'll go talk to her."

Alicia bobbed her short brown curls and squeezed Olivia's shoulder. "Atta girl."

"Praying for you, sweetie." Tammy gave Olivia a gentle prod.

"Oh, thank God. There she is." Mom turned on Olivia, tears filling her eyes. "Where have you been?" She looked back to Ben. "Do you just let these girls run loose?"

"I was with Tammy and Alicia, Ben's wife, Mom." Olivia sighed as her heart softened. Mom wasn't angry after all. She was hurting. Maybe even lonely. "Why did you come here? You know it's against the rules."

"There should never be rules that keep me from my daughter. That's just wrong." She dabbed a silk handkerchief at the corner of her eye.

Olivia stepped forward and took her mother's hand. "Listen. The rules are there for a reason. If I follow them, it doesn't mean I don't love you or need you. But what I do need is for you to let me do this right, Mom. It's the best thing for me—for us. Trust the program, and let me make it through the best way I can." Olivia squeezed her hand. "Please."

Mom stared at Olivia's face for a long moment then nodded slowly. "You're right. I'm sorry I came. I'm just. . .I'm so—" She dropped Olivia's hand and started backing away. "I'm sorry." She pivoted on one spike and ran toward a waiting taxi. She climbed in the backseat and rode away.

She never looked back.

🌀

"So health food isn't a real concern around here, huh?" Olivia scraped the remains of someone's fried chicken tenders and macaroni and cheese into the trash bin. A dollop of barbecue sauce dripped from the plate and plopped onto her sock. *Ick.*

Tricia groaned. "I totally know what you mean. You have to watch yourself or you'll blimp up." She patted her slightly chunky hips. "I'm still working on the eight pounds I gained in my first few months here. I'm afraid they might be here to stay."

"T, get over it. You're skinny, and you'll always be skinny. Eight pounds. . .right." Ju-Ju added a wad of used napkins to the garbage and turned to Olivia. "Just don't let them catch you dieting. We're not allowed, you know."

Olivia's jaw dropped. "Not allowed to diet? That's pure crazy."

Skye pointed to a poster on the wall. "All meals meet the state requirements like school-lunch programs have to. And they don't like for us to diet because, quote"—she wiggled her fingers in the air beside her face—" 'Moderation should make dieting unnecessary.' Unquote."

Olivia smirked. "Okay. That's plain absurd. I, Olivia Mansfield, am from this moment henceforth officially on a diet."

"You'll do anything to buck the system, won't you?" Ju-Ju chuckled and dried the counter she'd just scrubbed.

"I don't think I'm purposely *trying* to." Olivia shrugged. "But when the system makes no sense, it just begs to be bucked. I mean, I could stand to lose five pounds already. Heavy breakfasts, bread baskets at every meal, and desserts twice a day won't help that mission at all."

"Well, diet or not, no one's forcing you to eat *that* stuff."

"I'll tell you who's *always* on a diet." Skye gave Tricia and

Ju-Ju a knowing look. They nodded and all said one word at the same time: "Donna!"

"Donna's probably the only one who doesn't need to be on a diet." Olivia scowled.

"Yeah, but she'd tell you that she only stays slim by being very careful. You'll never see her with bread or sugar. Ever."

"But I thought dieting was against the rules."

Ju-Ju shrugged. "A lot of things around here are 'Do as I say, not as I do,' but not really in a bad way. I mean, I can sort of see their point. We're still growing. Blah, blah, blah."

Skye swiped a cloth at a stray crumb on the countertop. "And the counselors don't have any privileges they need to earn. They aren't in trouble like we are."

"I guess that's true. But all I know is I'm hitting the tread-mill as soon as I can tonight."

⟳

When the game room opened for free time, Olivia put on a pair of sleek yoga pants and grabbed her running shoes.

"You guys coming?"

"We'll be in there in a minute, but not to run." Ju-Ju laughed. "I'm allergic to sweat."

Tricia smoothed her sleek hairdo. "And if you'd spent an hour straightening your hair, you'd avoid it, too. Besides, I'm not feeling well—pretty sure that dinner is what did it. Ju-Ju, you and Skye go on ahead with Olivia. I'll join you in a little bit."

Skye flipped her legs out and hopped off her top bunk. "Yeah. I, for one, am not hanging around here. Maybe there's a good movie on or something."

"Hope you feel better, Trish," Olivia called over her shoulder as the three girls stepped into the hallway and hurried to the game room.

They walked in, Olivia with her water bottle filled and a

towel draped over her shoulder. A group already milled by the theater area, digging through the stacks of DVDs. Someone wanted to watch a classic and the others were arguing for a comedy. On the other side, girls were clustered around the Ping-Pong table, where it seemed a tournament was already under way. They sure hadn't wasted any time.

Olivia groaned when she turned toward the exercise area. All of the machines were in use. She'd have to come earlier next time. She wandered over to the treadmills and skipped past the gasping, red-faced runners to approach the walking girl who was breathing steadily. She'd be easier to talk to. "Hey, do you know if there's a sign-up sheet for people who want a machine after you guys are finished?"

"Sure. Kira's got it." The speed walker nodded in the direction of *her*. The crying girl from the bathroom. Her name was Kira? Olivia had done all she could to avoid the little blond ever since she'd arrived at Diamond Estates. Now, there she sat, holding court on a stool with her panting minions standing around her, seemingly waiting for her to toss them some crumbs.

Now what? Forget exercising or approach Kira? Olivia shook her head at her internal struggle. Nope. She was done giving in to bad people. If Kira wanted to be a jerk, that was her choice. Olivia had some running to do.

Tugging at the ends of the towel hanging across her shoulders, Olivia jogged over to Kira. "Mind if I sign up for a treadmill?" She reached out for the clipboard.

"I don't know. How bad do you want it?" Kira's steel-blue eyes looked Olivia over from head to toe. "Then again, from the looks of things, you sure do need it."

"Excuse me?"

"Oh, I'm only kidding. Lighten up, Petunia." Kira snapped

her gum and high-fived one of her followers.

Petunia? Who was Kira trying to impress, and how did she think *that* would do it? "Um, riiight." Olivia yanked the clipboard away from Kira and scrawled her name at the bottom of the list.

Thirty minutes later, the first group finished their session. Kira stepped up to the machines, her royal subjects close behind.

Olivia looked the list over and saw they had, indeed, signed in before her. What were the chances they would run for only thirty minutes and then give her a turn? No way. They'd never vacate a machine knowing Olivia wanted to use one. They'd run until they had a heart attack if it would keep the new girl from getting what she wanted. What had Olivia ever done to them anyway? Or more precisely, what had she done to Kira?

ᔕ

So it *was* true. Alarm clocks *did* work even in the middle of the night. They should have some sensor that at least required the sun to be up before they let off their cacophony and destroyed peace. Olivia rolled over and pulled her pillow over her head. It felt alien to try to pry her body from her bed. It wasn't like they had to start school at any certain time. Why couldn't the powers-that-be move the whole day back an hour or two and let them sleep in a little bit?

Light flooded the room.

"Oh, Skye." Tricia groaned and covered her head.

Skye laughed. "Race you to the bathroom."

Olivia pulled herself halfway up and rested back on her elbows. "How can you be so chipper this early in the morning?" She shook her head.

Ju-Ju moaned from under her pillow. "No kidding. I took my shower last night, so leave me alone for ten more minutes."

Olivia padded to the bathroom and stepped into the shower while thinking about Ju-Ju. She really was a contradiction. So motivated and focused on the rules, yet she had the biggest chip on her shoulder and toughest attitude Olivia had ever seen in someone her own age—actually, Ju-Ju wasn't even quite her age yet. There was a story there, and Olivia couldn't wait to hear it.

The thirty-minute primping allotment dwindling rapidly, Olivia finished her shower while Skye and Tricia readied at the sinks behind the partition. She towel-dried her wet hair and then twisted the damp mass into a clip. No time for blow-drying. A little bit of lip gloss and some mascara, and then she'd better get dressed fast or she'd be facing the day naked. She chuckled at the thought of showing up to the prayer room with no clothes on.

At least the house was all girls—unless she counted Ben— and she didn't have to worry about what she wore. Her mom had seemed enamored by Ben's rugged good looks, but Olivia didn't really see the appeal now that she'd gotten to know him. He was handsome, sure, if you liked that sort of thing. Kind of annoying with all of his rules and regulations though. And too spiritual. *Way* too spiritual.

His son, on the other hand—he was another story. But, thankfully, Justin had his own school and didn't hang around all day for a bunch of teenage girls to make fools of themselves over him. If he did, Olivia would have to get up at five o'clock to get ready.

A quick glance in the mirror disgusted her. Olivia could honestly say she hadn't left the house in a warm-up suit with her wet hair pinned up and hardly any makeup on in, well, ever. She'd have to get up earlier tomorrow. She couldn't live like this. A girl had her pride.

Tricia, perfectly made up and dressed to kill in skintight

jeans and a flowing tunic, stumbled toward the door like a half-asleep zombie. She picked up a folded piece of paper that someone had slipped under the door. "It's the new counseling schedule." She glanced down the list. "Olivia, you're today. I'm tomorrow." She passed the paper to Skye and looked at Olivia. "You'll go to Tammy's office—the first one of those office doors off the dining room—right after school."

Oh great. Sounded like loads of fun. Olivia nodded. What could she say? The work was about to start. That *was* what she'd come here for, right?

What would they talk about? How would she know how much to say to Tammy? Better yet, how could she avoid saying what she didn't want to? There was no way Olivia could tell her everything. If she did, Jake and Mom would find out. She couldn't let that happen.

But if she weren't honest, she'd never get the help she needed, and wasn't that what she was there for? She'd start slowly and see what happened. If Tammy was as smart as everyone said she was, she'd know how to get Olivia to open up.

Olivia imagined Jake's face if he knew what Charles had done to her. . .many times. No way. She'd rather die than tell anyone about that. Even if it meant she never got help.

Even if it meant she carried it alone forever.

No matter what, no one could ever find out.

ⓢ

After a light breakfast of toast and a banana—Olivia passed on the bacon and cheesy eggs—the girls filed down the hallway toward the library, ready for their school day. "I'm really curious about how the whole school thing works."

Tricia's long, french-manicured fingernails clicked on the heavy library door she held open for Olivia. "Think of it like being homeschooled. Most parents who do that aren't actually teachers—that's kind of how Tammy, Donna, and Patty do it here with us."

"I guess." Olivia didn't really care about the teachers. She could handle the work on her own if she had to. "My only concern is my oboe. I used to be able to go practice every day during study hall. We also had band practice twice a week, and then symphonic band practice two other times each week. I was hoping to try for a scholarship to a music school."

"If you're serious, you should really talk to Tammy about it. They always do their best to work out something important like that." Tricia sat down at a table and unzipped her backpack.

Olivia nodded. Tricia was right. If life after Diamond Estates included a music scholarship, she needed to have disciplined practice times. "I'll talk to her about it today during our counseling appointment." Besides, maybe that would get her out of some of the dumb stuff like snowshoeing. Then again, Justin had gone snowshoeing.

"I'd tell them I need time to practice my flute. But they'd just laugh at me since I haven't touched the thing in weeks." Tricia gave a wry grin.

"Yeah, I don't think I've gone this long without playing my oboe in years."

"Okay, girls. Let's get settled down so we can start on time." Patty stood in front of the two rows of wooden tables where the girls had taken their seats. "We're going to start the day off with math drills, so everyone take out your most current workbook." She counted heads and scribbled a note. "Once you're done with the assignment, pair up for the drill portion. Olivia, why don't you come on up here and have a seat by the desk so I can fill you in on how things work?"

Olivia joined Patty at the front of the room and sat in the wooden chair beside her desk. "Are you the teacher every day?"

Patty shook her head. "No one here is actually a teacher. We all take turns facilitating your self-directed studies." She piled seven—no, eight—books and papers on her desk and slid the stack in front of Olivia.

"Based on your grades and the classes you were enrolled in at your last school, we've determined that these courses are the best places for you to start." She flipped open the social studies book. "See here? There's a checklist at the beginning and end of each chapter. You must do everything on that checklist before you may take the test to pass on to the next segment."

Oh boy. This should be interesting. "What if I have questions?"

"Oh, I'm sure you *will* have questions from time to time." Patty smiled. "You can always feel free to ask the person in charge that day. If we don't know the answer, we always know how to find it."

"Okay. This *is* real school, right? I mean, this counts for college and everything, right?" What if she'd made a *huge* mistake and had disqualified herself from college by coming to a fake school?

"Oh, definitely. Everything you do is fully accredited, just like anywhere else. You don't have to worry about that at all."

Olivia sure hoped Patty knew what she was talking about.

"Now, it looks like most of the girls are ready for drills. Want to jump in with them or do the assignment first?"

Olivia shrugged. "Whatever you think."

"Well, then you go ahead and sit by Kira. She's in the same book as you and doesn't have a partner at the moment."

Perfect. Olivia slumped into the seat beside Kira and closed her eyes. Could the day get any worse?

Patty stood in front of the room of paired-up girls and held up a timer. "Okay, spread the flash cards out in front of you. When the buzzer goes off, you see if you can beat your opponent by solving the problems on more cards than she does. As you get the answer right, snatch the card into your pile, and we'll count them at the end. Ready. Set. Go." Patty clicked the button.

Kira stared into Olivia's eyes and pressed her hands and forearms over the cards.

"What are you doing?" Olivia kept her voice low and calm. "I can't see the cards. Move your arms." She glanced at Patty, who was watching the timer. The other teams were scurrying through their races, but Kira wouldn't budge. Olivia sat back in her chair. If Kira wanted to act like a child, there was nothing Olivia could do about it.

"Five more seconds." Patty held up the timer.

Olivia crossed her arms and waited for the buzzer.

Kira's steely eyes glinted with smug confidence as she swept the cards into her lap and gathered them in a pile. "I win."

That's what you think.

Chapter 19

Come on in, Olivia." Tammy gave her a big grin and gestured to a puffy tomato-red chair on the other side of her desk. "Have a seat. How's your day going?"

"Fine." Olivia sat on the edge of her seat, wringing her hands in her lap.

"Don't be nervous. I don't bite."

"I don't know why I'm so jittery." Olivia spoke slowly and signed her words.

"It's normal to feel anxious about talking to someone about your personal life and thoughts. Especially a relative stranger."

Olivia nodded and fought back tears. "It makes no sense that I'm about to cry." She made the motion for tears. "We haven't even started."

"You've got a lot bubbling just under the surface. Part of you is scared to face it, but the other part is so ready to let it all go. This will be an ongoing process, so don't think we're going to be able to fix everything today, or even this month." Tammy reached a hand across the desk to touch Olivia's shoulder. "It took a lifetime for you to get to this point. Give us some time to work out a breakthrough. Okay?"

"Deal." She'd try, but Olivia had no idea how much she would tell Tammy. Maybe everything. Maybe nothing.

Tammy reached across her desk and pulled her spiral notebook closer to her body. "I do have a few ground rules.

Number one is complete honesty. If you aren't honest with me, there's really nothing I can do to help you. Right?"

Omission wasn't really a lie though. "Makes sense."

"Number two is effort. You need to put forth your best effort every single time. Don't hide from the difficult things— let's hit them head-on, together. Got it?"

"Got it." *Maybe.*

"Number three is confidentiality. I'm obligated to protect your privacy and never discuss you with anyone outside the staff here at Diamond without your permission—you should know, though, that I am free to discuss anything I need to with Ben and that the staff prays together for you every day. On the flip side, I'd appreciate confidentiality, too. I might share things with you as part of our therapy. That information should stay in this room."

"Sounds fair." Olivia signed by tapping her fingertips together.

Tammy opened her notebook to a new page and poised her pen to write. "I'm going to ask you a few questions. I'm not really going to delve into your answers today. They're mainly meant to give me a kind of jumping-off point so I know where to direct our time together in the future."

Olivia squirmed. *Here comes the fun part. Might as well get it over with.*

"First of all, I've read your details and I've heard your story, but I'd like *you* to tell me why you're here. I don't need a play-by-play of your actions and mistakes; I'm looking for more of an understanding of what you're looking for."

Good question. What if Olivia didn't even know exactly what she hoped to find? She supposed she could just say that. "That's the thing, I don't even know what I'm looking for, really." She gazed at her shoe while Tammy waited for more. "I guess the short answer is that I'm searching for God." Olivia made sure her lips were readable and dragged the side of her flat hand along the length of her face.

Tammy gave a confused squint. "Short answer?"

"Yeah. I mean, I'm hoping to find God. But I really have no idea how to do that or what He'll even look like when *or if* I find Him. I don't feel Him, see Him, hear Him." Olivia threw up her hands, almost forgetting to sign her words. "I see the other girls praying." She put her hands together. "And I watch them sing songs and everything else that goes on. It seems like they really know Him. I guess I don't see that happening for me." Olivia pointed to herself.

"Then what's the long answer?"

"The long answer?" Boy, Tammy knew how to ask all the hard questions. Olivia shrugged. "Well, I guess I'm running from things. I have fears, memories, worries. . .but don't we all? I miss my daddy. I feel guilty about Jordyn's death—she's my best friend who died recently. I guess I feel guilty about my daddy, too. But that's just stupid. I was only a kid. Speaking of that, why would God take a little kid's daddy from her? If there's really a God, why. . . ?" Olivia could go on. But she'd said enough.

Tammy scribbled some notes on her page and gazed at Olivia. "What's the one thing in your life, the one event or trigger looming in your mind as a reason you've wandered down the path you've been on lately?"

How could she choose? There were so many. "I guess I'd start with my dad's death. I was there—I saw it happen and felt his blood." Olivia made the sign for *blood* and then shivered involuntarily. "I had it all over me."

Tammy nodded and scrawled on her paper.

"Then there's my stepdad, Charles. . ." Her breath caught

and tears welled up in her eyes. She shook her head, unable to continue. Why had she said his name?

Tammy wrote something down. "It's okay. That's enough about him for now."

"The last thing, my last defining moment I guess, was the accident I was in a little over a week ago." Olivia touched the scar on her cheek. "Jordyn, my best friend, died in that one." Bet Tammy wished she could pass Olivia on to someone else and wait for the next new girl—someone without so much baggage.

"Okay, that's great information, and it will help us as we move forward. I know it's difficult to bring this stuff up, but it's really necessary. My last question for you is this: what's one thing you're disappointed in or frustrated about the program since you got here?"

Finally—her chance. "Can I say two things?"

Tammy snickered. "It's really funny. No one *ever* has only one thing to say." She put her notebook on her lap and folded her hands on the desk. "Sure. Two things—go for it."

"Number one, I honestly don't understand why we need to get up so early every day." Olivia crossed her legs while signing then uncrossed them so she wouldn't seem combative. "I mean, it's not like we have to be anywhere at any certain time. Couldn't there be a little more flexibility?" She had to spell out the word with her fingers.

Tammy shook her head and smiled. "The short answer, as you called it, is no. We want to train you girls how to be contributing, functioning members of society. When you have a job, you'll be lucky if you can sleep until six in the morning. We do let you sleep in until eight on the weekends and even nine on holidays. So it's not completely inflexible. Studies have shown that the day is most productive when a person lives within a schedule and rises early."

Alrighty then. Guess that was a resounding no.

"What was your second thing?" Tammy smiled and nodded encouragingly.

"It has to do with my oboe." Olivia spoke slowly and signed an explanation of the amount of practice she'd been used to at home. "You see, I need to keep up my practice if I'm to have any hope of a scholarship. Do you think there might be a time during the school day when I could take an hour to go practice?"

"Absolutely. We definitely want to support those types of commitments. Give me a little bit of time to figure out what to do, but we'll get it worked out." Tammy made another quick note, clicked her pen, and then shut her book. "That's all the time we have for today. I now have a lot more insight into who you really are and what your needs are. Thanks so much for your honesty."

"How often do we get together for sessions like this?"

"For your first couple of months here, we'll meet three times a week." Tammy pulled out a calendar. "Let me see. How about Mondays, Wednesdays, and Fridays at ten thirty? That would get you back to the library before lunch prep."

Sure, why not? If nothing else, it would get her out of part of the school day. "Sounds fine to me." Olivia lifted her open hand with splayed fingers and touched her thumb to her chest. *Fine.*

"I'd like to pray for you before you leave. Okay?" Tammy smiled.

"I guess so." Olivia shrugged and fought off a groan as she closed her eyes. So much praying around here. They wouldn't ever expect her to pray out loud, would they? No way she'd do that. How strange—talking to someone you couldn't see, in front of other people who couldn't see Him either. It felt so weird. She remembered doing it as a kid. But she also sang nursery rhymes and believed in the tooth fairy once, too.

"Amen." Tammy stood up and smiled. "Come on. I'll escort you back to class."

Olivia stood and smoothed the front of her pants. "Um, I was wondering about something else. When can I call my mom?"

"Good question. Normally you'd have to wait until next week, but we'll be letting everyone call home for Thanksgiving."

"Thanksgiving?" Olivia searched her brain for dates and realized in horror that it was only three days away. Her eyes dampened at the thought of being alone for the holiday. How would it feel to spend it so far from home? What would she do? What would Mom do with only Charles to celebrate with? Maybe Jake would come home to be with Mom. Olivia pushed the thoughts from her mind and nodded. "Okay. I hadn't realized. It'll be nice to talk to her." She touched her lips.

Tammy gazed at Olivia for a moment then nodded. "It'll be okay. We have a great time on holidays. You'll see. And speaking of Thanksgiving, your assignment for our next session is to be thinking of what you're most thankful for. I'd love it if you came up with three things to share with me on Wednesday."

What have I got to be thankful for? And even if there were things, who would I thank?

❧

"Happy Thanksgiving, roomies," Skye's singsong voice called out from her bed.

Olivia pried open one eye to look at the clock. Six fifteen? Seriously? "No offense, but shh!" What was Skye doing awake when they could sleep in three extra hours until nine o'clock since it was a holiday? The sun hadn't even encroached on the darkness, and Skye had already started yakking.

Tricia moaned and yanked her covers up to her chin. "No kidding. Shh."

Ju-Ju threw a pillow and socked a giggling Skye in the head.

Olivia pulled her pillow over her face. What did she have to be thankful for on a holiday when she'd be away from home with no family? Several girls got to go home for the weekend because they were graduating the following month—just in time for Christmas. Others had visitors coming to celebrate right there in the house with them. Being so new, Olivia hadn't been granted any of those privileges.

Would she be able to do what it took to earn some extra rights by Christmas? It would be intolerable if she had to stay here and celebrate Christmas by herself. But what was the alternative? Go to *Chuck's* house? *No thanks.* Huddled with Mom and Jake around a roaring fire in a ski chalet sounded perfect—as if Charles would allow that. What did the other Diamond Estates girls do for the holidays? She'd have to ask some of them who'd been there longest what the holidays were like last year.

Thankful? She felt most thankful that her group had laundry duty and outside chores for the holiday week. The kitchen team would have a tough time cooking the Thanksgiving banquet and then cleaning up the destroyed kitchen after it. The dining room team would have an equally difficult time getting the fancy plates and dishes washed and put away—especially with their added guests. Way better to just tuck away in the steamy laundry room to fold sheets and tablecloths. She didn't even mind sorting everyone's socks by their initials if it meant no greasy pots of gravy to clean.

What else made her thankful? They had plans to leave the grounds the next day for a traditional Black Friday shopping trip. That would be fun—shopping was *always* something to be thankful for. Olivia had plenty of money to buy Christmas gifts and maybe a new outfit for herself—and a credit card in case the cash ran out. Some of the girls weren't really looking forward to going shopping, naturally. After all, how fun could it be with no money to spend? One of these days, once he knew she'd never be coming home, Charles would cut off Olivia's credit card. She was sure of it. But for now. . .she might as well get the most she could out of it.

Olivia rolled over and put her hands beneath her head, her eyes wide open, staring at the revolving ceiling fan in the slowly brightening room. She supposed she should be thankful she was there. Safe, away from Charles, headed in some kind of direction—whether it was the right one or not remained to be seen. But at least she wasn't still careening on a collision course with self-destruction. And she was safe. She'd never, ever let someone hurt her again.

Olivia's hand made an involuntary move for her front pocket. It was time for a smoke, and her body knew it. Oh, what she would give for a cigarette. Even one drag to relax her tense nerves and loosen the tightness in her chest. She could go run on the treadmill and get the same calming effect from the endorphins. But it was the cigarette she truly craved. Why wasn't that desire fading yet? She drew in her breath in a pretend inhale, letting her lungs expand, hoping they'd believe the air she breathed was nicotine.

No such luck.

🌀

"Who wants pie?" Patty steered a dessert trolley into the dining room. The pies had already been cut and placed in single-serving pieces on plates with a generous scoop of vanilla ice cream—the good kind with the specks of vanilla bean in it. She pushed the cart past each table. "Pumpkin or apple?"

When the cart got to their table, Olivia selected a slice of apple, fully intending to leave most of it untouched. She'd never be able to skip the ice cream though. Skye and Tricia each picked the largest pieces of pumpkin they could find.

"I'm going to pay for this later." Tricia eyed her pie like it might gobble her up, but she took a huge bite anyway. "Mmm, so good."

Ju-Ju stared at the dessert trays for a moment and then asked, "Can I go get a Ding Dong from my cupboard?"

Aha! Ju-Ju was the Ding Dong freak Ben had mentioned. She'd rather have one of those waxy, tasteless snack cakes than a piece of homemade pie fresh from the oven? Crazy.

Patty laughed. "If that's what you want, go ahead."

Ju-Ju made a record-breaking trip to the kitchen then slid back into her seat. She pulled the hockey-puck-sized dessert from its white plastic wrapper and placed it on her napkin.

Tricia nudged Olivia. "Watch this." She nodded toward Ju-Ju.

No worries. Olivia had no intention of looking away as Ju-Ju peeled the chocolate coating from the cake and ate the flakes one by one. Then, with only chocolate cake exposed, she picked up her spoon and cored the cream-filled center out and ate that in one bite. On her napkin remained only a donut-shaped chocolate cake, which she picked up and nibbled around the edges until it shrank and eventually disappeared.

Tricia giggled at Olivia's openmouthed expression. "Funny, eh?"

"I've never seen anything like it." Who knew eating a Ding Dong could be turned into such a spectacle?

Ju-Ju glared. "How do you eat your Oreos? You unscrew and scrape, right?"

Olivia nodded.

"Well, I basically dismantle my Ding Dong like you do your Oreo. Deal with it."

"Fair enough, weirdo." Olivia winked at Tricia and Skye.

"You girls going shopping tomorrow?" Kira pressed the palms of her hands on the table in front of Olivia and smiled a syrupy sweet smile. Her two cronies—what were their names anyway?—stood just behind Kira with a brainless smile in place, ready for orders.

"Yes," Ju-Ju hissed. "Pretty sure it's mandatory."

Kira's smile wavered. "Yes, well. I was just hoping to get some shopping tips from the rich girl over here." She tipped her head at Olivia. "Oh. Wait. On second thought, if I'm bargain shopping, I'd be better off asking *you* for help, Ju." She flipped her hair over her shoulder and spun toward the door. She spun around and looked at Tricia. "I'd ask you for help with fit, but, well. . ." She shrugged and pranced away.

Her followers parted like the Red Sea to let her pass through.

Tricia swallowed her pie with a loud gulp, put down her fork, and pushed her plate out of reach. "I've got to go to the bathroom." Her chair squeaked back as she left the table and hurried out the side door.

Ju-Ju squinted at Kira's retreating back. "I'm going to keep my eye on that girl. Olivia, I'd suggest you do the same."

✿

Seriously? Prayer time at 5:00 a.m.? Was God even awake at five o'clock in the morning? Standing in the foyer after their extra-early quiet time, the girls anxiously waited to load into the vans for their Black Friday trip to the mall.

Ben stood on the third step and spoke over the banister to the group, his eyes twinkling. "Girls, we're about ready to go. I just have to point out that most of you would only just now be rolling out of bed and whining about the time. Funny how, for a special event like shopping, you can get up even earlier than you normally do, with hardly any complaining. Hmm."

Well, what did he expect? Of course shopping on Black Friday was easier to get out of bed for than a prayer time that meant nothing to you and a breakfast you didn't even want to eat. Still, Olivia could see his point. She could probably try to make a better effort to wake up on time without complaining. But first, shopping!

They left no corner of the mall unexplored. Arms full of packages, Olivia had purchased more than anyone, and that was even with trying to hold back on some of her purchases so she wouldn't make the other girls feel bad. She was proud of herself for purchasing only Christmas gifts for other people, forgoing a new outfit or anything else for herself.

At the preset meeting time, Olivia, Ju-Ju, and Skye collapsed in orange plastic chairs in the food court next to Tammy while they waited for the rest of the group to arrive.

"Where's Tricia?" Tammy signed as she glanced around the noisy food court.

"She ran into the restroom." Olivia let her bags slide from her lap to the floor. "In fact, I think I'll go, too. Do you guys mind watching my stuff?"

"Naw. 'Course not. You go on." Skye waved toward the public bathroom. "We'll be right here when you get back."

Olivia navigated around strollers and shopping bags scattered on the floor near the tables she passed. Her shoulders sagged at the sight of the line extending out the restroom door and past the one for Taco Bell. No Tricia though. She must have made it in already. Olivia counted the people ahead of her—she could be all the way back home at Diamond Estates before making it through that line. Maybe she could at least go in just to wash her hands.

Standing at the sink, she peered into the mirror and wiped away the smudged eyeliner. *Ugh.* Dark circles. Puffy eyes.

Looking just like she'd risen before dawn.

A toilet flushed. Then another. Women milled around. Where was Tricia?

As a *whoosh* faded away, Olivia heard someone gag. Gross! A toilet flushed, more retching. Her stomach churned at the thought of some stranger vomiting only a few feet away. She shook the water off her hands and pulled the lever for the paper towels. Oh no—empty! Olivia looked at her wet hands and then rubbed them on her jeans as the door to the far stall swung open and she locked eyes with Tricia.

"Was that you in there? Are you okay?" Olivia went to Tricia's side and reached a hand out to touch Tricia's shoulder.

"Yeah. It's no big deal. Just something I ate, I guess." Tricia shrugged and turned her back to Olivia to wash her hands.

"Are you sure? That sounded awful." Olivia searched Tricia's face in the mirror. "Look. Your eyes are all red. You look terrible."

"I'm fine. Really. Please don't make a big deal out of it." Tricia left the crowded bathroom with Olivia following right behind.

Approaching the group after having crossed the packed commons, Tricia grinned and held up her few shopping bags. "Success!"

Weird. She looked totally normal. If Olivia threw up, she was in bed for at least a day. How had Tricia bounced back so quickly? She was Superwoman.

"Are you going to tell them you're sick?" Olivia whispered.

"Shh. Please don't say anything. I'm fine. Really."

"If you say so." Olivia shrugged.

"Oh, I almost forgot." Olivia rooted around in her largest bag searching for the CD she'd purchased for the prayer room. She had to remove several things before she uncovered it. "Here you go, Tammy. I really love this group, and it's a worship album, so it's allowed at the center. Do you think maybe we could have it on some morning during prayer?"

"Definitely. I know this group—it'll be perfect. Thanks for contributing. It's good for you guys to make the time personal to your own tastes." Tammy accepted the CD and tucked it into her bag.

"No problem." Olivia bent to replace the items she'd pulled from her bag. Something caught her eye on the bottom. She lifted a sweater and stifled a gasp as she uncovered a green-and-white dream come true.

An unopened pack of Newport Menthols.

Chapter 20

Glancing to her right and her left, Olivia tried to be discreet. Had anyone noticed? Where had the cigarettes come from? They were her favorite brand—she could almost taste them. Were they a gift from God? Manna from heaven? *Yeah right.* Someone put them there—someone who wanted her to get in trouble.

Should she tell Tammy and let her sort it out? But what if Tammy didn't believe Olivia and thought they really were her cigarettes? Plus it would cause a huge problem with the other girls. They were probably testing her. If she ratted them out, they'd hate her. No, she couldn't risk that by telling. Plus an unknown enemy was out to get her, and she didn't want to stir up even more trouble by making her mad.

Olivia rummaged in the depths of the big shopping bag, pretending to fold some items as she sorted through her purchases. She slipped the pack up her sleeve and collected some garbage from the table, intending to toss the cigs and then dump the messy trash on top.

On the way to the waste cans, Olivia felt the lump of the cigarette pack in her sleeve. What if she kept it? What if she hid the cigarettes and pulled them out only when she really, really needed one? The thought of a private walk through the woods with the warmth of the minty cigarette smoke coursing through her lungs almost brought tears to her eyes.

No one was watching her—that she knew of—so she'd

never get caught. But she still had no idea who'd slipped the pack into her bag. In all likelihood, the culprit was waiting to see what she did. Maybe she was watching Olivia right now. Since she had no idea who had planted the pack, where she was at the moment, or what her intentions were, Olivia needed to cover her tracks. Pretending to dig into her sleeve, Olivia let some items fall into the can and then dumped the food remains right on top. She made enough of a show of it that whoever knew about the cigarettes would think she tossed them, but anyone else would just think she had a bad itch on her arm.

Safe.

Now, who was out to get her? It couldn't have been one of her roommates. Skye and Tricia seemed to really like her. She and Ju-Ju may have had a rougher start, but Ju-Ju didn't seem the type to do something that mean and juvenile. Olivia really didn't know the others girls well enough yet for them to have any reason to do something so cold and hateful. Something that could have gotten her sent home.

Lost in her thoughts as she walked back to the table where her friends sat, Olivia tripped on something in the center of the aisle and went sprawling onto the ground. She popped right up, before she even realized what had happened, and whipped her head around to see what made her stumble. Kira's foot stuck out across the middle of the aisle. Had she tripped Olivia on purpose? Then Kira winked at her.

Of course. Kira had hidden the cigarettes. Olivia should have thought of her first thing because Kira had made no secret of the fact that she didn't like Olivia. But what had Olivia ever done to Kira? Or what did Kira *think* Olivia had done?

"Everyone is present and accounted for." Patty tucked her clipboard into her bag and pointed toward the doors. "Let's move out."

Everyone gathered their belongings. Olivia scooped up her bags and shouldered her purse. She tried to clear her mind, but the pack of cigarettes still hidden in her sleeve was calling her name. She'd better not let them fall out while they were riding in the van.

She took a seat and perched her things around her feet and on her lap.

Tammy popped her head in once they were all settled. "Inspection time, girls."

Obediently, everyone held their bags open as Tammy poked through the purchases to make sure nothing was against the rules.

When her turn came, Olivia's hands trembled as she held out each sack and even helped Tammy lift out the items and look in and under each thing. Kira knew about the bag check and probably assumed Olivia didn't. Her plan had likely been for Olivia to get caught with cigarettes during the inspection. Olivia could hear herself protesting that they weren't hers and imagined no one would have believed her. Why would they?

If she would stoop that low, what else was Kira capable of?

𖠿

Olivia stood straighter and squared her shoulders, immune to the stares she was sure pierced her back like lasers as she made her way up the sanctuary aisle to her seat between Ju-Ju and Skye. Had she already been there three weeks? In some ways it seemed like she'd arrived only the day before. But in other ways it felt like a lifetime. Nine counseling sessions, two phone conferences with Mom, a major holiday, new friendships. . .but no God. Maybe all the rest would be enough to get her through. She hadn't really hoped to make friends. She'd never expected to love her counselor. She hadn't even hoped for the opportunity to advance her oboe skills. So maybe it *was* enough. . .with or without God.

She stood to her feet as the service opened with a contemporary worship song. Becoming familiar with the practice of reading from the overhead screens and singing along, Olivia actually joined in. The same woman who did it every week sat on the stool on the far right of the stage, signing to several rows of hearing-impaired people. Olivia preferred to watch her rather than the preacher. It made her feel closer to Jake. Plus she thought the signing was such a great thing to offer hearing-impaired people. Maybe they'd let Olivia fill in sometime if the regular woman got sick or something.

Ack. Olivia shook her head at the thought. What was she thinking? She could never do something like that in front of all those people. For crying out loud, she could barely garner enough nerve to walk down the aisle to sit down.

After a few choruses, the worship director signaled for them to take their seats. He held out the microphone to a special guest who walked onto the stage. *Ah.* A solo performance. Olivia loved when they did that—it felt like a concert. The first few bars of the song came through the speakers, and Olivia peered a little closer at the singer. *Justin?*

Dressed in sleek black trousers with a crisp seam and a black and gray tweed sport coat over a royal blue knit shirt, Justin opened his mouth to sing.

Olivia had never heard anything like it in person. He sounded like an angel. She sat on the edge of her seat, never expecting him to do well throughout the whole song—surely he'd mess up and be embarrassed.

Skye nudged her and giggled. "Close your mouth. You might catch a fly."

Olivia snapped her jaw shut. She hadn't realized she'd been gawking, but she could hardly help it. "I had no idea he could sing like that."

"Justin can do just about anything musical. He's been attending Denver Fine Arts Academy on a full scholarship."

"He's amazing," Olivia whispered. She couldn't pull her eyes from the gorgeous guy who gripped the microphone and sang convincingly about the voice of truth calling him to get out of a boat. Olivia had no idea what it meant, but she wanted to know, and she didn't want the song to end.

Skye nodded. "Just don't let Kira hear you say that."

Kira? Olivia glanced over at the little firecracker who sat in the row ahead of her. Someone said she'd been a gymnast for years—had Olympic hopes until she got injured. She couldn't be more than five feet tall. Muscular but tiny—no big threat. Kira had eyes that bored holes through Olivia, but what did she have to worry about? Besides, why did Kira care what Olivia thought of Justin anyway?

As if she were a mind reader, Kira turned around and winked at Olivia again.

Olivia gasped at her nerve. "What's the deal with the winking? She keeps doing that to me," she hissed at Skye through the corner of her mouth.

"Don't bother trying to figure Kira out. Just know she's not going to make this easy on you."

"Well, there is nothing going on. But even if there were, Kira is the least of my concerns."

"I reckon I'd be a little worried if I were you." Skye chuckled. "Don't put nothin' past that girl."

Donna leaned over the laps of a couple of girls. "Shh. Pay attention to the song."

"Sorry." Skye grimaced.

Olivia faced forward and listened to the last words of the loveliest sound she'd ever heard, shaking her head the whole time. He did a beautiful job—as well as a professional singer at a concert hall—without a single mistake. The song ended, and Justin lowered the mic and dropped his head as he walked off the stage to thunderous applause. Right before he got to the end of the stage, he turned and pointed skyward.

How could such a simple gesture make her stomach do flip-flops?

What could Kira do to her anyway?

Olivia's flip-flops turned to nausea. Kira had already tried to get Olivia in trouble with the cigarettes. If she'd already stooped to that level, Kira would stop at nothing to get Olivia in some kind of mess. But why would she want to do that?

Unless. Did Kira have some claim on Justin, or think she did anyway? *Duh!* That must be the problem. But even if it were true, it wasn't like Olivia and Justin had ever even spoken but a few times. Well, there was the one incident with the snow. But Olivia would hardly call that flirting. Justin had meant the prank for his dad. Maybe Kira didn't know that. But Olivia had done nothing wrong. But that couldn't be it. Kira had had it in for Olivia since the time she first visited Diamond Estates, and Olivia wasn't pursuing Justin. Besides, the last she'd heard, Justin was forbidden from dating the Diamond girls. So there was really nothing to talk to Kira about. Rules were rules.

But rules are meant to be broken. . .right?

Chapter 21

Okay, girls, let's count off by twos." Patty stood on a chair holding her clipboard.

What was this? Kindergarten? When her turn came, reminiscent of elementary school, Olivia held up two fingers. "Two."

The girl next to Olivia said, "One."

Very good, boys and girls.

"Ones, you'll be going with Ben to select a Christmas tree. Twos, you'll be staying here with me and Alicia to get the tree trimmings ready." Patty jumped down from her chair, her short frame disappearing as she slipped in among the girls.

Phew! Olivia didn't want to have to go traipsing around outside in the snow. She and Ju-Ju could hang out while Tricia and Skye went outside. But then again, Kira was also a two. Olivia would have to keep an eye on her—steer clear of her if at all possible. That girl was nothing but trouble.

Christmas music was being piped in through the multiroom speaker system, and buckets of popcorn waited on the dining room tables for some of the girls to string. Ju-Ju and Olivia headed as far away from that project as they could get. Gingerbread cookies were spread on another table along with frosting, sprinkles, and all kinds of other decorations.

Olivia grimaced at Ju-Ju. "Should we?" She wrinkled her nose at the thought of decorating cookies.

"Nah." Ju-Ju shook her head.

That left one option—the kitchen and whatever crafty horror awaited them behind those doors. They passed through the entrance before Olivia realized they were joining Kira's group. They'd better get out of there. Suddenly stringing popcorn held infinite appeal.

"Come on in, girls!" Alicia flashed her deep dimples. "We could really use your help in here."

Too late to sneak away unnoticed. With dread like a lump in her stomach, Olivia approached the group standing around the center worktable and went to the corner, standing as far from Kira as she could and still be a part of things. Why did she let that girl get to her so much?

Ju-Ju grinned. "Ooh! Are we doing what I think we are?" She clapped her hands and rubbed them together.

"Yep." Alicia gestured to the cookbook. "We're making homemade candy canes."

Huh? Why bother going to all that trouble? "Candy canes are probably cheaper to buy than to make. Why go to all that extra work?"

"Cheaper is seldom better. Besides"—Alicia smiled proudly—"it's a Diamond Estates tradition that everything on the Christmas tree is homemade. Except for the lights, of course. And no Christmas tree is complete without candy canes."

Olivia leaned in to whisper in Ju-Ju's ear. "Let me guess, colored blinking lights?"

"Of course. What other kind are there?"

So much for the elegant, magazine-worthy trees her mom had professionally decorated with dainty white lights every year. Olivia made a mental note to pull up her online photo albums the next time they had computer access. Ju-Ju needed a lesson in taste—holiday style.

Alicia handed out little cards with the recipe printed on them and then demonstrated one candy cane. Then the girls divided into groups of two and spread out to separate work spaces in the kitchen. Olivia steered Ju-Ju to a corner opposite Kira's perch on a bar stool near Alicia.

Olivia and Ju-Ju mixed their first batch of candy, heating it to the precise temperature and adding red food coloring to half of it. "So, Ju, tell me your story. If you're ready to, I mean." She dropped the red candy mixture onto the powdered-sugar-coated cookie sheet and dragged it into a long, thin strip to cool just like Alicia had done.

Ju-Ju shrugged and did the same with the white candy. "It's no big secret. Basically, my mom and brother were killed when I was twelve. They were shot in a drive-by while watching TV in our living room." Ju-Ju shrugged again.

"You poor thing. That had to be awful." Olivia waited for her to continue.

"I was in my room asleep when it went down. I heard it all and knew instantly what had happened, but I was too scared to come out of my room. It took me over an hour to gather enough courage to go out there. I often wonder if they'd be alive if I'd gotten them help sooner."

Olivia nodded. "I know all about that kind of guilt. We can what-if ourselves to death, can't we?" She thought of her hands covered with her daddy's blood and of Jordyn behind the wheel.

"For sure. I'm so good at that." Ju-Ju's eyes grew dark for a moment before she shook herself out of it and began to twist the cooling strands of candy together. "So I was on my own. I didn't want to go into foster care because I'd heard so many horror stories about the things that happen to kids in those homes. So I ran away." She chuckled and made a grimace at the same time. "In a sense, I created a horror story of my own, but at least it was my own choice. At least I was the one in control—or at least I thought I was."

"What happened?" Olivia bent the end of her first twisted candy strip into a U shape and then snipped the scraggly ends off with kitchen shears.

"Well, that whole first year, I lived on the run. I slept wherever I found a place and stole money whenever I could find a way. I ate here and there, whatever. When I was thirteen, I realized I could make steady money plus sleep in a warm bed most of the time if I became a prostitute—New York businessmen love feisty little Mexican chicas." She wiggled her eyebrows.

Olivia lowered the new strings of candy she'd picked up to twist and fought against the tears burning behind her eyelids. "Oh, Ju-Ju. Really?"

"Hey now. You've had your own tragedy and pain. I won't cry for you if you don't cry for me. Deal?"

Olivia choked back a sob. "Deal." She dabbed the corner of her eye. "So what happened? How'd you end up here?"

"I stumbled upon a preacher one day while I was working a corner. He was a cop on a missions trip, evangelizing on the streets of New York. He posed as a john—a man who wanted to hire a prostitute—and actually paid my fee so I'd give him the time. He spent his whole hour talking to me about Jesus.

"His teenage daughter had run away and was never found—until it was too late anyway. Then his wife died of cancer. The man had suffered as much heartache as I had, but he'd still managed to find joy and peace somehow. I wanted that feeling."

You're not the only one.

Ju-Ju rolled out another strip of white candy. "So before he left New York, he put me on a plane to Denver." Her eyes grew wistful. "Officer Mark Stapleton from Chicago. I'll never forget him."

Olivia squealed. "I know him! He's the one who told *me* about this place." She shared the details of her recent association with him and how her mom knew him from way back. "Did you know he helped fund and build the game room?"

Ju-Ju's eyes widened. "I had no idea. Wow. It's a small world—either that or Mark Stapleton is an angel doing God's work all over the place."

That was certainly a possibility.

☙

"As is our tradition, now that we have a decorated Christmas tree, we'll gather around it and sing some Christmas carols in celebration of the start of the season." Patty hefted her keyboard onto its stand and pulled up a stool.

The twenty-four girls clustered in a half circle, facing the tree.

Olivia looked up into the evergreen boughs and watched a needle fall to the floor. The tree stood tall and regal in its homemade pride. It had heart and soul, unlike the commercial perfection of her mom's trees. The colored lights might not be as elegant as the white Italian lights, but they were homier somehow. Happy. Warm. But still, something was missing. Why wasn't she satisfied?

The smells were all there—cider steeping in the slow cooker on the banquet table along the wall and gingerbread notes lingering in the air from the day's baking. Brightly wrapped presents had already started popping up under the tree as some of the girls had spent their free time wrapping them. Frost on the windows gave away the cold temperatures outside, while the warmth of the roaring fire in the fireplace kept them toasty inside. What could be missing?

Lonely. That was it. She was lonely. The Christmas season was meant to be a family time for celebration and happiness.

Problem was, the celebrations rang hollow when there was no family around. Maybe she could sneak away and smoke one of her cigarettes later that afternoon. Breaking away from the group long enough to smoke had proven to be a more difficult task than she'd expected, even though she kept the unopened pack tucked somewhere in her clothes at all times. They just didn't leave a girl alone at this place. Ever.

Tammy had been trying to help Olivia see things differently. Her experiences were nothing more or less than what she made of them. Olivia could embrace the process and jump in with all her might. Or she could continue doing what she'd been doing and keep everyone and even the program itself at arm's length. Maybe it was time to put the past behind her and give it all she had. She'd come that far, and she sure wasn't doing herself any favors by not getting the most out of her time there.

". . .all is calm, all is bright. . ." Olivia joined in the singing with a grin on her face. She would find a way to enjoy Christmas no matter what. She had an idea and scrambled to her feet. She cupped her hand around her mouth and whispered in Patty's ear then scurried off to her room. Olivia returned in a flash with her oboe case and flipped open the latches.

She put her instrument together in record time, tuned it to match the sounds coming from the piano, and then stood beside Patty. As Patty began the next song, Olivia joined in with her rich oboe tones. Thankfully, she knew most of the Christmas carols they sang and could read the sheet music for the ones she didn't.

After they sang several songs, Tammy put up her hand. "I have a request. Olivia, will you play that solo from the *Phantom of the Opera* that you played for me during our session a couple of weeks ago?"

Tammy and Jake both loved to listen to her play. Should she be worried that her biggest fans were both deaf? "Sure. But just so no one gets confused, it's not really from *Phantom*. It's background music from the movie version. I just happen to love the oboe part." She raised her instrument to her lips, closed her eyes, and began to sway to the familiar melody.

As the last strains faded away, silence filled the room.

A tall man with slick black hair and a narrow English mustache that curled up on the ends stood from a chair in the back. "Young lady." He approached Olivia wearing a tweed coat and carrying a top hat. He reminded Olivia of a detective in a foreign film.

Her cheeks warmed as she realized a stranger had been listening to her play. Where had he come from? She'd played in front of so many people over the years, but it never got easy. Plus surprises like this always embarrassed her—like someone standing outside the door listening while she sang in the shower. Not cool.

The man placed his top hat under his arm and held out a business card. "I'm Sean Gables, the conductor of the symphony orchestra for the Denver Fine Arts Academy."

What was he doing here? Had Tammy invited him? *Ooh!* Maybe she was dating him. He didn't look like Patty's type—too tall and too. . .um. . .proper.

"Anyway, without taking up too much of your time, I'd like to know if you'd be willing to come to the academy and audition for a spot as an oboist in the group. We only have one playing with us right now, and as you know, that's not nearly enough since we play at various venues throughout the state and even compete."

"I. . .I'm flattered." Olivia could feel the heat rise from her neck and knew her face was beet red. "Thank you. But I don't know. I'm not sure how I can. And I don't go to school there."

Tammy leapt to her rescue by handing Mr. Gables her card. "If you'll contact me on Monday, I'll be glad to discuss the details and possibly set something up with you to audition Olivia."

He placed his hat on his head and nodded sharply. "I'll be sure to do that. I'll call you Monday morning around nine o'clock if that's all right."

"Nine would be fine, Mr. Gables. Thank you so much." Tammy shook his hand, and he stepped away.

Olivia half expected him to click his heels.

"Mr. Gables, great to see you." Justin came up behind Olivia and reached out a hand.

"Hey there, young man. How are your classes this year?"

"School's great. The vocal schedule is brutal though." Justin and Mr. Gables laughed at an inside joke.

Olivia felt awkward standing there while they talked, but she couldn't just walk away either. Could she? It was that or keep standing there looking like a crazy person with nothing to add to the conversation. Time to go. "Sorry, gentlemen, I have to get to my duties. It was nice to meet you, Mr. Gables." She scurried away before they could say another word.

§

Well, if that crazy turn of events didn't warrant a cigarette, Olivia didn't know what would. She hurried out to the tree line, hoping no one followed. She could see into the Diamond Estates windows where girls milled around the tree and drank cider. They would be busy for a while—no one would miss her.

Stepping deep enough behind the trees that she could dispose of the cigarettes if someone approached, but not so far that she'd get in trouble if someone found her out there, she pulled the pack out. With trembling fingers, she dragged the gold tab around the box to cut through the plastic wrapper. She reached in and pried out one cigarette as she plucked a match she'd swiped from the kitchen out of her shoe. Striking it on the nearest tree, she smiled faintly as it lit up.

With trembling hands, Olivia placed the cigarette between her lips and prepared to draw in a breath just as the match touched the end.

"What's up, Olivia?" Justin poked his head around a tree.

Olivia shrieked and dropped the match and the cigarette on the ground. The snow extinguished the flame instantly. "You shouldn't sneak up on someone like that, Justin."

"I wouldn't say I was sneaking, exactly. I had to run home for something Mom wanted, and it was faster to go back this way." He stooped down, picked up her cigarette, and held it up in front of her face. "Were you going to smoke this?"

"*Were* being the operative word." Olivia crossed her arms. "Are you going to give me a hard time about this? It's tough to quit, you know."

Justin shook his head. "I'm sure it is. But this is against the rules, not to mention disgusting and gross. Here, see how ridiculous I look with this?" He lifted the cigarette to his lips. "Completely unattractive, isn't it?" He bent his wrist a few times in an exaggerated motion toward his mouth.

Um, wouldn't exactly say that.

He handed it back to her. "I'm going to trust you to get rid of this."

Just *that* one? "Okay, okay. I promise."

"I have to get out of here before someone comes looking for me." He jogged off toward the house. "Remember, you promised," he called over his shoulder.

Sure. Olivia smiled and held up the cigarette to show him then dropped it to the ground and crushed it.

That left nineteen more.

Chapter 22

Try to look cool or go ahead and gawk? Olivia could barely contain her excitement as she and Tammy approached the regal Symphony Hall on the grounds of the Denver Fine Arts Academy. She wrung her hands together and wiped her damp palms on her slacks. What if her hands were so sweaty when she tried to play that she dropped her oboe? The thought made her laugh, but it came out a nervous snort.

Tammy cast Olivia a few sideways glances as they walked through the parking lot toward the main entrance. "You okay? You're kind of scaring me." She signed *scared*.

"I'm fine. I'm just nervous. I've never done anything like this before." Her fingers flew like lightning to keep up with her words. "I mean, who'd have thought I'd be here, today, doing this? It's a dream come true. I can't believe it." Finally. A stroke of good luck in her life.

Tammy stopped walking and grabbed Olivia's shoulders. "Calm down. Breathe. There you go. In. Out. In. Out." She laughed. "You need to relax, kiddo. You're going to do great, but only if you keep it together."

Olivia knew Tammy was right. Deep breath. This was no big deal. Just a regular day at oboe practice. These judges she'd be auditioning in front of—they were nobody special. Make it or not. . .it didn't matter. *Sure, Olivia. Just keep telling yourself that. Maybe you'll eventually believe it.*

Tammy held the door open and stood aside to allow Olivia to step into the lobby. The lights were off, probably because there wasn't a performance that night. But even in the dark hall, the ornately framed portraits on the walls were individually lit like in a museum, casting strange shadows on the faces of the famous composers. Almost as though they frowned upon what they feared Olivia might do to their beloved compositions. She'd try not to disappoint them.

Strains of music came from the one lit hallway to their right. "I think we should go this way," Olivia whispered and pointed. She started tiptoeing toward the sounds. Did the eerie eyes in the paintings follow her movements?

Tammy tugged on her arm. "Why are you so scared? You have every right to be here—you were invited personally. Now, be confident."

She's right. This is ridiculous. Get it together. Olivia squared her shoulders, tucked her oboe under her arm, and strode for the inhabited hallway. She had no idea what she'd find, but if she were about to wander into a place she shouldn't be, then they should have given clearer instructions about where she was to go. Right?

Two gray aluminum doors beckoned at the end of the hallway. A sign on the front read AUDITIONS TODAY: ONLY ENTER BETWEEN SONGS. Not allowing her confidence to waver, Olivia listened at the door as someone played a clarinet solo. Finally, when the last note filtered through the air, she heard conversation but couldn't make out a single word. Within moments, the door swung open and a girl burst into the hallway with her hand over her mouth. She stumbled down the hall without a glance at them. What had they said to make her so upset?

Her turn. *Be confident.* Olivia pulled the door open with a little more force than necessary. No matter. Better more than not enough. She was in charge. As long as she could keep up the personal pep talk, she'd be fine. A cigarette sure wouldn't hurt though.

The room was three times, maybe four times, the size of her band room back home and proportionately cluttered and disorganized. Suddenly she felt at ease. Two tables had been pushed together into one long one across the front of the room. Six sour-faced judges—five women and Mr. Gables—sat in seats behind the table.

Now or never. And if she didn't storm right over there, she'd lose her nerve. Olivia approached the table.

Mr. Gables jumped to his feet and began pumping Olivia's hand.

"Fellow judges, this is Olivia Mansfield, the musician I was telling you about. She's amazing on that oboe. I got lost in her song and forgot to pay attention to technique—that seldom happens to me, as you know."

They nodded, and a few even cracked a little smile.

"What are you going to play for us today?" The judge on the far right consulted a clipboard.

"Oh, Olivia, would you please play that oboe solo you did the other day? Don't tell them what it is. Let's see if they can guess."

"Sure, Mr. Gables."

Olivia settled in her chair, tuned her instrument, and raised it to her lips. She began to play and, as usual, closed her eyes and lost herself in the song. As the last note wafted up toward the acoustic panels and settled around them, Olivia opened her eyes to the sound of applause.

The clipboard judge shook her head. "Clapping at an audition is highly unprofessional. I hope you'll excuse us, Miss

Mansfield. It's safe to say that we were quite moved by your performance. Thank you for coming. We'll be in touch."

Olivia stood up and glanced at Mr. Gables, hoping for assurance.

He winked.

☙

Heart thumping, Olivia sat on a bolt of electricity outside Ben's office listening to him debate with Donna, Patty, and Tammy about whether or not Olivia should be allowed to play oboe in the orchestra. Didn't they know she could hear them? They had to know. Probably wanted her to sweat it out a little.

"I just wish we'd had this meeting before she tried out." Ben's chair squeaked like it did when he leaned back all the way. "I mean, you had to know that she had a chance at making it. What did you think we would do if that happened?"

"I figured we'd work it out if it was God's will," Tammy said quietly.

Patty cleared her throat. "There are a lot of factors that we have to consider."

Olivia had never hungered for anything more than to have the opportunity Mr. Gables offered when she spoke to him on the phone just a few minutes before. Playing for the Fine Arts Academy would catapult Olivia's college plans like nothing else she could have conspired. Still shocked that the school even considered adding a nonstudent to its roster, Olivia waited for the verdict—her future hanging in the balance.

"I can't even believe we're discussing this. She's not ready!" Donna practically shouted. "She hasn't even gotten to the heart of this program yet. We can't put her out there to fend for herself. It's completely against our policies—especially the new rules. We put those into place for very important reasons. We mustn't forget that."

Olivia pictured her banging a gavel or slamming her fist down on the table.

"You make some good points, Donna." Tammy sounded like she might be weakening. "Especially with all that's gone on lately. . ."

What did she mean by that?

"I mean, if it's meant to be, the opportunity will still be there in a couple of months when the time is right for her." Donna sighed. "That's only my opinion. I don't know her like the rest of you do. I just don't want us to get sucked into the hype and let Olivia do something to jeopardize the most important thing."

Even Olivia had to admit that Donna made sense from the standpoint of the Diamond Estates program. But this was a once-in-a-lifetime opportunity. And a once-in-never chance for someone who didn't even attend the academy. They had found her a loophole to slip into the spot because homeschooled students were afforded the opportunity to participate in some extracurricular activities at area schools—Diamond Estates qualified—but Olivia would be the first Diamond girl ever to have the chance to do something like this. It was a miracle. If they said yes. Which, knowing Olivia's luck, they wouldn't.

"Tammy, you know Olivia best." Ben cleared his throat. "I'm going to leave this one up to you."

Yes! Olivia punched the air and leaned a little closer to the door, her chair wobbling as it almost dumped her on the floor.

Tammy chuckled. "I had a feeling it was going to come to that. I'm not sure what's right, but I do know this kid needs a break, and she definitely has a God-given talent. If it's really up to me, I want to let her do it."

"Okay. I'll support your decision." The rollers on Ben's chair squeaked as he scooted backward and stood up. He poked his head out of the office and beckoned for Olivia to come in.

She moved to the empty seat in Ben's office and waited, sitting on her hands to contain her excitement.

"You heard all of that, right?"

"Yeah, I did. I really appreciate this opportunity, Ben." She turned to Tammy. "I know you put your neck out for me. I won't disappoint you. I promise." Olivia touched her finger to her lip and then pressed her flattened palm over her fist.

"I know." Tammy grinned. "I'm really proud of you and think you deserve this chance. It would be sad if you had to pass it up."

"There is one other issue we have to figure out though. How are we going to get her back and forth to practices and scheduled events?" Ben pulled out his calendar. "According to Sean. . .er, Mr. Gables. . .you'll have to get to orchestra practice three times a week and concerts once or twice a month. I think we can cover the concerts because the schedule is lighter on the weekends, and since her promotion, Alicia doesn't work weekends at the hospital so she'd be available to help, too. But the practices are in the middle of the afternoon, which could be a problem."

He tapped his fingernails on the desk as he thought out loud. "We can't really let a counselor leave at those times on such a regular basis. Paying a taxi would be a ridiculous expense." Ben put his fingertips together under his chin and spun on his chair. "Maybe we can have someone run you down the mountain, and then we'll have to ask Justin to bring you home. He can find an empty room to do his homework or study after school while he waits."

"Are you sure that's wise? They really shouldn't spend time alone like that. It's inappropriate, don't you think?" Donna sat up straight. "Not to mention against the rules."

Oh wow. Kira wouldn't like it one bit. Why did that thought thrill Olivia to no end?

"I hear you. I'm concerned about that aspect, too." Ben shook his head. "We really could be asking for trouble, but I can't think of an alternative." He blew out his air with a loud *whoosh.* "I'm open to other suggestions. . . ." He looked around the group.

"I think it would be fine as long as there's someone else with them." Tammy signed even though they could hear her. "Maybe one of the more senior girls could ride down with Olivia and then hang out at practice until Justin picks them up."

Ben nodded. "Yeah. That's what they'll have to do. Maybe we could rotate girls—ask for volunteers who are far enough along in the program. They could do homework while they wait there. It would give them each a chance to get out a little more, too, and experience some culture." He looked at Tammy and Donna. "Anything else?"

"Nope. That sounds like as good of a plan as we're going to come up with." Donna sighed. "I'm not sure I like it though. Just for the record."

That was fine with Olivia. She only needed Tammy in her corner. "Thanks so much, you guys." Olivia jumped to her feet. "You're not going to regret this!"

Olivia plowed out of the room, right into Kira.

Kira stumbled back a few steps from the impact. "Hey! What's your problem?"

"Sorry!" Olivia backed away from Kira's glare. Boy, she was good at that. "I. . .I. . .oh, never mind."

Olivia scurried away to find her friends. She ran full-speed up and down several hallways before she finally found them right outside the game room. "You guys are never going to believe this." She skidded to a stop right before barreling into

Skye, who was down on one knee, tying her shoe.

"Whoa." Tricia laughed and held up a hand to block Olivia. "Hold on or we won't hear your news because we'll be in the hospital or something."

"Okay." Olivia raised one finger and leaned forward with her hands on her thighs, trying to catch her breath. "You'll. . .never believe. . .this," she panted.

"So you mentioned." Ju-Ju smirked.

"Remember my audition yesterday?" Olivia waited until they nodded. "Well, they offered me a spot in the academy orchestra."

"Oh, is that what all this is about?" Tricia waved her hand. "We all knew you'd make it. This isn't big news."

"Yeah, really. Oh, I mean, congratulations!" The corners of Skye's mouth fought against a grin as she tried to get serious.

"No. Hang on. I'm getting to it." Olivia squinted down the stairs and peeked around the game room door to make sure no one was trying to eavesdrop. "Guess how I'm going to get home from practices three times a week." She wiggled her eyebrows up and down and gave a flirtatious grin.

"No way." Skye squealed. "Justin?"

Olivia pressed a finger over Skye's lips. "Shh. No need to alert the enemy to my attack."

Ju-Ju laughed. "Well said, *and* well played." She shook her head. "Kira's going to throw such a fit she'll split her leopard leotard."

"Well, I certainly didn't set out to make this happen. And it's not like Justin offered. His dad's going to make him do it. Oh, and we won't be alone. Someone else has to be with us at all times."

"Somehow I don't think those tidbits of information are going to be of any comfort to Kira." Skye grimaced.

What was the deal with Kira? Something was going on that Olivia didn't know about. "Okay. That's it. Someone is going to have to tell me the story of what happened between those two." Olivia held out her arm to usher the girls to a private table in the game room. They all took a seat and eyed each other. No one seemed too eager to speak.

Olivia drummed her fingernails on the table. "Someone start talking."

Chapter 23

Skye looked at Tricia. Tricia turned to Ju-Ju. No one opened her mouth.

"I'm waiting." Olivia sat back in her seat with her hands behind her head like Ben.

Skye covered her mouth and giggled. "All right. You win." She sighed. Her face grew serious, and she glanced in every direction. "You just can't tell a soul, y'hear? There aren't many people who know the whole story, and they forced us to promise we wouldn't tell anyone. I think they hoped it would just go away."

"Hoped *what* would go away? I'm not just anyone off the street. Start talking." They were so close to spilling it. If Olivia backed down even an inch, they'd chicken out.

Tricia picked at her fingernails.

"Look, something happened, and I think I deserve to know what it was. I mean, I'm sort of involved, if only by default. Kira hates me because I'm the new girl. . .because Justin pays attention to me. . .because. . .why? Why does she hate me?"

Skye looked at Ju-Ju and shrugged. "You want to take it from here?"

Ju-Ju leaned forward. "Okay. Here's the deal. Kira moved in a few months ago. And oh boy, she was an even more *delightful* young lady than the one you know today." Ju-Ju rolled her eyes at Tricia, who laughed.

"Boy, ain't that the truth?" Skye nodded.

"Well, right away she started in on Justin—like day one. Every time he came around, she pretended to be weak, like she needed him to help her with something. She played poor helpless girl to a big strong man. Kira sucked him into her little web—flirted, teased, made up reasons to be near him. You know what I'm talking about."

Olivia nodded. *Yeah. Keep going.*

"He seemed to like it—to like her. I never understood why." She shuddered. "But they became sort of a thing—as much as two people could be at this place anyway."

Ju-Ju cleared her throat and leaned farther across the table. "Well, then she tried to. . .um. . .you know, with him." Ju-Ju opened her eyes wide and implored Olivia to catch on. "You *know*."

"Oh? Really?" Olivia's volume rose enough to make several girls turn and look. How could Kira have thought something like that even could have happened here? The girls were never left alone with Justin or anyone. She dropped her voice back to a whisper. "Here? At Diamond Estates?"

"Yep." Skye jumped in. "At that time it might have been a possibility, actually. There were ways to get off alone if you really wanted to. Go for walks. Hike in the woods—stuff like that. The rules got a lot stricter after Kira's junk happened. Justin used to hang around here much, much more than he does now."

"Okay. . . ?" Olivia squinted, confused. "So what happened? Did she and Justin—"

"No. Justin turned her down flat, and she stormed off mad as a hornet. End of story." Tricia averted her eyes.

"That's it? That can't be it." Olivia waited. There had to be more to it.

Ju-Ju shook her head. "No, the story isn't finished. Hang on. So the day after that happened, I found her in the downstairs bathroom—the one off the main hallway."

"Yeah, that's where I had my first encounter with her, too. Was she crying?"

"Nope. She was taking a pregnancy test."

No! "What? You have *got* to be kidding me." Kira couldn't be pregnant. If she was, that would mean. . .

"Hold on." Ju-Ju held up her hand. She checked behind her and to both sides before dropping her voice to a whisper. "This is where the whole thing gets crazy. Not that it wasn't already. The test was positive. I could see the big blue plus sign all the way from the doorway. They never did find out how she got a pregnancy test into the house."

Exactly how I got the cigarettes in here, that's how. But who cared about the stupid test? *Get on with the story.* Olivia scooted to the edge of her seat and leaned in. "Then what happened?"

"Turns out, Kira had been pregnant since before she came to Diamond Estates, and she'd been trying to set things up to name Justin as the baby's daddy. Luckily he didn't fall for it, or things might have turned out much differently. If he'd had sex with her, he'd never have known the baby wasn't his." Ju-Ju raised her eyebrows and waited.

It sounded like a soap opera. "Wow. I can't wrap my brain around how someone could be so cold." Olivia closed her eyes. "So Kira is pregnant?"

"Hang with me a little longer. I'm about to wrap it up." Ju-Ju glanced around her. "So later that day—after I found her with the test—I overheard her tell one of her friends that she planned to try to get an abortion without telling anyone, since she couldn't snag Justin. I have no idea how she would have pulled it off, but that was her plan. She probably would have found a way, knowing her." Ju-Ju snapped her gum. "So I told Ben."

"You did?" Olivia's mouth fell open.

"I had to. I might not like Kira, but I don't want *anyone* to have to go through the aftereffects of an abortion—even her." Ju-Ju's eyes clouded, and she clenched her fists. "Trust me, you never get over it. I wouldn't wish that on my worst enemy. Not to mention the fact that there was an innocent baby whose life was on the line."

Hmm. Did Ju-Ju know that from personal experience? Olivia would have to revisit the abortion issue with her some other time. "So it's true? Kira is pregnant right now?"

"No. As luck would have it—"

"More likely divine intervention." Tricia looked around the room.

"Right on, T." Ju-Ju nodded. "Kira had a miscarriage before it went on much longer. She lost a lot of blood and was in the hospital for a few days. But, physically, she's fine now. Emotionally, not so much."

The hospital? "That must have been when I came for my first visit. Justin said someone was in the hospital, and Ben was bringing her home that day."

"Yep. That would have been Kira." Ju-Ju smirked. "Great timing, huh?"

"Yeah. That explains why she was sobbing in the bathroom. I caught her in a private moment. Explains a lot, actually. But wait. I thought you had to, quote, 'want to change' to be allowed to come here. How could someone who really wanted help do something so devious?"

Tricia sighed. "There's no telling what goes on in someone's head. She convinced herself that her situation was special, and she would have done anything she could have to get out of it or make it okay somehow. It's easy to justify bad actions when you're under fire like she felt, you know?"

That was the most Olivia had heard Tricia say at one time. "I guess. But seduction, abortion, deception? That's pretty huge. And she's only, what, sixteen?"

"She's seventeen as of a few weeks ago. Not that age matters. She's a troubled soul." Skye's face softened. "I try to remember to pray for her every day. We all should."

Ju-Ju shook her head and gazed at Skye then patted her hand. "Sweet, simple little Skye."

"What? Are you saying we shouldn't pray for Kira?"

"Nope. I just think you put a little too much stock in the hope of answered prayers and too little trust in your own common sense. But that's just my opinion."

"Whatever. I'd rather have extra faith and believe in people than be tough as nails."

"Okay. Now's not the time to fight. I need you to stay with me here." Olivia shook her head. It didn't make sense. "I don't get it, you guys. I wasn't here for any of this. I'm the new girl. What did I ever do to make Kira hate me besides catch her crying?"

"Ah!" Skye held up her finger. "It's not what *you* did, sugar. It's what Justin does every time he sees you."

Tricia giggled.

"Huh? What does he do?"

"Come on, chica." Ju-Ju tilted her head and squinted. "You can't seriously be trying to tell us that you don't see him look at you differently than he looks at the rest of us. Really?"

"Differently how?" If they saw it, too, then it might actually be real. *Don't blush.* But what if Ben or Tammy—or worse, Donna—saw it?

"Like the sun's coming up behind you." Skye's face softened, and she batted her long eyelashes. "Like you're the first woman he's ever seen. Like. . .like he could devour you."

"Giiirl. From the looks of things, you read a few too many of those contraband romance books your daddy tried to hide from you." Tricia fanned Skye's face with a notebook.

Ju-Ju stared at Skye then turned back to Olivia, shaking her head. "Anyway. He looks at you like you're special. He watches you. If we see it, Kira must see it, too. But who cares about her?"

"Did I hear my name?" Kira peeked around the corner and flashed her dimples as she came through the door. She posed with her hands on her hips like she'd just completed a gymnastics routine.

"I don't think you did." Ju-Ju didn't exactly lie.

Oh no. What had Kira heard? It couldn't have been much because the door just opened. "Ju-Ju said, 'Who cares.' Maybe that's what you heard." It wasn't really a lie, was it? More of an evasion.

"Okay. Well, if you decide to talk about me, let me know." She grinned. "I'll join you—I'm my favorite subject." Kira sashayed away.

"Ugh. She grates on my last nerve." Ju-Ju gritted her teeth.

"Yeah. That girl's meaner'n a snake."

"But you think we should pray for her, right, Skye?" Tricia snorted.

" 'Course we should. It's the Christian thing to do."

"But you guys, she's had it in for me since I had a little clash with her when I visited a few months ago. She didn't like me then, and that couldn't have had anything to do with Justin."

Ju-Ju nodded. "Fresh meat—new competition. That's all the reason Kira needs to start hating someone. Time only makes it worse."

Olivia threw her hands up in the air. "So what do you think I should do about Justin?"

"Don't *do* anything. Keep being yourself." Ju-Ju peered around the room. "And watch your back."

Chapter 24

"Cool. Nap time." Ju-Ju dove into the backseat.

Olivia climbed into the front seat beside Justin. "Hey. I thought Marilyn was going to be driving me down to practice."

"Oh, you're stuck with me today." Justin's eyes sparkled. "I had a half day."

Stuck? Hardly. "What are you going to do while I'm at practice, Ju?"

"Probably more sleep. If not"—she wriggled her arms out of her puffy coat and balled it up beneath her head—"I brought a book."

"How about you?" Olivia turned to Justin. What if he said he planned to just wait in the van? She'd feel horrible.

"I have a grocery list for Mom and stuff Marilyn needs for the center. That will take me at least as long as your practice."

"Okay. I just—I feel bad taking up so much of everyone's time." Olivia looked down.

"Don't think anything of it. If I wasn't driving you, I'd be shoveling manure in the barn or something."

Eww. "I'm curious, do you ever get tired of helping so much? Do you ever get to have fun?"

Ju-Ju let out a big snore.

Olivia giggled.

"I think if I didn't believe in the importance of Diamond Estates then I might feel differently, but I love it. I feel like we're missionaries with a purpose that God has called our family to. I'm proud to be able to be a part of it in whatever way I can."

Olivia nodded. She couldn't remember a time when helping someone else had been rewarding like that. Would she sacrifice so much for God's work? Probably not. Olivia had to admit that she and the other girls complained nonstop. That had to be wearing on the staff who had sacrificed so much to be there for them—from what she heard, they didn't get paid that much. Olivia vowed to stop the griping. She'd do her part happily from now on. Or at least try to.

"Most kids our age can't stand to be around their parents so much. But you're with yours all the time, and you don't seem to mind. How come?"

"I think Dad's amazing—it's inspiring to watch him work. I know my mom wishes she could be around more though. But she's doing her part in a different way." Justin pulled the van under an awning in front of Symphony Hall. "Here we are."

Olivia reached back and nudged Ju-Ju. "Come on, sleepyhead. You can continue your nap in the theater." They climbed from the car and waved as Justin pulled away.

The car squealed to a stop and backed up. The window came down, and Justin leaned across the seat, making eye contact with Olivia. "Knock 'em dead." The window buzzed up, and he drove away.

"Earth to Olivia." Ju-Ju waved her hand in front of Olivia's face. "Hellooo?"

"Huh? What?" Olivia shook her head in an unsuccessful attempt to free Justin from her thoughts.

"Oh boy. You've got it bad, girlfriend." Ju-Ju shook her head and pulled open the door for Olivia.

"I don't have anything bad."

I've got it good.

ॐ

"I can't believe you're going to miss free day." Tricia rolled over in her bed at ten o'clock in the morning. She stretched her arms over her head and yawned.

"Oh, I didn't miss it. Sleeping in is the best part of the day." Olivia latched her oboe case. "Next to that is staying up late tonight—I'll be back in plenty of time for that. Besides, after all these weeks of cramming to learn the music for the holiday concert, an actual performance will be a nice change." Plus, since it was the weekend, Justin would probably be driving her. She zipped her jacket over her sparkly red dress, grabbed her music folder, and waved to her roommates.

"Have fun." Skye winked. "Don't do nothin' I wouldn't do, y'hear?"

"That leaves the door wide open for just about anything." Tricia ducked under her covers as Skye threw a pillow at her.

"Break a leg?" Ju-Ju squinted through her sleepy eyes at the bright light. "Do people still say that?"

"I don't know, but I'll take it." Olivia bustled out of the room and hurried down the stairs toward the conference room to make a quick phone call to Mom before heading out.

Tammy waited in the conference room to set up the call as they'd prearranged. Her laptop sat open on the table. "Here you go, Liv. There are some people who wish to see you." She grinned and held out a hand toward the chair.

Olivia stepped over to the seat in front of the computer and sat down to peer at the screen. People? She gasped when she saw a face looking back at her. How cool! They'd never had video for their calls before.

"Olivia?" Mom sounded breathless—like she'd been running around. Knowing her, she probably couldn't get the computer set up and thought she'd be late.

"Yep. It's me, Mom."

"Okay. Hang on. I have a surprise for you."

Another surprise? Hang on? She didn't have all day—why waste the time they did have? Olivia waited while Mom did something on the keyboard.

A window popped up asking if a third party could be accepted into the chat session and be viewable by webcam. Huh? The instant she clicked ACCEPT, the window on her screen split and Mom moved into the right-side window as the left window came into focus.

"Hello?" A familiar male voice came through before the picture's pixels caught up to real time.

Olivia's heart skipped. "Jake? Is that you?"

"It's me, sis. It's so good to talk to you. The school has this cool voice-to-text software so I can read what you say." Jake squinted. "Oh, there you are. I can see you now. You look beautiful. How are you?"

"I'm fine now. I missed you both, but I hadn't realized just how much until I actually saw you." Olivia sniffled.

"Don't cry, sweetie. This is a big day for you. A happy day." Mom grinned.

Wow. She remembered? "I wish you guys could be here."

"We wish that, too." Jake cleared his throat. "Liv? I just want you to know how proud I am of you." He put his fingertips up to the webcam so she could reach out and touch them on her screen.

Olivia waited for Mom to chime in. No words came. Oh well. Baby steps. "I can't believe I have to make this short, but I really have to go." The tears fell in earnest.

"It's okay. We'll be talking in a few days for Christmas. Give it all you've got today, sweetheart."

"I love you, Liv." Jake's piercing eyes came through the camera.

"I love you, too. Both of you."

The line went dead.

ᔪ

"Morning. Who's coming with us today?" Olivia smiled at Justin from her perch on the foyer bench, where she waited for him for once. "My mom is, actually. We have some last-minute Christmas gifts to buy in town, and since everyone else has a free day, we decided to go together. She's already sitting all the way in the back making some work calls so she can be freed up the rest of the day."

"Okay. I'll force myself to behave, then." Like she'd have the guts to do anything else. She could barely formulate a coherent sentence when talking to Justin.

Why could she talk to her friends nonstop all day long, then get in the presence of Justin and have nothing intelligent to say at all? Forget intelligent—she'd settle for interesting. Or even mildly amusing. He would think she was a big bore if she didn't spark up a little. She climbed into her seat and waved at Alicia.

"Hi, sweetie. I'm on hold." She pointed to the phone in her hand. "Oh. Yep. This is she." Alicia turned away.

"What's wrong? You seem kind of sad." Justin studied her after they turned onto the road.

Oh, other than missing my mom and brother, nothing. "Oh, I'm fine. I guess it just feels strange to be doing something this important without any family or friends here or anything." She reddened. "I mean, no offense. It's just. . ."

"No offense taken at all. I'd probably feel that way, too. I'll cheer extra loud for you, okay?" Justin's cheeks turned a touch pink.

Time to change the subject. "So how did you get into music and performing?"

"Oh, I've loved to sing since I was a little boy. It's just part of me. And when you go to church as much as I have in my life, you get plenty of chances to practice singing if you even remotely want to." Justin flipped the turn signal then peeked at Olivia. "How about you? The oboe?"

"For me, it was the sound it made. It seemed to echo my soul. It thinks. It feels." Olivia looked out the side window. *It hurts.* "That probably sounds stupid. But it's true. I feel like it speaks for me. It says things I'd like to say but can't, either because no one's listening or because I don't have the guts to say them." *Ugh! Stop talking.*

"That's one of the best descriptions of an instrument I've ever heard." Justin's gorgeous blue eyes twinkled. "You know what? I can't wait to see you play it again now that I know what it means to you."

Olivia clamped her mouth shut as her cheeks flamed. He was just toying with her. He couldn't possibly be serious.

Justin maneuvered the van between some construction cones into the parking lot and drove up to the awning by the main entrance. "I'm going to let you off here and go take care of some things. I'll be back in plenty of time for the concert. Okay?"

"I do appreciate you coming. But I hope you don't feel like you have to." Olivia turned away. "I mean, you've been driving me to all my practices, and now this, too. I'll be fine if you just want to pick me up when it's over." She peeked at his face to gauge his response. *Please say you'll come.*

"Absolutely not. I can't wait to see it. It's been a year or more since I've been to one of these shows. Plus I get extra credit." He winked and gave her a smile that flipped her belly like a pancake.

Olivia knocked on the back window and waved to Alicia

before the van pulled away.

⟲

Hands shaking, Olivia took her seat to the right of the other oboist. The first-chair violinist stood and directed Olivia to play the tuning A, as was the customary role for the first-chair oboist. She lifted her instrument to her lips and let out a long, solid note. The orchestra erupted in a melee of sounds as the other instruments strove to match her tone. The violinist motioned for Olivia to hit the note one more time. Satisfied, he sat down, and they waited silently for the conductor.

Olivia gazed around the packed auditorium. She'd ask someone how many seats there were if she remembered later. A balcony wrapped around both sides and the back, and she counted six sections on the sloped floor. Something caught her eye in the far left corner. *Ju-Ju?* Olivia's heart raced as she realized that the people in three rows of seats were waving at her. By her best estimation, the entire gang from Diamond Estates—all twenty-three girls, the three counselors, and Ben and Alicia—had come to see her play. Where was Justin? *Oh, there he is.* Olivia spotted him making his way to a seat beside his mom.

What an amazing surprise. Justin and Alicia must have driven all the way back up the mountain to get everyone. No one had ever done anything like that for her before. Why would he go to so much trouble for her? He must pity her, or maybe his dad made him. On second thought, Ben obviously went along with the plan, but Olivia doubted he had forced Justin to do it. It seemed more Justin's style—thoughtful and sensitive. He'd probably have done it for anyone though—she wasn't anything special to him. Or was she?

⟲

The last symphonic measure filled the auditorium and faded

away to an explosion of applause. Olivia opened her eyes, aware of the audience for the first time since the performance had begun. They were on their feet. Every single one of them. The sound was nothing like the polite applause from the video-camera-wielding parents in the school gym after the band concerts twice a year. This was the real thing.

Olivia stood to her feet along with the rest of the orchestra and took a bow. The curtain lowered slowly and turned the thunderous applause into a dull roar. She fell back in her seat and listened to the sound. She'd always played for the love of the music, the way it affected her soul. But the standing ovation, the approval of the crowd, moved her even more. Not because they cheered for her—but because it meant that she'd had a part in reaching them, too. It meant something. Skill, talent, hard work, practice—it all meant something. To her and to them.

Olivia gasped. She was alone backstage, save for a few stragglers. How much time had passed? Everyone would be waiting for her. She packed up her oboe, gathered her things, and walked across the stage to the back door. She turned one last time to see the place where she'd found her true calling. Home.

She hurried through the back hallway to the lobby where they were probably waiting for her. There! They huddled in the back corner and waved as she approached.

Each of them reached behind their backs and pulled out a single red rose. Everyone, that is, except for two people. Justin, because he was nowhere to be found.

And Kira.

Chapter 25

Wake up!" Skye bounced on her bed and reached over to pull up the window shade, which flapped open, bright light flooding the room.

"What are you doing?" Ju-Ju covered her head with a pillow and turned her back.

"Merry Christmas, everyone!" Skye flopped back on her bed, the shiny waves of her hair flowing out beneath her head. "I just love Christmas."

"Funny, I just love sleep," Tricia murmured and dove under her covers.

"Okay. You guys sleep. I'm going downstairs to see if I can help Marilyn with the homemade cinnamon rolls." Skye jumped down from her bunk. "You've seriously never tasted anything like them. We only have them on Christmas." She paused. "I take that back. We had them last Thanksgiving, too. But still."

"Last Thanksgiving? You mean you've been here since—" Olivia noticed Tricia shaking her head with her finger pressed to her lips. Olivia closed her mouth and waited until Skye had scampered off for the kitchen—still in her peppermint-striped pj's.

"What's the deal?" Olivia propped up on an elbow. "Has she really been here since before last Thanksgiving?" Why didn't Olivia know this already? Come to think of it, she didn't have very much information at all about Skye's past. Strange, since she'd been Skye's roommate for more than six weeks.

"Yeah. Skye's in no real hurry to leave Diamond Estates." Tricia cringed. "It's kind of a sore spot with her though."

"What do you mean? Why doesn't she want to go home?" Not that Olivia could blame her. She tried to remember Skye phoning her parents since she'd been there. Not a single call came to mind. No letters either.

"She has no home to go to. At least not anymore." Tricia grimaced. "I don't want to gossip about her."

"Fine. Then I will." Ju-Ju groaned and sat up. "Skye got herself kicked out before she came here. Her dad thinks she's a disgrace, and he disowned her. She isn't welcome back at home."

"But I thought her dad was a preacher." How could a parent do something like that? Let alone a pastor?

"He is. He forgets to listen when he teaches about forgiveness. Don't matter. She don't need them. We're her family now." Ju-Ju pounded her chest with her fist.

What about when Skye graduated from the program? Where would she go? "How long will Ben and Alicia let her stay here? Do girls ever stay all the way until they graduate high school?"

"Well, the program is designed so that once you're finished, you go back home and reenter your old school. But they'll never kick her out of Diamond Estates if she has nowhere to go." Tricia unfolded her long, lean body from her bunk and padded off to the bathroom, holding on to the waistband of her drooping pants.

Had she lost weight?

"This is home for me, too. I won't be leaving anytime soon." Ju-Ju flopped back onto her pillow. "That's life."

Olivia lay back with her hands behind her head. She

couldn't believe what she'd heard. The more she learned, the more it became apparent that everyone had a story. . .and a need.

The door flung open and banged on the wall behind it. Skye barreled in and shouted, "Come on, you guys! You're never going to believe it! You've gotta see this!" The door slammed shut behind her as she twirled into the room.

Skye pulled Olivia from the bed.

"Okay. Okay. Just let me brush my teeth first." It was tough to deny Skye anything.

"Hurry. Hurry!"

"Simmer down, shortcake." Ju-Ju smiled and pulled a sweatshirt over her head. "What's the big rush anyway? It's not like we're seven and can't wait to see what Santa brought."

Skye gave a mischievous grin and tapped her foot. "Oh yes, you are. Come on. Y'all are slower'n molasses." She bounced up and down, barely containing her excitement.

"What's going on?" Tricia came out of the bathroom with a plastic shower cap covering her hair.

"You showered?" Skye squealed. "Y'all have no idea what you're missing. Hurry it up."

BANG! BANG! BANG! BANG!

"Merry Christmas!" Shouts and bells filled the hall outside their room.

"Wha–?"

Their door rattled as someone pounded on it. "Come on, girls!" It sounded like Patty.

"That's it." Ju-Ju pulled on her shoes. "Even I want to see what's up." She pulled the door open with Olivia, Skye, and Tricia close at her heels.

All the girls were lined up in the hallway—except for the five who were far enough along in their program they were allowed to travel home for the holiday. Most looked confused; some were dressed and eager—like Skye—while others were still in pajamas, rubbing their eyes as they shuffled toward the stairs. A jumble of Merry Christmases rang throughout the group as they made their way down to. . .somewhere.

When they arrived at the library door, Patty made them wait for Tammy, Donna, Ben, and Alicia. What on earth was going on? Why did red and green construction paper cover the window and block their view into the room? Confused, she looked to her right and saw that the door to the dining room was covered the same way. She nudged Ju-Ju. "Why do you think the dining room, too?"

"You know that wall between them?"

Olivia nodded.

"It's removable. It kind of collapses and slides into the back wall." Ju-Ju tried to peek behind a loose corner of the paper. "What do they have cooked up? Guarantee you, it's Alicia's doing, whatever it is. She's the creative one. She always tries to make things like holidays and birthdays special so we don't feel bad."

"Merry Christmas!" Ben and Alicia, costumed as shepherds, poked their heads around the corner. Justin, dressed in normal clothes, looking scruffy and unshaven—yet somehow even more gorgeous than usual—shuffled closely behind, stifling a yawn.

Ben pulled a lamb on a leash.

Olivia did a double take. It wasn't exactly a leash, but there certainly was a small lamb trailing behind Ben, trying to pull at the rope that tugged him along.

Alicia motioned for them to follow. "Come! Let's go see the baby Jesus. Born in Bethlehem. Born to take away the sins of the world."

The girls pressed in behind them and filled the library in stunned silence.

In front of the roaring fire, lay a baby in a manger, wrapped in threadbare cloths, playing with his chubby feet. Gazing down upon his sweet little cherub face were Mary and Joseph. Joseph stood like a proud daddy behind his wife, who knelt beside her baby's bed. Flanking them stood the shepherds and wise men with their gifts. Lambs, chickens, and even a goat filled the bright room.

Ben opened the french doors to the huge porch and let the falling snow fill the doorway as carolers in a sleigh drawn by two horses approached the house. *Wait a second.* Those weren't horses; they were reindeer.

The carolers began singing "Away in a Manger." No one moved while the sweet song and rich harmonies floated on the snowflakes. Olivia had never seen anything so holy or heard anything so pure. The singers climbed down from the sleigh and entered the house, continuing to sing. The girls joined them in "O Holy Night" and then "Silent Night."

Ben spoke up from behind the nativity scene. "Carolers, thank you so much for filling our home with festive praise this morning." He led the group in a round of applause. "We'd love for you to join us for breakfast. We also welcome some of our family members who are here to celebrate the holiday with us. Now, shall we? We're going to step into this winter wonderland"—he gestured to the wall that Alicia was sliding open—"to partake of a decadent Christmas morning meal while gazing upon the live scene of our Savior's birth."

The wall squeezed together like an accordion and latched into place. The scene on the other side was another world entirely. The floor was blanketed with inches of real-looking snow. A snowman stood in the corner, and the reindeer had been led in to feast from a trough near a decorative sleigh. The sounds of tinkling bells and Christmas songs filled the air.

Everyone scurried for a seat. Extra chairs had been set at each table to accommodate their guests. Once everyone was seated, Ben stood in front of them and smiled. "I just love Christmastime at Diamond Estates. I'm reminded why we're here. Why Alicia and I do what we do. It refocuses my mind and my purpose for the coming year. I pray it will do the same for you this year. Let's enjoy this meal together after we give thanks to God."

He lifted his hands and looked down on the baby in the manger with love in his eyes. "Precious Lord Jesus. Our Savior. Our God who became flesh to live with us. Thank You. Thank You for leaving Your heavenly home, the presence of Your Father, to come to us in this evil, sin-filled world. I don't know that I could have done it. That's why You're God and I'm not. Thank You.

"Lord, we pray for our loved ones we are unable to be with today. We pray that their Christmas morning is as rich and bright as ours is here today. Remind them, as You've so elegantly reminded us, that this day is about Your Son, Jesus. Let us all honor You in everything we say or do this day. Please bless this rich, delicious meal to our bodies in remembrance of You. Amen."

"Amen." Olivia reached for her cloth napkin to dab at her eyes and noticed that most everyone else did, too. There was a certain sense. . .something palpable. Was that the presence of God? It felt peaceful. She felt loved. If only she could take that feeling with her always.

More strangers sailed through the swinging doors with trays of piping hot food resting on their shoulders. They went to each table and served the food onto the fine-china place settings in front of the diners. "Who are all these people?" Olivia whispered to Ju-Ju.

"Some of them are family members of a few of the girls—
the ones who were allowed to have visitors come. The others
are people from church. It's really cool of them to come here on
Christmas morning like this." Ju-Ju leaned back so her crystal
goblet could be filled with orange juice. She flipped open her
napkin and placed it in her lap. "I think they all contributed
their china sets on loan, too. That probably makes you feel at
home, huh?"

"Wow. They left their families at home to come serve
us?" No one had ever gone to any trouble like that for Olivia
before—not that she could remember anyway.

She glanced at Skye. How hard this day must be for her
most of all. In Olivia's case, she wouldn't have wanted to go
home even if she had earned the privilege. Ju-Ju had no home
to go to, and Tricia had a little ways to go before she'd earn the
right to travel away for a weekend. But Skye had a family at
home celebrating without her. They didn't want her. What was
she thinking about as she watched the reindeer foraging in the
trough? Probably imagining the Christmases of her youth—
when she was wanted. . .loved. Years when she wore smaller
versions of her peppermint pajamas and smiled a toothless grin
for the camera while she opened gifts.

"It's weird." The corners of Skye's mouth turned up ever so
slightly. "I can picture my little brothers diving at the presents
under the tree. I can almost smell the hot cocoa my mom has
simmering in the kitchen."

Olivia felt her heart would break as she imagined the
magnitude of Skye's suffering. Olivia had lost her dad—she
knew the pain of endless grief. But the thought of having
parents alive, on the earth, who had no interest in her, who had
sent her away—unfathomable. "Do you hate them, Skye? Your
mom and dad?"

"No. No." Skye raised her watery gaze to Olivia's eyes. "I feel sorry for them."

How could Skye be so kind and happy all the time? She'd probably say it was Jesus in her. But how? And how could Olivia have that same thing for herself?

"Oh no." Olivia snapped out of it as trays of goodies passed by. "I can feel my muffin top coming back as we speak." Biscuits and ladles full of sausage gravy. Thick french toast with powdered sugar sprinkled all over it. Homemade donuts and bowls of fruit. Seasoned potatoes and scrambled eggs. Delicate crepes filled with strawberries or blueberries. Every time Olivia thought they had to be done bringing things out, more appeared.

Skye eyed the tray of still-steaming cinnamon rolls. "Honey, no diet is strong enough for this. Besides, it's Christmas."

A man wearing a chef's hat wheeled out a cart with a succulent glazed ham in the center and a carving knife beside it. He paused beside the first table and sliced a piece for each plate. Good thing the music played—otherwise the room would have been silent except for the clinking silverware.

Olivia gazed around the table and felt warmth fill her heart. As usual, Ju-Ju rolled her eyes at something naive Skye said in her Southern drawl, and Tricia gave a radiant smile then shrank back into her shyness. They each had their special qualities. . .and their pain. She couldn't have asked for more perfect roommates. They had become her family. What would she do when they left or when she did? *Don't think about that right now. It's Christmas.*

She lifted her eyes to take in the rest of the room. Directly across from her sat Ben and Alicia with Justin between them. He took a bite of the gooey cinnamon roll then glanced up and caught Olivia's gaze. The corners of his mouth turned up, and his eyes crinkled. *Merry Christmas.* He mouthed the words with his sticky lips and tipped his glass of orange juice toward her.

Olivia blinked once and gave a soft smile. *You, too.*

He turned to respond to something his mom said while Olivia let her wistful eyes rove the room again. Everyone looked so happy, and warmth filled her belly once more—contentment. Just as she was about to fork another bite, her gaze stopped dead on a bitter face.

Kira.

If looks could kill.

🌀

Trudging up the hill with a group of girls to the pasture beyond the barn, Olivia filled her lungs with the crisp mountain air. For once she didn't even want to ruin it with a cigarette. At least not at that moment. Why hadn't she seen the beauty around her before this? The snowcapped trees whose limbs gave out under the weight and dumped a fresh pile of snow every few minutes. The crackling fire where Ben was burning some brush. The horses whinnying in the pasture as they stood for their saddles in anticipation of the upcoming ride.

Olivia mounted Cinnamon, her favorite mare. They had a special bond, so Olivia chose her whenever she could. Cinnamon pranced around the corral, as eager to get going as Olivia. Steam rose from the horse's mouth as her warm breath mingled with the frigid January air. She snorted and whinnied, begging for freedom.

Finally, Ben released the gate and let them out for their ride. "You have a walkie?" he called to Justin, who led the group.

"Yep, channel two, Dad."

Ben waved them on and patted Cinnamon's flank as they passed him. "Have a nice ride."

Since there weren't enough horses for everyone, the rest of

the girls had free time and those who wanted to would get to ride later that day. Olivia felt bad to leave anyone behind on such a beautiful afternoon. She couldn't think of anywhere she'd rather be or anything she'd rather be doing.

The snow crunched beneath Cinnamon's hooves as she followed the horse in front of her up a steady grade. Olivia let Cinnamon handle things and closed her eyes to feel the wind on her cheeks. It smelled heavenly—a heady blend of the bonfire smoke that had wafted up from the ground below and pungent evergreen needles.

They came to a small clearing where the horses spread out a bit. Olivia let Cinnamon roam as she wished. She listened to the forest noises and imagined the wildlife in the trees around and above her. A whole different world. Someone had to have created all of it. There was no way it was an accident. No way.

"There you are." Justin's voice startled Olivia out of her thoughts.

"Oh, you scared me. You seem to do that a lot."

"We almost went on. Luckily I took a count. Not that I wouldn't have noticed you were missing eventually." Justin blushed.

"Oh?" Olivia tipped her head coyly. "You'd have noticed?" Where had that come from? She wasn't a flirt. The thin mountain air must have given her an extra dose of self-confidence.

" 'Course I'd have noticed. I'm too afraid of my dad to leave someone behind." Justin winked and rode away.

"Giddyap, girl. Follow that horse."

Chapter 26

Olivia picked at her breakfast and spread it around on her plate, trying to look like she was actually eating the fattening fare she'd been trying to avoid since Christmas. "Uh-oh. Here comes Patty." Olivia popped a bite of scrambled egg into her mouth.

Ju-Ju and Skye munched on their bagels, and Tricia drank some juice.

"What's up, Patty?" Ju-Ju asked with her mouth full.

"Morning, girls." Patty pulled up a chair and sat on it facing backward. "I just wanted to talk to Olivia for a sec. The service coordinator from church called. The woman who usually does sign language is pretty sick and won't be going today, and her usual backup is out of town. We were wondering if you'd be willing to sign on stage for this morning's service."

In front of all those people? Olivia's stomach flopped.

"Oh, you should totally do it, Liv." Skye grinned.

Signing definitely *was* something she loved to do, and Jake would be so proud. And maybe getting involved at church in some way would help her figure things out. "Sure. I'll give it a try. Sounds like fun." *Gulp!*

"Great. You'll just go wait right where the signer usually sits in the front row and then take her spot whenever it's time. I'll let the coordinator know about the change." Patty started to leave.

Olivia bit her lip. "But will they mind?"

Patty furrowed her eyebrows. "Mind about what?"

"Well, that I'm. . .you know."

"That you're what? A teenager? No, they love using the youth for service things."

"That's not really what I meant." Olivia swallowed. "I mean, will they mind that I'm a Diamond girl? Don't they think I'm kind of. . .um. . .troubled?"

"Oh." Patty waved a dismissive hand. "Olivia, everyone starts off troubled when they don't have Jesus. The day you decided to get help, you weren't *troubled* any longer; you were *seeking*. You're on your path." Patty nodded. "Trust me, it'll be fine. You might even get something out of it. Now, I have to go round everyone up. We're pulling out in five minutes." She jogged out of the room.

Appetite replaced by nerves, Olivia dumped the remains of her breakfast into the garbage can on her way to her room and picked up her pace. If she had to stand up in front of everyone, she'd better look herself over once more.

Olivia pirouetted in the full-length mirror attached to the back of the bathroom door in her room. Her black pants fit fine—nice, actually. The violet sweater was the perfect color for her dark features. It went great with her dark hair and her streak. *Oops*. Maybe it would be wise to hide the streak when she'd be standing up in front of the whole church so no one would judge her a rebel.

Olivia rummaged for a pin in her box of hair supplies. She gathered the clump of purple hairs and twisted them under a layer of black then secured the knot with the bobby pin. There. That seemed more appropriate—for this occasion anyway. Her roots had grown out enough that the purple was completely hidden.

After the drive down the mountain and the trek across the huge parking lot, it was almost an hour later when Olivia padded into the church in the middle of the pack of twenty-four teens. She felt on display for a different reason this time. Could they see her nerves? She clenched her trembling hands into fists as they made their way up the center aisle and over to their seats on the right.

This time Olivia didn't crawl into a seat, stepping over her roommates' feet as she usually did. Instead she sat in the very front row, looking at her sweaty hands, waiting for the service to begin. It would have been a great time to pray—if she did that sort of thing. Why was it so difficult for her to call out to God? Even in church. She'd obviously done it before, but now, every time she seemed to get closer to grasping Him, He slipped away. Or she did.

The musicians took their places and began an instrumental segment as people filed in—her cue to take her place. She rose from her seat and made her way to the stage.

As the worship band started to sing, Olivia started to sign. Her body took over for her head, and she forgot her nerves. Her hands and arms moved, communicating words that had grown unfamiliar to her. Praising God? Hallelujah? What did it all mean?

From her vantage point on the stage, it was amazing to see the people as they worshipped—Pastor had said to worship God in spirit and truth. That had to be what she saw before her. Eyes closed, some with a hand in the air, swaying their bodies to the music as they focused on God. It was a beautiful sight. Even the hearing-impaired folks in the first few rows seemed to feed off of her emotion. She began to sway her own body so they could get the feel of the music. With her movements, the bass even she could feel through the floor, and the words that seemed to be familiar to them, some of them even closed their eyes while they sang along by memory. By then, it seemed like everyone in the place had their eyes closed.

Whoops. Everyone, that is, except for one person.

Justin.

His lips weren't moving in song. His hands hung limp beside his hips. His body stood rigid and unmoving. He simply stared. At her.

Olivia peered a little closer, trying to read his expression. Was he angry that she was onstage, knowing about her recent past? *No.* Justin wasn't that judgmental. Did he think she was weird for doing sign language like that? *No.* That sure didn't seem like Justin either. What was he thinking as he watched her? Olivia couldn't tear her eyes away.

Maybe all he could think about was how unattractive she had looked with a cigarette between her lips. That was what he had said about smokers. Disgusting. Gross. Unattractive. *That's it. No more smoking.* Not only did she want to avoid looking gross to Justin, but she also wanted to move forward with good things in her life. Smoking, sneaking things, and being a slave to nicotine weren't going to help her do that. It was time. She'd said that before—about a lot of things—but it really was. Time for change.

Justin gave an almost imperceptible shake of his head as if clearing his thoughts. A smile lit up his face and crinkled his twinkling blue eyes. He nodded once at Olivia then shut his eyes as he sang the worship song.

Olivia's gaze shifted a few rows up and to the right of where Justin sat. Her heart sank as she saw Kira looking at the row behind her. Olivia didn't have to wonder too long to figure out who had caught Kira's attention.

Kira inched her shoulders back toward the front and shot

Olivia a venomous glare that felt like it could burn holes right through her.

Her hands raised in midsign, Olivia faltered. She lost her place and had to pause to pick it up again a few words later. Kira lifted her chin with a smug look on her face. She might have messed her up once, but Olivia had no intention of giving Kira the satisfaction of looking at her again. She needed to focus on what she was there to do and the people who needed her. Not Justin. And certainly not Kira. That girl didn't deserve a moment's pause from Olivia.

Now, focus. Too bad Jake couldn't see her like this. He'd be so proud. Mom, too, most likely. Maybe the service was video recorded and she could send them a copy. *Argh. Focus, Olivia.*

The pastor took the podium as the bars of the last worship song faded into the air. The musicians continued to play background instrumentals as he prayed.

Olivia tried to get every word of his prayer just right. He spoke quickly—his words tumbling out much faster than the words to the songs had. She enjoyed the challenge—good practice, like oiling rusty hinges. After the prayer, when the congregation sat down, Olivia sat on a stool, but it still felt strange to be alone and exposed, above the people's line of vision. Thank heaven she hadn't worn a skirt.

Other than her select audience, most weren't watching her as she continued signing through the service. But two people hadn't peeled their eyes from her. Kira and Justin. Olivia tried not to look, but she felt their very opposite stares. One enthralled her; one terrified her.

Oh boy. What had she gotten herself into?

ॐ

The game room door flew open and banged with such force against the wall that it left a dent. Kira, with a pink digital camera in her hand and two cronies following closely behind, sauntered over to the treadmill area where Olivia raced against her personal best.

"Who you trying to look good for, little lady?" Kira's voice oozed poison.

Little lady? Who did Kira think she was? Olivia kicked up her speed in a fury-induced adrenaline boost.

"Not going to talk to me?" Kira walked right in front of the machine and got as close as she could. "Still going to try to ignore me?"

Olivia punched up her speed. *Don't fall for it. Don't give her the pleasure.*

Ju-Ju stood up from her chair across the room and took a step toward Olivia.

Olivia caught her eye and shook her head slightly. All she needed was a gang fight in the game room. Not going to happen. She could handle Kira all by herself.

"It's no use, you know. He's in love with me." Kira winked.

Her hands on the grips, Olivia hopped up and placed one foot on each side of the speeding belt. She leaned forward and peered down over the treadmill at Kira. "If you really believe that, then I feel sorry for you." She held Kira's gaze for a moment then jumped back on, notched the speed up a tad more, and put in her earphones.

Kira lifted her camera, pressed a few buttons, and then turned the display screen toward Olivia.

Olivia's shoe caught on the edge of the treadmill platform, and she fumbled to grab on to the handrails to keep herself from falling flat on her face and then being thrown off the machine by the moving belt. She ripped the earphones from her ears and grabbed the camera for a closer look. Her jaw dropped at the close-up image of Justin in the woods lifting her cigarette to his lips with Olivia looking on. In the picture it appeared that Justin was enjoying a cigarette—not at all depicting what really happened. "Where did you get this?" A drop of sweat fell onto the display.

"You know where I got it. And in case you get any idea of erasing it, I have copies."

"What are you trying to pull?"

"I don't have to try to pull anything. You and Justin handed me all I needed on a silver platter. With evidence. I'm just waiting for the perfect time to use it."

Olivia stared into Kira's eyes. They were cold. Dead. "What do you want from me?"

"Ideally, I'd like you gone. But I'll settle for you leaving Justin alone. Completely."

"Or?"

"Or else."

⑤

"Ready when you are." Justin leaned back against his family's white Ford sedan, looking like he belonged on a billboard. He blew away a lock of long wavy brown hair covering one eye.

"We're just waiting for Tricia. Where's the van?" Olivia acted casual, like her heart wasn't racing and her hands weren't trembling as she pulled her legs into the car and laid her oboe beside her.

Justin closed the door for her then climbed into the driver's seat. "Dad thought I should save on gas by not taking the beast down the mountain to school so often just so we could use it."

We? A bolt of electricity shot from her toes to the top of her head.

Olivia checked her watch. What could be keeping Tricia? There wasn't much she could have been doing while Olivia practiced.

They waited in silence for a few minutes before Justin cleared his throat. "So, I have an idea. A sort of proposition." He glanced at her.

He's proposing already? Olivia wanted to giggle at her silly thought that fizzled just as quickly as it ignited. He wouldn't be proposing anything if he found out about Kira's picture. In fact, Olivia probably shouldn't even be talking to him. "I'm all ears."

"I saw you onstage on Sunday." He fidgeted and turned the heat up then down a little.

Was he nervous? "Yeah. . . ?"

"So, I've been thinking." Justin cleared his throat again. "How about we put together a duet for Easter?"

"A duet?" Olivia scoffed and waved her hand at him. "You've obviously never heard me sing."

"No, no. Just hear me out. It would be so cool. We'll do one of my favorite songs ever. 'It Is Well.' I'll sing the first verse a cappella while you sign." His nervousness fading, he talked quickly, his excitement mounting. "You'll play the second verse on the oboe while I sign—you'll have to teach me the sign language though. Then we'll rotate again for the third and fourth verses."

Olivia bit her lip. Would that work? They'd have to practice a lot. That would mean even more time together. Would Ben go for that? What would Kira do? It might push her over the edge. And she had that picture to hang over Olivia's head.

"Liv?" Justin peered at her.

Ugh. Another belly flop. Why did he have to call her that? So familiar—like he knew her well. Or wanted to. It just made her like him more. Just as he was slipping from her grasp forever. She had to cut him loose or he'd wind up in trouble—the last thing she wanted.

"What are you thinking?" He held his breath. Was he afraid

she might shoot him down?

Like that would ever happen if she weren't being forced. "I'm just trying to get a feel for how it would work—how it would go over with people." Kira, mainly.

"You know, I've been singing and performing for a long time. I think it would be really cool—different. They always look for something special for days like Easter. It will be televised, too—not that that's the reason to do it. But still."

Olivia nodded. *Say no. Say no.* "If you think we should do it, I'm up for it. I do have an idea to make it even cooler though." Why couldn't she just say no to him?

His eyes brightened. "You do? What is it?"

"What if we bring Tricia in on it with her flute? That way there would be music playing the whole way through." And Kira might not get so jealous.

Justin grinned. "That's an awesome idea. Do you think she'd do it?"

"That's going to be the problem. She's really shy. It'll take some convincing, that's for sure."

"Well, I hope you can pull it off. That way there wouldn't be any issue about us being alone to practice either."

Us. How could one little word send such warmth coursing through her veins? "I'll do my best. Oh, here comes Tricia now."

Tricia opened the door and tucked her long legs into the backseat. "Hey, guys. Sorry I'm late. Had to use the restroom. You ready?"

"Yep." Olivia glanced at Justin and then turned to face almost backward in her seat. "Trish, we need you to do something. Promise me you will?"

"Oh no. I'm not falling for that. You're going to have to tell me what I'm getting myself into."

Olivia explained Justin's idea while Tricia shook her head

the entire time. "No way. I can't get up onstage in front of all those people." She crossed her bony arms.

"You have to do it. It's going to be so cool." Olivia stuck out her bottom lip. "Please?"

Justin flashed a pearly smile toward the back. "I'm afraid we can't take no for an answer. I'm really sorry, but the situation is completely out of my hands."

"All right, all right. I'll do it since I still have time to lose a few pounds." Tricia laughed and waggled a finger at Justin. "I get it now. You get your way all the time because of that irresistible charm of yours."

Tell me about it.

෯

"Ju? Can we talk before the others come back?" Olivia put her open book facedown on her bed. Tricia was at her counseling session—much needed after agreeing to do the song with Justin and Olivia—and Skye was in the shower.

Ju-Ju knitted her eyebrows in concern. "Everything okay?"

"Yeah. I just wondered about something." Olivia chewed on her bottom lip. How to start such a topic? "You said some things that led me to believe that you had an abortion. Is that true?"

Ju-Ju turned her face away and nodded. "Only Tammy and Ben know. It was two abortions, actually."

"Oh, Ju. I'm so sorry." Olivia's eyes welled up with unshed tears. "Are you okay?"

"Honestly?"

Olivia nodded.

"No. I'll never be okay with those decisions. Never." Ju-Ju's voice caught as she struggled to keep it together. "I mean, sure. Time heals all wounds, and God's grace is enough—I know He forgave me a long time ago. It's forgiving myself that I'm having a hard time doing."

Should she speak? Reach out a hand to touch Ju-Ju? Just let her talk? Olivia had no idea what to do. So she waited.

"I never thought I'd feel this way." Ju-Ju shook her head. "To me, it seemed like the easy way out of a very difficult situation. I mean, what was I going to do with a baby at fourteen? Then fifteen? Impossible." She fingered the fringe on her pillow. "Turns out, it wasn't the easy way out at all." The tears started to flow. "It would have been easier to give my babies life and know they were healthy, growing, and happy than it is to live with the knowledge that I. . .didn't. And not a day goes by that I don't feel the guilt and think of who they might have been."

"Oh, Ju. I don't know what to say."

"Why do you ask? Did you. . . ?" Ju-Ju gazed with sympathetic eyes.

"No. I never had to." Olivia sighed. "But I planned to if it came up. If I had to."

"You had a boyfriend?"

"No." Olivia shook her head and whispered, "Stepfather." She lifted her eyes.

Ju-Ju nodded and held her gaze. "I'm glad you never had to make that decision. Sounds like you have enough baggage to deal with. Something to be thankful for in the middle of all the garbage, huh?"

"Yeah. I guess that's one way to look at it." Olivia looked away. "Ju?"

"Hmm?"

"How do you move on from your past?"

"One day, one hour, one moment at a time. I have to constantly remember that part of God's grace is that He asks me to forgive myself. If I don't, then I'm kind of wasting His forgiveness of me. Does that make sense?"

"I guess." Olivia shrugged. "No. It doesn't, actually. I mean, what am I supposed to forgive myself for? Not stopping Jordyn from driving that night? Not making my daddy put on his seat belt? Hating my stepfather?"

"In your case, you just need to feel the love of a true Father. God wants to be your Daddy."

"What if I can't get over it all? What if I can't let go? What if I never find God?"

Ju-Ju grinned. "Not an option. You will."

"But how do you know I will?"

"Your Daddy doesn't break His promises. You'll see."

Chapter 27

"H ow much do you remember of the crash?" Tammy banged her hands together in the sign for *car accident*.

"I was only seven, but I remember every moment. Every heartbeat. Every breath." Olivia peered through the blinds on Tammy's office window then looked back at her so she could read Olivia's lips. "Those visions are with me all the time. I wish I could forget." She swiped her hand across her forehead.

"Which of your memories stick out to you the most?"

"I remember thinking that I had warm glue on my hand. Turns out it was Daddy's blood." Olivia shuddered. "It felt sticky, so I thought it was glue—like when a little kid puts Elmer's on her hand and rubs her fingers together. When they shined the light in the car, I saw what it was. I can't get the picture of my hand covered with his blood out of my head no matter how hard I try."

"What were you thinking at that moment?" Tammy moved her finger in a circle beside her head.

Olivia shook her head. "I heard myself screaming, but my mind went blank. I overheard someone say I was in shock."

Tammy nodded.

"What else do you remember?"

"Daddy prayed as the car was rolling." Olivia put her head in her hands, her shoulders shaking. "Why didn't God listen?"

"What did he pray? What were his words? Do you

remember?" Tammy leaned forward.

Like she'd ever forget. "He shouted, 'Oh God, save my angel.' "

Tammy gasped and grabbed Olivia's hands. "Olivia? Don't you see? God *did* answer his prayer. He heard the cry of your daddy's heart, and He answered."

Maybe. But He didn't hear mine.

৯

"When can I come for a visit, Liv?"

"I don't know, Mom. It's going to depend." Olivia played with the spiral phone cord in one of the semiprivate conference rooms the girls used when calling home.

"Depend on what?" Mom's exasperation came loud and clear through the phone lines.

"On a lot of things. I really don't know when they'll move me to the level of the program where I'm allowed visitors."

"But I'm your mother. Enough's enough. I've put up with these restrictions far too long, actually. What kind of mother lets someone else keep her from her daughter?"

That—from the Mother of the Year. Olivia leaned against the wall and gripped the phone. *Please don't make this harder than it has to be.* "I know it's hard, Mom. We've been over this before. There are steps I have to take, progress I have to make, before they'll let me have the distraction of visitors." Especially when the visitor had been the cause of many of her problems. "It's the way the program works. It's what I signed up for. What *we* signed up for."

"But you've been there for four months. What's the holdup?"

"It's not about the length of time, Mom."

"Have you gotten into trouble? Why haven't they told me about it?"

"No. No. Nothing like that. I don't know why this is so hard for me and not for others. I just. . .I just can't seem to figure things out, to let go like the other girls have." Not for lack of trying.

"What do they want from you? I mean, what would prove that you'd made it?"

"I'm not sure. I think it's more about what I feel than it is about what they observe. As long as I'm honest about my confusion, they'll keep trying to help me through it." Did Mom want her to lie to them and fake a religious epiphany?

Silence.

"How's Jake?"

"Don't try to change the subject, Olivia."

Like Mom wouldn't if she were under scrutiny? Like she did every day of her life. "I'm not, Mom. I want to know how my brother is before I have to go. I wish we could just have nice conversation instead of it always being a battle."

"You're right. That's what I want, too." Mom sighed. "Jake's doing great. His grades are up. He's made lots of friends. His basketball season is almost over, and they're in the play-offs. He's pretty stoked."

Stoked? "That's wonderful. Would you tell him. . .tell him I miss him."

"If you want to come home, Liv, all you have to do is say the word."

Olivia bit her lip and looked up at the ceiling. "I believe in what I'm doing here, Mom. I wish you would, too."

Mom heaved a heavy sigh. "What do you want me to do?"

"Just support me." *Love me.*

🌀

Olivia perched on a stool on one side of Justin, and Tricia sat on a chair on the other as he stepped up to the microphone.

How could his hands not be shaking? The sight of hundreds of people sitting silently, staring wide-eyed at them, waiting to be entertained, almost made Olivia crumple to the floor. She trembled so much she thought she might fall off her stool. It was different than being just one member of a large orchestra. This time the spotlight was on her. It took all of her focus not to turn her eyes on Kira. Olivia could only imagine the rage on that girl's face when she saw the trio on the stage.

Olivia lifted her hands in feigned confidence, prepared to sign when the words started.

Justin stepped closer to the microphone, raised his face, and began to sing softly as Olivia signed the words and Tricia let the delicate tinkling notes flow from her flute.

When peace, like a river, attendeth my way,
When sorrows like sea billows roll;

Olivia closed her eyes and let her arms fall into a peaceful rhythm to accompany the beautiful music coming from Justin's lips.

Whatever my lot, Thou has taught me to say,
It is well, it is well with my soul.

As the last note of the first chorus faded, Olivia reached for the oboe that hung by a strap around her neck. She pointed the bell at the microphone while Justin prepared to sign the verse they had chosen to be next, just as she'd taught him.

He finally looked a little nervous.

My sin, oh, the bliss of this glorious thought!
My sin, not in part but the whole,
Is nailed to the cross, and I bear it no more,
Praise the Lord, praise the Lord, O my soul!

Olivia played those notes on her oboe as if they came from her soul. The words flashed on three screens—two behind her on either side of the stage and one on the back wall of the auditorium—but the emotion best came through in the sign language and the contrast of the somber oboe and hopeful flute.

The third verse reversed back to Justin singing, Olivia signing, and Tricia playing the flute. Then, for the final verse, they crescendoed and Justin sang *and* signed while both girls played their instruments.

> *And Lord, haste the day when my faith shall be sight,*
> *The clouds be rolled back as a scroll;*
> *The trump shall resound, and the Lord shall descend,*
> *Even so, it is well with my soul.*

As the song ended, the trio walked off the stage to the coveted sound of no applause. Reverent silence. After his last performance, Justin had explained to her that clapping was great, but no applause was even better. It meant the congregation was so moved they wanted to sit quietly and contemplate what they'd heard. To have their own private moment of worship as the notes faded away.

That was all Olivia wanted to do, too. She'd have loved to just crumple onto the couch that sat backstage for guests who were waiting to be called out. But she had to join the group in the auditorium or someone would come looking for her. "Justin, I'll be right out. I need to use the restroom."

He opened the door to the sanctuary. "I'll save you a seat."

Olivia hurried to the bathroom and splashed some cool water onto her face. She startled as a toilet flushed behind her. A door banged open with force that shook the walls.

Kira thundered out from the stall. "I hope you're happy with yourself, you piece of slime."

Olivia reared back like she'd been slapped. "What? Are you serious? I don't—"

"Blah. Blah. Blah." Kira made talking motions with her hand. "You say lots of words, but none of them mean anything.

Here's something maybe even *you* can understand." Kira stepped up on her tiptoes and lifted her nose to just barely an inch from Olivia's. "Stay. Away. From. Justin." She huffed toward the door and then spun around with her hand on the handle. "Or. Else."

"Or else what, Kira? You keep saying that, but what exactly are you going to do about it?"

"Don't forget that I have that picture, and I'm not afraid to use it. Not only would you get kicked out of Diamond Estates, but Justin would be in so much trouble."

"There's no way I'd get kicked out—not after what you've done and still managed to stay."

"You don't know anything about me, so don't pretend to think you do."

"Kira, you know as well as I do, that picture isn't what it looks like. Ben will believe me. Maybe *I'll* get in trouble, but Justin is innocent and you know it."

"Prove it." Kira grinned. "In fact, I think I'm going to forward it to Ben right now." She reached into her pocket and pulled out her cell phone.

Could she dive for it and knock it out of Kira's hands? Nah. It wasn't worth it. Olivia would keep her dignity and deal with the fallout later.

Kira backed away as she pressed buttons. "There. It's sent. We'll let Ben decide about guilt or innocence." She took a step toward the door and then turned back to Olivia by the sink. "Hey, can I have your bed once you're gone?"

A beep came from the back stall. A toilet flushed, and the door swung open. Tricia came out, her eyes a little bloodshot, but sporting a grin on her face. "I don't know what picture you just sent to Ben, but I just sent him a recording of this conversation. So. . .you're right. We'll let him figure out the truth."

If looks could kill.

ᔕ

"I thought God didn't want people to work on Sundays." Olivia poured pasta into a pot of boiling water.

Tricia laughed. "In our hearts, we're not supposed to be working, even though our bodies slave away."

Olivia narrowed her eyes. "What? I'm standing over a steaming stove. I'm sweating in this sweltering kitchen. I don't even want to eat the food. How can this not be considered work?" Kitchen detail was the *worst*.

"Ah. It's better to give than to receive, right?" Ju-Ju swatted her with a damp dish towel. "You're supposed to want to serve everyone. Like it's your mission for the day."

"Riiight. I see *that* happening." This place got crazier and crazier.

"I wanted to tell you." Ju-Ju's voice grew serious. "You guys were awesome today. It was really moving."

Olivia waited for sarcasm, but none came. "Thanks, Ju." A compliment from her meant more than the hundred others she'd received that day.

"No, I'm serious. It was something special."

Skye stepped up to the stove and stirred the spaghetti sauce. "I agree. I had to wipe tears away, it was so beautiful."

"Really?" Tricia almost whispered when she spoke up. "I was most nervous about what you two thought about it more than anyone else."

"Us?" Ju-Ju jerked her head back in shock. "Why?"

"Oh, she's right. It's just easier to get vulnerable for strangers than it is for people you care about. I feel that way all the time when I practice with you guys around." Olivia sighed. "Anyway, at least it's over."

"It's not over. That will stick with me for a long time. I just wanted you to know." Ju-Ju's neck reddened, and she turned away.

"Thanks, Ju. I mean it." Olivia turned back to her cooking. No sense making her uncomfortable. It took a lot for her to say those things.

Skye's eyes twinkled. "I will add this, though. That Justin. . .ooh, honey. He has it *bad* for you."

"Oh, he does not." Olivia blushed. "I wish you guys would stop it. It's not like we can date or anything anyway." Especially not with Kira around. She locked eyes with Tricia. Should they tell the other two what happened in the bathroom? They'd probably make a big scene out of it. Probably best to wait it out. Let Ben respond.

Marilyn bustled into the kitchen, the inner thighs of her tight polyester chef's pants rubbing together. One day, those things were going to let off a spark. She engulfed Olivia in the crooks of her meaty arms.

Help me!

Ju-Ju smirked. She seemed to be enjoying Olivia's suffocating plight.

Marilyn lifted one arm and dragged Tricia into the hug.

Olivia couldn't help but giggle at Tricia's squished cheeks and eyes that looked about to fall out.

"You girls made me so proud today. I thought my buttons were going to pop." Marilyn bounced a little, gave one last squeeze, and then released the girls.

"Um. . .thanks, Marilyn."

Ju-Ju shot her a *Better you than me* grin.

"What you did with that song—I've never heard or seen anything so beautiful."

"Thanks." Tricia blushed. The pink tint made Tricia's cappuccino skin even more beautiful, if that were possible.

"Okay. That's enough attention—don't want it to go to your heads. We've got dinner to cook, and from the looks of things, you need a double helping. You're getting too skinny, Tricia." Marilyn sampled the sauce and started shaking spices into the pot.

"Marilyn's right, T. You're not trying to lose any more weight, are you?" Ju-Ju looked her over.

"Yeah, you lose any more and you'll be invisible. Look"— Skye wrapped her hand around Tricia's wrist—"you're just skin and bones."

Tricia shrugged. "Oh, I don't know. I'm not really trying. Whatever happens, happens." She strode across the kitchen and busied herself in the pantry.

"Oh. Olivia. I almost forgot. Ben wants you in his office for a few minutes." Marilyn looked at her watch. "About five minutes ago."

Great. Here it comes. Olivia wiped her hands on her jeans and hurried from the kitchen. All the way to Ben's office, she recited her defense. *They weren't my cigarettes in the first place. I made a mistake. Justin wasn't smoking.* Though true, they all sounded like excuses—hollow.

Would she get kicked out of Diamond Estates? She'd never go back to *Chuck's,* but even worse, she didn't want to leave.

Her hand poised to knock on the door, Olivia took a deep breath as the door opened.

"Come on in, Olivia." Ben stood back to let her pass. "Kira and I have been sorting some things out. I must say, we have several things to deal with. Seems there are cigarettes involved. Some bribery. Some contraband cell phones. What's going on with you girls?"

Oh no! Would Tricia get in trouble for her cell phone?

"I'll tell you what, let's start at the beginning. I think I have a fairly good idea, but why don't you tell me where the cigarettes came from and what you were doing out in the woods smoking them with my son?"

"Ben, no. Justin wasn't smoking. He just happened upon me and was showing me how ridiculous and gross it looked. He was right."

"I know Justin wasn't smoking. I know my boy. Trust me. But your explanation makes sense. Where did they come from though—the cigarettes?"

Olivia recalled the details of the Black Friday shopping trip, smuggling the pack, then hiding them for weeks.

"So where are they now?" Ben's eyes narrowed.

He would never believe her. "In the incinerator. I didn't want them anymore. I have no use for them."

Ben nodded and turned to Kira. "I have no proof, but I would stake my life on the fact that you planted the cigarettes in Olivia's bag. What's up with you, Kira? What are you thinking? And the picture, your threats. . .I thought we'd been getting somewhere with you."

He rocked back in his chair with his hands behind his head. Thinking. That was almost never a good sign.

"Kira, I'm going to have to call your dad. I'm not sure what to do about all of this. I'll have to take some time to pray about it and consult with the staff. You and I will meet back here at ten tomorrow morning."

"What about her?" Kira sputtered and jabbed her finger at Olivia. "You don't have to call *her* parents?"

"Not that I have to explain my reasoning to you, Kira, but Olivia has no prior offenses, and she fixed her mistake the best way she could think of. I will give her a break—just like I've given you pass after pass in hopes that you'll soften one of these days." He closed his eyes. "Please, Lord."

Kira jumped to her feet and stormed from the room.

Olivia was so relieved when dinner was over and all cleaned up. People hadn't stopped talking about the performance at church. And if *she* was embarrassed at the attention, she could only imagine how Tricia was faring under it.

On their walk to the game room, Olivia slipped her arm across Tricia's shoulders. "You making it, superstar?"

"Very funny. It's not easy." Her eyes twinkled.

Olivia took a sharp breath and pointed at Tricia's face. "You're enjoying it! You can't fool me. You're loving every minute of it."

"Well, I wouldn't say *every* minute." Tricia grinned. "But it *is* kind of fun to have everyone say such nice things about something I did. It feels nice."

Then it was all worth it—even the mess with Kira. "You deserve it."

Ju-Ju feigned a yawn. "If you two are finished with your little lovefest, I'm kind of curious about what we're going to do for fun tonight."

"Movie." Skye turned and walked backward in front of the group.

"Fine with me. I'm too tired for much else anyway." Tricia rested a hand on Skye's shoulder so she could pull off her shoes and walk the rest of the way barefoot.

"Sure. I just need to run up to the room and take care of something." Olivia made a quick detour. "I'll meet you there."

She sprinted up the stairs to her room. Olivia wanted to make sure she had saved the program from that morning's church service so she could show her mom and Jake.

Whistling her "Phantom of the Opera" oboe solo, Olivia hurried down the hall. Her door stood open just a crack. Odd. They always shut it. There were no locks on the individual bedroom doors—only on the main one to the hallway—but they'd never had a problem before.

Olivia put her hand on the door and gently pushed it open. "Hello? Someone in here?"

No answer.

Pressing the door open a little farther, Olivia stepped inside. Light filtered in through the window blinds onto the neat beds and orderly shelves. Everything seemed just fine.

Then she saw it.

Chapter 28

Olivia fell to her knees and touched the ruins of her beloved oboe. The reed was still attached to the top body section, which had been shattered in half. The bottom piece was just a mass of splintered wood that didn't hold any resemblance to the custom-made professional-grade oboe Olivia had caressed in her hands just hours before.

It looked like it had been struck against something. She lifted her teary eyes and gazed around her room. *Aha.* The back of the desk chair stood scratched and dented as evidence. She looked back at the remains of her dear friend.

How could. . . ? Who could. . . ?

Kira. It had to be her. Who else would have done such a thing? None of the other girls had anything against her. Why the oboe though? Probably to keep Olivia from being able to go to practice, so Justin would have nowhere to drive her. And because Justin loved it.

The image of Kira holding the oboe over her head and swinging it down like a mallet against the seat back made her shiver. How could someone do something so cold? Kira was sick.

Olivia sank onto the floor, her stomach clenched in knots, and gathered up as many of the pieces as she could. She leaned back against the bed in defeat, her heart thundering. What should she do? Tell Tammy? Confront Kira? Both? Neither? As she pondered her options, the door opened and Ju-Ju poked her head in.

"Hey, chica. What's happenin'? We're waitin' for ya."

Olivia gazed up at her through brimming eyelids.

"What's that? Is that your oboe?" Ju-Ju gasped and dropped to her knees beside Olivia. "What happened?"

"I wish I knew."

"You mean someone did this on purpose?" Ju-Ju picked up one of the broken pieces.

Olivia nodded. "Sure looks that way."

"Kira." Ju-Ju sighed.

Of course Kira. "Most likely. And you don't even know what happened earlier today. But how can I prove it?" Olivia's shoulders sank as the weight of her loss set in. She caressed the broken pieces. But where was the bell? She dropped flat onto the floor and looked under the desk and then under the bunks. She finally saw it all the way across the room under Ju-Ju's bed where it must have rolled against the wall. She crawled over and shimmied under the bed, reaching for it with her fingertips. She scooted it toward her hand and grabbed hold. Not that it would matter.

The oboe was ruined. Her future was ruined. The symphony! What about her big concert next weekend? Olivia had a solo. She looked up at Ju-Ju, who was shaking her head.

"How much do these things cost?" Ju-Ju tried to fit two of the broken pieces together like a puzzle.

"For a good one like this? Anywhere from three to four thousand dollars—more, probably."

Ju-Ju exhaled with a whistle. "That much? What will you do?"

"I have no idea. I could probably find a cheap used one for about five hundred bucks. But it won't sound anything like this one did. Besides, I have a concert next weekend." She'd never be able to get an oboe before then. No way Charles would pay for it—not that Olivia wanted anything from him ever again.

Maybe she could get an increase on her two-hundred-dollar credit card limit. But wouldn't that still be like Charles paying for it? What other option did she have? At least charging it felt different than coming right out and asking him for money.

Still holding the bell, she scurried to her bedside and dug in her purse for her wallet. Olivia pulled out her credit card and flipped it over to read the back. There was an 800 number she could call, so she slipped it into her pocket, hoping to find an opportunity to use the phone later.

Olivia put the pieces on the front of her sweatshirt and pulled the hem up around them like a cradle then went to the door. "I guess I'd better go spread the joy and let Tammy in on what's happened."

"Want me to come with?"

What's the point? "No need. Nothing either of us can do anyway." *Kira wins.*

Olivia let herself out the door and slumped down the hall toward Tammy's office, still holding her bundle inside the front of her shirt.

The door stood wide open, but Olivia knocked hard enough for Tammy to feel the vibrations so she wouldn't be startled. "Mind if I come in?" She drew her finger to her body and pointed to the chair.

Tammy nodded, her eyebrows knit together. "What's wrong?" She placed her thumb and forefinger on either side of her chin and shook her head.

Stepping up to the desk, Olivia dropped the hem of her shirt and let the pieces spill out into a jumbled heap of rosewood and chrome.

Tammy gasped. "What happened?" She jumped up and ran around her desk to Olivia's side. She picked up the pieces of the instrument.

"I wish I knew. Someone did this." Olivia twisted her fists apart. "Broke it."

Tammy shook her head. "Why? Who? Do you know?"

"Yes. But I can't prove it." She filled Tammy in on what had happened in the church bathroom.

"Oh boy. I sure wish you'd told me about this right away. We'll have to get Ben down here." She pressed numbers into her phone and waited. In the space of no more than a few heartbeats, Olivia heard the beep of a return text. "He'll be right here."

Olivia nodded. "Can I use your phone real quick while we're waiting?" She held her hand up to the side of her face. "I mean, we have to get to the bottom of this—that's a big priority. But my first concern is about my concert next weekend. It's a big deal. I have an important solo." Olivia fought against the tears. "I h–have to buy a new oboe."

"How will you do that?"

Olivia felt her cheeks reddening. "I'm going to call and see if I can get a raise in my credit card limit." Now that she said it out loud, it sounded crazy even to her. She'd never be allowed to place that call.

"Oh." Tammy hesitated. "I can't let you do that, hon. It's not your money. You'd have to call home for permission."

It figured. Olivia slumped down even farther. "Just forget it, then. Charles will never agree to it."

"Then you definitely have to know it wouldn't be right to go behind his back with the credit company. Right?"

"What's right about any of this?" Olivia shouted—not that Tammy could hear her volume. But she couldn't mistake the tears. "Everything. Every. Single. Thing. Everything I care about gets destroyed. Everything. God truly hates me. That's all there is to it." She pulled her flattened palm down across the length of her face—*God*—then flicked the fingers of both hands outward from her chest—*hates*. She pressed her fists hard into her chest—*me*.

"What's this I hear?" Ben boomed as he came through the door, his usual grin replaced by a comforting smile. "God hates you? Whatever drew you to that conclusion?"

Tammy gestured to her desk. "Someone did this to Olivia's oboe."

"Oh dear." He put his hand on Olivia's shoulder. "Olivia, you must understand, this isn't the work of God. This is the work of His enemy, Satan, trying to keep you from seeking the Lord. He wants nothing more than for you to run from God, to think He hates you or doesn't answer your prayers. This is how Satan works. You can't let him have that victory."

Hmm. That actually made sense. Didn't change anything though. "But he's already won." Olivia gestured to the pile on the desk.

"No. His victory only occurs if he turns your heart from seeking God. He doesn't care a bit about that oboe. He wants you." Ben held her gaze. "Don't let him win, Olivia. He's trying to beat you down with this oboe. The Lord *will* win if you trust Him."

Transfixed, Olivia nodded. What Ben said really rang true. At least it was some kind of explanation. "Okay. Then what do I do?" Why couldn't Mom have married someone like Ben?

"You fight."

Olivia nodded. "I fight."

"Yes, but Olivia, your fight isn't against an enemy in this house. It's not against the person who did this." He gestured at the desktop. "Or who sent me that text message earlier today. It's not against your stepfather, or the person driving the car that killed your daddy. It's not against your mom. Most of all,

Olivia, your fight is *not* against yourself."

Olivia stared at Ben's eyes—not blinking, not moving a muscle, afraid she was about to get the answer to her search and any movement would break the spell of the moment. "Who, then? Who do I fight?" *Tell me. Please tell me.*

"You fight the lies."

"The lies?"

"The lies that tell you you aren't good enough. The lies that tell you you're at fault. The lies that keep you from opening up to us about your pain. The lies that keep you from turning your heart over and trusting Jesus." Ben looked deep into Olivia's eyes. "Those lies. Face them so you can fight them."

Olivia nodded slowly. *He's right.*

"Are you ready to do the hard work?"

"Yes." Whatever it took.

Ben looked at Tammy, all business again. "This is it. This is the week. She's ready."

Tammy nodded. "I'm ready, too." She smiled softly at Olivia. "But Ben, what about. . . ?" Tammy gestured to the oboe.

"No problem. God will work that out."

"But if I can't do my solo, I need to let Mr. Gables know."

Ben put his hand on Olivia's shoulder. "God will work it out. Do you trust Him?"

Did she? Olivia had no idea. She pressed her lips together in a tight line and shook her head. "I don't know."

"Do this for me. Say, 'I trust You, Lord,' whether you mean it or not, at least once an hour until you see His answer. Can you do that?"

"I'll try." Sounded like a kooky idea to Olivia. But nothing else had worked. She might as well give it a shot.

"Good enough." Ben grinned, his eyes sparkling. "This is

my favorite part. This is when God moves—big-time." He spun on his heels and left in a flurry.

🌀

"I. Trust. You. Lord." Olivia let the words form a cadence as she ran on the treadmill, thankful to have beaten Kira to the machine. Only three hours had passed since she found her destroyed oboe. Six hours since the confrontation with Kira and Ben about the cigarettes. Nine hours since the performance at church. How could nine hours feel like a lifetime had passed? She let Ben's words wash over her thoughts and tried to stay focused on the fight. He'd been so right about that. She had been held back by lies.

"I. Trust. You. Lord." Did she? Maybe this was how it started. What did they call that? A step of blind faith? That's definitely what it was. Blind faith. Trusting Someone who'd seemingly never helped her before.

"I. Trust. You. Lord." Ben had said once an hour. But more often couldn't hurt, right?

"Oliiivia. Seems like you're really trying to get somewhere on that treadmill. When you figure out your destination, send us a postcard."

Kira. Olivia continued at her same pace with her face forward. She wasn't going to let Kira get the best of her.

"You did such a wonderful job today. It was simply beautiful." She turned to walk away then turned back with a snide grin. "Oh, and thanks for teaching my boyfriend how to do that sign language. He's never looked hotter to me."

Her boyfriend? Olivia's face must have registered the shock she felt.

"Yeah. Didn't you hear? Justin and I are back together. Isn't that great?" Kira's syrup slithered over her tongue. "In fact, he said he almost had a little crush on you, but the cigarettes and that horrid scar were just too much for him to take." Kira turned and bounced away, flinging her blond ponytail over her shoulder.

"I. Trust. You. Lord."

Olivia's pace slowed. Could Kira be telling the truth? Was Justin still interested in her? Olivia was pretty sure Kira was lying. But what if Justin really did find Olivia's scar hideous? Her fingertips crept to her cheek. She felt the raised jagged line. Hardly visible from the front, but from the side—that was another story. What if he had been doing all of this because he felt sorry for her? Oh no. What if he was simply following orders from his dad?

Olivia gasped as she remembered Justin's words from their first meeting. *"It's just more of the same. Girls come and go. . . . Every girl here knows it's only temporary. Dating like that makes no sense to me."*

Who was she kidding? Justin was too smart to get involved with someone like her. And her scar *was* hideous. Another reason for someone not to love her.

Did she even stand a chance at love. . .ever?

Chapter 29

I t's time to talk about Charles." Tammy closed the door to her office, sat down in her chair, and waited.

What did Tammy want from her? Olivia wasn't about to spill out the details as casually as telling a joke or chatting about the weather. It wasn't as easy to spew out the raw truths as Tammy seemed to think it should be. Olivia couldn't turn her horror on and off like flipping a light switch. With her arms crossed over her chest, she held Tammy's gaze.

"Tell me." Tammy leaned forward.

"Tell you *what*?" Olivia didn't want to have this conversation—not now, not ever. But Ben had said she needed to face it in order to fight it. *Sigh.*

"Tell me what happened so I can help you," Tammy coaxed with a gentle tone, but she gave no sign of backing down.

"What happened?" Olivia pointed to her head and banged her fists together then pointed to herself. "Trust me. You don't want to know what happened. But fine." She poked her thumb into her chest. "I'll tell you." She took a deep breath and pushed the words out like water surging through a broken dam before she had second thoughts and stopped them. "My stepfather molested me from the time I was twelve until just a few months ago. There. You happy?"

"Happy? Nowhere near." Tammy sighed and pressed on her eyes.

Olivia blew out her breath like a deflating balloon. She had thought the world would feel different to her once that information floated out on the airwaves, but it didn't. Ju-Ju knew and now Tammy did, but Olivia's reality remained the same, and voicing it didn't erase it or change it in the slightest. But, she had to admit, it did free her in a way. She no longer carried it alone, and that was a strangely comforting realization. But now what?

"How often?" Tammy only signed her words as though she didn't trust her voice.

Was that a quiver in her lower lip? "Total?" Olivia brought her fingertips together in front of her body.

Tammy nodded.

"Sixteen times."

"Olivia, you need Jesus."

"Tell me something I don't know. He just doesn't seem very interested in me."

Tammy drew back like she'd been slapped. "What do you mean?"

"Let's see, where do I even start? He let my dad die in front of me even though He could have stopped it. He let my mom marry *Chuck*. He let Chuck abuse me for years. He let my friend die in yet another car accident I was in. I either did some royal damage in a past life or He just gets His jollies out of watching me suffer. Or—and I'm sincerely considering this possibility—He simply doesn't exist."

"Oh, sweetie." Tammy shook her head. "You've got it all wrong. It's like Ben said. God didn't *let* your dad die; He held you through the pain of the unthinkable. He didn't *let* your mom marry Charles or *let* Charles abuse you; He held you up in the face of the darkest evil in the world. He didn't *let* Jordyn die to make you suffer; rather, He kept His hand on you in the light of the natural consequences of her actions. Do you see?"

Olivia listened intently. Could Tammy be right? "If He's there, why don't I feel His presence?" She scooped her open palms up into the air. *Presence.* Then she signed an unspoken word by touching her fingertip to her forehead and pressing her fist outward. *Ever.*

"But you do, Liv." Tammy smiled. "Remember when you told me how you knew deep in your heart that you had to come here?"

Olivia nodded.

"That was the voice of the Holy Spirit. Um. . .remember when Mr. Gables showed up here from the fine arts school?"

"Yeah?" *What did that have to do with God?*

"It was a total coincidence he came here that day. No one invited him. He popped in unannounced and uninvited. He's a big financial supporter of Diamond Estates, and he's always welcome here for a visit. . .but he's never just popped in like that before. And the one day he did, it *happened* to be at the exact time you were playing. And he *happened* to be in desperate need of an oboist."

Hmm.

"Listen. You have these big things in your life. They're like benchmarks of pain so when you look back, you see only those glaring reminders sticking up like skyscrapers on the horizon behind you. But you're missing all the beauty beneath them."

Go on. Please. Tell me about the beauty.

"You're a loving, amazingly talented girl with a heart of gold. You have a brother you've cherished and given your time and attention to. You helped him become the man he is. And your dad, whether you can see it yet or not, he lives on in you. All of the wonderful things about him, the things you shared together, are a part of you. You are his legacy."

Some legacy. "But wow—I'm not honoring his memory, am I? By living in the past, in guilt, in fear. . .I'm just making it all a big waste."

"Right. I'm not going to say that bad things haven't happened to you. You've sure had more than what would seem like your share. But you see, God has kept His hand on you, guided you and girded you with strength through all the junk life has thrown your way." Tammy grew animated and signed every other word. "Now, in His timing, He's about to restore some of what the locusts have eaten."

"Huh? Locusts?"

"It's in the Bible. God wants to give you back what your enemy stole from you. You just need to surrender to Him. And then, once He's healed you from the inside, He can work through you."

Olivia nodded. The walls seemed to inch closer and closer until she felt like she might suffocate. "Would it be possible to have permission to go for a walk? I won't go far. I just need some air and the chance to think some things through."

"You bet. Make sure you take a walkie-talkie." Tammy smiled. "Take as long as you need."

Olivia smiled as she closed the door to Tammy's office. There wasn't a doubt in Olivia's mind that Tammy was on her computer at that very moment, instant messaging the staff to appear at an emergency prayer meeting for Olivia's soul.

It was time.

I trust You, Lord.

The pine needles crunched beneath her feet like the chant of the monks who had paced the forest two hundred years before on their own quest for the Almighty. Her search was different, but it was her own.

"Lord? You said You'd be here for me when I called for

You. Are You there?"

Olivia fell to her knees on the blanket of evergreen needles. She clutched her hands to her heart. "I can't do this alone anymore, Lord. I need You."

You've never been alone, My child. You've only needed to reach out to find Me.

She fell flat, barely noticing the needles that prickled her cheeks. "Then why? Why?" She pounded her fists into the frozen earth. "Why—if You've been there all along—did You let all that stuff happen to me? What did I ever do to deserve it?"

The earth grew damp as her warm tears melted the snow. Why didn't God defend Himself? Why couldn't He just answer her one question: *Why?*

Olivia drew herself to her elbows and glanced around the forest. The fog in her thoughts began to clear as the answer became clear. Jesus, as her Savior, never promised to keep her from pain; He'd promised to hold her through it. The pain might have been inevitable, but her loneliness and misery—those were optional.

༄

"How did things go for you on your walk yesterday?" Tammy closed her door as Olivia stepped into the office for an unscheduled counseling session.

"Pretty good. Me and God? Well, let's just say we're getting some things worked out," Olivia signed as she took her usual seat. "I wish I wasn't so analytical and could just take things by faith. I was out there for a long time. But I kind of feel like He wanted me to know that He made me exactly like He wanted me. Now I guess I'm supposed to trust Him and watch Him do His thing."

"You feel like He spoke all of those things to you?" Tammy leaned forward.

"I think so. No. I *know* He did." Olivia stood up to pace but made sure to let Tammy see her face when she spoke. "I don't know how to be sure that I'm—quote, unquote—'a Christian.' But I do know He promised that He's working on me and that He's never left my side."

"Well, Liv, 'Christian' simply means 'Christ follower.' The Bible says if you confess your sins—if you admit you need God's grace—then He is always faithful to forgive your sins and make you clean and righteous before Him."

Olivia pressed her lips together and nodded slowly. "Yeah, I did that yesterday. I told God I needed Him and that I was sorry for doubting Him and being angry with Him. I told Him I couldn't do it on my own."

"That's it, Liv. That's what it means to surrender yourself to Him. Now you have to walk in faith, believing you're forgiven, and watch for God's hand in your life."

Olivia shook her head. "I was making it way too difficult, wasn't I?"

Tammy nodded. "Yes, you were."

"There wasn't ever going to be lightning bolts or earthquakes, was there?"

"Usually not. Usually God calls out to us with a quiet voice."

Olivia let the truths sink in. They rang true in her heart. She knew she'd met Jesus even though she didn't feel very different.

"Now, unless you have other questions about this subject, I want to get back to what we spoke about yesterday—because this is all wrapped up together. It's all part of your ultimate healing."

"Okay. I figured that was coming." Olivia had thought of nothing else since their talk.

Tammy leaned forward and grasped Olivia's hands. "I really, really think we need to involve your mom in this. She needs to know."

Olivia whipped her head side to side. "No way. I've tried so many times to tell her. It's like she knows what I'm going to say and refuses to hear it. I'm done trying."

"Can I approach her about it? You don't even have to be a part of the conversation."

Now, that idea had merit. Even if Mom didn't believe Tammy, at least Tammy would get a good feel for what Olivia had been dealing with. She nodded. "I think that might be okay." Scary, but better than having to do it herself.

"All right. I'm going to get a few more details from you; then I'll set up a call with your mom. Let's see—" She consulted her calendar. "We're scheduled to have a counseling call with her this coming Friday. I'll make sure your mom and I speak before then so the three of us can talk together on Friday."

Olivia gulped. "Can you let me know when you're going to do it and then fill me in right after?" The thought of wondering all day, every day until Friday was too much to bear.

"I'll keep you informed every step of the way." Tammy pulled Olivia in for a hug. "After we get things ironed out with your mom, we'll know what to do about the legal issues."

"Legal issues?" Wait. She didn't think Olivia was going to press charges and fight Charles in court about this. Did she? How could Tammy expect Olivia to face him ever again?

"You'll definitely have some choices to make about whether you want him walking the streets or not."

How can I be expected to make a decision like that?

Chapter 30

The room was bustling with activity when Olivia returned. A fully dressed Skye climbed across her bed, trying to smooth the covers. Ju-Ju applied a little makeup at the mirror in the corner. They were almost ready to go to prayer. Olivia had better hurry. No time for a shower.

She opened the bathroom door, expecting to see Tricia preening at the mirror, but the room was empty. Water streamed from the showerhead, but there were no sounds of movement on the creaky floor. Olivia stepped over to the cubicle and called out Tricia's name as she peered behind the partition.

Olivia screamed.

Tricia lay in a crumpled heap on the shower floor in a puddle of watery vomit.

"Help me! Someone!" Olivia shouted toward the door as she slid the glass door open and flipped off the running water. She tugged on Tricia's hands to pull her out, but Olivia's bare feet slipped on the wet surface. She landed on her back beside Tricia, her hair mopping up water and vomit. Finally, reaching under Tricia's arms, Olivia pulled her out and let the limp body flop onto the rug. Olivia gasped as she surveyed Tricia's naked, skeletal body. Her hip bones jutted out like arrows. How had that happened?

Was she breathing? Olivia watched closely until she saw

Tricia's chest rise and fall in a shallow breath. Olivia threw a bath towel over her nude body and slid to the door. "You guys. Someone. Go in the hallway and pull the fire alarm right now."

Skye gasped and sprinted away.

Ju-Ju ran into the bathroom and locked eyes with Olivia. "Is she alive?"

"Barely."

"Oh no. Why didn't I act sooner? I was getting worried about her." Ju-Ju shook her head. "I can't believe I waited too long to do something."

"Don't talk like that." Olivia knelt on the floor and gathered Tricia into her arms like a little girl clutching a rag doll. "Shh. It's going to be okay. It's going to be okay." She recited the promise for her own sake as much as Tricia's.

A siren blared throughout the building. Help would come. But would it be too late?

"What's going on? Who pulled the alarm? Is everyone okay?" Ben's worried voice thundered down the hallway.

"In here," Skye shouted out their door and grabbed the comforter off of her bed and threw it over Tricia.

Ben shot into the room. He took one look at the scene and punched three numbers into his cell phone. "Yes. It's a real emergency. There's no fire, but we're in need of an ambulance right away."

Olivia looked at Ju-Ju and whispered, "Pray."

Tammy whisked Ju-Ju and Olivia out of the bathroom as soon as the EMTs arrived. "Come on, girls, let's get back so they can do what they need to do to help Tricia." She leaned her back against the wall, slid down to the floor near the window, and patted the area around her for the three girls to join her. "This is a good time for praying. Don't you think?"

The four huddled there together until they heard the

ambulance driver say, "Okay, she's stable enough to move. Let's get her out of here before her blood pressure drops again."

He spoke into his radio: "I've got a seventeen-year-old malnourished female, approximately 105 pounds. She appears to have fainted. Possible head injury. BP 110/60, which is up from the first reading of 80/55. We're moving now."

The other EMT pushed the gurney from the bathroom and into the hallway.

Ben followed, his face ashen as he looked at Tammy. "How did we miss this?"

Tammy shook her head. "I don't know."

Olivia rose from the floor. "Can I go with her to the hospital?" *Please.* Never mind the vomit in her damp hair. She had to go be with Tricia.

"Alicia and I are going. You need to stay here for now. We'll have someone bring you girls later this afternoon, once we know what's happening." Ben turned and left without another word.

"I can't believe this happened." Olivia searched Ju-Ju's eyes for answers.

"Has she been eating normally lately?" Tammy asked softly, with no accusation evident in her voice.

"I think so. I mean, she's always talking about needing to lose weight. But I've never noticed anything unusual. She eats pie and stuff, too. Complains about it, but eats it. Sometimes a lot of it."

"And then what?" Ju-Ju's shoulders slumped.

Skye stood up from the floor. "What do you mean, then what?"

"T might eat like a pig sometimes. But then what does she do?"

Realization hit Olivia's stomach like a lump of clay.

"Bathroom. She always goes to the bathroom after she eats." The mall! "Oh man, you guys, I've heard her vomit before. She said it was just something she ate."

"Yeah. It was something she ate all right." Ju-Ju slumped on the chair. "Why didn't I do something sooner? I knew something was up."

"If this is your fault, then we're all to blame." Tammy smiled softly. "You girls love her. You'd do anything to protect her. She was good at hiding it. This is not your fault. Tell me you know that."

Olivia nodded. "I know it's not our fault."

Easier to say than to believe.

✺

"Hey, T." Ju-Ju pushed the door to the hospital room open and held it back for Olivia and Skye to enter.

Tricia's head wavered as she lifted it off the pillow, the dark circles under her eyes in stark contrast with the bleached white sheets. "Are you guys mad at me?"

"Mad at you? Are you kidding? We're just so glad you're okay." Skye sat down on the edge of the bed and gave Tricia a side hug and a kiss on her pale forehead.

Why? Olivia wanted to ask, but stuck with a safer question. "What can we do to help?"

Tricia shrugged. "I have to have more counseling for a while. I'm not sure what happens from here. Ben says I'm not going to be leaving Diamond Estates for a while—that I need some more help." Tears filled her eyes. "I guess he's right, but with this setback, there's no way I'll graduate from the program with you guys in a couple of months."

"Well, you know that Ju-Ju and I aren't going anywhere anytime soon." Skye rubbed Tricia's forearm.

"No. But you'll be through with the program even if you

still live in the house for a while. It'll be different."

"It'll be better." Skye smiled.

Did anyone actually believe that? Olivia gazed out the window. Someone needed to say something funny to break the ice.

"Why, T?" Ju-Ju grabbed her hand. "Why did you want to be so skinny even to the point of risking your life?"

Not quite what Olivia had in mind.

Tricia shrugged. "Look. You have to understand. I'm not tough like you. And I don't have brains like you." She nodded at Olivia. "And I'm not sweet and lovable like Skye. All I have going for me are my looks. It's why I always wanted attention from boys. It was like confirming that I was worth something."

"But you *are* beautiful—inside and out. What made you think a few pounds one way or another would change that?"

"Oh, in my world—the world of modeling—it can make you or break you. Everything can rest on those few pounds."

"Then why be a part of that world? That's ridiculous. You're worth so much more than that." Ju-Ju shook her head. "I don't get it."

"You wouldn't get it. You're tough enough—strong enough—not to cave under pressure like that. I guess I'm not. And then when Kira. . ."

"Kira has done a lot of things to hurt a bunch of people. She only wanted to get to you. She was jealous. But she's coming around." Olivia crouched down to be at eye level with Tricia. "We need you, Tricia. You're important to so many people. Please don't hurt yourself in order to match up to someone else's ridiculous ideal. Just be yourself. We love you just like you are."

"I'll try."

"Good." Olivia nodded. "They say you're coming home tomorrow. Tell us how we can help you."

"You know, the thing I'm most afraid of is that everyone will treat me weird. I mean, watch what I eat and what I don't eat, follow me into the bathroom, offer me treats. . ." Her shoulders slumped. "I just want things to be normal."

Ju-Ju gave a resolute nod. "You know what, T? I think we can handle all of that. You'll get enough focus on this stuff in counseling. Between the four of us, we'll try to keep everything the same. Right?" She looked at Skye and Olivia.

"Yeah, I agree." Skye nodded.

"Sure. As long as you let me measure your food and count your calories." Olivia winked. "I'm totally kidding. I think you make a fair point, and I'm on board with keeping things normal—whatever that is."

"Thanks, you guys." Tricia yawned. "Now, I'm kind of tired. I think I need to take a nap."

Olivia, Ju-Ju, and Skye let the heavy door close softly as they left the room. Olivia slumped against it and looked at Ju-Ju and Skye. "We have lots of work to do with her."

᎒

"Hey. I'm back." A very tired-looking Tricia tiptoed into the room and heaved her duffel bag onto her bunk.

"Welcome home, girlfriend." Ju-Ju jumped from the desk chair where she sat. "How are you?"

Tricia laughed. "Oh, I'm fine. My head still hurts a little from my fall, but that's about it."

Olivia gave her a hug.

"Glad to have you back, Trish."

"Thank you, Skye." Tricia's smile quickly faded. "Now I have to do something difficult."

"Can we help?" Olivia stepped closer.

Tricia moved to her bedside. "I wish. First of all, I need to apologize to you three. I, um, have something in here that isn't allowed—that's actually illegal." She lifted her mattress and felt around underneath it. When she pulled her hand out, she had a baggie full of little blue pills.

Olivia gasped. "What are those?"

Ju-Ju nodded. "Speed. Diet pills, huh, T?"

Skye shook her head. "I can't believe you had those in here and none of us ever noticed."

"I didn't realize it, but I've been living a lie. I mean, I thought my weight and diet issues were private and no one's business—I thought they had nothing to do with my program here. I realized when I was in the hospital, though, that anything that has to be hidden from your loved ones isn't right. My family, my friends, Ben and Alicia, Tammy—they all want the best for me. So if I have to hide something, it can't be good. You know?"

The three girls nodded.

Olivia tipped her head at the bag. "What now?"

"I've got to turn myself in. It's the first step toward real recovery."

"I'm proud of you, T."

"Me, too." Skye hugged her.

"Want me to go with you?"

"Thanks, Liv. But no. I need to do this on my own." Tricia's smile faltered. "You could all pray for me while I'm gone, though. I think I'm going to need it."

Chapter 31

Olivia sat on her hands to keep them from shaking, which only made her teeth chatter.

"Okay, Liv. I've got your mom on Skype and webcam." Tammy pushed a button to amplify the call.

"Mrs. Whitford, it's me, Tammy, with Olivia and Ben on the call."

"Good afternoon, everyone." Mom's jaw tightened.

"Ben, would you like to take it from here?" Tammy gestured to the computer.

He nodded and adjusted his tweed blazer. "I understand things didn't go very well when Tammy delivered some difficult news to you. Have you had a chance to process the information, Mrs. Whitford?"

"I wouldn't exactly call it information, Mr. Ben. It's more like unfounded accusations dropped out of nowhere." Mom crossed her arms. "What kind of ideas are you people putting into my daughter's head anyway?"

Here we go again. Olivia's stomach retched. She put her head in her hands and breathed deeply.

"Mrs. Whitford, it was very difficult for Olivia to open up about this." Ben used an even tone. "She said she tried to talk to you about this many times."

Mom leaned forward and glared at the webcam. "Oh? Name one time."

"After your trip to Chicago. After Charles ripped the lock off my door. After the funeral." Olivia spoke into the camera in an emotionless, monotone voice. "Those times were all this year. I have other examples if you want them."

Mom's eye twitched, and her shell seemed to crack a teeny bit when Olivia spoke. "I don't know, Liv. It's just so hard for me to believe."

"Mom, respectfully, I find *that* hard to believe." Olivia spoke in almost a whisper. "You've shown me many times you don't trust Charles's reactions, and you've stepped between us sometimes."

"You noticed that?" Her shoulders sagged ever so slightly.

"Of course. I used to think you stepped in front of Charles so I'd be forced to look his direction—which made me so mad because I could always see him. Then I realized you were trying to get between us." Olivia locked eyes with her mom on the computer screen.

"Remember the day Officer Stapleton brought me home? What happened that night, Mom? I mean, you don't have to tell me, but the last thing you said to me on the driveway was that I was to go to my room, lock the door, and not come out. That tells me you knew what he was capable of, and you expected it." Olivia gripped her armrests until her fingers cramped. "Did you not notice that Charles was nowhere to be found when you went back into the house? Did it *never* occur to you he might have been waiting for me in my room?"

Mom gasped and covered her mouth with a tissue.

Olivia looked at Ben and Tammy, who both nodded encouragingly. She'd never meant to say this much, but now that she'd started, she had to finish. "Mom—if you want to know what I think—I think that somewhere in the recesses of your mind, you knew this was going on, but you didn't know how to deal with it and wanted to pretend it wasn't happening."

Mom openly sobbed.

"What about the night before I left to come here? Did you honestly not have any idea that I snuck out of the house on the rope ladder to get away from Charles? He came home drunk that night, crashed his car into the garage wall, and was coming after me!"

"What do you mean? You said you went for a walk in the morning." Mom shook her head and tears flew in every direction.

"Mom. I don't believe you." Olivia tried to remain calm. "I don't believe for one second you never wondered about that night."

Ben leaned in closer to the camera. "Mrs. Whitford, is it possible that you've protected your husband all these years because you didn't want to believe the truth about what was going on?"

Mom gulped back her sobs and lifted her head. She nodded. "You're right about all of it. It's all true." Her body trembled, and her face drained of all color as her eyes lifted to the space above her computer.

Charles's face came into view of the webcam, and he leaned in until they could see the blood vessels in his eyes. The sneer on his face was pure evil. "I heard every word."

The screen went black.

"Oh God, please." Olivia reached out and clutched the laptop screen. "No. No!" she screamed.

Tammy put her arms around Olivia while Ben pulled out his cell phone. He scrolled through the contacts and punched a button—a lifeline.

"Mark? I need a favor, and right away. It's an emergency. Are you in your cruiser?" Ben nodded. "Great. Turn your siren on and head to the Whitfords' place, stat. I'll explain while you drive. And you might want to call for backup. This is a matter of life and death."

Chapter 32

Olivia dropped to her knees and pressed her forehead into the carpet. "God, You told me You loved me. You told me You were with me and that You would protect me. I believed You—I still do. But would You please forget about me right now? Please, God, please protect my mom." Olivia rose on her knees and clasped her hands together. She rocked back and forth as sobs tore through her body. "She's. . .she's. . .a–all I've g–g–got."

"Yes, Father." Tammy grasped Olivia's hands. "Please place Your angels around Olivia's mom and protect her from evil. We trust You and will give You the glory for this."

"You've arrived at the Whitford house, Mark?" Ben stood and paced the room while he talked into his phone.

Tammy dropped her volume to a whisper.

"Uh-huh." Ben ran his fingers through his unruly hair and turned away. "No one? You don't see anyone? You should probably wait for backup before going in. We don't want you to—" He stepped from the office into the hallway and lowered his voice.

Olivia gasped and covered her mouth with a trembling hand. "She's dead—I just know it. Everyone I love dies." She collapsed on the floor in a heap, her entire body shaking. She stared straight ahead with empty eyes. *Will Jake be next?*

Tammy put her hands on Olivia's upper arms, squeezed gently, and prayed.

Ben's usually tan face looked ghostlike and frozen when he stepped back into his office. He looked from Tammy to Olivia then squeezed his eyes shut and slipped his phone in his pocket.

Olivia jumped to her feet from where she'd been kneeling. She rushed to Ben, scraping her thigh on the corner of his desk before she grabbed the lapel of his jacket. "Why did you hang up your phone? Why aren't you talking to my mom? She's dead, isn't she?" Olivia's voice turned shrill. "Isn't she?"

Ben gently peeled her hands from his jacket and helped her to a seat. "I don't know. They haven't found her yet."

Olivia put her head in her hands, but not before she caught the look Ben gave Tammy over her head. Not good. *So this is what it feels like to be alone in the world? Empty.* Had Mom suffered? Of course she had. Charles wouldn't have had it any other way. Olivia never got to say good-bye. She never got to tell her mom that she'd been right about a few things. Never. . .

Oh God, You promised.

Tammy moved to the chair beside Olivia and put an arm around her shoulders while they waited in silence.

Olivia traced a crack in the wall with her eyes. Up and down. Jagged like her scar. The ticking minutes thundered from the clock on the wall, mocking Olivia's helplessness with every passing moment.

"Oh-livia. Where are you?"

Olivia cowered in the corner, behind her heavy window drapes. Why wouldn't Charles leave her alone? She gripped the curtains like a shield around her shaking body. Please, God. Please don't let him find me.

"Oh-livia?"

She heard banging and rustling as he searched for her. Olivia knew he'd find her soon. He always did when Mom wasn't home. At first, he just talked to her and said nice things—he told her it

*was their special time. He talked to her about her favorite books
and what she wanted to be when she grew up. She even kind of
liked him. . .then.*

"Isn't twelve a little old to be playing hide-and-seek?"

Yeah, that's right. I'm just playing a game, you creep. Please
just go away. Please, God.

*Olivia longed for the days of playing and chatting. Those ended
when Charles started getting weirder and weirder. Last time—
Olivia shuddered at the memory—Charles had. . .touched her.
What would he do this time?*

*"Ah, there you are." Charles pulled back the curtain and
exposed a trembling Olivia. "What's wrong? You cold? Come here.
I'll warm you up." He took her hand and led her—*

Ben's phone rang, startling Olivia. It was all she could do to
stop herself from grabbing it out of his hands while he answered
it. She swiped the tears off her cheek while she listened.

He turned away and listened to the caller. "Okay. I'll pass
that along. Please keep us informed, Mark." Ben looked at
Olivia. His eyes were kind, sad, scared, and wise—all at the
same time. "I need you to be calm, Olivia." He crouched down
and looked into her eyes.

Oh God. "What's going on?" Part of her didn't want to
know.

"Officer Stapleton found your mom and Charles. They're
in the house. Charles has her in the attic, and there's kind of a
standoff. She's okay though."

"A standoff? What does that mean?" Olivia shook Tammy's
hand off her arm and stood to her feet. "Does he have a gun?"

Ben nodded.

"But she's still alive? You're sure?"

He nodded again. "Mark's waiting for backup to arrive."

Olivia dropped on her knees to the carpet again and prayed

out loud. "Lord, You know what's happening right now. You know what's happened in the past. Please don't let evil win. Please protect my mom. I'm not saying this as an ultimatum—I'm really not trying to bribe You. But the fact is, it's the only way I'll know You're even interested in me. I thought so yesterday—but now this happened. You can make something big come out of this, though—something that makes me know for sure You're up there and You're on my side. Just. . .just save her. One word from You—one nod to an angel to help her out of this—that's all it would take. Please."

What was it that Ben had told her to say? "I t–t–trust You, Lord."

It sure didn't sound like a typical churchy prayer. But a flowery prayer full of thees and thous wouldn't have been real coming from her at that time, and He would know that. The best she could do was to speak from her heart. If God was who people said He was, that's what He'd want anyway.

Still on her knees, Olivia glanced up at Ben. "What will I do? What if something happens to her?"

Tammy crouched down beside her. "Let's not think about that right now. Have faith, Olivia. Let's trust God to protect her."

"Based on previous experience, that might not be the best plan." Olivia shook her head. "I'm holding out hope though. I'm trying to trust."

Ben jumped like he'd been awakened. "I'm going to go alert the prayer chain. I don't know why I didn't think of it sooner. Too shocked, I guess." He hurried from the room, already pressing buttons on his cell phone.

Olivia collapsed back against Ben's desk with her legs splayed out in front of her. She leaned her head back and stared straight ahead.

Tammy got up and went to a chair. She sat forward with her

elbows on her thighs and rocked in her seat, praying quietly.

BANG!

The door burst open, and Donna, Patty, Skye, Tricia, and Ju-Ju came barreling in.

"We just heard." Ju-Ju dropped down beside Olivia. She put her arms around Olivia's shaking shoulders and pulled her close. "Shh. Don't worry, chica."

Tricia looked at Tammy with a question in her eyes.

Tammy shook her head. "Nothing yet. Prayer teams are rallying all over the country by now, if I know Ben."

Olivia let her head fall against the desk. Waiting was the worst part. Shouldn't they have gotten to Mom by now? Shouldn't she have heard Ben's phone ring out in the hallway? No news was good news, right? Maybe not in this case—maybe the longer things went on. . . Olivia had to shake her head to clear the thoughts. She tried not to keep going to that dark place, but it was difficult. She almost couldn't imagine a favorable outcome—she'd never had one before, so why expect one now?

Ben paced back into the office, his hair seeming even more silvered than it had been that morning. His eyes were drawn and his face gaunt. He seemed to be taking it as hard as Olivia—a strangely comforting thought for her, since she was used to carrying the weight of the world by herself.

He stepped over to Olivia and squatted down to eye level.

Tammy scooted her chair to the side a few inches—in better line with Ben's face—and stared at his lips.

Ju-Ju clutched Olivia's hand tighter.

Skye took her other one.

Wait. He's not just coming to me to offer comfort. He has something to say. It's not good news. Olivia's stomach turned and threatened to empty. Judging by the lack of a smile and a sense of urgency, Olivia already knew the words that would come from Ben's lips. She'd heard them too many times. They amounted to one simple truth.

Olivia, you lose.

Her shoulders slumped even more, and she hung her head. She'd run out of tears.

"Liv. The situation has ended." Ben sighed. "Your mom is okay. She's going to be just fine."

Olivia raised her head slowly, not believing what she'd heard. "She's what? She's okay?"

Ben nodded with a hint of a smile. "She's not hurt at all."

Thank You, God.

"Thank You, Jesus." Tammy raised a hand toward heaven.

Ju-Ju grinned, and Tricia squealed.

Not so fast. "But why do you look so upset?" Olivia asked Ben. *Here comes the bad news.*

"Charles shot at the police officer. Thankfully, he missed. But Officer Stapleton had to shoot him." Ben closed his eyes. "Charles is in critical condition and is being transported by LifeFlight right now."

Olivia nodded and looked at the floor.

"What are you thinking right now?" Ben gave up his crouch and sat down beside her.

"Honestly?" Olivia shuddered. "I'm wondering if God is mad at me for hoping Charles dies."

Ben nodded. "I had a feeling you'd say that. You know what? You're human."

Olivia felt some slight relief even at those few words.

"God forgave you, and He expects you to forgive others— even when they don't ask for that forgiveness—and even Charles. But that will come in time. It's a process He'll work in you."

Olivia nodded. Enough about Charles. "I just can't believe

my mom is okay. When can I talk to her?"

"Officer Stapleton said he'd finish taking her initial statement and then call me back." Ben looked at his watch. "I'd figure maybe ten more minutes." Just as his words trailed off, his phone rang. Ben glanced at the display and handed it right over to Olivia.

"Hello?" She gripped the receiver.

"Livvie Love?" Mom's voice sounded weak.

Olivia gasped. "I'm so glad you're okay, Mom. I was so worried."

"Olivia. I'm. . .I'm just. . .I'm s–s–s–sorry." She coughed a sob. "I can't believe. . .what you've. . .b–b–been through, and it's all my f–f–fault."

"Shh, Mom, don't even think of that right now. Just take care of yourself. We'll talk about all that later."

"They're taking me to the police station to give a statement." Mom's breathing was ragged. "Hold on, Liv. They're telling me something."

Olivia heard rustling, like her mom had covered the phone with her hand. The muffled background voices were indistinguishable. Olivia picked at a burn in the carpet while she waited. She imagined the hole came from a rebellious teen who'd lit up a cigarette right in front of Ben and then dropped it to the floor in defiance when he told her to put it out.

"Liv?" Mom let out a shuddering breath when she came back on the line. "It's over."

"I know, Mom. You're safe."

"No, I mean it's all over." She drew a sharp breath. "He's dead."

Olivia nodded. "Are you okay with that, Mom?" *I know I am.*

"I don't have much of a choice. It's not the real Charles I'm going to grieve over; it's the ideal of what I'd hoped for." Mom sighed. "I have some real soul searching to do."

"We both do."

"I have to go with Mark now. I'll call you later, okay?" She started sobbing again.

"Okay. I'll be praying for you. Just get through all of this and then get some sleep." Olivia paused. "I love you, Mom."

But it was too late. She'd already hung up.

Olivia stared at the lifeless phone in her hand. Had the past few hours, weeks, months, years been real? Or were they all just one big nightmare? Was it over?

Her body jerked when she felt a light touch on her shoulder. Ben. She'd forgotten that she wasn't alone in the room. She looked around at her friends—her family—and then back to Ben's eyes. "It's finished."

Chapter 33

Maybe life wasn't meant to be easy. Maybe that's what made Olivia's search so difficult. She'd been looking for something that didn't exist. Demanding something she'd never been promised. Olivia stared at the ceiling, wishing she could take a nap. She needed to forget the past few days, forget about the concert she'd missed, forget about all she'd lost, even for just a little while, to make the time go faster.

She should have been at practice already. It broke her heart to have to stay home. Not only did she miss the music and the time with the orchestra, but she missed spending time with Justin on the ride down. Well, the Justin she'd thought he was anyway.

"Yo, Liv." Ju-Ju poked her head into the bedroom.

"Ah! You scared me."

"Sorry about that. Um. . .would you come with me? Ben wants you for something."

Sigh. She wanted nothing more than to sleep away her sorrows and heal from the past week's events. That wasn't going to be possible apparently.

Olivia shuffled along after Ju-Ju. "What does he want? Do you know?"

"I have no idea. You know Ben. It's all a big mystery."

"Right." The last thing she needed was any more drama.

"Here. He said to come into the dining room." Ju-Ju

pointed down the hall and let Olivia go first. When they arrived at the door, she swung it open wide and hundreds of people yelled.

"Surprise!"

Olivia stumbled back like she'd walked smack into a wall of noise.

Ju-Ju grabbed her elbow to steady her.

Olivia surveyed the room in dazed silence. Okay, maybe there weren't hundreds of people packed in here, but there had to be close to fifty. Who were they, and why were they surprising her?

Mr. Gables? What was he doing here? Why wasn't he at orchestra practice? Olivia's conductor stood in the center of the group, holding—wait. What was that he had hidden behind his top hat? An oboe? He held what looked like a Marigaux—one of the priciest and most professional oboes on the market—or at least an excellent replica. Where had he gotten that?

Having trouble adjusting her eyes to take in the full scene, Olivia only then realized that many of the people in the room were fellow orchestra members. Her eyes moved to Ben. "Can someone explain what's going on?"

"Mr. Gables, why don't you do the honors?" Ben waved his arm with a flourish.

"Miss Olivia, I have several things I'd like to say to you, if I may."

Olivia nodded then remembered her manners. "Yes, sir."

"You are a rare student, a brilliant oboist, and a pure heart. I knew the moment I heard you play your oboe that God had a special plan for you. I hoped I'd get to be a part of it, and now I do." He smiled down at her like a kindly father. "Following the tragedy of what happened to you the other day, the Denver School of Fine Arts dipped into its specialty fund to purchase this spectacular instrument for you." He held out the oboe.

Olivia gasped. "I'd hoped maybe you were offering me a loan until I could find a decent used one somewhere. But this is mine?" She took it with hesitant fingers, unsure of how or where to hold it so she wouldn't leave fingerprints.

"Ah, so you do recognize its value?" Mr. Gables's grin boasted his pride in his student.

"Of course. It's a Marigaux." Olivia shook her head. "How can I? It's too much."

"No. No. It's not too much. You haven't heard the terms." He winked.

"Terms?" Olivia had to force herself to focus on his words while she held the amazing French-made oboe in her hands.

"Yes, my dear Olivia. With the acceptance of this gift, you are agreeing to attend the Denver Fine Arts Academy next year on a full scholarship." He grinned as the whole room erupted in cheers.

The whole room, that is, except for Kira, who stormed out the doors in a huff. Her stomps up the stairs shook the floor.

Donna followed her.

"Anyway"—Mr. Gables shook his head in disdain and twisted his slick mustache between his fingers—"I'm jesting about the oboe requiring your attendance at the academy. It's yours regardless. But we would like nothing more than for you to graduate from our hallowed halls and bring honor to the name of the Denver Fine Arts Academy when you go on to do great things."

Olivia wiped her eyes, but the tears continued to flow. "I never. . . No one ever. . . How can I ever thank you?"

"Don't thank me. Turn all your gratefulness to Jesus. He's the One who gave you life, and He gave you your incredible talent. He deserves the praise, Miss Olivia."

She nodded. *I wish my mom were here.*

Ben stepped forward and cleared his throat. "Now, will you play for us?" He brought a chair to the center of the room where Olivia stood and motioned for her to sit.

In a daze, Olivia perched on the edge of the seat, turning the instrument over and over in her hands. What a thing of beauty. She moistened the attached reed and then played a tuning note. Her stomach flipped at the sound that escaped. She closed her eyes and began to play.

The first few measures filled the silent room. Then one by one, the audience began to sing along.

When sorrows like sea billows roll;
Whatever my lot, Thou has taught me to say,
It is well, it is well with my soul.

When she finished the song, everyone offered congratulations and the room began to clear. The girls had chores to finish and dispersed in different directions. The musicians filed out one by one to climb on the bus and head back down the mountain. Olivia shook Mr. Gables's hand. "I truly can't thank you enough, sir."

"Your presence for another year is thanks enough, young lady." His dark eyes twinkled. "Now, go practice."

"Yes, sir." Olivia grinned as he walked away. Right behind where Mr. Gables had stood sat Justin. Her grin faded just as quickly as it had appeared. Hidden like a coward. Olivia would have hidden, too, if she'd treated someone so despicably. She folded her arms across her chest and clenched her jaw.

"That was awesome, Liv. I think of that as *our* song."

"What are *you* doing here?"

Justin scrambled to his feet, his face white.

"Olivia? What's the matter? What did I do?"

Boy, he was a great actor. "Tell me the truth, Justin Bradley.

I'm going to ask you one time—God is your witness. Did you ever say one word about my scar to Kira?"

Justin's eyebrows knitted together in apparent confusion. "That's what this is about? Yeah, I said something to her, but—"

"That's all I wanted to know. Thanks for at least being honest about it." Olivia jogged for the door, trying not to cry until she escaped into the hallway. "I have to go."

The last thing she saw as the doors swung shut was Justin's wide eyes and open mouth.

Olivia ran to her room and collapsed on her bed with her brand-new oboe tucked in beside her—where it would stay. She was too tired to cry, too worn out to think.

Sleep.

෨

Olivia opened her eyes to startling pitch-black silence. She squinted and tried to see if anyone else was in the room. Skye's bed looked lumpy, and Tricia's long arm hung down from her bed, her hand resting on the floor. What about Ju-Ju? Was she in the bed beneath Olivia?

Ju-Ju stirred and let out a snore.

How had she slept through their coming in and getting ready for bed? She peeked at the clock on the desk. Already five o'clock in the morning. Her alarm would go off in an hour, and there was no way she could fall back to sleep after sleeping more than ten hours. She sat up slowly and swung her legs over the side, letting herself down to the floor as quietly as possible. No sense waking everyone else up.

The little light on the desk gave off only a small amount of light, so Olivia clicked it on. She carefully pulled out the top desk drawer and reached in for a few sheets of paper and a pen. Settling into the desk chair, she thought about how to convey what she'd needed to say for a long time.

Dear Mom,

I love you.

I just wanted to tell you that, and I hope you believe I mean it. Not only that, but I forgive you. The forgiveness I'm extending is as much for my sake as it is for yours. It's so I can be free of the anger—free of the bitterness and resentment I've had toward you for things you've done or haven't done over the years.

There, that feels so much better already.

I want to move on, Mom. I want us to move on. I'm sorry you're alone because I know you don't like to be. But I'm so glad you're safe. I don't know what I would have done if. . .

I made a deal with God. Did you know that? I told Him that if He saved you, if He brought you back to me, I'd give my whole life to Him because I'd fully believe, with my whole heart, that He cared about what happened to me.

He cares about you like that, too, Mom. You once knew that. In fact, you once taught me all about the things of God. I remember now.

Would you do me a favor? Would you please go back to church? And really think about getting counseling. You have a lot of junk to get through. We'll face it together as much as we can, but some of it you'll need to do on your own. Promise me you'll reach out and find a way? And that you'll go to church?

I have one other request, Mom. And it's a big one.

Move to Denver. Please? Why don't we just start over here? A new place, new home, new scenery. There's no reason not to. What's left for us there? Alicia said she'd help you get a job at the hospital if you want to work. Plus I just found out yesterday that I have a scholarship for next year.

I'll be able to graduate from Denver Fine Arts Academy—
what a dream come true for me!

Why can't we take what the devil meant for evil and
let God turn it around for good? Ben said that God loves it
when we give Him the chance to do that.

Let's do it. Okay? Please.

Love, Livvie

Olivia folded the paper and slipped it into an envelope out of the stationery pack Mom had given her. As she licked the glue and sealed the stamped envelope, she realized it was her first handwritten letter, other than all the thank-you notes Mom had made Olivia write when she was little. *Hmm.* She'd almost forgotten about being forced to write a note to her relatives or friends' parents after every gift, every trip to the movies, every dinner out. She'd hated doing it, but Mom still made her. Something else she'd been right about.

Olivia slipped from the room into the brightly lit hallway and let the door click into place behind her before heading down the stairs. The sconces cast eerie shadows on the walls of the rustic lower level. Finally at her destination, she pulled the handle and held her letter over the slot in the mailbox.

Please let Mom take this letter well. Whatever Your will is for our future, I trust You, Lord. Amen.

She dropped the letter and let the door slam back into place. Olivia stepped away but hurried back to pull the lever and make sure the letter had fallen. It was gone. Satisfied, she wiped her hands on her pajama pants and turned to head back to her room.

Olivia screamed as she felt a light touch on her shoulder. She whirled around with her hands raised to ward off an intruder.

Kira.

Chapter 34

Don't touch me, Kira." Olivia forced power into her dark eyes. "You don't want to mess with me."

"Don't be crazy. I'm not going to hurt you." Kira looked down. "I just heard someone leave your room and hoped it might be you."

"Why? So you could follow me and torment me with your insults? There's nothing you could say that will hurt me anymore, Kira." Olivia held out her arms. "Give it your best shot."

Kira closed her eyes and sighed. "That's not why I'm here."

"Great. Then we're through here." Olivia lifted her chin and stormed away.

Kira followed right behind. "Wait. I need to talk to you."

"I have nothing to say to you." *Just keep walking.* Kira meant nothing but trouble. But what could she want to say? Didn't everyone deserve a chance? Olivia slowed to a stroll, but she didn't look back. "Talk."

"I. . .I'm sorry."

Putting on the brakes completely, Olivia came to a dead stop. "You're sorry? For what, exactly?" *Breaking my oboe? Breaking my heart?*

"For all of it." Kira lowered her eyes.

Not getting off that easy, honey. "What's *all* of it, Kira? What exactly are you apologizing for?" As if she was really repentant about anything.

"I broke your oboe."

Duh. "Why did you do it?" Besides being cold and heartless. "And why are you telling me now?"

"I guess I did it because I was jealous. I. . .I'm sort of used to getting all the attention—most popular girl in school, gymnast, you know. Everyone was making such a big deal over you."

"Everyone?" Olivia raised one eyebrow.

"Well, especially Justin." Kira looked at Olivia for the first time. "I wanted to hurt you because of some things that happened. But none of it was your fault."

"I don't know what to say." Olivia crossed her arms over her chest. What did Kira expect? Everything was supposed to be fine all of a sudden? Just because she sort of apologized? "Do you know how much that oboe cost?"

"I do now. I didn't then. Not that cheaper would have made it okay." She looked down again. "There's more." Kira wrung her hands until her knuckles turned white. "It's about Justin." Her eyes welled up with tears. "We're not back together. Actually, we never were together. Justin's too smart—too good—for someone like me. He never fell for it. Not even for a second."

"But people said you guys were a thing. That you were like boyfriend-girlfriend."

Kira shook her head. "That's what I wanted everyone to believe, but that's not what happened. Justin spent a lot of time with me, that much is true. But it wasn't because he had any interest in me that way. He just saw me as a sort of personal mission. He saw through me and knew I wasn't for real."

Ah. Much like he'd tried to get Olivia to stop smoking. Was she only a personal mission? Someone else for Justin to fix? "Okay, so what about that picture you took and sent to Ben? Did you really believe that Justin was smoking that cigarette?"

"No. Of course not." Kira bit her lip.

"You could have gotten him in a lot of trouble. Thankfully, Ben knows his son too well for that." Now for the big question. "But what about me?"

"What about you?"

"I'm guessing Justin never said that about my scar? That it was horrid?" Olivia realized she was tracing the line on her cheek and jerked her hand away.

Kira shook her head. "No. He didn't say that." She took a deep breath. "In fact. . ."

Olivia waited a moment. "In fact, what?"

She raised her eyes and looked at Olivia. "He didn't say it was horrid. In fact, he told me that he loved that about you. Let's see, how did he put it? Oh, right. He said it made you vulnerable and reminded him that even though you're so strong, you've been through a lot and you're fragile. He said he felt the need to protect you. Or something like that."

Olivia let tears course down her cheeks. "You hurt me when you told me what you did about my scar. But you know what else? You hurt Justin, because I pushed him away after that. Just like you wanted." Olivia shuddered at the memory of the look on Justin's face when the dining room door closed on him the last time she saw him.

"I know." Kira hung her head.

"That proves you never loved him, Kira. The only person you've loved up until now is yourself. You've forgotten something though."

Kira looked up, her eyes rimmed with tears but sparkling with hope.

"You've forgotten that Jesus loves you, too. He has your back. You don't need to do all these manipulations to make life go well for you. You just need to follow Him."

Kira nodded. "I just don't get that whole thing."

"You need to do what Ben told me to do."

"What?" Kira seemed eager, like she'd do anything. Like Olivia had felt when she came to the end of herself. She and Kira had something in common after all.

"Say, 'I trust You, Lord,' every hour until you feel like you do trust Him."

"That's it?" Kira looked skeptical, just like Olivia had.

Olivia smiled and nodded. "That's it."

Ben stepped around the corner. "Well, there's a tad more to it than that, but you've done a fantastic job at getting her started, Olivia." He turned to Kira. "I heard everything. We're going to need to talk—a lot's been going on with you the last few months, Kira. It's time to get to the bottom of it." He slipped his arm across her shoulders and steered her to his office.

Kira cast one more glance at Olivia; then her head hung low in defeat as she walked away.

"Hey, Kira."

Kira turned to look at Olivia. Her eyes were wide.

"I forgive you."

Chapter 35

H appy birthday, dear Olivia. Happy birthday to you."
Olivia closed her eyes and wished for a real family. She wished for a future of love and happiness—peace and security. She opened them and blew out the seventeen candles with one breath—the breeze helped. She loved having a June birthday so she could have her cake outside as had been tradition since she was a toddler. The smell of spring was always in the air—even in Chicago, but especially this year in Colorado. The trees were covered with leaves, and the birds chirped in the boughs. Who'd have thought she'd turn into such a lover of the outdoors?

Her birthday. That meant she'd spent every major holiday alone at Diamond that year. Thanksgiving, Christmas, Easter, and her birthday without any family. But it was strangely okay somehow. She gazed up at the Rocky Mountain landscape. *I hope I never have to leave.*

Patty and Tammy cut the horse-shaped chocolate cake and passed out Styrofoam bowls of vanilla ice cream. Olivia almost turned hers down because of the hour she'd have to spend on the treadmill later, but then she thought of what Tricia had put herself through. Life was too short, and Olivia wasn't about to spend it worrying about her weight to the point of not having a piece of her own birthday cake. So she reached for a big piece of the mane with extra frosting.

She tried to force herself not to watch what Tricia did when

offered a piece of cake, but she couldn't help herself. *Phew.*
Tricia selected a small piece and just a dab of ice cream. A treat
without going overboard. That meant she didn't intend to visit
the restroom after she ate it. The best gift Olivia could receive
for her birthday.

Ben and Alicia burst through the doors and strode across
the yard to the picnic area. "Happy birthday, Olivia!" He put
his arm around his wife and beamed at Olivia. "We have a big
surprise for you. Let's see. What's the one thing you'd want to
do on your special day?"

That was easy. "I'd love several hours to ride Cinnamon up
the mountain."

"Well, that's fine. But I mean something you really want,
but wouldn't think possible." Ben grinned.

Alicia's eye sparkled. "Think big."

Ugh. Seemed like they had done something special for her.
What if she guessed wrong? Olivia hated to hurt their feelings
by not coming up with the right answer. "The only other thing
I can think of definitely isn't possible, so I don't want to say it."

"Try me." Ben folded his arms across his chest and gave her
an *I've got a secret* grin.

He asked for it. "I'd love to be with my mom."

Ben put two fingers between his lips and let out a loud,
shrill whistle.

The patio door swung open and there she stood, right on
the deck.

Olivia dropped her fork full of cake on the picnic table, and
it bounced onto the grass, sending crumbs and frosting flying
everywhere. "Mom? How? Did you?" She turned to Ben.

He shook his head. "Justin did it all. He set it up—with
permission, of course."

Mom stood rooted to her spot, her eyes wide. "Liv?"

She opened her arms.

Olivia ran to her and fell into the embrace she'd needed for years. She laid her head on her mother's shoulder.

"Happy birthday, Livvie Love. Everything is going to be okay." Mom pulled back a little, put her hands on each side of Olivia's face, and looked into her eyes. "I love you."

Olivia crumpled. The years of fighting to be strong, begging to be noticed, hiding from the pain. . .they all washed away in the final wave of God's healing.

It was finished.

ꙅ

On her way out to the stable to saddle up two horses, Olivia saw a bent-over figure in the garden. She stopped walking and just watched. His arms bulged as he pulled at the wire fencing. The sprigs of vegetables that poked up from the dirt were about to attract the rabbits and other hungry animals. Time to fence them out.

Justin wiped the sweat off his forehead. He reached into his pocket and pulled out a bandanna that he folded and tied around his head to keep the sweat from dripping into those gorgeous blue eyes of his.

"Need some help?"

Startled, Justin lost his grip on the fencing, and it sprang back into the tight roll he'd been fighting against.

Olivia winced. "Sorry. Here, let me hold the end and you unroll."

Silently, Justin followed her instructions without looking into her eyes.

Olivia stood still while Justin pulled his side around the post he'd already placed. "I think I've got it now. Thanks." He took the end she held with one hand and grabbed her hand with the other. "Olivia. It's been over a month since we last spoke—it's been so hard to be around here knowing you're avoiding me. I don't know what I said to offend you, but I'm sorry. I wouldn't hurt you for anything. Ever."

"I know that now." Olivia's chin quivered. "The truth came out eventually. It was all Kira's work. She came to me and apologized, believe it or not." She looked into Justin's eyes. "I'm the one who's sorry. I didn't believe in you. You should be angry with me, not me with you."

Justin shook his head. "Liv, you probably have good reason to assume that people will betray you. I won't. Ever. But it will take you time to learn that and believe it." He released her hand.

Olivia nodded. "I hope not too much time—I don't want you to run off on me."

He held her gaze. "Never."

"Olivia? Where are you?" Mom called from the deck.

"I'm out here, Mom. You all freshened up? I'm just getting saddles on the horses. Come on out." Olivia looked at Justin. "Thank you for bringing her here."

He winked. "No problem."

Mom approached them just as Justin turned back to his work.

Olivia finished cinching Buttercup's saddle for Mom and then mounted Cinnamon. "Ready to go?"

Olivia tugged lightly on the reins and turned to see if Mom was following her up the trail. "You doing okay on Buttercup?"

"Oh yes. She and I are getting along beautifully. She's a darling." Mom leaned down and patted the horse's neck.

"She really is." Olivia pointed up the trail. "Just beyond that ridge is a clearing. We'll let them wander a bit in there. They like to explore." She flicked her reins and tapped her heels into Cinnamon's side to get her moving a bit faster. No real need though. The horse knew exactly where to go.

The sun beat its warmth down on her head, but Olivia felt

the cool mountain air on her face. The blend was invigorating. Snow melted and fell from the trees while green grass poked from the earth, searching for sunlight and nourishment. The promise of spring. So much hope.

Olivia reined Cinnamon to a stop when they reached the clearing. She closed her eyes, breathed in the fresh air, and let it cleanse her lungs. "I miss Daddy."

"I miss him, too." Mom lifted her face to the sunshine. "Life would have been so different."

"I'll never forget the day of his funeral. I think about it all the time." Olivia patted Cinnamon's neck.

"Yeah. I wish I remembered more of it, but I fainted and spent most of it in the foyer getting medical attention."

Olivia's jaw dropped. "What? You fainted? That's where you were?"

"Where did you think I was?"

"I just always wondered why you didn't come to me while I was crying on the floor in front of his casket. I felt so alone." Olivia turned her head away so Mom wouldn't see the tears. "I'd just lost my daddy, and all I wanted was my mommy."

Mom gasped. "Liv, I didn't know you felt that way. I had no idea. You've been carrying that all these years?"

Olivia nodded. "I thought you didn't care."

"Oh, sweetie. No. It kills me that you've been hanging on to that—that you ever had to wonder." Mom reached out and took Olivia's hand and gazed through the trees at the blue sky above. "It's all going to be different now. Do you believe that?"

"I do." *Deep breath.* "Mom, I mailed you a letter a few weeks ago. Did you get it?"

She smiled and nodded. "I was waiting for you to bring that up."

Olivia nodded but said nothing, hoping Mom would

make the next move.

"Congratulations on the scholarship, Liv. That's amazing."

Olivia twisted the reins between her fingers. "Thanks. We talked about that on the phone already." *What else?* And why hadn't she brought the letter up before?

"I agree with everything you said—church, counseling, job. You're right about all of it."

"So you've gone to church?"

"I did go Sunday, but I've decided not to get involved."

Olivia's shoulders slumped. "Why not, Mom?" Nothing would change if she didn't start with the basics. Church was step one.

Mom's eyes twinkled. "Wouldn't it make more sense to just start going to church here?"

"Do you mean. . . ? You're going to move here? I get to stay in Colorado?" Olivia's eyes lit up. School. Friends. Mountains. Church. And Justin. Her heart swelled as the blessings poured into her mind. As long as Mom really meant it.

Mom nodded. "Why not? It's not like my choices have led us anywhere worth hanging on to. Why not a fresh start? And Liv, you deserve this shot at a future. When I think of all you've been through—" She took a shuddering breath and wiped her eyes.

"Thanks, Mom." Olivia held her gaze. "It really means a lot to me." She looked up at the sky and let the sun bathe her face. "You know, it's not just this place I love." She spread her arms at the expanse of the outdoors. "It's also *that* place. Diamond Estates. Ben, Alicia, and the counselors are doing amazing work with the girls who come here. It's so sacrificial. I want to live like that. I'd love to be a counselor here after I finish school—or do something like this."

"I could see you doing that, Liv. I mean, you sure won't get rich." She chuckled.

Money. Wealth. Stuff. Why did her mother always have to go there? Some things never changed.

Mom went on. "But I know now that riches aren't even close to being important to the big picture. It took me awhile, but I figured it out."

Olivia gasped and looked up and down Mom's body. "Wait! Mom. Are you wearing off the rack?"

"Come on, now. You can't be serious." Mom looked down at her clothes in horror. "Does it look like I am?" Her eyes blazed with panic.

"I'm just teasing you." Apparently the materialism would be tackled with baby steps. Olivia smiled. Some things never did change—but that didn't have to be all bad.

"I want you to know something, Liv. I'm putting most of Charles's money and investments in a trust for you."

Olivia's stomach turned at the mention of his name, and she opened her mouth to protest. She didn't want a dime of his money.

Mom held up her hand. "No, Liv, hear me out. You can do whatever you want with it. Maybe it will fund your own place like Diamond Estates after college. Think about it. You said you wanted to take what Satan meant for evil and let God use it for good. Why not let God win in a big way?"

Wow. She was right. Again. Olivia nodded. "What a great idea, Mom. Thank you."

"I kept out enough to get us a place to live, nothing extravagant. We'll start house hunting tomorrow so it can be ready when you graduate from here in August—that's only a couple of short months away, you know. And then I'll get a job."

Could it be true? Did Olivia have a shot at one of those happy families like she saw at church? Bumped and bruised along the way—but happy in the end?

Wait a second. Olivia pulled on her reins and brought Cinnamon to a stop. "Mom, about the house. . .I have an idea."

🌀

"Where are we going, and when are we going to get there?" Skye whined from the far back seat of the van.

Ben laughed and looked back at his son seated beside Olivia. "Skye, you remind me of Justin when he was three— impatient as all get-out."

"Thanks, Dad." The tips of Justin's ears reddened.

"Patience, Skye. You'll see when we get there." Olivia tossed a neck pillow at her.

Tricia wiggled her eyebrows at Ju-Ju beside her in the next-to-last row. "I know where we're going. Nah-nah-nah-nah-nah."

"Real mature, T!"

"Soon enough, girls. Turn left up here at the stop sign," Mom directed Ben. "Then an immediate right." She leaned forward and pointed out the front window. "It's that one right at the end."

"Here we are." Olivia climbed from the van and waited until everyone stood on the driveway. "Welcome to our new home."

"This is yours?" Ben whistled. "It's awesome."

It sure is. Olivia looked up at the modest, two-story redbrick exterior and the wide porch with its rocking chairs and porch swing. Large backyard, wooded on three sides. *It's perfect.*

"Yep." Mom put her hands on her hips and leaned back to gaze up toward the gables. "I closed this morning. I'm hoping to get it painted and all ready before the Diamond Estates graduation—only three more weeks."

"Let's go in." Olivia skipped up the steps and opened the white front door. The hardwood floors gleamed, and the white trim looked like it had been freshly painted. They passed through the foyer into a sunny yellow kitchen with white cabinets. The tiny breakfast nook was big enough for a round table with four chairs. Its sliding glass doors led out to a large, weathered deck.

The group stepped out to see the backyard.

"This is awesome." Justin gestured to the mountain view and the thick trees.

"I have to admit, I'm partial to that." Ben pointed to the built-in grill. "You've chosen a beautiful home, Ginny. I know Alicia will agree." He gazed up at the white siding on the back of the house.

Olivia chuckled. *Wonder what he'd say if he could see where we used to live.* The foyer of that house would swallow the entire first floor of this one. But *this* was home.

"There's a finished basement—I'm going to let Olivia do whatever she wants in that space. She'll make it a hangout of some kind, I'm sure."

"Yeah, but let's go upstairs. That's the best part." She led them through the house, past the dining room and family room, up the carpeted staircase with its wooden handrails. She passed the first few doors and went right to the master bedroom. "This one's Mom's." She gave them just a second to peek in at the vaulted ceilings and the bathroom with its jetted bathtub. It was half the size of the one she'd had in Illinois.

"Come on, there's more. This one is my room." Olivia stepped back so everyone could peek inside. "That's enough. Come on." She hustled them into the hallway, her stomach knotted.

"Why are you in such a hurry?" Justin laughed. "You said this was the best part."

"Yeah, really. *Chica es muy loco.*" Ju-Ju rotated a finger by her head.

"I'm not crazy, you'll see." Olivia stopped beside two closed doors and winked at Tricia, who grinned. If only she could be a part of this, too. "Ju-Ju and Skye. . .pick." She bowed to the doors.

"Pick? Pick what?" Skye shook her head. "I don't understand."

Mom stepped in front of them and bent to eye level. "Girls, what Olivia is trying to tell you is that we have a place for you here. We want you to come live with us here in our new home. I want to give you girls a fraction of the love you've given my girl. I'm not a perfect mom, but I'm learning." She clasped her hands, her eyebrows wrinkled in nervous anticipation. "Will you come?"

Ju-Ju's jaw dropped. Tears rained from her eyes and dropped heavily on her shirt. It was the first time Olivia had seen Ju-Ju cry. "You mean it? A real bedroom, in a real home, with a real family?" Her eyes looked hopeful, but she shook her head. "It sounds too good to be true. What's the catch?"

"There's no catch, silly. We want you here." Olivia reached out her arms, and Ju-Ju fell into her grasp. It had been years since her friend had been held in a loving embrace. Years since she'd had a family or any permanent security. She clung to Olivia's shirt, her shoulders still shaking with sobs.

Skye was next. "Do you mean it?" She blinked rapidly. "Is it okay?" Skye turned to Ben in a panic.

"Yes, girls. We've worked it all out. This is your home starting today, after graduation." Ben rocked back on his heels, his pride evident on his face. Talk about a happy ending.

"Want to see your rooms?" Mom grinned and motioned to the doors.

Ju-Ju put her hand on the doorknob closest to her and looked at Skye. "Ready?"

Skye bit her lip and nodded.

They opened the doors at the same time and stepped into

their very own rooms with white, primed walls.

"I'd have had the walls painted, but I want you to pick your own colors. I want you to make your room special, a place you want to be. We'll pick out furniture, curtains, and bedding once you know exactly what you want."

Skye and Ju-Ju rotated in full circles, trying to take it all in.

"Now, the bathroom." Mom gestured to the large bathroom that divided the two rooms. "You'll have to share this one. We'll choose a color that works with both of your rooms—you know, something you both like."

"Mrs. Whitford. . ."

"Please call me Ginny, Mrs. Mansfield, or even Mom. I'm leaving Whitford behind in Illinois."

"Mrs. Mansfield, then. . .I just can't thank you enough."

"You already have. I wish you could come, too, Tricia. But God's got you right in the palm of His hand—you'll graduate Diamond Estates when the time is right. Then you'll go home to your family."

"Believe me, I've had a few pangs of jealousy, but on the plus side, I'm thrilled that none of you guys are leaving the area." Tricia gave a weak smile. "I'll be fine, I promise. I'm really happy for you all."

Ben looked at his watch. "Yep. The three of you are ready to embark on new things. Your time at Diamond Estates has come to a close. You've all done me proud, and I'm going to miss you."

"We won't be far away." Olivia turned to Justin.

He squeezed Olivia's hand. "I have a feeling you'll be seeing a lot of them, Dad."

Chapter 36

B en took his place at the pulpit and looked out at the rows of Diamond girls cheering on the graduates and the family members in the rows behind them. Then he turned his gaze down to the three girls who were leaving the program that day.

Olivia felt tears already welling up within her. She'd come to love Ben, Alicia, Tammy, and everyone else like they were family—a unique blend of parents and special friends. Surely a combination of hearts blended by God with the express purpose of bringing His love to Olivia in so many ways. It would be difficult for her to walk away from that place in a few hours and get into her mom's car and drive away, never to live like family with them again—well, most of them.

Misty-eyed himself, Ben took a steadying breath. "I'm so proud of you girls, and I'm thankful that the Lord saw fit to give me the opportunity to guide you to Him. I will treasure the memory of each one of you. In fact, Alicia and I look forward to a lifelong friendship with you."

His eyes moved down the row, stopping on Ju-Ju. "Julia, you have changed me with your humor and the strength with which you face the world around you. You were handed a plate of garbage, but you turned it into a. . .well, a Ding Dong."

Olivia grinned as the audience burst into laughter.

Ben turned to Skye. "Dear, sweet Skye, you have brought a bright light into my life that wasn't there before. Your joy is infectious, and once Jesus got ahold of you. . .wow. What a sight to behold. I'm very grateful that you and Ju-Ju have found a family and a home. You both deserve it.

"I also want to say something to another one of your special foursome." He let his gaze travel to the seat beside Skye. "Oh, Tricia. I worried that you'd be a handful when you arrived at Diamond Estates. You're exquisite, and I expected you to be anything but what you really are—humble, gracious, and as beautiful inside as out." He leaned forward and pointed at her. "You might have a little more work to do, but I want you to know and believe that you're important. Let the Lord prove that to you. Stand up and be counted. When you leave, you're going to go on to do mighty things for God."

"Olivia." Ben choked up on her name. "Words can't express how I've been affected by your presence here. You haven't been here that long compared to some, but my life will be forever changed by knowing you. You've endured so much, yet you came out victorious in Jesus."

He stepped back and grinned at them all. "One of the most difficult parts of my job is to love you and then let you go. We've had some great times and also some really difficult times over the past months. I want to keep you here, under the shelter of my wings, protected from the world. But that would limit what God wants to do in each of you. And, on the flip side, one of the greatest joys that comes with my job is getting to sit back and watch the Lord move in your lives in ways you can't even imagine.

"Allow me to close this service with a word of prayer. Then you're all invited to the fellowship hall for refreshments."

As he prayed, the butterflies in Olivia's tummy kicked up their fluttering. It was easy to follow the Lord while she lived it, breathed it, ate it, and drank it. . .all day, every day in a house full of people who shared the same goal. How would it be to go to a real school? Live in a normal community? Spend time with non-Christians? Time would tell, she supposed.

What about prayer time? She'd grown to love those early morning hours in the chapel, with praying teenagers scattered around the room. Donna, Patty, and Tammy kneeling with their elbows on a chair. Worship music playing softly on the stereo and Ben walking around the room, touching each girl on the head as he whispered heartfelt petitions to a mighty God on their behalf.

Would she keep praying in the morning? Again, totally up to her. Maybe Ju-Ju and Skye would want to do it together. That would probably help her keep the commitment. But what if they didn't want to or wanted to do it at a different time? Olivia had to make up her own mind and do it for herself, no matter what her friends decided to do.

Ultimately, she was on her own. Just her and God.

She shifted her eyes to the row on her right and caught Justin staring. He winked.

Okay, her, God, and Justin—if God willed it.

". . .Amen." Ben finished his prayer and smiled at Ju-Ju, Olivia, and Skye. "Go with God."

The rows of onlookers erupted into a round of applause, and the girls rose and hugged each other. "I'm sure going to miss having you girls around here." Tricia wiped away a tear. "Tammy says it'll be good for me. I'm sure she's right. I can't believe you're leaving, though."

Olivia squeezed her tighter and held on for a moment. When she released her, Tricia pointed over Olivia's shoulder. "I think someone's waiting to talk to you."

Kira. For once, Olivia's stomach didn't clench at the sight of her.

"I know you have a lot of people to talk to, so I won't take a lot of your time." Kira raised her gaze to lock with Olivia's. "I just wanted to say thanks."

Olivia nodded. "Changes. Once and for all. Right?"

"Yep. I promise." Kira's eyes shifted to just over Olivia's shoulder. "Your public awaits."

Turning, Olivia expected to find her mom and Jake, but she ran right into Justin.

"Where are you off to so fast?" Piercing blue eyes sparkled just inches from her face.

Welcome back, butterflies. Olivia had wondered how things would change between her and Justin once she was no longer under the umbrella of Diamond Estates' rules. She was about to find out. "Hi there." She tilted her face down and looked up at him.

"Have any plans this weekend?" Justin tipped his head to one side, his wavy hair draping across his shoulder.

Olivia shook her head but didn't trust herself to speak. This weekend? Nothing but getting to know the new house and helping Ju-Ju and Skye unpack and get settled in their new rooms down the hall from hers.

"May I take you out to dinner? Maybe a movie?"

Her first date. Hopefully it would be her last first date. "I'd like that very much." Olivia felt her cheeks turning pink.

Justin took her hand in his and turned her toward the door to the fellowship hall. "Shall we?"

He intended to hold her hand in front of all those people? Well, it wasn't against the rules anymore. *Fresh start.* Funny how those once-dreaded words had recently taken on new meaning in more ways than one.

They headed up the sloped center aisle of the church when Olivia saw her mom and Jake standing off to the side, waiting. She dropped Justin's hand and ran into her mom's arms and squealed. "I did it."

She jumped from her mom's hug into Jake's—the first time since he'd left for college. Oh, how she'd missed him.

He lifted her and swung her around in a circle. "I'm so sorry for. . .for not. . .knowing," he whispered in her ear. "I would give anything to go ba–"

Olivia placed her hand gently over his mouth and shook her head. They'd covered it all on the phone over the past months— no need to let a dead man poison this perfect day.

Jake set her down and gave her a gentle smile.

Olivia lifted her hand in the universal sign for *I love you*.

Jake nodded and grinned. He held up his hand in the same sign and pointed to Olivia. Nodding his head toward Justin, Jake opened his palms. "Who's this?"

"Ack! I'm sorry I haven't introduced you two." She pulled Justin over and signed as she spoke. "Justin, my brother Jake. Jake, this is. . .my Justin."

৯

"My Livvie Love." Mom smiled down on her as she looked over Olivia's shoulder into the backstage mirror. "You've grown up so much this year. You're a real lady. I'm so very proud of you."

Olivia smiled. "It's been a long road. But it was worth it to get to this moment. I feel like everything in my life has led me to this. Everything that has ever been important—you, God, music—it's all been made right in my life. There's only one thing missing." Her eyes clouded over as she imagined how proud her dad would have been of her at that moment.

"I have something for you." Mom reached into her purse and pulled out a purple velvet box. "Your dad wanted to give you this on your wedding day, but I think now is the right time. I'm sure he would have agreed."

"Dad knew about whatever's in this box?" Olivia's hand

shook as she reached for it.

"He didn't just know about it—it was his doing." Mom gestured for her to go ahead and open it.

Olivia savored the moment. Once she knew what lay inside, she could never go back to the magic of wondering. She gingerly lifted the hinged lid that her daddy had once touched with his own hands. That was gift enough even if the box were empty. But inside, resting on a white velvet pillow, lay a delicate pearl necklace. In the center was a large pink pearl nestled between two smaller white ones. A pink pearl lay on each side of those white ones and then two more white pearls finished off each end of the strand. "It's beautiful, Mom. You mean Dad picked this out?"

"Not exactly. Here, I'll explain." Mom lifted the necklace and slipped it around Olivia's neck. "See the big pink pearl in the center?"

Olivia nodded and touched it with two fingers as she gazed into the mirror. The necklace draped elegantly across her neck. Her hair in a loose updo with cascading tendrils, along with her black velvet ball gown, set it off perfectly.

"Your dad bought that one the day you were born. For the next seven years, he added a new pink pearl on your birthday. He kissed each one as he selected it and prayed that the new year would find you blessed with all of your greatest wishes." Her breath caught as a sob welled in her throat.

Olivia wiped away a single tear that coursed down her cheek.

"Your eighth year. . .I had to. . .take over the duty." Mom laid her fingertips gently on each of the white pearls nestled between the pink ones. "I wanted to leave the pink ones to your dad, so you'd always know exactly which ones he'd chosen for you. And I also wanted to spread them out over the years so his prayers and wishes for you could be a part of your whole lifetime, not just the first seven years. So I put my white ones between them."

Oh Daddy. Olivia's pearls swam in her eyes as she peered through her tears. "I never could have imagined anything more beautiful."

"There are still a few more pearls to add before it's finished. One for your eighteenth birthday, and one for your wedding. Maybe even one for my first grandchild." Mom winked. "But I'll just borrow it back from you when I need to add to it."

Someone cleared his throat. "Miss Mansfield, I'm sorry to interrupt, but it's time to take your place." The stagehand held back the velvet drape as he waited for her to join the orchestra in the pit.

Olivia took a deep breath and touched the center pearl one more time before turning away. "How did I ever get so lucky?"

"It's not luck, Liv. None of it."

"No. I don't suppose it is. Blessed. We're blessed." Olivia took her place in the symphony orchestra and raised her oboe to give the tuning note.

After the notes faded into silence, Mr. Gables stepped up to his music stand and waited. He lifted his arms to begin *The Phantom of the Opera.* Just beyond his right shoulder, in the audience, Olivia saw Justin in the front row holding a bouquet of roses so large it almost blocked his view.

He raised his hand and made the universal sign for *I love you.*

Discussion Questions

1. What kept Olivia from seeking God?
2. What keeps you from fully realizing God's will in your life?
3. How did Olivia's relationship with her daddy mirror her relationship with God?
4. Who or what has helped you understand God's love for you?
5. How were the words Olivia's dad prayed just before he died a reflection of Christ's love for you?
6. What was the defining moment for Olivia?
7. Was that change easy for her?
8. What has been a defining moment in your walk with Christ?
9. Do change and growth come easy for you?
10. Did Olivia learn more about God from the good things or the bad things?
11. How are you like Olivia? How are you different?
12. What have you learned about your own choices from reading about Olivia's life?

Chapter-by-Chapter
Discussion Guide

Chapter 1
- What are some words you might use to describe how Olivia feels about her life?
- What do you think she's afraid of?

Chapter 2
- Why do you think Olivia's mom won't hear her out about Charles?
- What makes Olivia begin to think it's okay to do things she'd once thought were wrong?
- Can you understand her choices?

Chapter 3
"If it feels good, do it."

- What does that statement mean to you in light of this chapter?
- What does it mean to you when you consider God's Word?

So let God work his will in you. Yell a loud no to the Devil and watch him scamper. Say a quiet yes to God and he'll be there in no time. Quit dabbling in sin. Purify your inner life. Quit playing the field. Hit bottom, and cry your eyes out. The fun and games are over. Get serious, really serious. Get down on your knees before the Master; it's the only way you'll get on your feet. (James 4:7–10 MSG)

Chapter 4

- Describe Olivia's downward progression and how sin has become easier for her.
- In what ways have you already seen God at work in her life up to this point?
- What are her thoughts about God?

Chapter 5

- Olivia admitted to herself that the miracle of the music, especially the solo, was that she felt heard. Why do you think being heard is so important to her?
- She mentioned that she's smart enough to know when to stop doing certain things. Is that how it usually works?
- Do you think she regrets her actions? Or is she just mad that she got caught? Why?

Chapter 6

- This chapter leaves Olivia with some real tension. Should she be in trouble?
- What would be a logical way for a parent to respond?
- What is Olivia afraid of?
- How does God respond to sin?

Don't let sin rule your body. After all, your body is bound to die, so don't obey its desires or let any part of it become a slave of evil. Give yourselves to God, as people who have been raised from death to life. Make every part of your body a slave that pleases God. Don't let sin keep ruling your lives. (Romans 6:12–14 CEV)

Chapter 7
- Describe Olivia's hopelessness at this point in her story.
- She believes that God is out to get her. What makes her think that?
- What does God say about that?

No test or temptation that comes your way is beyond the course of what others have had to face. All you need to remember is that God will never let you down; he'll never let you be pushed past your limit; he'll always be there to help you come through it. (1 Corinthians 10:13 MSG)

Chapter 8
- How do you feel about Olivia's mom at this point in the book?
- Do you think Olivia is completely right about her mom?
- What could Olivia be doing differently to improve the communication between herself and her mother?
- How is your communication at home?

Chapter 9
- How do you feel about Justin's thoughts on dating?
- In high school, is a dating relationship a temporary thing?
- Why do you think teens place so much importance on having a dating relationship?

Chapter 10
- Do you think it was fair for Ben to say he would have sent Olivia home if she had planned to stay? Why?
- Do you want someone to be your friend because she's forced or because she wants to?
- Do you think Jesus feels like that, too?

Chapter 11

- What could Olivia have done differently when Jordyn said she was okay to drive?
- How would you have handled the exact same situation?
- What can Olivia do about it now?
- Olivia thinks God hates her. What do you think?

In Psalm 10:1 (NIV), David felt a lot like Olivia does; he asked, "Why, LORD, do you stand far off? Why do you hide yourself in times of trouble?" But David pressed on, and he learned the truth about God:

I love you, Lord, my strength.
The Lord is my rock, my fortress and my deliverer;
my God is my rock, in whom I take refuge,
my shield and the horn of my salvation, my stronghold.
I called to the Lord, who is worthy of praise,
and I have been saved from my enemies.
(Psalm 18:1–3 NIV)

Chapter 12

- Olivia has to face the funeral of her best friend while carrying the guilt of her own involvement in the accident. Does she share in the responsibility for Jordyn's death?
- She has fears about not making it to heaven. Are those fears justified?

The truth about heaven:

> *God has given us eternal life, and this life is in his Son. Whoever has the Son has life; whoever does not have the Son of God does not have life.* (1 John 5:11–12 NIV)

Chapter 13

- Do you think it was difficult or easy for Olivia to finally decide to go to Diamond Estates? Why?
- Olivia talks about luck quite a bit. She blames God for the bad things and then praises luck for the good things. What do you think about that?

Chapter 14

- What do you think about the rules at Diamond Estates?
- Is it unfair that the girls have to get up at such an early hour, have meals at the same time, keep their rooms clean, and so on?
- Do you think Olivia can handle that lifestyle after what she's used to?

Chapter 15

- What does Tricia mean when she says it's better not to be beautiful at all than to be gorgeous and have to try to stay that way?
- How do you think she's feeling about herself?
- Do you think she has a good grip on how God sees her? Why or why not?

Chapter 16

- Where do you feel God's presence most? Or do you struggle with that like Olivia?
- How does God make it easy to find Him?

If I climb to the sky, you're there!
If I go underground, you're there!
If I flew on morning's wings

to the far western horizon,
You'd find me in a minute—
   you're already there waiting!
Then I said to myself, "Oh, he even sees me in the dark!
   At night I'm immersed in the light!"
(Psalm 139:8–11 MSG)

Chapter 17

- What might be standing in the way of Olivia's knowing Jesus like she did as a child?
- What hinders you from approaching God?

Chapter 18

- What about prayer time? Do you have your own daily quiet time with God?
- Olivia struggles with feeling judged by the people at church. Do you ever feel that way?
- What does God say about forgiveness and the sins of the past?

He has removed our sins as far from us as the east is from the west. (Psalm 103:12 NLT)

Chapter 19

- Can you understand why Olivia doubts God's existence?
- Why do you think God lets bad things happen to people, especially kids?
- Olivia has trouble thinking of things to be thankful for. What are you most thankful for in your life?
- When Olivia finds the cigarettes in her bag, what should she do?

Chapter 20

- How do you think Officer Stapleton could suffer such loss and still have joy and peace, when someone like Olivia blames God for her pain? What's the difference between the two?
- Is there any grief or pain in your life that keeps you from drawing close to God?

Chapter 21

- How would you handle the situation with Kira?
- What do you think is really going on there?
- In real life, we don't have the benefit of seeing into people's motives like we do in fiction. How can you apply that fact to future conflicts that come up?

Chapter 22

- Was it luck that got Olivia the audition for the orchestra?
- Why can't she see God's blessings?

Chapter 23

- Compare how Ju-Ju, Skye, Olivia, and Tricia feel about gossip.

Mean-spirited slander is heartless;
quiet discretion accompanies good sense.
A gadabout gossip can't be trusted with a secret,
but someone of integrity won't violate a confidence.
(Proverbs 11:12–13 MSG)

- How do you feel about Kira now that you know more of her story?
- What should the girls do about Kira?

Chapter 24

- Olivia is starting to admit to herself that she has feelings for Justin. What do you think about that?
- How might her feelings for Justin affect her focus at Diamond Estates?
- Olivia's mom never says, "I love you," to her daughter. How do you think that makes Olivia feel?
- Why do you think her mom is like that?

Chapter 25

- The staff goes all out for Christmas. Why do you think they put so much work into it?
- Where is Olivia now in her quest for Christ?
- What does Olivia have in common with Cinnamon the horse?

Chapter 26

- Do you think Olivia got a different picture of what worship is from her onstage view?
- What should she do about Kira and the picture?
- Ju-Ju admits to having had two abortions. Does she regret them?
- Describe how she feels about her choice.

Chapter 27

- What needs to happen in Olivia before she can accept the love of God?
- What needs to happen in you?
- Do you need to forgive yourself or forgive others?
- What signs of trouble are popping up in Tricia's life?
- What signs should you be on the lookout for with your friends?

Chapter 28

- Why did Ben think Satan was at work against Olivia?
- Can you think of a time when Satan worked in your life to try to keep you from seeking God or to make you blame Him?
- Why did Kira get in more trouble than Olivia? Do you think that was fair?

Chapter 29

- Olivia tells Tammy everything. How difficult do you think that was for her?
- Do you think it was freeing to get it out, or do you think she wished she'd kept it to herself?
- Is there anything in your life that you need to share with a parent or trusted adult? Just think about it and be open to it.
- If Olivia was mistreated, why does she have things to confess? Read Romans 3:23.

Chapter 30

- What motivated Tricia to do such dangerous things to be skinny?
- What does God think of Tricia?
- Why do you think she couldn't see just how skinny she'd become?
- Do you think it's fair that Tricia will have to stay at Diamond Estates longer? Is it a punishment?

Chapter 31

- It must have been very difficult for Olivia to confront her mom like that. What might you have said or done differently?

- Holding people accountable is part of God's calling for Christians.

"If your brother sins against you, go and tell him his fault, between you and him alone. If he listens to you, you have gained your brother. But if he does not listen, take one or two others along with you, that every charge may be established by the evidence of two or three witnesses." (Matthew 18:15–16 ESV)

- How has Olivia followed that biblical guideline without even really knowing it?

Chapter 32

- What if Olivia's mom had died in the standoff? Would that have meant that Olivia was right about God?

And we know that in all things God works for the good of those who love him, who have been called according to his purpose. (Romans 8:28 NIV)

- How do you think Romans 8:28 applies to God's intervention with Olivia's mom?

Chapter 33

- So everything gets better. Olivia's mom is safe. Her evil stepfather is dead. She finds Jesus. Then she gets an oboe and a scholarship. It's all too good to be true, isn't it? What's the one thing that still bothers her?
- What do you feel insecure about?
- Do you think it makes sense for Olivia to offer her mom forgiveness? What did she need to be forgiven for?

Chapter 34

There are things Olivia has to resolve to do on her own, like being committed to her personal prayer times, even if her friends don't want to.

- What things in your life remind you of that?
- What do you do about it?
- Olivia is a little worried about being on her own away from Diamond Estates. Do you think those concerns are reasonable and helpful? Why or why not?

Chapter 35

Think of Ju-Ju, Skye, Tricia, and Olivia.

- What types of backgrounds do they come from?
- Where is each of them in their walk with God?
- What kinds of different roads did they take to get there?
- Is it okay to travel different paths to arrive at the same goal: Jesus?

Chapter 36

- What is the significance of the pearl necklace?
- What do you think happens next in Olivia's life?
- How have you been challenged through this book?

Here's a sneak peak at book 2 in the Diamond Estates series:

THE EMBITTERED RUBY

Chapter 1

I f only heaven and hell shared the same zip code," Carmen Castillo sputtered into her cell phone as she huddled on the rusty fire escape. Anything for privacy. Even if it did put her at risk of a drive-by.

"You having a tough day, babe?"

"To say the least. I mean, I'm stuck here in Hackensack, New Jersey—some weird version of Hades on Earth. You're still in Briarcliff Manor, New York, otherwise known as Heaven."

"Let's pretend. Close those gorgeous brown eyes and lay that pretty face on my chest. Now I'm squeezing. Do you feel it?"

Ah. Nate McConnell's deep, velvety voice massaged the tension from her body. Her fingers tingled as she imagined stroking the prickly stubble on his face and then running them through his blond buzz cut. Next she tried to envision her dark waves lying across his thick biceps. That didn't quite work. "It's surreal. It's like I'm watching someone else's life fall apart on a TV special. Except it's mine. All mine."

Silence.

What could he say to her, after all? Carmen knew he loved her. They'd been together since Nate's junior year and her freshman year. Her move must have hurt him, too—but obviously not like it had destroyed her. He still lived in luxury and kept the same elite zip code they'd both enjoyed all their lives. And he clearly wasn't hurting enough to fight for her. But really, what did she expect him to do? Marry her? Yeah right. Like his parents would go for that. They barely tolerated Nate's dating Carmen because of her Mexican heritage—though they didn't know their disdain was so obvious.

Carmen wondered if his mom lay in bed at night and whispered, "Well, at least she's half white," as she tucked her silk sheets around her feet. Then Nate's dad would turn out the light and mumble, "Yes, thank the Lord for small favors."

Finally, Nate cleared his throat. "So where's everyone else?"

"You mean you can't hear the construction racket? I can barely think over the hammering and drilling. Mom and Kimberley are in my—er, *our*—room setting up. . .get this: bunk beds. Bunk beds? You've got to be kidding. I get to play Rock, Paper, Scissors with my little sister over who gets the top bunk. After never having shared a room for a day in my life."

"Yeah. That must be a pain. I wouldn't like sharing with Charlie."

"At least your little brother is cute and you can kind of overlook his immaturity because he's only three. Kimberley, well, she's a spoiled brat. I'd almost rather share with Harper. She's only ten, so she falls asleep early and is still kind of cute." Carmen peered around the cracks to peek in the window. "Speaking of Kim, there she goes now. Towel across her shoulder, off to take a bath in the claw-foot tub. Would you believe she sees that as an adventure?"

"She's only thirteen. Give her a break maybe?" Nate's words sounded clipped.

Carmen gritted her teeth against her turbulent emotions. *Bet he's glad he called.* "I'm sorry. I'm being horrible company. I can let you go and talk to you later."

"Okay. You know I love ya, babe. But if you want to go,

that's fine." The lilt in his voice gave away his relief. "Give me a call when you feel like it."

It wasn't at all what she wanted. What Carmen really wanted was a genie in a bottle to grant her three wishes. She'd even take just one wish. Or some ruby slippers. *There's no place like home.* But if she couldn't have that, she'd take time with her boyfriend. Was that too much to ask the universe? Carmen stared at the lifeless phone in her hand. *Apparently.*

How would she see Nate anymore? Maybe she could talk her parents into letting her live with Dad. Ugh. No matter how bad Hackensack was, it couldn't be as bad as being around Dad's girlfriend, Tiffany, and her pom-poms. Tiffany, who turned simple, everyday tasks into a cheer. "The coffee's. . .ready? Okay!" *Rah, rah. Gag.* But Tiffany wouldn't be around forever. No way. At least not if Carmen could help it.

Not ready to go back inside, Carmen closed her eyes. Maybe if she could imagine hard enough, she'd think she was back home taking a dip in the pool or soaking in the hot tub. She breathed air deep into her lungs, expecting the familiar smell of the cedar planks in the sauna. Instead, exhaust fumes from the buses and grease from the diner across the street attacked her senses.

No use.

Carmen slipped her phone into the pocket of her jeans and pried herself from the stucco wall she'd been leaning against. Crumbling plaster pelted the metal grid of the fire escape and then rained onto the street below.

A whistle pierced the din of street traffic.

Shielding her eyes against the sun, Carmen squinted up the street. Nothing there but two old men on a bus stop bench outside the drugstore. Down the street, little kids played on the uneven sidewalk. Where had that whistle come from? Finally, her gaze settled on four menacing teens leaning on the lamppost across the street. One dark pair of eyes drew hers like magnets. He cocked his head and stared holes into Carmen's flaming cheeks.

Shirtless, he touched the black and gold bandanna tied around his bulging bicep. Then he shifted position, and Carmen saw the largest tattoo she'd ever seen in person. A huge lion head with a five-pointed crown on its head was inked on his right side, starting at his ribs and winding around to the middle of his back.

Carmen's eyes roved to take in the dress of the others. All black and gold. The tattoos among them too numerous to count. Latin Kings.

Did that mean. . . ? Oh, yep. There it was. A polished handle stuck out of the waistband of the tallest of the group. How many of the others had guns?

Great. Now she was alone on a narrow fire escape, in a place God had forgotten about, being leered at by a gang. Carmen wanted to be safe inside huddled on her bunk bed, but she had frozen under their glares. Too scared to move—too afraid to appear nervous or show any sign of weakness. What were they doing there outside her apartment? More importantly, why were they watching her?

The leader snapped his fingers, and a cigarette appeared at his lips. Another pair of hands flicked a lighter, and it sparked to life. He took a long drag and blew out the smoke in slow motion. Then he winked one dark eye at her and ran his tongue along his lips.

Carmen shivered as goose bumps speckled her body from head to toe. She flung the sliding door to the side and scurried back through the opening. She slid it shut, latched the lock, and lowered the bar until it clicked into place.

Don't look. Don't even turn around. Keep moving, and don't look back.

She could feel their laser-sharp gazes burning holes between her shoulder blades as she moved though the family room. A quick right and she was in the hallway. Three more steps to her room. Was she safe there? Were any of them?

Those jerks were going to be trouble. Carmen could feel it in her bones.

゜

Main Street, Hackensack, New Jersey. Now there was a place to take a sightseeing tour. Carmen scuffed along the sidewalk, careful to avoid the side of the street where those guys had been standing and ogling her the day before. "Find a market," Mom had said. Should have been easy enough.

Carmen walked past a run-down library that probably survived on nothing but castaway books from other libraries—like the one in Briarcliff. The grease smell from several hole-in-the-wall restaurants seemed to follow her down the street. And the gym boasted a life-size mural of a steroid junkie punching a bag.

There was no shortage of nail salons, barbershops, pawnshops, and lawyers' offices. But a market? Maybe she could ask someone for directions. She lifted her eyes just enough to peek around for a friendly-looking pedestrian, but from the looks of things, she'd better explore on her own. She reached in her pocket and gripped her cell phone. . .just in case.

Ah. There, across the street, Giant Farmers' Market. That should do it. Carmen waited for a car to pass and then jogged to the other side. Her head down, she pulled the glass door open and stepped inside. As her eyes adjusted to the fluorescent lighting, she glanced around the store. Now, this place had some merit. Fresh. Bright. Almost happy.

Piles of colorful produce. Artichokes, chutney, guava,

pomegranate. Some things even she didn't recognize. Wow. The Latin aisle alone boasted rows and rows of bottles Carmen had never seen. Ethnic oddities, rare herbs, and. . .um. . .pig ears? Those might have to wait for another time. This was supposed to be a "milk, eggs, bread" kind of shopping trip. Maybe, since there was nothing else to do around here, she'd be able to practice for culinary school.

Thirty minutes later, Carmen hurried back to the apartment with plastic bags dangling from her wrists, cutting off her circulation. She'd had enough culture for one day. Odd, though—no one glanced her way as she shuffled along. Didn't she stand out at all? Couldn't they tell she didn't belong here—that it wasn't her home? Probably a good thing she blended in. Not like Kimberley, who was blond like their dad. Wonder how it would be for her?

Dead bolt. Lock. Second lock. The door swung open three inches then jerked. She shoved her face into the opening to see into the room. "Hey. Can someone come take the chain off the door so I can get in? These bags are getting heavy."

Little Harper cartwheeled across the room, her·tongue poking through the space where her tooth had once been. "Coming." She closed the door and slid the chain off before skipping toward the kitchen.

Did that girl ever walk?

Carmen rushed through the door, reached her foot back to nudge it shut, then hurried to the galley kitchen. She heaved her packages onto the gold-flecked countertop and freed her wrists from the bags. Red rings remained where they'd cut into her skin. "Phew. I thought I was going to drop something. Where's Mom?"

"In your room." Harper flashed a dimpled smile and bounded down the short hallway.

Carmen took a deep breath before entering her room. She'd been a real grump lately. Maybe surprising Mom would help make up for some of her bad attitude. "Hey, Mom. I'm back." She stepped over the tools and packing material strewn across the stained and tattered carpet of her bedroom. After all, it wasn't Mom's fault they'd had to move into the dingy apartment. Which was probably rat infested. And should be condemned.

Well. . .not entirely Mom's fault anyway. There had to have been a place across the river they could have rented. Yeah, yeah. This was close to Mom's new job. Affordable. Carmen had heard it all. But did she buy it? She just hoped they hadn't been dragged out to never-never land to make Dad feel guilty.

"You're still at it, huh?" Carmen sank to the floor and picked up the instructions. "Want some help?"

"I think I'm almost done. Finally. How was the shopping?"

"I found this neat market—they have lots of fun cooking stuff. I'm going to make a surprise dinner tonight."

"Okay, but remember, God's sure been faithful to us, but we don't have extra money for you to buy all kinds of exotic foods to play chef with."

Carmen took a deep breath. The God stuff again. "I know, Mom. Just trying to do something nice." *Change the subject.* "But hey. Since the bunk beds aren't finished, how about we just separate them and put one on each side of the room? Or better yet, put Kimberley's in the living room."

The hammer clanged as Mom dropped it on the drill. "We've been over this. We have no choice, Carmen. You've got to share a room with Kimberley, and trying to squeeze two separate beds in here is silly. It would take up way too much room. That's all there is to it." She sat back on her heels. "You know, it's not like I'm thrilled to share with Harper. At my age, I didn't expect to be roommates with a ten-year-old."

"But. . ." Oh, what was the point in arguing? She had to stop thinking about her big bedroom at home. . .er. . .at Dad's. That wasn't her life anymore—at least it stood waiting for her to visit two weekends a month. Carmen looked around the tiny space and up at the water spots on the ceiling—one of them reminded her of an elephant with its trunk raised. This was her new home—whether she liked it or not. "Why can't I at least go to my old school? I mean, I could take the bus. Nate and I Googled it."

Mom pressed her fingers into her temples until her knuckles turned white. "You Googled *what* exactly?" She uttered each word with what seemed a huge effort.

Oh no. Mom appeared done in. Why hadn't Carmen waited to bring this up after dinner? Too late though. "Um, the bus schedule. All I'd have to do is catch the one-sixty-five a block away at State Street. Then hop on the number seven subway at Times Square. A quick ride to Grand Central, and then I'd get on the Metro-North's Hudson Line to Ossining, and then I'm basically there."

"Right. And what time is that first bus at State Street—4:00 a.m.?" Mom shook her head. "You're talking to a native New Yorker. I know full well that what you just described is at least two hours' traveling time each way."

Two and a half, actually. But telling Mom that wouldn't help Carmen's cause. "I don't mind that. Really. I can do homework, read, or even nap."

"No way, Carmen. It's just not safe to have you traipsing all over two states twice a day."

It had to be safer than going to school in Hackensack. Not that Mom would appreciate that comment.

"And walking around outside this apartment while it's still dark? I don't think so. Plus, what about your sisters—how are they supposed to get to school? But I have an idea. If you and Nate want to be together so much, why doesn't he do the daily bus pilgrimage and transfer to college in New Jersey to be with you? That would be the chivalrous thing to do, rather than expecting you to do it."

"Right, like his parents are going to let Nate McConnell, heir to the throne of their political empire, slum it in Hackensack, New Jersey." Carmen wrinkled her nose and gazed out the tiny window at the billboards and barred store windows below. He wouldn't do it anyway. No way. "Just forget about it. Besides, it's a lot harder to transfer colleges than high schools, and I'd have already started the year in Briarcliff a month ago."

Mom ignored her. She grunted and leaned back at her hips, rotating her upper body. "I'm getting too old for this," she muttered.

"You're thirty-five. That's not old." They'd certainly had that discussion before. Mom was still young and pretty. She could lose a few pounds, sure, but who couldn't, really? Maybe if she did, maybe if she bought some new clothes and got a trendy haircut, then maybe Dad would want her back and they could all go home.

And makeup. Hopefully Mom's new Mary Kay venture would add a little color to her own face. Maybe they'd teach her to get rid of those dark circles and bags under her eyes. She'd never be as young and, um, perky as Tiffany. . .but she could be a better version of herself.

"Hey guys, what's up?" A tiny blur of flowing black hair bounded across the room and rolled onto the bottom bunk. Harper rested her elbows on the bare mattress and propped her chin in her hands.

"Get off my bed." Carmen swatted her little sister down and fitted the bottom sheet onto the bed.

"Um. You might want to know, Kim says she gets the bottom bunk." Harper shrugged. "Just giving you a fair warning."

"Hah. I don't think so. Kimberley's in for a rude awakening if she thinks I'm climbing to the top bunk every day. That ain't happening."

"Well, I'm going to leave you two to battle that one." Mom rose from the floor, her knee popping on the way up.

Yeah. Not going to be a battle.

"I have a facial party tonight. So you'll be in charge of course." She nodded at Carmen.

Thanks for asking. Not like she had a life anyway. "Okay. But for now, Harper, you're going to have to go. I've, um, got to change clothes."

"Okeydoke." Harper scurried out of the room behind their mother, pulling the door shut behind her.

Finally. Carmen ran to her dresser and rummaged through the drawers; then she turned to the closet and dug through the three unpacked boxes. Not there. She pulled her purple nylon duffel bag from under her bed and plowed through the contents. Not there either. Where were they? She'd missed two of her birth control pills already in the hustle of the move, and now they were nowhere to be found. In an entire year of taking them, these were the first she'd missed. If she could find them, she'd just double up for two days—that should do it.

Carmen rubbed her chin and turned in a circle, looking at everything in her room. Had she said something to Nate about where she put them? But she couldn't ask him—then he'd know she'd missed some, and they were supposed to get together after tennis practice tomorrow. He had a special evening all planned while his parents were away, and then he planned to stay over with her at Dad's. Carmen sure didn't want to mess that up.

Where were those pills? *Think. Think....*

Nicole O'Dell and her husband, Wil, have six children ranging from nineteen down to the most recent additions: triplets, born in August 2008. Nicole writes fiction and nonfiction focused on helping teens make good choices and bridging the gap in parent/teen communication. Nicole is also the host of Teen Talk Radio at www.choicesradio.com, where she talks with teens and special guests about the real issues young people face today, and she loves getting out among teens and parents when speaking at youth groups and conferences. Over the years, Nicole has worked as a youth director, a Bible study leader for women and teens, and a counselor at a crisis pregnancy center. Her writing also includes devotionals and Bible studies for women of all ages. Visit www.nicoleodell.com to follow Nicole's blog and participate in the active Choices! Community.